KINCAID'S DANGEROUS GAME

"So who a̶ ̶ ̶ ̶ ̶ ̶ ̶?"

She seem̶ ̶ ̶ ̶ ̶ ̶ ̶ ̶ ̶ ̶ ̶ ̶ ̶ ̶ er eyes behind tho̶ ̶ ̶

"Nobody yo̶ ̶ ̶ ̶ ̶ ̶ he could have sworn he saw her re̶ ̶ ̶ ̶ btly – but then, with her, how could he be sure?

He watched her finish off the skewered meat and then carefully lick the stick clean of barbecue sauce. Watched the ways her lips curved with sensual pleasure, and her little pink tongue slipped tantalisingly between them to lap every possible morsel from the skewer. When he realised hungry juices were pooling at the back of his own throat, he tore his eyes away from her and tackled his own plate.

"So…let me get this straight. You're a private investigator, hired by someone I don't know. So what is it, exactly, you want with me?"

He pointed with his fork at the card she'd left lying on the table. "If you read that, it says I specialise in finding people." He paused, took another bite. "I've been hired to find someone…and I believe that person is you."

First published in Great Britain 2010
Harlequin Mills & Boon Limited,
Eton House, 18-24 Paradise Road, Richmond, Surrey TW9 1SR

The Rancher Bodyguard © Carla Bracale 2009
Kincaid's Dangerous Game © Kathleen Creighton-Fuchs 2009

ISBN: 978 0 263 88216 2

46-0410

Harlequin Mills & Boon policy is to use papers that are natural, renewable and recyclable products and made from wood grown in sustainable forests. The logging and manufacturing processes conform to the legal environmental regulations of the country of origin.

Printed and bound in Spain
by Litografia Rosés S.A., Barcelona

THE RANCHER BODYGUARD

BY
CARLA CASSIDY

KINCAID'S DANGEROUS GAME

BY
KATHLEEN CREIGHTON

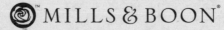

MILLS & BOON

THE RANCHER BODYGUARD

BY
CARLA CASSIDY

Carla Cassidy is an award-winning author who has written more than fifty novels. In 1995, she won Best Silhouette Romance from *Romantic Times BOOK-reviews*. In 1998, she also won a Career Achievement Award for Best Innovative Series.

Carla believes the only thing better than curling up with a good book to read is sitting down at the computer with a good story to write. She's looking forward to writing many more books and bringing hours of pleasure to readers.

Chapter 1

As he approached the barn, Charlie Black saw the sleek, scarlet convertible pulling into his driveway, and wondered when exactly, while he'd slept the night before, hell had frozen over. Because the last time he'd seen Grace Covington, that's what she'd told him would have to happen before she'd ever talk to or even look at him again.

He patted the neck of his stallion and reined in at the corral. As he dismounted and pulled off his dusty black hat, he tried to ignore the faint thrum of electricity that zinged through him as she got out of her car.

Her long blond hair sparkled in the late afternoon sun, but he was still too far away to see the expression on her lovely features.

It had been a year and a half since he'd seen her, even though for the past six months they'd resided in the same small town of Cotter Creek, Oklahoma.

The last time he'd encountered her had been in his upscale apartment in Oklahoma City. He'd been wearing a pair of sports socks and an electric blue condom. Not one of his finer moments, but it had been the culminating incident in a year of not-so-fine moments.

Too much money, too many successes and far too much booze had transformed his life into a nightmare of bad moments, the last resulting in him losing the only thing worth having.

Surely she hadn't waited all this time to come out to the family ranch—his ranch now—to finally put a bullet in what she'd described as his cold, black heart. Grace had never been the type of woman to put off till today what she could have done yesterday.

Besides, she hadn't needed a gun on that terrible Friday night when she'd arrived unannounced at his apartment. As he'd stared at her in a drunken haze, she'd given it to him with both barrels, calling him every vile name under the sun before she slammed out of his door and out of his life.

So, what was she doing here now? He slapped his horse on the rump, then motioned to a nearby ranch hand to take care of the animal. He closed the gate and approached where she hadn't moved away from the driver's side of her car.

Her hair had grown much longer since he'd last seen her. Although most of it was clasped at the back of her neck, several long wisps had escaped the confines. The beige suit she wore complemented her blond coloring and the icy blue of her eyes.

She might look cool and untouchable, like the perfect lady, but he knew what those eyes looked like flared with desire. He knew how she moaned with wild abandon when making love, and he hated the fact that just the unexpected sight of her brought back all the memories he'd worked so long and hard to forget.

"Hello, Grace," he said, as he got close enough to speak without competing with the warm April breeze. "I have to admit I'm surprised to see you. As I remember, the last time we saw each other, you indicated that hell would freeze over before you'd ever speak to me again."

Her blue eyes flashed with more than a touch of annoyance—a flash followed swiftly by a look of desperation.

"Charlie, I need you." Her low voice trembled slightly, and only then did he notice that her eyes were red-rimmed, as if she'd been weeping. In all the time they'd dated—even during the ugly scene that had ended *them*—he'd never seen her shed a single tear. "Have you heard the news?" she asked.

"What news?"

"Early this afternoon my stepfather was found stabbed to death in bed." She paused for a moment and bit her full lower lip as her eyes grew shiny with suppressed tears. "I think Hope is in trouble, Charlie. I think she's really in bad trouble."

"What?" Shock stabbed through him. Hope was

Grace's fifteen-year-old sister. He'd met her a couple of times. She'd seemed like a nice kid, not as pretty as her older sister, but a cutie nevertheless.

"Maybe you should come on inside," he said, and gestured toward the house. She stared at the attractive ranch house as if he'd just invited her into the chambers of hell. "There's nobody inside, Grace. The only woman who ever comes in is Rosa Caltano. She does the cooking and cleaning for me, and she's already left for the day."

Grace gave a curt nod and moved away from the car. She followed him to the house and up the wooden stairs to the wraparound porch.

The entry hall was just as it had been when Charlie's mother and father had been alive, with a gleaming wood floor and a dried flower wreath on the wall.

He led her to the living room. Charlie had removed much of the old furniture that he'd grown up with and replaced it with contemporary pieces in earth tones. He motioned Grace to the sofa, where she sat on the very edge as if ready to bolt at any moment. He took the chair across from her and gazed at her expectantly.

"Why do you think Hope is in trouble?"

She drew in a deep breath, obviously fighting for control. "From what I've been told, Lana, the housekeeper, found William dead in his bed. Today is her day off, but she left a sweater there last night and went back to get it. It was late enough in the day that William should have been up, so she checked on him. She immediately called Zack West, and he and some of his deputies responded. They found Hope passed out on her bed. Apparently she was the only one home at the time of the murder."

Charlie frowned, his mind reeling. Before he'd moved back here to try his hand at ranching, Charlie had been a successful, high-profile defense attorney in Oklahoma City.

It was that terrible moment in time with Grace followed by the unexpected death of his father that had made him take a good, hard look at his life and realize how unhappy he'd been for a very long time.

Still, it was as a defense attorney that he frowned at her thoughtfully. "What do you mean she was passed out? Was she asleep? Drunk?"

Those icy blue eyes of hers darkened. "Apparently she was drugged. She was taken to the hospital and is still there. They pumped her stomach and are keeping her for observation." Grace leaned forward. "Please, Charlie. Please help her. Something isn't right. First of all, Hope would never, ever take drugs, and she certainly isn't capable of something like this. She would *never* have hurt William."

Spoken like a true sister, Charlie thought. How many times had he heard family members and friends proclaim that a defendant couldn't be guilty of the crime they had been charged with, only to discover that they were wrong?

"Grace, I don't know if you've heard, but I'm a rancher now." He wasn't at all sure he wanted to get involved with any of this. It had disaster written all over it. "I've retired as a criminal defense attorney."

"I heard through the grapevine that besides being a rancher, you're working part-time with West Protective Services," she said.

"That's right," he agreed. "They approached me about a month ago and asked if I could use a little side work. It sounded intriguing, so I took them up on it, but so far I haven't done any work for them."

"Then let me hire you as Hope's bodyguard, and if you do a little criminal defense work in the process I'll pay you extra." She leaned forward, her eyes begging for his help.

Bad idea, a little voice whispered in the back of his brain. She already hated his guts, and this portended a very bad ending. He knew how much she loved her sister; he assumed that for the last couple of years she'd been more mother than sibling to the young girl. He'd be a fool to involve himself in the whole mess.

"Has Hope been questioned by anyone?" he heard himself ask. He knew he was going to get involved whether he wanted to or not, because it was Grace, because she needed him.

"I don't think so. When I left the hospital a little while ago, she was still unconscious. Dr. Dell promised me he wouldn't let anyone in to see her until I returned."

"Good." There was nothing worse than a suspect running off at the mouth with a seemingly friendly officer. Often the damage was so great there was nothing a defense attorney could do to mitigate it.

"Does that mean you'll take Hope's case?" she asked.

"Whoa," he said, and held up both his hands. "Before I agree to anything, I need to make a couple of phone calls, find out exactly what's going on and where the official investigation is headed. It's possible you don't need me, that Hope isn't in any real danger of being arrested."

"Then what happens now?"

"Why don't I plan on meeting you at the hospital in about an hour and a half? By then I'll know more of what's going on, and I'd like to be present while anybody questions Hope. If anyone asks before I get there, you tell them you're waiting for legal counsel."

She nodded and rose. She'd been lovely a year and a half ago when he'd last seen her, but she was even lovelier now.

She was five years younger than his thirty-five but had always carried herself with the confidence of an older woman. That was part of what had initially drawn him to her, that cool shell of assurance encased in a slamming hot body with the face of an angel.

"How's business at the dress shop?" he asked, trying to distract her from her troubles as he walked her back to her car. She owned a shop called Sophisticated Lady that sold designer items at discount prices. She often traveled the two-hour drive into Oklahoma City on buying trips. That was where she and Charlie had started their relationship.

They'd met in the coffee shop in the hotel where she'd been staying. Charlie had popped in to drop off some paperwork to a client and had decided to grab a cup of coffee before heading back to his office.

She'd been sitting alone next to a window. The sun had sparked on her hair. Charlie had taken one look and was smitten.

"Business is fine," she said, but it was obvious his distraction wasn't successful.

"I'm sorry about William, but Zack West is a good man, a good sheriff. He'll get to the bottom of things."

Once again she nodded and opened her car door. "Then I'll see you in the hospital in an hour and a half," she said.

"Grace?" He stopped her before she got into the seat. "Given our history, why would you come to me with this?" he asked.

Her gaze met his with a touch of frost. "Because I think Hope is in trouble and she needs a sneaky devil to make sure she isn't charged with a murder I know she didn't commit. And you, Charlie Black, are as close to the devil as I could get."

She didn't wait for his reply. She got into her car, started the engine with a roar and left him standing to eat her dust as she peeled out and back down the driveway.

Grace drove until she was out of sight of Charlie's ranch and then pulled to the side of the road. She leaned her head down on the steering wheel and fought back the tears that burned her eyes.

A nightmare. She felt as if she'd been mysteriously plunged into a nightmare and couldn't wake up to escape, didn't know how to get out.

She'd barely had time to mourn her stepfather, the man who had married her mother when she'd been sixteen and Hope had been a baby.

William Covington had not only married their mother, Elizabeth, but had also taken on her two children as if they were his own. Grace's father had died of a heart attack and William had adopted the two fatherless girls.

He'd guided Grace through the tumultuous teen years with patience and humor. He'd been their rock when their mother had simply vanished two years ago, taking with her two suitcases full of clothing and her daughters' broken hearts.

Grace raised her head from the steering wheel and pulled back on the road. She couldn't think about her mother right now. That was an old pain. She had new pains to worry about and a little sister to try to save.

No way, she thought as she headed toward the hospital. No way was Hope capable of such a heinous crime. And Hope had always been the first one to declare that she thought drugs were stupid. She couldn't be taking drugs.

But how do you know for sure? a little voice in her head whispered. She'd been so busy the last couple of years, working at the shop and flying off for buying trips. Since the disappearance of her mother and her subsequent breakup with Charlie, Grace had engaged in a frenzy of work, exhausting herself each day to keep the anger and the heartache of both her mother's and Charlie's betrayals at bay.

Sure, lately, when she'd spent time with Hope, the young girl had voiced the usual teenage complaints about William. He was too strict and old-fashioned. He gave her too little freedom and too many lectures. He hated her friends.

But those were the complaints of almost every teenager on the face of the earth, and Grace couldn't believe they had meant that Hope harbored a killing rage against William.

She turned into the hospital parking lot and slid into an empty parking space, then turned off the engine. She stared at the small structure that comprised the Cotter Creek hospital, her thoughts filled with Charlie Black.

Six months ago, everyone in town had been buzzing with the gossip that Charlie Black had finally come home. She knew his father had died from an unexpected heart attack and had left Charlie the family ranch, but she'd assumed he'd sell it and continue his self-destructive path in the fast lane. She'd been stunned to hear that he'd closed up his practice in Oklahoma City and taken over the ranch.

She'd met Charlie two months after her mother's disappearance. She hadn't told him about her mother, rather she'd used her time with him as an escape from the pain, from the utter heart break of her mother's abandonment.

With Charlie she'd been able to pretend it hadn't happened. With Charlie, for a blessed time, she'd shoved the pain deep inside her.

She'd refused to tell him because she hadn't wanted

to see pity in his eyes. She'd needed him to be her safe place away from all the madness, and for a while that's what he'd been.

As soon as she'd heard about William's murder and Hope's possible involvement, Charlie's name was the first one that had popped into her head. All the qualities she'd hated in him as a man were desirable qualities in a defense attorney.

His arrogance, his need to be right, his stubbornness and his emotional detachment made him a good defense attorney and would make him a terrific professional bodyguard, but he was definitely a poor bet for a personal relationship, as she'd discovered.

That was in the past. She didn't want anything from Charlie Black except his ability to make sure that Hope was safe.

As she got out of her car, she recognized that she was in a mild state of shock. The events of the past three hours hadn't fully caught up with her yet.

She'd been at the shop when she'd gotten the call from Deputy Ben Taylor, indicating that William was dead and Hope had been transferred to the hospital. He'd given her just enough information to both horrify and terrify her.

Her legs trembled as she made her way through the emergency room entrance. She hadn't been able to see Hope when she'd been here before, as Hope had been undergoing the stomach pumping. Surely they would let Grace see her now.

She told the nurse on duty who she was, then sat in one of the chairs in the waiting room. She was the only person there. She clasped her hands together in her lap in an attempt to stop their shaking.

Was Hope okay? Who had really killed William? He'd been a kind, gentle man. Who would want to hurt him?

She blinked back her tears and straightened her shoulders. She couldn't fall apart now. She had to be strong because she knew this was only the beginning of the nightmare.

"Grace."

She looked up to see Dr. Ralph Dell standing in the doorway. She started to stand but he motioned her back into her chair as he sat next to her. "She's stable," he said. "We pumped her stomach, but whatever she took either wasn't in pill form or had enough time to be digested. I've ordered a full toxicology screen."

"Is she conscious?" Grace asked.

"Drifting in and out. She'll be here until the effects have completely worn off." Dr. Dell eyed her soberly. "The sheriff is going to want to talk to her, and even with her condition I can keep him away only so long."

"I know. Charlie Black is supposed to meet me here in the next hour or so."

"Good. Deputy Taylor has been here since she was brought in."

Grace frowned. "Has he talked to her?"

Dr. Dell shook his head. "Up until now Hope hasn't been in any condition to talk to anyone. And I promised you I wouldn't let anyone in to see her while you were gone. I'm a man of my word."

"Thank you." Grace raised a trembling hand to her temple, where a headache had begun to pound with fierce intensity.

"How are you doing?" Dr. Dell reached out and took her hand in his. He'd been both Hope's and Grace's doctor since they'd been small girls. "You need anything, you let me know."

She realized he wasn't just holding her hand, but rather was taking her pulse at the same time. She forced a smile. "I'm okay." She withdrew her hand from his. "Really. Can I see Hope?"

He nodded his head and stood. "However, I caution you about asking her too many questions. Right now what she needs is your love and support. There will be plenty of time for answers when she's feeling more alert."

Grace heartily agreed. The last thing she wanted right now was to grill Hope about whatever might have happened at the Covington mansion that morning. All she wanted—all she *needed*—was to make sure that the sister she loved was physically all right. She'd worry about the rest later.

"I've got her in a private room," Dr. Dell said, as he led Grace down a quiet corridor.

She saw the deputy first. Ben Taylor sat in a chair in the hallway, a magazine open in his lap. He looked up as they approached, his thin face expressing no emotion as he greeted her.

"Grace." He nodded to her and shifted in his seat as if he found the whole situation awkward.

She knew Ben because his wife worked part-time

for her at the dress shop. "Hi, Ben," she replied, appalled by the shakiness of her voice.

"Bad day, huh?" He averted his gaze from hers.

"That's an understatement." There were a hundred questions she wanted to ask him, but she wasn't sure she was ready for any of the answers. Charlie would be here soon and would find out what she needed to know.

She pushed open the door of the hospital room and her heart squeezed painfully tight in her chest as she saw her sister. Hope was asleep, her petite face stark white and her blond hair a tangled mess.

Grace wanted to bundle her up in the sheet, pick her up and run out the door. Nobody could ever make her believe that Hope had anything to do with William's murder.

Pulling up a chair next to Hope's bed, Grace fought against a tremendous amount of guilt. In the past couple of months had she been too absent from Hope's life? Had there been things she wasn't aware of, things that had led to this terrible crime?

Stop it, she commanded herself. She was thinking as if Hope was guilty, and she wasn't. She wasn't! As soon as Charlie arrived, everything would be okay.

A knot of simmering anger twisted in her stomach. She shouldn't be alone here, waiting for Hope to wake up. Their mother should be with her, but she'd run from her responsibility and her family and disappeared like a puff of smoke on a windy day. Hope had been far too young to lose her mother. *Damn you, Mom,* Grace thought.

Hope stirred and her eyes opened. She frowned and looked at Grace in obvious confusion. "Sis?" Her voice was a painful croak.

Grace leaned forward and grabbed Hope's hand. "I'm here, honey. It's all right. You're going to be all right now."

Hope looked around wildly, as if unsure where she was. Her gaze locked with Grace's once again, and in the depths of Hope's eyes Grace saw a whisper of terror. "What happened?"

"You got your stomach pumped. Did you take something, Hope? Some kind of drug?"

Hope's eyes flashed with annoyance and she rose to a half-sitting position. "I don't do drugs. Drugs are for losers." She fell back against the bed and closed her eyes, as if the brief conversation had completely exhausted her.

Grace remained seated next to her, clasping her hand even after she realized Hope had fallen back asleep. If Hope hadn't taken any drugs, then why had the authorities found her unconscious on her bed when they'd arrived?

Had she been hit over the head? Knocked unconscious by whoever had committed the murder? Surely if she'd had a head injury Dr. Dell would have found it.

Hope slept the sleep of the drugged, not awakening even when a nurse came in to take her vital signs. The nurse didn't speak to Grace. She simply did her job with stern lips pressed tightly together.

Minutes ticked by with nauseating slowness.

Grace checked her watch over and over again, wondering when Charlie would arrive. Hopefully he'd have some answers that would unravel the knot of dread tied tight in her stomach.

She leaned her head back against the chair and thought of Charlie. The moment she'd seen him again, an electric charge had sizzled through her. It had surprised her.

He was as handsome now as he'd been when they'd dated, his dark hair rich and full and his features aristocratically elegant, holding just a hint of danger. She knew those slate-gray eyes of his could narrow with cold intent or stoke a fire so hot a woman felt as if she might combust.

She'd been more than half in love with him when they'd broken up. She'd thought he felt the same way about her, but the redhead in his bed that night had told her different.

On that night she'd hated him more than she'd loved him, and in the past eighteen months her feelings hadn't changed. She rubbed her fingers across her forehead, thoughts of Charlie Black only increasing her headache.

Maybe he'd come in and tell her that Hope wasn't in any trouble, didn't need the expertise of a criminal defense lawyer or a bodyguard. Then she'd go back to the mess that had suddenly become her life and never see Charlie again.

She glanced at her watch and frowned. He was late. He was always late. That was something else she'd always found irritating about him—his inability to be on time for anything.

She didn't know why she was thinking about him anyway, except that it was far easier to think about Charlie than what had happened.

Somebody murdered William. Somebody murdered William. The words thundered through her brain in perfect rhythm with her pounding headache.

Who would want him dead? He'd been a wealthy man, a generous benefactor to numerous charities. He'd been well liked in the community and loved and respected by the two stepdaughters he'd claimed as his own.

Although he was the CEO of several industrial companies, he'd stopped working full-time a year ago and went in only occasionally for meetings.

He was kind and gentle, and his heart had been broken when Hope and Grace's mother had left him, left *them.* Tears burned her eyes again and she struggled to hold them back as she realized she'd never again see his gentle smile, never again feel the touch of his hand on her shoulder.

It was just after seven when the hospital door creaked open and Charlie motioned her out of the room. She got up from the chair and joined him in the hallway, where he took her by the arm and led her away from Ben Taylor.

"We've got a problem," he said when they were far enough down the hallway that Ben couldn't hear their conversation. His gray eyes were like granite slabs, revealing nothing of his thoughts.

"What?" she asked.

"I have every reason to believe that as soon as Hope is well enough to be released by the doctor, she's going to be arrested for the murder of your stepfather."

Grace gasped. "But why? How could anyone think she's responsible?"

He shifted his gaze and stared at some point just over her head. "Hope wasn't just found passed out on her bed. Her room had been trashed as if she'd been in a fit of rage."

"But that doesn't make her a murderer," Grace exclaimed. Although it *was* definitely out of character for Hope to do something like that. Hope had always been a neatnik who loved her room neat and tidy.

Charlie sighed and focused his gaze back on her. The darkness she saw there terrified her. "The real problem is that Hope was found covered in William's blood—and she had a knife in her hand. It was the murder weapon."

Chapter 2

Charlie watched as the color left Grace's cheeks and she swayed on her feet. His first impulse was to reach out to her, but before he could follow through, she stiffened and took a step back from him.

She'd never been a needy woman— that was one of the things he'd always admired about her and ultimately one of the things he'd come to hate. That she wasn't needy— that she had never really needed him.

"So, what do we do now?" Her strong voice gave away nothing of the emotional turmoil she must be feeling.

"Zack West wants to question her tonight. I just saw him in the lobby and he's chomping at the bit to get to her. Give me a dollar."

"Excuse me?" She looked at him blankly.

"Give me a dollar as a retainer. That will make it official that at least for now, I'm Hope's legal counsel. She's a minor. She can't be questioned without me, and we can argue that as her legal guardian you have the right to be present, too."

She opened her purse and withdrew a crisp dollar bill. He took it from her and shoved it into his back pocket. "I'll go find Zack and we'll get this over with."

As he walked away, her scent lingered in his head. She'd always smelled like jasmine and the faintest hint of vanilla, and today was no different.

It was a scent that had stayed with him for months after she'd left him, a fragrance that had once smelled like desire and had wound up smelling like regret.

This was a fool's job, and he was all kinds of fool for getting involved. From what little he'd already learned, it didn't look good for the young girl.

If he got involved and ended up defending Hope, then failed, Grace would have yet another reason to hate his guts. Even if he defended Hope successfully, that wasn't a ticket to the land of forgiveness where Grace was concerned.

Still, Charlie knew that in all probability Hope was going to need a damn good lawyer on her side, and he was just arrogant enough to believe that he was the best in the four-state area.

Besides, he owed it to Grace. Although at the time of their breakup they'd been not only on different pages but in completely different books, he'd never forgotten the rich, raw pain on her face when she'd been confronted by the knowledge that he hadn't been monogamous.

Maybe fate had given him this opportunity to right the wrong, to heal some wounds and assuage the guilt he'd felt ever since.

He found Zack in the waiting room. The handsome sheriff was pacing the floor and frowning. He stopped in his tracks as Charlie approached him. "If you want to question Hope, then Grace and I intend to be present," Charlie said.

Zack raised a dark eyebrow. "Are you here as Hope's lawyer?"

"Maybe." Charlie replied.

Zack sighed. "You going to make this difficult for me?"

"Probably," Charlie replied dryly. "You can't really believe that Hope killed William."

"Right now, I'm just in the information-gathering mode. After I have all the information I need, *then* I can decide if I have a viable suspect or not."

Zack had only been sheriff for less than a year, but Charlie knew he was a truth seeker and not a town pleaser. He would look for justice, not make a fast arrest in order to waylay the fears of the people in Cotter Creek. But if all the evidence pointed to Hope, Zack would have no choice but to arrest her.

"I heard you were working for Dalton," Zack said.

Dalton was Zack's brother and ran the family business, West Protective Services, an agency that provided bodyguard services around the country.

"I told him I'd be interested in helping out

whenever he needed me," Charlie replied. "But I need to get this situation under control before I do anything else."

"Then let's do it," Zack said. He headed down the hallway toward Hope's room and Charlie followed close behind.

Dr. Dell met them at her door, his arms crossed over his chest like a mythical guardian of a magical jewel. "I know you have a job to do here, Sheriff, but so do I. She's still very weak, so I want this interview to be short and sweet."

Zack nodded, and the doctor stepped away. Grace's eyes narrowed slightly as Zack and Charlie entered the room. She sat next to the bed, where Hope was awake.

The kid looked sick and terrified as her gaze swept from Charlie to Zack. "Hope, you remember Zack West, the sheriff," Grace said. "And Charlie is here as your lawyer."

Hope's eyes widened, and Charlie had a feeling she hadn't realized just what kind of trouble she was in until this moment. Tears filled her eyes and she reached for her sister's hand.

"I want to ask you some questions," Zack said. He pulled a small tape recorder from his pocket and set it on the nightstand next to the bed. "You mind if I turn this on?"

Hope looked wildly at Charlie, who nodded his assent. Charlie stood next to Grace, trying to ignore the way her evocative scent made him remember the pleasure of making love with her and how crazy he'd been about her.

He couldn't think about that now—he knew he shouldn't think about that ever again. He couldn't go back and change the past and that terrible mistake he'd made. All he could do was step up right now and hopefully redeem himself just a little bit.

"I told her about William," Grace said to Zack, her chin lifted in a gesture of defiance. "She knows he was murdered but insists she had nothing to do with it."

A knot of tension formed in Zack's jaw. "I need to hear from her what happened today," he said, and focused his gaze on Hope. "What's the first thing you remember from this morning?"

Hope raised a trembling hand to her head and rubbed her temples. "I woke up around nine and went downstairs to get some breakfast. Nobody was around. It was Lana's day off, and I figured William was still in bed. Lately he'd been sleeping in longer than usual."

She stopped talking as tears once again filled her blue eyes. "I can't believe he's gone. I just don't understand any of this. Why would somebody do this to him? What happened to me?"

"So, you made yourself breakfast, then what did you do?" Zack asked, seemingly unmoved by her tears.

Grace's lips were a thin slash, and her pretty features were taut with tension. Several more strands of her shiny blond hair had escaped her barrette and framed her face.

Charlie was surprised to realize he wanted to do something, anything to erase that apprehensive look on her face, to alleviate the tortured shadows in her eyes.

"After I ate breakfast, I was still tired, so I went

back to bed," Hope replied. "And I woke up here." Her features crumbled. "I don't know what happened to William. I don't know what happened to me." She began to cry in earnest, deep, wrenching sobs.

Grace got up from her chair and put her arms around Hope's slender shoulders and glared at Zack as if he were personally responsible for all the unhappiness on the entire planet.

"Isn't this enough?" she asked, those blue eyes of hers filled with anger. "Can't you see what this is doing to her?"

Unfortunately, Charlie knew that Zack was just getting started. "Grace, let's just get this over with," he said. "Zack has to question her sooner or later. We might as well get it finished now. We'll give her a minute to pull herself together."

Zack waited until Hope calmed down a bit before asking about any tensions between her and William and probing her about any fights her stepfather might have had with anyone else.

Charlie protested only a couple of times when he thought the questions Zack asked might incriminate Hope if she answered.

Despite Charlie's efforts to protect Hope, what little information Zack got from the girl offered no alternative suspect and merely added to the mystery of what exactly happened in the Covington mansion that morning.

After an hour and a half of questioning, it was Grace who finally called a halt to the interrogation. "That's enough for tonight, Zack," she said firmly, as she rose from her chair. "Hope is exhausted. She isn't going anywhere. If you have more questions for her, you can ask them another time."

Zack nodded and reached over and turned off the tape recorder, then slipped the small device into his pocket. "I'll be in touch. I guess I don't have to tell you and Hope not to leave town."

"Innocent people don't leave town," she replied vehemently.

Zack left the room and Grace leaned over her sister. "We're going to go now, honey. We need to take care of some things. Nobody will bother you for the rest of the night. Just get some sleep and try not to worry. Charlie is going to fix all this, so there's nothing to worry about."

Charlie nearly groaned out loud. Sure, that was easy for her to say. But he was a defense attorney turned rancher, not a miracle worker.

They left the room together, and once out in the hallway Grace slumped against the polished wall. For the first time since arriving at his ranch, she looked lost and achingly fragile.

His need to touch her—to somehow chase away that vulnerable look in her eyes—was incredibly strong. "Do you need a hug?" The ridiculous words were out of his mouth before he'd realized he was going to say them.

She released a bitter laugh and shoved off the wall. "I'd rather hug a rattlesnake," she said thinly.

If he had any question about the depth of her dislike for him, her curt reply certainly answered it.

"It doesn't look good, does it?" she asked.

"It doesn't look great," he replied.

"So what happens now?" she inquired, as they continued down the hallway to the hospital's front doors.

"Nothing for now. Questioning Hope is only the beginning. We really won't know how much trouble she's in until Zack's completed his investigation into the murder."

They stepped out into the unusually warm spring night air, and again he caught a whiff of her sweet floral scent. He wanted to ask her if she was dating anyone, if she'd found love with somebody else in the eighteen months since they'd been together.

He reminded himself he had no right to know anything about her personal life, that he'd given up any such right the night he'd gotten drunk and fallen into bed with a woman whose name he couldn't even remember.

"I don't want to wait for Zack," she said. "I want us to investigate this murder just as vigorously as he will."

Charlie looked at her in surprise. "That's a crazy idea!" he exclaimed.

"Why is it crazy? You told me once that you worked as an investigator before you became a lawyer."

"That was a long time ago," he reminded her.

She crossed her arms, a mutinous expression on her face. "Fine, then I'll investigate it on my own." She turned on her heels and walked off.

Charlie sighed in frustration. "Grace, wait," he

called after her. "I can't let you muck around in this alone. You could potentially do more damage than good for Hope."

"Then help me," she said, her voice low with desperation. "I'm all that Hope has. The only way to make sure she isn't railroaded for a crime she didn't commit is for me to find the guilty person, and that's exactly what I intend to do—with or without your help." She paused, her eyes glittering darkly. "So, are you going to help me or not?"

He shoved his hands in his jeans pocket and shook his head. "I'd forgotten just how stubborn you could be."

"I don't think you want to start pointing out character flaws in other people," she said pointedly.

To Charlie's surprise, he felt the warmth of a flush heat his cheeks. "Touché," he said. "All right, we'll do a little digging of our own. The first thing you should do is make a list of William's friends and business associates. We need to pick his life apart if we hope to find some answers."

"I can have a list for you by tomorrow. Why don't you meet me at my shop around noon, and we can decide exactly where to go from there."

"You're going into work?" he asked in surprise.

"I'd rather meet you at the shop than at my place," she replied.

"All right, then, tomorrow at noon," he agreed reluctantly. Charlie had worked extremely hard over the last six months to gain control and now felt his life was suddenly whirling back out of control.

She nodded. "Charlie, you should know that just because I came to you for help—just because I need you right now—doesn't mean I like you. When this is all over, I don't want to see you again." She turned and left without waiting for a response.

Jeez, he seemed to be watching her walking away from him a lot, especially after throwing a bomb at him. Still, he couldn't help but notice the sexy sway of those hips beneath the suit skirt and the length of her shapely legs. A surge of familiar regret welled up inside him.

He was a man who made few excuses or apologies for the choices he made, but the mistake of throwing Grace away would haunt him until the day he died.

The morning sun was shining brightly as Grace parked in front of her dress shop on Main Street. She turned off the engine but remained seated in the car, her thoughts still on the visit she'd just had with Hope.

Hope had been no less confused about the events of the day before and didn't seem to understand that at the moment she was the best suspect they had.

Fortunately, Dr. Dell wanted to keep her under observation for another twenty-four hours, and that was fine with Grace. The tox screen had come back showing a cocktail of drugs in Hope's system but Hope was still vehemently denying taking anything. At the hospital, Hope was safe and getting the best care.

Grace wearily rubbed a hand across her forehead. The day was just beginning, and she was already exhausted. Her sleep had been a continuous reel of nightmares.

She'd been haunted by visions of Hope stabbing William and then taking the drugs that knocked her unconscious. And if that hadn't been bad enough, images of Charlie also filled her dreams.

Charlie. She got out of the car and slammed the door harder than necessary, as if doing so could cast out all thoughts of the man.

She focused her attention on the shop before her. Sophisticated Lady had been a dream of hers from the time she was small. She'd always loved fashion and design, and five years ago for her twenty-fifth birthday, William had loaned her the money to open the shop.

Grace had worked her tail off to stock the store with fine clothing at discount prices, and within two years she'd managed to pay back the loan and expand into accessories and shoes.

Now all she could think about was whether she'd sacrificed her sister's well-being for making her shop a success. She'd spent long hours here at the store, and when she wasn't here she was away on buying trips or at Charlie's place for the weekend.

As much as she hated to admit it, she didn't know what had been going on in Hope's life lately, but she intended to find out

She entered the shop, turned on the lights and went directly to the back office, where she made a pot of coffee. With a cup of fresh brew in hand, she returned to the sales floor and sat on the stool behind the counter that held the register.

Much of her time the night before had been spent thinking about William, grieving for him while at the same time trying to figure out who might want him dead. The list of potential suspects she had to give to Charlie was frighteningly short.

The morning was unusually quiet. No customers had entered when Dana Taylor came through the door at eleven-thirty. "Hey, Grace," she said, her tone unusually somber. "How are you holding up?"

"As well as can be expected," Grace replied. "Right now I'm having trouble wrapping my mind around it all."

"I'm so sorry," Dana replied sympathetically.

"I was wondering if maybe you'd be available to take some extra hours for a while. I'm going to be busy with other things."

"Not a problem," Dana replied, as she stowed her purse under the counter. "When Ben got home from the hospital last night, he told me not to expect to see a lot of him for the next week or two." She didn't quite meet Grace's eyes.

"There's a new shipment of handbags in the back. If you have time this afternoon, could you unpack them and get them on display?" Grace asked, desperate to get over the awkwardness of the moment.

"Sure," Dana agreed. "Any business this morning?"

"Nothing. It's been quiet." Grace turned toward the door as it opened to admit Charlie.

An intense burst of electricity shot through her at the sight of him, and instantly every defense she possessed went up.

"Morning, ladies," he said as he ambled toward the counter. Clad in a pair of snug jeans and a short-sleeved white shirt, he looked half rancher, half businessman and all handsome male.

His square jaw indicated a hint of stubbornness and his eyes were fringed with long, dark lashes. His nose was straight, his lips full enough to give women fantasies of kissing them. In short, Charlie was one hot hunk.

His energy filled the air, and despite her wishes to the contrary, Grace felt a crazy surge of warmth as she gazed at him.

"Good morning, Charlie," Dana replied. "How are things out at the ranch?"

"Not bad. The cattle are getting fat, and I've got a garden full of tomato and pepper plants that are going to yield blue-ribbon-quality product."

Pride rang in his voice, a pride that surprised Grace. Two years ago, the only things that put that kind of emotion in his voice were his fancy surround-sound system, his state-of-the-art television and the new Italian shoes that cost what most people earned in a month.

He turned his gaze to Grace. "We need to talk," he said. His smile was gone, and the enigmatic look in his gray eyes created a knot in Grace's stomach.

"Okay. Come on back to my office," she said.

He followed her to the back room, where she turned and looked at him. "Something else has happened?"

"No, I just have some new information."

"What kind of information?" She leaned against the

desk, needing the support because she knew with certainty whatever he was about to tell her wasn't good.

"Did you know that Hope has a boyfriend?" he asked.

She frowned. "Hope is only fifteen. Their relationship can't be anything serious."

One of his dark eyebrows quirked upward. "When you're fifteen, everything is serious. His name is Justin Walker. Do you know him?"

Grace shook her head, and a new shaft of guilt pierced through her. She should have known her sister's boyfriend. What other things didn't she know? "So, who is he?"

"He's a seventeen-year-old high school dropout with a bad reputation," Charlie replied. "And there's more. Apparently Justin was a bone of contention between William and Hope. William thought he was too old and was bad news and had forbidden Hope from seeing him."

Grace sat on the edge of her desk. "How did you find out all of this?"

"I had a brief conversation with Zack this morning. I wanted to be up-to-date on where the investigation was going before meeting you today. And there's more."

She eyed him narrowly. "I'm really beginning to hate those words."

"Then you're really going to hate this," he said. "On the night before the murder, Hope and William went out to dinner at the café. An employee told Zack that while there, they had a public argument ending with Hope screaming that she wished he were dead."

Grace's heart plummeted to her feet, and she wished she didn't hate Charlie, because at the moment she wanted nothing more than his big strong arms around her.

Chapter 3

Justin Walker lived with a buddy in the Majestic Apartments complex on the outskirts of town. The illustrious name of the apartments had to have been somebody's idea of a very bad joke.

The small complex had faded from yellow to a weathered gray from the Oklahoma sun and sported several broken windows. The vehicles in the parking lot ran the gamut from souped-up hot rods to a rusty pickup truck missing two tires.

"You sure you want to do this?" Charlie asked dubiously, as he parked in front of the building and cut his engine.

Grace stared at the building in obvious dismay. "Not really, but it has to be done. I want to know exactly what his relationship with Hope was…is. I want to hear it from him, and then I want to hear it from my sister." She turned to look at Charlie. "Does he work?"

"He's a mechanic down at the garage, but he called in sick this morning."

"You managed to learn a lot between last night and now," she observed.

He shrugged and pulled his keys from the ignition. "It just took a phone call to find out if he was at the garage today. Somehow I knew you'd want to talk to him." He directed his gaze back at the building. "But, just because he isn't at work doesn't mean he's here."

"There's only one way to find out." She opened her car door and stepped out.

Charlie joined her on the cracked sidewalk and tried not to notice how pretty she looked in the yellow skirt that showcased her shapely legs and the yellow-flowered blouse that hugged her slender curves.

This whole thing would have been so much easier if during the time they'd been apart she sprouted some facial hair or maybe grown a wart on the end of her nose.

"Which unit is it?" she asked.

"Unit four." He pointed to the corner apartment, one that sported a broken window. Grace grimaced but marched with determined strides toward the door, on which she knocked in a rapid staccato fashion.

Charlie stepped in between her and the front door, protective instincts coming into play. He had no idea if Justin was just a loser boyfriend or an active participant in William's murder.

The door opened and a tall young man gazed at them with a wealth of belligerence. He looked like he wasn't having a good day. "Are you more cops?" he asked, his dark eyes wary and guarded.

Grace moved closer to the door. "No. I'm Grace Covington, Hope's sister, and this is her lawyer, Charlie Black. Are you Justin?"

He hesitated a moment, as if considering whether or not to tell the truth, then gave a curt nod of his head, his dark hair flopping carelessly onto his forehead. "Yeah, I'm Justin. What do you want?"

"Sheriff West has already talked to you?" Charlie asked.

Justin's eyes darkened. "He was here half the night asking me questions."

"May we come in?" Grace asked.

Justin's eyes swept the length of her and he scowled. "You don't want to come in here. The place is a dump." He stepped outside and closed the door behind him.

"You were dating my sister?" Grace asked.

Justin barked a dry laugh. "I wouldn't exactly call it dating. She's not allowed to date until she turns sixteen. We hung out, that's all. When she'd show up down at the garage after school, I'd take a break and we'd just talk. It was no big deal."

There was hostility in his voice, as if he expected them to take issue with him. "Were you sleeping with her?" Grace asked. Charlie wasn't sure who was more surprised by the question, himself or Justin.

Justin gave her a mocking smile. "Don't worry, big sister. As far as I know your baby sister is still as pure as the driven snow."

"Where were you yesterday morning?" Charlie asked. "Your boss told me you weren't at work." He felt Grace stiffen next to him.

"Funny, the sheriff asked me the same thing." Justin clutched his stomach. "I've been fighting off this flu bug. Yesterday I was here in bed, and if you don't believe me, my roommate will vouch for me. I didn't leave here all day."

"And your roommate's name?" Charlie asked.

Justin stepped back toward his apartment door. "Sam Young, and now I'm done answering your questions." He stepped back inside and shut the door firmly in their faces.

"Do you believe him?" Grace asked when they were back in Charlie's car and headed for the hospital.

He cast her a wry glance. "In the words of a famous television personality, I wouldn't believe him if his tongue came notarized."

Her burst of laughter was short-lived, but the sound of it momentarily warmed his heart. Charlie always loved to hear her laugh, and there had been a time when he'd been good at making her do so.

"After we speak with Hope, I need to find out if I can go to the house and get some of her things," Grace said. "Dr. Dell thought he would release her at some point this evening or first thing in the morning, and we'll need to get some of her clothes and things to take to my place."

"When we get to the hospital, I'll call Zack and see what can be arranged."

"I'd like to talk to Hope alone. I don't think she'll be open about her relationship with Justin if you're there, too."

"Okay," he replied. He glanced at her and caught her rubbing her temple. "Headache?"

She nodded and dropped her hand back into her lap. "I think it's a guilt thing."

"Guilt? What do you have to feel guilty about?" he asked in surprise.

A tiny frown danced across her forehead, doing nothing to detract from her attractiveness. "I should have been paying more attention to what was going on in her life. I should have been putting in less hours at the store and spending more time with her."

"Regrets are funny things, Grace. They rip your heart out, but they don't really change anything," he replied. He was an old hand at entertaining regrets.

"You're right." She reached up, massaged her temple once again and then shot him a pointed look. "You're absolutely right. The past is over and nothing can change the damage done. What's important is to learn from the mistakes made in the past and never forget the lesson."

Charlie frowned, knowing her words were barbs flung at him and had nothing to do with the situation at hand. They spoke no more until they arrived at the hospital.

As she disappeared into Hope's hospital room, he called Zack West to find out what was going on at the Covington mansion. Zack informed him that the evidence gathering was finished and said Grace was free to get whatever she needed for Hope.

When Charlie asked him for an update, he merely replied that it was an ongoing investigation and there was nothing new to report.

As he waited for Grace, he sat in one of the plastic chairs in the waiting room. Charlie had a theory that murder happened for one of three reasons. He called it his "three *R*" theory. Rage, revenge and reward were the motives that drove most murderers.

At the moment, the officials were leaning toward rage—a young girl's rage at being stymied in a love relationship by an overbearing father figure.

The news was certainly filled with stories of young people going on killing rampages against authority figures. Had Hope snapped that morning and stabbed William while he slept and then, filled with remorse, taken drugs in a suicide attempt?

Hopefully they would be successful in coming up with an alternative theory that would explain both William's death and Hope's drugged state.

He looked up as Grace entered the room. She sat next to him as if too exhausted to stand. "What did she have to say about Justin?" he asked.

"She told me she's crazy in love with him, and she thinks they belong together forever, but she hasn't gotten physical with him yet."

"That's different from Justin's story. He made it

sound like she was no big deal to him," Charlie observed.

"Maybe he doesn't feel the same way she does. Maybe he was afraid to tell us how he really feels about Hope," she replied.

"Maybe," Charlie agreed.

Grace reached up and tucked a strand of her shiny hair behind her ear. "She's not being released today. She's running a fever and Dr. Dell wants to get to the bottom of it."

"You still want to go by the house?" She sat so close to him he could feel the heat from her body. He used to tease her about how she was better than a hot water bottle at keeping him warm on cold wintry nights. He wished he could tell her how he'd been cold ever since he'd lost her.

She nodded. "Whether she's here or at my place, I'm sure she'd be more comfortable with some of her own things. Besides, I'd like to talk to Lana, William's housekeeper. She'd know better than anyone what was going on between William and Hope, and if anyone else was having a problem with William."

Grace jumped up from the chair, newfound energy vibrating from her. "We need to find something, Charlie, something that will point the finger of guilt away from Hope. I can't lose her. She's all I have left."

She looked half frantic, and again a soft vulnerability sagged her shoulders and haunted her eyes. This time Charlie didn't fight his impulse—his need to touch her. He reached out for her hand and took it in his. Hers was icy, as if the heat of her body was unable to warm her small, trembling hand.

"We'll figure it out," he said. "I promise you that we'll get to the bottom of this. I won't let Hope be convicted of a crime she didn't commit."

What he didn't say was that if Hope was guilty, not even the great Charlie Black would be able to save her.

The Covington estate was located on the northern edge of town, a huge two-story structure with manicured grounds, several outbuildings and a small cottage in the back where Lana Racine and her husband, Leroy, lived.

As Charlie pulled into the circular drive and parked in front, Grace stared at the big house and felt the burgeoning grief welling up inside her.

The sight of the bright yellow crime-scene tape across the front door nearly made her lose control, but she didn't. She couldn't.

She'd spent her life being the strong one—the child her mother could depend on, the teenager who often took responsibility for her baby sister, and the woman who'd held it together when her mother deserted them.

Charlie didn't know about her mother. When they'd been dating, she told him only that her mother had moved away, not that she'd just packed her bags and disappeared from their lives.

Without an explanation.

Without a word since.

Was she sunning on a beach in Florida? Eating

crab cakes and lobster in Maine? Or was she out of the country? She'd always talked about wanting to go to France.

Grace welcomed the raw anger that took the place of her grief—it sustained her, kept her strong.

She glanced back at Charlie, wondering if she should tell him about what had been going on in her life when she'd met him. She dismissed the idea. She couldn't stand the idea of seeing pity in his eyes, and after all this time, what difference did it make?

"Are you sure you're ready to go in there?" Charlie asked.

She focused back on the house and nodded. "I'll just get some of Hope's things, then we can go talk with Lana and Leroy."

She almost wished Charlie weren't here with her. He'd stirred old feelings in her, made her remember how much she'd once cared about him. She'd thought her hatred of him would protect her from those old feelings—that it would vaccinate her against the "wanting Charlie" emotion. She'd been wrong.

All day she'd been plagued by memories of the taste of his lips on hers, the feel of his hands stroking the length of her. Their physical relationship had been nothing short of magic. He'd been an amazing lover, at times playful and at other times intense and demanding.

But it wasn't just those kinds of memories that bothered her. Remembering how often they had laughed together and how much they'd enjoyed each other's company had proved equally troubling.

Amnesia would have been welcome. She would have loved to permanently forget the six months with Charlie, but spending time with him now unlocked the mental box in which she'd placed those memories the night she'd walked away from him.

Focus on the reason he's in your life, she told herself. Hope. She had to stay focused on Hope and finding something, anything, that would reveal the young girl's innocence.

She got out of the car, grateful to escape the small confines that smelled of him—a wonderful blend of clean male and expensive, slightly spicy cologne. It was the same scent he'd worn when they'd been dating, and it only helped stir memories she would prefer to forget.

Charlie pulled away the crime-scene tape, and Grace used her key to open the front door. They walked into the massive entry with its marble floor and an ornate gilded mirror hanging on the wall.

"Wow," Charlie said, obviously impressed. "I'd heard this place was a showcase, but I had no idea."

"William was an extremely successful man," she replied. "He liked to surround himself with beautiful things."

"I know you said your mother married him when you were sixteen. What happened to your father?"

"He died of a heart attack when mom was pregnant with Hope. We were left with no insurance and no money in the bank." Grace paused a moment, thinking about those days just after her father's death. There'd been a wealth of grief and fear about what would happen to them now the breadwinner was gone.

She walked from the entry to the sweeping stair-case that led to the second floor. Placing a hand on the polished wood banister, she continued: "William was like a knight in shining armor. He and Mom met at the grocery store, and he swooped into our lives like a savior. He was crazy, not just about Mom, but also about me and Hope."

"He didn't have children of his own?" Charlie asked.

"No. He'd been married years before, but it ended in divorce and there had been no children. We were all the family he had."

"Who is his beneficiary?"

Grace looked at him in surprise. "I have no idea. I hadn't even thought about it."

"Maybe your mother?" he asked.

"Maybe," Grace agreed, although she wasn't so sure. Grace's mother had ripped the very heart out of William when she'd disappeared. William had been a good man, generous to a fault, but he hadn't been a foolish man, especially when it came to money.

"Let's get Hope's things and get out of here," she said, her heart heavy as she climbed the stairs.

Charlie followed just behind her as she topped the stairs and walked down the long hallway toward Hope's room. The door was closed and she hesitated, unsure she was ready for whatever was inside.

Hope had been found covered in blood, clutching the knife in her hands, her room trashed. Grace grabbed the doorknob and still couldn't force herself to open the door.

Charlie placed a hand on her shoulder. "We don't have to do this. We can buy Hope whatever she needs for the time being."

How could a man who had been incredibly insensitive eighteen months ago, a man who had been so thick he hadn't recognized the depths of her feelings for him, be so in tune to what she was feeling now?

She didn't have the answer but was grateful that he seemed to understand the turmoil inside her as she contemplated going into Hope's room. Deep within, she knew she was grateful that he was here with her.

"It's all right. I can do this," she said, as much to herself as to him.

She straightened her shoulders and opened the door. A gasp escaped her as she saw the utter mess inside. She took several steps into the room and stared around in horror.

Ripped clothes were everywhere. The French provincial bookshelf had been turned over, spilling its contents onto the floor. A hole was punched in the Sheetrock wall, as if it had been angrily kicked.

The bed had been stripped. She imagined that the investigators had taken away the bedclothes. "Definitely looks like somebody had a temper fit in here," Charlie said from behind her.

Grace's mind whirled with sick suppositions. Was it possible that a rage had been festering in Hope for some time? Their mother's defection had been difficult on Grace, but it had been devastating for Hope. Grace had been twenty-eight years old when their mother had left, but Hope had been a thirteen-year-old who desperately needed her mom.

"I'll just grab some clothes," Grace said. She'd taken only two steps toward the closet when her foot crunched on something.

She looked down and saw the arm of a porcelain doll. She knew that arm. She knew that doll. It had been Hope's prized possession, given to her on the birthday before their mother had disappeared.

Crouching down, she found the rest of the doll among the mess of clothes and books and miscellaneous items that had fallen from the bookcase.

The porcelain arms and legs had been pulled from the cloth body. The head was smashed beyond repair, and the body had been slashed open.

Rage. There was no doubt that rage had destroyed the doll. The rage of a daughter whose mother had left her with a man who hadn't been able to understand her needs, her wants?

Hope's rage?

The breakdown that began in Grace started with a trembling that seemed to possess her entire body. Her vision blurred with the hot press of tears, and for the first time she wondered if her sister had committed the crime, if it was possible that Hope was guilty.

Chapter 4

Charlie saw it coming: the crack in her strength, the loss of her control. Until this moment Grace had shown an incredible amount of poise in dealing with the mess that had become her life.

Now she looked up at him with tear-filled eyes and lips that trembled uncontrollably, and he knew she'd reached the end of that strength.

"Grace." He said her name softly.

"She couldn't have done this, Charlie? Surely she didn't do this?" They weren't statements of fact but questions of uncertainty, and he knew the agony the doubts must be causing her.

Again the crazy, overwhelming need to hold her, to be her soft place to fall, swept over him. He touched her shoulder, then placed his hand beneath her arm to help her to her feet.

The tears in her eyes streamed down her cheeks, and when Charlie wrapped his arms around her, she didn't fight the embrace—she fell into it.

Her body fit perfectly against his, molding to him with sweet familiarity. A rush of emotions filled him—compassion because of the ordeal she was going through, fear for what she might have to face, and finally a desire for her that he couldn't deny.

The vanilla scent of her hair coupled with that familiar jasmine fragrance filled his head, making him half dizzy.

The embrace was over soon after it began. Grace jumped back as if stung by the physical contact. "I'm okay," she exclaimed as a stain of color spread across her cheeks.

"I never thought otherwise," he replied dryly. He'd be a fool to think that it had been *his* arms she'd needed around her, *his* comfort she'd sought. She'd just needed a little steadying, and if it hadn't been him, it would have been anyone.

She didn't need steadying anymore. Her shoulders were once again rigid as she went around the room, gathering clothes in her arms. After he took the clothes from her, she went into the adjoining bathroom and returned a moment later with a small overnight bag he assumed held toiletries.

"That should do it," she said. Any hint of tears was gone from her eyes, and they once again shone with the steely strength they'd always possessed.

They left the bedroom and went back down the stairs. She relocked the front door, then they stowed Hope's things in the car and headed back to the caretaker cottage where Lana and Leroy Racine lived.

If Charlie was going to mount a credible defense for Hope, he knew that to create reasonable doubt he had to identify another potential suspect with a motive for murder.

He'd never met the Racines, and as he and Grace walked across the lush grass to the cottage in the distance, he asked her some questions about the couple.

"How long have Lana and Leroy worked for William?"

"Lana was William's housekeeper when my mother married him. She married Leroy about ten years ago and soon after had their son, Lincoln."

"Leroy works the grounds?" he asked.

She nodded. "William hired him when he and Lana got married. As you can see, he does a great job."

"Theirs is a happy marriage?"

She shrugged. "I assume so. I'm not exactly privy to their personal life, but they seem very happy. They're both crazy about Lincoln."

They fell silent as they reached the house. It was an attractive place, painted pristine white with black shutters. The porch held two rocking chairs and several pots of brilliant flowers.

Grace knocked on the door, and an attractive redhaired woman who looked to be in her forties answered. She took one look at Grace and broke into torrential sobs.

Grace's eyes misted once again, and she quickly embraced the woman in a hug. "I can't believe it," Lana cried. "I just can't believe he's gone."

"I know. I feel the same way," Grace replied.

Lana stepped away from her and dabbed at her eyes with a tissue from her pocket. "Come in, please." She ushered them into a small but neat and tidy living room, where Grace introduced Charlie.

"Would you like something? Maybe something to drink?" Lana asked as she motioned for them to sit in the two chairs across from the sofa.

"No thanks. We're fine. I wanted to ask you some questions," Grace said. "Is Leroy here?"

"He just left to pick up Lincoln from school." Lana looked at Charlie. "Lincoln goes to the Raymond Academy in Linden."

Charlie had heard of the exclusive private school located in a small town just north of Cotter Creek. Tuition was expensive, especially for parents working as a housekeeper and a gardener.

On the end table next to him, he noticed the picture of a young boy. He picked it up and looked at it. The dark-haired boy looked nothing like his red-haired mother. "Nice-looking boy," he commented, and put the picture back where it belonged.

"He's a good boy," Lana said, pride shining in her brown eyes. "He's smart as a whip and never gives us a minute of trouble."

"Must be tough paying to send him to the Raymond Academy," Charlie observed.

"It is, but Leroy and I agreed early on that we'd

make whatever sacrifices necessary to see that he gets the best education possible." She twisted the tissue in her lap. "Although with William gone, it looks like both of us are going to be without jobs, so I don't know how we'll manage Lincoln's school costs."

"I'd like to talk to you about William and Hope," Grace said. "You know Hope is in the hospital—that the sheriff believes she killed William and then took some sort of drug to knock herself unconscious?"

"That's nonsense. I spoke to Zack West and told him it was ridiculous to think that Hope would do such a thing. She's a sweet child and couldn't possibly do something like this. Did Hope and William argue? Absolutely. She's a teenager and that's what they do, but there's no way anyone will make me believe she killed him."

"Then that makes two of us," Grace said with fervor. It was obvious that Lana's words completely banished whatever momentary doubt had gripped her while in Hope's bedroom.

"Do you know of anyone William was having problems with?" Charlie asked. "A neighbor? A business associate? Anyone?"

Lana shook her head. "Believe me, I've racked my brain ever since I found him dead in his bed." Again a veil of tears misted her eyes.

"I can't think of anyone. He was a wonderful and gentle man. He was so good to me. One time, before I was married to Leroy, I wasn't feeling very well. I called William and told him I thought I had the flu and shouldn't come cook dinner for him. He showed up on my doorstep thirty minutes later with a pot of chicken soup he'd bought at the café. That's the kind of man he was. Who would want to kill a man like that?"

"That's what we're going to try to find out," Charlie said. He stood and pulled a business card from his back pocket. "If you think of anything that might help our defense of Hope, would you please give me a call?" He handed the card to Lana.

At that moment the front door opened, and Leroy and Lincoln came in. After Lana made the introductions, she told Lincoln to go to his room and do his homework.

As the well-mannered young boy disappeared into the back of the house, Charlie felt the chime of a biological clock he didn't know men possessed.

Since moving back to the family ranch in Cotter Creek, he'd been thinking about kids and recognizing that if he intended to start a family, it should be soon. He wasn't getting any younger.

Charlie sat down and turned his attention to Leroy. He was a big, burly man with a sun-darkened face and arms. His face seemed better suited for prize fighting, but at the moment his rough-hewn features held nothing but concern for his wife.

Leroy sat next to her and put an arm around her shoulder, as if to shield her from any unpleasantness.

Charlie asked Leroy the same questions he'd asked Lana and got no different answers. Leroy talked about what a wonderful man William had been and how he'd even helped pay for their wedding.

"I wish to God I knew who was responsible for this," Leroy said, his blunt features twisted with pain. "But, like we told the sheriff, we don't have a clue."

"We appreciate your time," Charlie said, recognizing that nothing more could be learned here. Once again he stood, and Grace followed suit.

"Grace?" Lana looked decidedly uncomfortable. "I know this probably isn't the time or the place, but Leroy and I don't know what we're supposed to do. Should we move out of here?"

Grace frowned thoughtfully. "I wouldn't do anything right now. We'll see what's going to happen with the estate. I'll check into it and let you know what's going on. Although I think Leroy should keep up the grounds, I'd prefer you stay out of the house for the time being." She took Lana's hand and smiled. "Consider yourself on paid vacation at the moment."

They all said their goodbyes, then Charlie and Grace left. "They must be terrified, not knowing what will happen to them now that William is gone," Grace said, as they walked back to the car.

"You should probably talk to William's attorney and find out about his will. Maybe he made some kind of provisions for them in the event of his death."

"His attorney is in Oklahoma City. I wonder if anyone has told him William is dead."

"I'll check with Zack," Charlie said. "And you might think about making funeral plans."

He could tell by the look on her face that she hadn't thought of that. "Oh God. I've been so overwhelmed. Of course, I need to take care of it." She looked stricken by the fact that she hadn't thought about it. "I'll speak with Mr. Burkwell tomorrow to find out what needs to be done." Jonathon Burkwell owned the Burkwell Funeral Home, the only such establishment in the town of Cotter Creek.

When they got to the car, Grace slid into the passenger seat and Charlie got behind the wheel. He started the engine, but then turned to look at her. "Have you called your mother, Grace? Maybe she should come help you take care of things."

Before replying, she averted her gaze and stared out the window. "No, there's no point in contacting her. She's out of the country, and there's really nothing she can do here. I'll be fine without her. Hope and I will be fine."

He studied her pretty profile. As a criminal defense attorney, Charlie was accustomed to people deceiving him, and he knew all the subtle signs of a liar. Right now he had the distinct feeling that Grace was lying to him about her mother.

It had been a day from hell. Grace sat at her desk in the back of the dress shop finishing up the payroll checks. The store had closed at seven, but on the night before payday she always stayed late in case any employees wanted to pick up their checks early.

She didn't mind staying. She was reluctant to go home and face the emptiness of her house and the tumultuous emotions that had been boiling inside her all day.

She'd spoken with William's attorney first thing that morning. He hadn't heard about the murder and was shocked. He, in turn, surprised Grace—she and Hope were the sole beneficiaries to William's fortune. Grace only hoped that fact didn't add to the body of evidence building against her sister.

The rest of the morning was spent making the necessary arrangements at Burkwell's funeral home. It was one of the most difficult things she'd ever done.

At noon, she and Charlie had taken the clothes and personal items to Hope. Grace visited with her sister while Charlie went to the cafeteria for a cup of coffee.

After the hospital visit, they'd gone back to the Covington mansion, where she went through William's desk, seeking something that might tell them who would have wanted him dead.

She still hadn't made herself open the door to William's room—the place where he had died — although she knew eventually she'd want to search it for anything that might help build a defense case for Hope.

She'd returned to the store at three-thirty, and now it was almost eight. She was exhausted but made no move to head home.

She'd just finished writing the last check when she heard the faint whoosh of the store door opening. "Grace?" a familiar voice called.

Grace jumped up from the desk and hurried out of her office. Standing just inside the door, with an eight-month-old baby boy on her hip, was Rachel Prescott, Grace's best friend.

"Oh honey, I just heard the news." Rachel approached her with a wrinkle of concern dancing across her forehead. "Jim had a three-day conference in Dallas, and I decided to go with him. We just got home a little while ago. How are you doing?"

"I'm okay. At least I'm trying to be okay." Grace smiled at the baby boy, who gave her a sleepy smile in return, then leaned his head against his mother's chest. "How's my Bobby?" She reached out and stroked his silky dark hair.

"He's pooped. He didn't have his nap today. So, tell me, what's this I hear about Hope being a suspect?"

"The medical examiner determined that William was killed between six and ten in the morning. Hope was the only one home. There were no signs of forced entry, and the murder weapon was found in Hope's hand." As Grace ticked off the pertinent points, a wave of discouragement swept over her.

Rachel laid a gentle hand on Grace's shoulder. "Sounds bad, but we both know Hope isn't capable of killing anybody." Grace smiled gratefully.

"I also heard you've hooked up with Charlie Black again," Rachel added, a hint of disapproval in her voice.

"Not hooked up as in 'hooked up,' I've just hired him to investigate the murder, and if the world goes crazy and Hope is arrested, I want him to defend her."

Rachel raised an eyebrow. "And who is defending you from Charlie?"

Rachel was the only person who knew the truth about how Charlie had broken Grace's heart, and she'd proclaimed him the most black-hearted, vile man on the face of the planet. At the time, Grace had relished her friend's anger on her behalf.

"Don't worry, I have no intention of making the same mistakes where Charlie is concerned. I just need him right now. He's good at what he does, but that doesn't mean I want him in my life on a personal level. I haven't forgotten, and I certainly haven't forgiven him."

Unfortunately, that didn't mean she didn't want him on some insane level. Over the last couple of days, she'd realized there was a part of her that had never really gotten over him.

"I just don't want to see you hurt again," Rachel said. "It's bad enough that you haven't dated since the breakup."

"That has nothing to do with him," Grace protested. "You know how busy I've been here at the shop."

"I know this place has become the perfect excuse for you," Rachel replied dryly.

Grace didn't respond. She couldn't exactly argue the point because she knew there was more than a kernel of truth to Rachel's words.

"Take that baby home and put him to bed," she finally said.

"Is there anything I can do? Any way I can help?" Rachel asked.

"Just pray they find the guilty party and that they don't arrest my sister," Grace replied. At that moment, the door to the shop opened once again, and one of her young, part-time employees came in to get her paycheck.

When Rachel and Bobby left, Grace gave the high school girl her check and then returned to her desk in the back room. She'd give it another half an hour or so before locking up the store and going home.

She kicked off her shoes beneath the desk and reached for the mug that held the last of the lukewarm coffee she'd been drinking all evening.

Charlie. Drat the man for being as attractive as he'd been eighteen months ago. From all indications, he appeared to have settled into ranching and small-town life with his usual aplomb.

The hard edge he'd possessed before seemed to be missing. He was still strong and self-assured, but he somehow seemed a bit more sensitive than he'd been during their six months together.

Not that it mattered. The familiar saying flitted through her mind: *Screw me once, shame on you. Screw me twice, shame on me.* She would be a fool to allow Charlie back into her heart in any way, shape or form. Charlie had proven himself unable to keep his pants on around other women.

Her present attraction to him was surely just due to her belief that he could save her sister and somehow make sense of the senseless.

She closed her business checkbook and locked it in the bottom desk drawer. Time to go home. Maybe tonight she would sleep without nightmares.

Maybe tonight visions of a blood-covered, knife-wielding Hope wouldn't haunt her. Maybe images of a dead William wouldn't visit her dreams.

Once again she heard the *whoosh* of the shop door opening. She quickly unlocked the desk drawer, pulled out the checkbook and then walked in her stocking feet from the office into the other room.

"Hello?" She frowned as she looked around the room. It was dimly lit with only a few security lights on, and she didn't see anyone inside.

Odd, she could have sworn she'd heard the front door open. Maybe she'd just imagined it. She glanced around one last time, then returned to her office, sat back in her chair, put the checkbook away and locked the drawer.

She moved her feet beneath the desk, seeking the shoes she'd kicked off minutes before. Suddenly Grace was eager to get home to the two-bedroom house she rented. She'd lived there for the past five years, long enough to fill it with her favorite colors and fabrics and make it a home where she enjoyed spending time.

Successful in finding her shoes, she stood and stretched with arms overhead, grateful that this trying day was finally at an end. Maybe tomorrow won't be so difficult. One could hope, she thought.

She grabbed her purse, turned off the office light and stepped out. Just as she was about to head for the front door, she felt a stir in the air and saw in her peripheral vision a ruffling of the dresses hanging on the rack.

"Hello? Is somebody here?" Her heartbeat quickened, and she gripped her purse handle. "Who's there?"

A dark shadow with a bat or length of pipe raised over his head exploded out of the clothes rack. He didn't make a sound, and the scream that rose up in the back of Grace's throat refused to release itself as she threw her purse at him and turned to run back to the office.

A lock. There was a lock on the office door. The words thundered through her brain as her heart threatened to burst out of her chest.

She had no idea who he was or what he wanted, but she didn't intend to stick around and ask questions. She ran past a mannequin and knocked it over, hoping to block his attack and gain an extra second or two to reach the office.

The mannequin banged to the floor, and she heard a hissed curse. Deep. Male. Oh God, what was he doing in here? What did he want?

She gasped as she reached the office door, but before she could grab the knob and turn it, something hard crashed into the back of her head. She crumpled to her knees as shooting stars went off in her brain.

The intruder kicked her twice in the ribs and frantic thoughts raced through her scrambled brain as she struggled to regain her breath. She knew if she didn't do something he was going to kill her.

"Grace?" The familiar female voice came from the front door, although to Grace it sounded as if it came from miles away. "Grace, are you here?"

It was only then that the scream that had been trapped inside her released itself. The attacker froze, then raced for the back door of the store. As he went through it, the alarm began to ring. The loud, buzzing noise was the last sound Grace heard as she gave in to the shooting stars and lost consciousness.

Chapter 5

Charlie stepped on the gas, breaking every speed limit in the state of Oklahoma as he raced toward the hospital. His heart beat so hard he felt nauseous and every nerve ending he possessed screamed in alarm.

He'd called Grace at home to make arrangements for meeting the next day, and when he didn't get her there, he'd tried Sophisticated Lady to see if she was working late. Deputy Ben Taylor answered and told him there'd been an attempted robbery at the store and that Grace had been transported to the hospital. He had no information on her condition, and Charlie jumped into his car almost before he could hang up the phone.

Now he squealed into the hospital lot and parked, his heart still pounding the rhythm of alarm. How badly had she been hurt? Had they caught the person who had broken in?

He raced into the ER and nearly ran into Zack coming out. He grabbed the man by his broad shoulders. "What happened? Where's Grace? Is she all right?"

Zack held up his hands. "Calm down, Charlie. She's going to be fine. She's got some bruised ribs and a possible concussion."

Charlie's heart dropped to his toes as he released his hold on Zack. "And you call that fine? Ben Taylor said something about a robbery at the store."

"We think that's what it was, but he was interrupted by Ben's wife showing up to get her paycheck. I've got to get back to the store, but if you want to see Grace, she's in examination room two."

Charlie hurried down the hallway, his hands clenching and unclenching. Bruised ribs? A possible concussion?

A simmering rage began to burn in his stomach as he thought of somebody hurting Grace. He hoped to hell Zack would find out who was responsible.

Charlie wasn't a violent man. He was accustomed to using his brain and mouth to solve fights, but at the moment, he wanted nothing more than to find the person who hurt Grace and beat the holy hell out of him.

The door to the examination room was closed. Charlie gave a soft knock but didn't wait for an answer before opening the door.

Clad in a worn, pale-blue-flowered hospital gown,

Grace sat on the edge of the examining-room table, her arms around her waist as the doctor sat in the chair before her.

Her eyes widened slightly at the sight of Charlie, and she winced as she shifted positions. "You didn't have to come here." Her normally strong voice was weak, reedy. The sound of it squeezed his heart.

"Of course I had to come here," he replied. "How is she?" He looked at the doctor, who wore a name tag that proclaimed him to be Dr. Devore.

"I have sore ribs and a headache. Other than that I'm fine," she answered. "In fact the doctor was just releasing me."

"Against my better judgment," Dr. Devore muttered beneath his breath. "She has quite a goose egg on the back of her head."

Charlie shot a look at Grace. She sighed and raised a trembling hand to her head. "He's worried that I might have a concussion and thinks I should spend the night."

"Then you should stay," Charlie said.

"I don't want to," she said crossly and dropped her hand from her head. "I'm a grown woman, Charlie. I know what's best for me, and I just need to go to bed. I'll be fine after a good night's sleep."

"If she goes home, somebody should stay with her throughout the night," Dr. Devore said, as he stood. "And if she suffers any nausea, vomiting or blurred vision, she needs to come right back in. I'll write you a pain prescription for your ribs, and the nurse will complete your discharge papers. Then I guess you can go."

"You aren't going home alone," Charlie said the moment the doctor left the room. "You have two choices, Grace. You can either have me as a house-guest for the night or you can come back to the ranch with me."

He saw the mutinous glare in her eyes and quickly continued, "Be reasonable, Grace. You shouldn't be alone. What if you get dizzy in the middle of the night and fall? What if you start throwing up and can't stop? Somebody needs to be with you."

"I don't want you in my house," she said hesitantly.

"Then come to mine," he replied. "I have a comfortable guest room, and if you're worried about being alone with me, don't be. Rosa will be there."

Once again she raised a hand to her head and winced. "Okay, I'll go to your place."

Her relatively easy capitulation surprised him and made him wonder just what had happened tonight in the shop and what was going on in her head. He intended to find out before the night was over.

"Can you take me by my house to get a few things?" she asked.

"Absolutely."

The nurse came in with her prescription and discharge papers. She reminded them of all the signs to watch for and to return to the emergency room should Grace experience anything unusual.

Charlie stepped out of the room so Grace could

get dressed, and while he waited for her he called Rosa to make sure she had the guest room ready.

When Grace opened the door of the examining room and stepped out, Charlie wanted to wrap her in his arms, hold her tight and make sure that nobody else ever hurt her again.

She was in obvious pain as they walked to his car, and once again rage coupled with fierce protectiveness filled him.

Their first stop was at the pharmacy, where they filled the prescription for her pain pills. He wanted her to wait in the car while he ran in, but she insisted on going in.

From the drugstore, he drove to her house. He'd never been inside it before. Their dates had usually taken place in Oklahoma City when she was there on business.

They'd had two dates here in Cotter Creek when he'd come back to visit his father, and it had been on those dates he'd met Hope, but he'd never been invited into her personal space.

As he stepped into her living room, two things struck him: the lime and lavender color scheme that was both soothing and sensual, and the magnificent scent of jasmine and vanilla that lingered in the air.

When Grace disappeared down the hallway to her bedroom, he walked around the living room, taking in the furnishings and knickknacks that showed the nuances of her personality.

The sofa looked elegant yet comfortable, and the

bookshelf held an array of paperback books and framed photos of both Hope and William. What was curiously missing were any photos of her mother. Again Charlie wondered about the whereabouts of the elusive Elizabeth Covington and the relationship she had with her daughters.

Right now, what he really wanted to know was what Grace's bedroom looked like. Was her bed covered with luxurious silk sheets that smelled like her? Did she still own that sexy little red nightgown that hugged her curves and exposed just enough skin to make his mind go blank?

He sat on the sofa and mentally chastised himself. He had to stop thinking about things like that—had to stop torturing himself with memories of how her long hair had felt splayed across his bare chest and how she loved to cuddle and run her finger through his thatch of chest hair.

He remembered the two of them running naked into his kitchen to bake a frozen pizza after a bout of hot, wild sex, slow-dancing on his balcony and the philosophical debates that usually ended in laughter.

She was smart and sexy—everything he'd wanted in a woman—but he'd thought she was playing for fun and hadn't realized she was playing for keeps. She'd breezed into his life every weekend or so. She hadn't been inclined to share much information about her personal life. Instead they had spent their time together living in the moment.

Now, as he sat on the sofa with those old regrets weighing heavy, he realized that despite their intense relationship there were many things he didn't know about her, many things they hadn't shared.

He stood up when she returned to the living room with a small, flowery overnight bag in her hand. He took the bag from her, and moments later they were in his car, headed toward his ranch.

"You want to tell me exactly what happened tonight?" he asked.

"I figured you already knew. Somebody tried to rob the store."

He glanced at her. She was ghostly pale in the light from the dashboard. "That's the short version. I want all the details," he said gently.

She leaned her head back against the seat, winced slightly and closed her eyes. "I was in the back in the office and went out to greet whoever had come in, but I didn't see anyone so I went back to the office to lock up my desk and get ready to leave. I was halfway to the front door when he came out of the rack of clothes."

Charlie's hands tightened around the steering wheel as he heard the slight tremor in her voice and felt her fear grow palpable in the car.

"And then what?" he asked.

"He had a bat or something like that in his hands. I ran back toward the office. I knew if I could get inside I could lock the door and call for help." She drew a tremulous breath. "I almost made it." She opened her eyes and gave him a wry smile. "I guess I shouldn't have stopped to admire that cute blouse on the mannequin."

Her smile began to tremble and fell away as tears filled her eyes. "I'd just reached the office door when he hit me in the back of the head. I fell to my knees and he started to kick me." A small sob escaped her, but she quickly sucked in a breath to stop her tears. "If Dana hadn't come in for her paycheck, I don't know what would have happened."

"You didn't see who it was? You couldn't make an identification?"

"No. All I saw was a big, dark shadow." She sucked in another breath and wiped her eyes before the tears could fall. "I guess I should be grateful that he didn't get the money in the cash register." Once again she leaned her head back and closed her eyes.

Charlie said nothing, but his blood ran cold. What kind of a robber would walk right past the cash register and hide in a rack of clothes? If he'd truly been after quick cash, why not take the money from the register and escape out the front door?

His hands clenched tighter on the steering wheel as alarms rang in his head. What she'd just described didn't sound like an attempted robbery. It sounded like attempted murder.

Under any other circumstances, Grace would have never agreed to go to Charlie's for the night, but the truth was that she was afraid to be alone. The attack had shaken her up more than she wanted to admit, and even now as she closed her eyes, all she could see was a vision of the big shadow leaping out at her.

Almost as upsetting as the attack itself was the fact that she couldn't think of a single friend who would welcome her into their home. Over the last couple of years she'd been so focused on the store, she hadn't taken the time to nurture friendships. Her relationship with Rachel was the only one she'd managed to maintain, and she was reluctant to barge into Rachel's happy home where she lived with her adoring husband and baby boy.

With William gone and Hope in the hospital, she really had no place else to turn but to Charlie. At least Rosa would be there.

A surge of anger swelled up inside Grace. Her mother should be here. Her mother should be the person calming her fears, offering her support and comfort. The anger was short-lived. She was unable to sustain it as her head pounded and her ribs ached.

She was grateful when Charlie pulled up to the ranch. Lights blazed from almost every window. All she wanted was a pain pill and a bed where she'd feel safe for the remainder of the night.

Rosa greeted them at the front door, fussing like a mother hen as she led Grace to the airy, open kitchen. "I'm going to make you a nice hot cup of tea, then it's bed for you, you poor thing."

As Grace eased down into a chair at the table and Charlie sat across from her, Rosa bustled around, preparing the tea. Despite the pounding of her head, Grace found the hominess of the room comforting. Maybe a cup of tea would banish the icy knot inside her chest.

It smelled like apple pie spices, and a vase of

fresh-cut daisies sat in the center of the round oak table. The yellow gingham curtains added a dash of cheer.

"Tell me again what happened," Charlie said.

"She will not," Rosa said, her plump face wrinkling in disapproval as she shot a stern look at him. "There will be time for you to talk tomorrow. Right now what she needs is to drink that tea and get into bed. Haven't you noticed that she's pale as a ghost and in obvious pain?"

Grace looked at Charlie, and in the depths of his gray eyes, she saw compassion and caring and a flicker of something else, something deeper that both scared her and sent a rumbling shock wave through her.

She quickly broke eye contact with him and stared into her cup. Coming here had been a mistake. She didn't want to see Charlie here in his home environment, one so different from his apartment in Oklahoma City.

"You want one of those pills?" Charlie asked.

She nodded. "I'd like a handful, but I'll settle for one."

"Your head still hurt?" he asked, as he got the bottle and shook out one of the pills.

"The only thing that takes my mind off how bad my head hurts is the pain in my ribs." She forced a small smile that turned into a wince.

"I'm just going to go turn down your bed and fluff your pillows," Rosa said, and left the kitchen.

Grace took the pill and sipped her tea, the warmth working its way into icy territory. She'd been cold since the moment the attacker had leapt out of the clothes rack. She would have given him any money she had if he'd demanded it. He hadn't needed to hit her over the head and kick her.

She was aware of Charlie's gaze on her, intent and somber. "What?" she finally asked. "What are you thinking, Charlie?"

"I'm thinking maybe we have a lot to talk about tomorrow."

Instinctively she knew he was talking about more than William's murder case, about more than the attack on her tonight. She frowned.

"Charlie, if you think I'm going to talk about anything that happened before three days ago, then you're wrong. I have no desire to go back and hash out our past. I told you what I want from you. I want you to keep Hope out of jail. I appreciate what you're doing for me tonight, but don't mistake my need for your abilities as an attorney and investigator for a need for anything else. Don't mistake my gratitude for anything other than that."

Her speech exhausted her. Thankfully at that moment Rosa returned to the kitchen and Grace stood, a bit unsteady on her feet.

Charlie was at her side in an instant, his arm under hers for support. "Let's get you into bed," he said.

She was already feeling the initial effect of the pain medication, a floating sensation that took the edge off and made her legs a bit wobbly. She rarely took any kind of pain meds. She hated the feeling of being even slightly out of control.

Charlie led her down the hallway, and for a single, crazy moment, she wished he were going to crawl into bed with her. Not for sex—although sex with Charlie had always been amazing.

No, what she yearned for was his big, strong arms around her. He'd always been a great cuddle partner, and she'd never felt as loved, as safe, as when she'd been snuggled against him with his arms wrapped around her.

"You should be okay in here," he said as they stepped into the room.

The guest room was large and decorated in various shades of blue. The bed was king-sized, the bedspread turned down to reveal crisp, white sheets.

"Do you want me to send in Rosa to help you get into your nightclothes?" he asked.

"No, I'll be fine," she replied. Her voice seemed to come from someplace far away. She looked up at him, his face slightly blurry, and again she was struck by a desire to fall into his arms—to burrow her head against his strong chest and let him hold her through the night.

"You need to go now, Charlie," she said, and pushed him away.

He stepped back toward the door. "You'll let me know if you need anything?"

"You'll be the first to know."

He turned to leave but then faced her once again. "Grace? I could kill the man who did this to you." His deep voice rumbled and his eyes flashed darkly.

She sat on the edge of the bed. "I appreciate the sentiment," she said. "Good night, Charlie."

"'Night, Grace." He closed the door, and she was alone in the room.

It took what seemed like forever to get out of her clothes and into her nightgown. She went into the adjoining bathroom and brushed her teeth, then returned to the bedroom, where she turned out the bedside lamp and fell into bed.

It was only when she was finally alone that she began to cry. She didn't know if her tears were for William, for Hope, for her mother or for herself.

And she feared they just might be tears because, in the past, Charlie Black hadn't been the man she'd thought he was, the man she'd wanted him to be.

Chapter 6

It was just after two in the morning, and Charlie sat in the recliner chair by the window in the living room, staring out at the moonlit night.

He'd grown up on the ranch, and some of his happiest memories were of things that occurred here. He'd loved the feel of a horse beneath him and the smell of the rich earth, but in college, his head had gotten twisted, and suddenly the ranch hadn't seemed good enough for him.

He'd been a fool. A shallow, stupid fool.

A year ago he would have never dreamed that he'd be back here on the ranch. He'd been living in the fast lane, making more money than he'd ever dreamed possible and enjoying a lifestyle of excess.

Meeting Grace had been the icing on the cake. He'd eagerly looked forward to the two weekends a month she came into town and stayed with him. Although he would have liked more from her, he got the feeling from her that he was an indulgence, like eating ice cream twice a month. But nobody really wanted a steady diet of ice cream.

He'd thought he was her boy toy. They'd never spoken about their relationship, never laid down ground rules or speculated on where it was going. They'd just enjoyed it.

Until that night. That crazy Friday night when things—when *he*—had spiraled out of control.

He shoved these thoughts from his mind and closed his eyes and drew a weary breath. He was tired, but sleep remained elusive. The attack on her earlier tonight worried him because it didn't make sense.

If the goal of the person in the store had been to rob it, then why carry in a bat, why not a gun? Why leave the cash register untouched and go after Grace? Had he thought that her cash might be locked away in the office? Possibly.

He sat up straighter in his chair as he sensed movement in the hallway. He reached over and turned on the small lamp on the table next to his chair.

Grace appeared in the doorway. She was wearing a short, pink silk robe tied around her slender waist, and her hair was tousled from sleep. She didn't appear to be surprised that he was still awake.

"Can't sleep?" he asked.

"I had a bad dream. I tried to go back to sleep, but decided maybe it was time for another pain pill." She walked across the room to the sofa and curled up with her bare legs beneath her. "What's your excuse for being up this time of the night?"

"No bad dreams, just confusing thoughts."

"What kind of confusing thoughts?" she asked, and then held up a hand. "Wait, I don't want to know, at least not tonight." She reached up and smoothed a strand of her golden hair away from her face. "Talk to me about pleasant things, Charlie. I feel like the last couple of days have been nothing but bad things. Tell me about your life here at the ranch. What made you decide to move back here?"

"You heard about Dad's heart attack?"

She nodded. "And I'm sorry."

"Initially I was just going to come back here to deal with whatever needed to be taken care of to get the place on the market and sold, but something happened in those days right after I buried Dad."

He paused a moment and stared back out the window, but it was impossible to see anything but his own reflection. In truth, his life had begun a transformation on the night that Grace left him, but he knew she wouldn't want to hear that, probably wouldn't believe him, anyway.

He looked back at her. "I realized that I hated my life, that I missed waking up in the mornings and hearing the cows lowing in the pasture, that I missed the feel of a horse beneath me and the warm sun on my back. I realized it was time to come home to Cotter Creek."

She leaned her head back against the cushions. "When I was planning to open a dress shop, William told me I could use the money he loaned me to open one anywhere in the country, but it never entered my mind to be anywhere but here," she said. "Cotter Creek is and always will be home. I love it here, the small-town feel, the people, everything. Has the transition been tough for you?"

"Learning the ins and outs of ranching has been challenging," he admitted. "Even though I grew up here I never paid much attention to the day-to-day details. I already had my sights set on something different than the ranch. My ranch hands have had a fine time tormenting the city boy in me. The first thing they told me was that cow manure was a natural cleaner for Italian leather shoes."

She laughed and that's exactly what he'd wanted, to hear that rich, melodic sound coming from her. She was a woman made for laughter, and for the next few minutes he continued to tell her about the silly things that had happened when he'd first taken over the ranch.

He embellished each story as necessary to get the best entertainment value—needing, wanting, to keep her laughing so the dark shadows of fear and worry wouldn't claim her eyes again.

"Stop," she finally said, her arms wrapped around her ribs.

"You need that pain pill now?" he asked.

"No, I don't think so. To be honest, what I'd like

is something to eat. Maybe I could just fix a quick sandwich or something. I didn't eat dinner last night," she said with a touch of apology.

"I'll bet there's some leftover roast beef from Rosa's dinner in the fridge. Want to come into the kitchen or do you want me to fix you a plate and bring it to you?"

She unfolded those long, shapely legs of hers. "I'll come to the kitchen." She stood and frowned. "We won't wake up Rosa, will we?"

"Nah. First of all she sleeps like the dead, and secondly her room is on the other side of the house." Charlie got up and followed her into the kitchen, trying not to notice how the silky robe clung to her lush curves.

He flipped on the kitchen light, and as she slid into a chair at the table, he walked over to the refrigerator, then turned back to look at her. "If you'd rather not have leftover roast, I could whip up an omelet with toast."

She looked at him in surprise. "You never used to cook."

He knew she was remembering that when they had been seeing each other he'd always taken his meals out, keeping only prepared food in his apartment that required nothing more than opening a lid or popping it into the microwave.

"When I came back here to the ranch, I learned survival cooking skills. Rosa takes three days off a week to stay with her son and his family, and during those days I'm on my own. So, cooking became a necessity, and to my surprise I rather like it."

"The roast beef is fine," she replied.

He felt her gaze lingering on him as he got out the leftover meat and potatoes and arranged them on a plate, then ladled gravy over everything and popped it into the microwave.

Was she remembering those midnight raids they'd made on his refrigerator after making love? When they'd eat cold chicken with their fingers or eat ice cream out of the carton?

Did she remember anything good about their time together, or had his betrayal left only the bad times in her head?

"Are you dating, Grace? Got a special fella in your life?" he asked.

She raised a perfectly arched blond eyebrow. "If I had somebody special in my life, I wouldn't be sitting here now," she replied, confirming what he'd already assumed. "I've been too busy at the shop to date, besides the fact that I'm just not interested in a relationship."

The microwave dinged and Charlie turned around to retrieve the food. He wanted to ask her if he was responsible for the fact that she didn't want a relationship, if he'd left such a bad mark on her heart that she wasn't interested in ever pursuing a relationship again. If that was the case, it would be tragic.

He placed the steaming plate before her, got her a glass of milk and sat across from her as she began to eat.

"What about you?" she asked between bites. "Are you dating somebody here in town? I'm sure there were plenty of fluttering hearts when the news got out that you had moved back."

"I would venture a guess that yours wasn't one of those that fluttered?"

She raised that dainty eyebrow again. "That would be a good guess," she replied.

He leaned back in his chair and shook his head. "I'm not seeing anyone, haven't for quite some time. Apparently Dad hadn't been feeling well for a while before his death, and the ranch had kind of gotten away from him. I've been incredibly busy since I moved back. I haven't had the time or the inclination to date."

"Charlie Black too busy for fun? Hold the presses!" she exclaimed.

He gazed at her for a long moment. "You've got to stop that, Grace," he finally said. "If you want my continued help, you need to stop with the not-so-subtle digs. I understand how you feel about me. You don't have to remind me with sarcastic cuts."

She held his gaze as a tinge of pink filled her cheeks. "You're right, I'm sorry." She turned her attention to her plate and set her fork down. "I'm just so filled with anger right now and you're an easy target."

He leaned forward and covered her hand with his, surprised when she didn't pull away from him. "We'll sort this all out, Grace. I promise you."

She surprised him further by turning her hand over and entwining her fingers with his. "I hope so. Right now everything just seems like such a mess."

"It is a mess," he agreed. "But messes can be

cleaned up." Except the one he'd made with her, he reminded himself.

She let go of his hand and picked up her fork once again. As she continued to eat, Charlie once again spoke of ranch life, trying to keep the conversation light and easy.

When she was finished eating, she started to get up to take her plate to the sink, but he stopped her and instead grabbed the dish himself.

"I'm not used to somebody waiting on me," she said.

"You never struck me as a woman who wanted or needed anyone to wait on you," he replied, as he rinsed the dishes and stuck them in the dishwasher. "One of your strengths is that you're self-reliant and independent. And one of your weaknesses is that you're self-reliant and independent." He smiled and pointed a finger at her. "And no, that doesn't open the door for you to point out all my weaknesses."

She laughed, then reached up and touched her temple. "Now I think I'm ready for a pain pill and some more sleep."

When she got up from the table, Charlie tried unsuccessfully not to notice that her robe had come untied. As she stood, he caught a glimpse of the curve of her creamy breast just above the neckline of the pink nightgown she wore beneath.

Desire jolted through him, stunning him with the force of it. Maybe this was his penance, he thought, as he followed her out of the kitchen. Fate had forced them together, and his punishment was to want her forever and never have the satisfaction of possessing her again.

As they passed through the living room, he turned out the lamp, knowing that if he didn't get some sleep tonight he wouldn't be worth a plugged nickel the next day.

When they reached the door to her room, she turned and looked at him. Her gaze seemed softer than it had since the moment she'd pulled up in her convertible and demanded his help.

"Thank you, Charlie, for feeding me and letting me stay here tonight. I really appreciate everything." She reached up and placed her palm on the side of his cheek, and he fought the impulse to turn his face into her touch. "Part of you is such a good man."

She dropped her hand to her side. "I just wish I could forgive and forget the parts of you that aren't such a good man."

She turned and went into the bedroom, closing the door firmly in his face.

Grace woke with the sun slashing through the gauzy curtains and the sound of horse hooves someplace in the distance. She remained in bed, thinking about her life, about what lay ahead and, finally, about Charlie.

Funny that the man who had hurt her more than any man in her life was also the one who made her feel the most safe. She'd slept without worry, comforted by the fact that Charlie was in the room across the hall.

Surely it was just because of all that had happened, that she'd so easily let him back in her life.

She was off-kilter, careening around in a landscape that was utterly foreign to her. Was it any wonder she'd cling to the one person she'd thought she'd known better than anyone else in the world?

With a low moan, she finally pulled herself to a sitting position on the side of the bed. She'd felt awful the night before, and although her head had stopped pounding, her body felt as if it had been contorted in positions previously unknown to the human body.

Her ribs were sore, but not intolerably so. No more pain pills, she told herself, as she headed for the bathroom. What she needed was a hot shower to loosen her muscles and clear her head. Then she needed to get Charlie to take her home.

Before falling asleep last night, she'd come to the conclusion that the attack in the shop had been an attempted robbery. It was the only thing that made sense.

The robber had obviously thought there was nothing in the register and probably assumed she had a safe or a cash box in the office. He probably wouldn't have attacked her at all if she'd gone directly to the front door and left instead of noticing the sway of the clothes on the rack in front of his hiding place. She went to the bathroom and turned on the shower.

She'd never felt such terror as when he'd jumped out of the clothes rack and raced toward her, the long object held over his head. If he'd hit her just a little harder, he could have bashed her skull in and killed her.

Shivering, she quickly stepped beneath the hot spray of water, needing the warmth to cast away the chill her thought evoked.

The shower did help, although her ribs still ached when she drew a deep breath or moved too fast. She dressed in the jeans and blouse she'd packed in her overnight bag, then left the bedroom in search of Charlie.

She found Rosa in the kitchen by herself. The plump woman sat at the table with a cup of coffee in front of her. When she saw Grace, she jumped to her feet with surprising agility.

"Sit," Grace exclaimed. "Just point me to the cabinet with the cups. I can get my own coffee."

"What about breakfast?" Rosa asked, as she pointed a finger to the cabinet next to the sink. "You should eat something."

"Nothing for me. I'm fine. I had some of your roast beef at about three this morning. It was delicious, by the way." Grace poured herself a cup of the coffee and joined the housekeeper at the table. "Where's Charlie?"

"Out riding the ranch. He should be back in a little while. How are you feeling this morning?"

"Sore, but better than last night." Grace took a sip of the coffee.

"Charlie was worried about you. I could see it in his eyes. He used to get that look when his mama was having bad days. She had cancer, you know. She was diagnosed when he was ten and didn't pass away until he was fourteen. Those four years were tough on him, but I'm sure you knew all that."

"Actually, I didn't," Grace replied. She'd known that Charlie's mother had passed away when he was a teenager, but that was all she'd known.

At that moment, the back door opened and he walked in, bringing with him that restless energy he possessed and the scent of sunshine and horseflesh. The smile he offered her shot a starburst of warmth through her.

"Grace, how are you feeling?" He shrugged out of a navy jacket and hung it on a hook near the backdoor, then walked to the cabinet and grabbed a cup.

"Better. A little sore, but I think I'm going to live." She didn't want to notice how utterly masculine he looked in his worn jeans and the white T-shirt that pulled taut across his broad shoulders. With his lean hips and muscled chest and arms, he definitely turned women's heads.

She'd always thought he was born to wear a suit— that elegant dress slacks and button-down shirts were made for him. But she'd been mistaken. He looked equally hot in his casual wear.

"I'm glad you're feeling better," he said, as he joined them at the table. "Did you get breakfast?"

"Said she didn't want any," Rosa replied.

"And I don't. What I'd like is for you to take me home now." She looked at Charlie expectantly.

He frowned and Rosa stood, looking from one to the other. "I'm going to go take care of some laundry," she said, and left the two of them alone at the table.

Charlie took a sip of his coffee, eyeing her over

the rim of the mug. "I wish you'd consider staying here for a couple more days," he said.

"There's no reason to do that. I'm feeling much better." She wrapped her fingers around her cup as his frown deepened.

"You might be feeling better, but I'm not. I don't like what happened to you last night, Grace."

She laughed. "I wasn't too excited about it, either, but it was an attempted robbery. It could have happened to anyone."

"But it didn't happen to anyone. It happened to you." His gaze held hers intently. "And given what happened to William, it just makes me nervous. It makes me damned nervous."

She leaned back in her chair and looked at him in surprise. "Surely you can't think that one thing had anything to do with the other?" she exclaimed. "You're overreacting, Charlie."

"Maybe," he agreed, and took another sip of his coffee.

"How can you possibly connect what happened to William to the attack on me at the store last night?"

"I can't right now." His lips were thin with tension. "But, I'd prefer we be too cautious than not cautious enough."

"Then I'll do things differently at the store. I realize now how incredibly stupid it was of me to leave the shop door unlocked when I was in the back room. Maybe whoever came in knew that it was payday and hoped I'd have some of the payroll in cash. I just can't believe it was anything other than that, and there's no reason for me to stay here another night."

She wasn't going to let him talk her into staying. Last night after he'd fixed her the meal and walked her back to the bedroom, she'd almost kissed him. When she'd placed her palm on the side of his face, she'd wanted to lean in and take his mouth with hers.

It had been an insane impulse, one that she was grateful she hadn't followed through on, but she felt the need to gain some distance from him.

There was no way she wanted to stay here another night with him. She was more than a little weak where he was concerned.

"I suppose you're going to be stubborn about this," he said.

"I suppose so," she agreed.

He drained his coffee cup and got up from the table. "Just let me take a quick shower and I'll take you home."

"Actually you can just drop me at the shop."

"You're actually planning to work today?" He raised an eyebrow in disapproval. "Don't you think it would be wise to give yourself a day of rest?" He carried his coffee cup to the sink.

"Actually, I think you're right. While you're showering, I'll make arrangements for somebody else to work both today and this evening. My ribs are still pretty sore, and I didn't get a lot of sleep last night. A day of lazing around sounds pretty good."

He nodded, as if satisfied with her answer. "Give

me fifteen, twenty minutes, then I'll be ready to take you to get your car."

As he left the kitchen, Grace sipped her coffee. Although she didn't want to admit it, there was a part of her that dreaded going back into the store, where last night she'd thought she was going to die.

She heard a phone ring someplace in the back of the house. It rang only once and then apparently was answered. It reminded her that she needed to make some calls.

She dug her cell phone out of her purse, grateful that Rosa had left it on the kitchen table where she would find it easily this morning. She made the calls to arrange for the shop to run smoothly without her today. Thankfully she had dependable and trustworthy employees to take over for her. She also needed to check on the final funeral arrangements for William.

When the calls were finished, she got up from the table and carried her cup to the sink, then went back to the bedroom to retrieve her overnight bag.

She could hear running water and knew Charlie was in the shower. She sat on the edge of the bed as memories swept over her—memories of hot, steaming water and Charlie gliding a bar of soap over her shoulders and down her back, of the feel of his soapy hands cupping her breasts, of his slick body pressed against her. More than once they'd left the shower stall, covered with suds and fallen into Charlie's king-sized bed to finish what they'd started.

She shook her head to dislodge the old images.

Rising from the bed, she grabbed her bag, then went back into the kitchen to wait for Charlie.

Grace pulled out her cell phone and called the hospital. "Hi, honey," she said when Hope's voice filled the line.

"Grace!" Hope instantly began to cry.

"Hope, what's wrong?" Grace squeezed the phone more tightly against her ear. "Honey, why are you crying? Has something happened?"

"I heard from a nurse this morning that something bad happened to you last night, that you were attacked. I thought I'd never see you again, that it would be just like Mom and you'd be gone forever."

Grace wished she could reach through the line and hug her sister. "I'm not going anywhere, Hope. You can always depend on me," she said fervently.

Again she mentally cursed her mother for abandoning them, for going away and leaving behind so many questions and so much pain.

"It was a robbery attempt, Hope, but I'm okay. I promise and we're going to be okay. You and I together, we're going to be just fine. We're going to get through all of this." She glanced up as Charlie entered the room, bringing with him the scent of minty soap and shaving cream. "I'll be in to see you sometime this morning, okay? You just hang in there. You have to be strong."

She hung up and stood to face Charlie. "I'm ready," she said.

"You'd better sit back down."

It was only then that she saw the darkness in his

eyes, the muscle working in his jaw. A screaming alarm went off inside her.

"Why? What's going on?" Her heart began to beat a frantic rhythm and her legs threatened to buckle as she sat once again.

"I got a call from Zack." He frowned, as if searching for words, which was ridiculous because Charlie was never at a loss for them. "Hope is being arrested this morning. She's going to be charged with first-degree murder."

Grace grabbed hold of the top of the table, her fingertips biting into the wood as his words reverberated through her head.

Chapter 7

If there was any chance of Charlie becoming a drinking man again, the events of the past three days certainly would have driven him to the bottle.

Hope had been arraigned on Tuesday morning in front of the toughest judge Charlie had ever butted heads against. The prosecuting attorney, up for reelection in the fall, had come with both barrels loaded. He'd suggested the judge send a message to the youth around the country, that no matter what the age or the circumstances, murder was never acceptable.

He'd requested no bail be set, and although Charlie had argued vigorously, nearly garnering himself a contempt charge, the judge had agreed with the prosecutor.

Hope would await trial at the Beacon Juvenile Detention Center in Oklahoma City. A plea deal had been offered to her. The authorities believed it was probable she hadn't acted alone, that it was her boyfriend, Justin, who actually killed William.

Hope refused to accept the deal, sticking to her story that she had no idea what had happened that morning at the house.

William's attorney had traveled to Cotter Creek and sat down with Charlie and Grace to go over the will. The estate had been left to Grace and Hope, with Grace as executor. He'd left some of his money to local charities and a generous amount to Lana for her years of service. He'd also left a small amount of money to Grace's mother.

After the meeting with the lawyer, they had visited with the Racines. Grace assured Lana and Leroy that she had no intention of selling the house anytime soon and would continue to pay their salaries if they wanted to stay on doing their usual duties. She also told them about the money William had left to Lana.

Hope's incarceration at the detention center was difficult for Grace, although as usual she kept a stiff upper lip and didn't display the emotions Charlie knew had to be boiling inside her.

Charlie now checked his watch with a frown. Time to leave. He was picking Grace up at ten for William's funeral. After the ceremony was over, they were driving into Oklahoma City to visit Hope. It was going to be a grim, long day.

He left the ranch and headed toward Grace's place. Charlie felt that tingle of excitement, a crazy swell of emotion in his chest—the same feeling he'd always gotten when he knew she was coming into Oklahoma City for the weekend. He would spend the entire week before filled with eager anticipation, half sick by wanting the days of the week to fly by quickly. By Saturday night, he'd be sick again, dreading the coming of Sunday when she'd return to Cotter Creek. He'd never asked her for more than what she gave him, was afraid that in asking he'd only push her away from him.

He shoved these thoughts out of his head as he pulled up in front of her house. She was waiting for him on the porch, a solitary woman in an elegant black dress. He got out of the car as she approached, and his heart squeezed at the dark, deep sadness in her eyes.

"Good morning," he said, as he opened the car door to let her in. "Are you ready for this?"

"I don't think you're ever ready for something like this," she replied.

He closed the door, went back around to the driver's seat and got in. "You look tired," he said, as he headed toward the cemetery. The wake had been the night before and was followed by an open house at Grace's place.

"After everyone left last night, I had trouble going to sleep," she said. "I'm sure I'll sleep better once the funeral is over and I get a chance to see that Hope's okay."

He nodded. "Zack turned over copies of William's financial records to me. I spent last night going through them looking for any anomalies that might raise a flag."

"Let me guess, you didn't find anything."

"Nothing that looked at all suspicious." He felt the weight of her gaze on him.

"We aren't doing very well at coming up with an alternate suspect," she observed.

"Unfortunately it isn't as easy as just pulling a name out of a hat. I intend to make a case that Justin is responsible."

"Then why hasn't he been arrested?" she asked. "Zack has made it pretty clear he thinks Justin was involved."

"Thinking and proving are two different things. Unfortunately Justin's roommate has provided him with an alibi for the time of the murder." His roommate, Sam Young, certainly was no paragon of virtue. Sam worked in a tattoo parlor and had a reputation for being a tough guy.

They fell silent for the rest of the drive to the cemetery. When they arrived, the parking lot was already filled with cars, indicating that there was a huge turnout of people to say goodbye to William Covington.

The Cotter Creek Cemetery was a pretty place, with plenty of old shade trees. Wilbur Cummins, the caretaker, took particular pride not only in maintaining the grounds but also in making sure that all the headstones were in good shape. A plethora of flowers filled the area.

As they waited for the ceremony to begin, people walked over to give their regards to Grace.

"I'm so sorry for your loss," Savannah West said, as she reached for Grace's hand. Savannah worked for the Cotter Creek newspaper and was married to one of the brothers who ran West Protective Services.

"Thanks." Grace turned and looked at Charlie. "Savannah is one of my best customers at the shop."

Savannah shoved a strand of wild red hair away from her face. "Still no arrest in the attempted robbery and assault?"

Grace shook her head. "I wasn't able to give Zack any kind of a description, so I'm not expecting any arrest."

"The criminals are running amuck in Cotter Creek. Zack is just sick about it and about what's happening with Hope," Savannah said.

Charlie felt the wave of Grace's despair as she nodded stiffly and her eyes grew glassy with tears. Savannah grabbed Grace's hand once again. "Zack was against making the arrest, but that ass of a prosecutor Alan Connor insisted."

"It doesn't matter," Charlie said. "Hope is innocent, and we'll prove it where it counts, in a court of law."

Grace placed a hand on his arm and smiled gratefully. Then it was time for the service to begin. As the preacher gave the eulogy, Charlie scanned the crowd.

Grace was right. Other than Justin, they hadn't managed to come up with a single lead that would point them away from Hope.

It was an eclectic crowd. Ranchers uncomfortable in their Sunday suits stood beside men Charlie didn't know, men who wore their expensive power suits with casual elegance. He assumed these were business associates of William's, and he noticed Zack West had those men in his sights as well.

Was it possible that William had been working on a business deal nobody knew about? Something that might have stirred up a motive for murder? At this point, he was willing to grasp at any alternative theory to Hope being a murderer.

Lana and Leroy Racine stood side by side, Leroy's big arm around his wife's shoulders as she wept uncontrollably. Certainly they had nothing to gain by William's death; rather, it was just the opposite. They stood to lose both their jobs and their home.

The only people who had a lot to gain by William's death were Grace and Hope, both of whom Charlie would have staked his life were innocent. But how had Hope gotten drugged? Who had managed to get into the house without breaking a window or a door? Who had killed William?

What he hoped was that Zack was doing his job and would give him a heads-up if he discovered any leads. Right now, coming up with a reasonable defense for Hope seemed impossible.

Grace remained stoic throughout the funeral, standing rigidly beside him. An island of strength, that was how he'd always thought of her. An island of a woman who took care of herself and her own needs, a woman who had never really needed him. And he was a man who needed to be needed.

When the ceremony was finally over and the final well-wishing had been given, most of the crowd headed for their cars, and Charlie gently took hold of Grace's arm.

"You ready to go?"

She nodded wearily. "I loved him, you know. He was as loving and kind a father as I could have ever asked for." She leaned into Charlie.

They were halfway to the car when a tall, gray-haired man who greeted Grace with a friendly smile stopped them. She introduced him as Hank Weatherford, William's closest neighbor.

"I was wondering if we could sit down together when you get a chance," Hank said. Grace looked at him with curiosity. He continued, "I've been trying to talk William into selling me the five acres of land between his place and mine. It's got nothing on it but weeds and an old shed. Now that he's gone I thought maybe you'd be agreeable to the idea."

Charlie narrowed his eyes as he stared at the older man. Interesting. A land dispute over five acres hardly seemed like a motive for murder, but Charlie smelled a contentious relationship between Hank Weatherford and William.

"Mr. Weatherford, I'll have to get back to you. I haven't decided yet what I'm going to do with the estate," Grace said.

He nodded. "Just keep in mind that I'd like to sit down and talk with you about those five acres."

"I'll keep it in mind," Grace agreed.

"That was interesting," Charlie said once he and Grace were in his car. "What's the deal with these five acres?"

"William always talked about having it cleaned up and maybe putting in a pool or a tennis court, but he never got around to it. I imagine Hank is tired of looking at the mess." She shot him a sharp glance. "Surely you don't think Hank had anything to do with William's death."

"Take nothing for granted, Grace. You'd be amazed at why people commit murder."

From the cemetery they went to her place, where they both changed clothes for the drive to Oklahoma City. Charlie had brought with him a pair of jeans and a short-sleeved light blue dress shirt, and he changed in her guest room.

She changed from her somber dress into a pair of jeans and a peach-colored blouse that enhanced the blue of her eyes and her blond coloring.

By one o'clock they were on the road. They hoped to get to the detention center by three, which would let them visit with Hope for an hour.

Grace seemed a million miles away as they drove. She stared out the window, not speaking, and she had a lost, uncertain look that was so unlike her, and it broke Charlie's heart just a little bit more.

She was still in his heart, as deeply and profoundly as she had been when they'd been seeing each other. He didn't want to love her anymore and knew that she certainly didn't love him, but he didn't know how to stop loving her. Over the past week it had become the thing that he did better than anything else.

He'd known when he'd gotten involved in this case that it was going to end badly. He could live with a broken heart, but if he didn't figure out how to save Hope, he knew he'd break Grace's heart once again. Charlie wasn't sure he could live with that.

As Grace stared out at the passing scenery, she was surprised to realize she was thinking of her mother. There were times when she glanced at herself in the mirror and saw a glimpse of the woman who had deserted them.

How could a woman who'd been a loving mother and good wife just pack her bags and leave without a backward glance?

And how long did it take before thoughts of her didn't hurt anymore?

She hadn't told anyone about Elizabeth, although she was sure most people in town knew about the vanishing act. Now she wanted to talk about it, especially to Charlie. She turned to look at him.

He looked so amazingly handsome, so cool and in control. She knew it was a façade, that he was worried about Hope, about her.

"You've asked me several times over the last couple of days about my mother." She tried to ignore the coil of tension that knotted tight in her stomach.

He shot her a quick glance. "You said she was out of the country."

She twisted her fingers together in her lap,

fighting both the anger and despair the conversation worked up inside her. "The truth is I don't have any idea where she is."

He said nothing, obviously waiting for her to explain.

She sighed and stared out the window for a long moment, then looked at him once again. "Two years ago while William was at a meeting and Hope was at school, my mother apparently packed a couple of suitcases and left."

Charlie frowned. "And you don't know where she went?"

"Don't have a clue." Grace tried to force a light tone but couldn't. She heard the weight of her pain hanging in her words. "I don't know where she went or why she left us without an explanation."

"And you haven't heard from her since?"

"Not a letter, not a postcard, nothing." She twisted her fingers more tightly together. "I don't mind so much for me. I mean, I'm a grown woman, but how could she walk out on Hope?"

"What did William have to say about it?" he asked.

"He said they'd had a fight the night before. At first he thought she'd just gone to a friend's house to cool off and would be back before nightfall. But she didn't come home that day, or the next, or the next. He was utterly heartbroken."

"Did you go to the sheriff?"

"Yeah, but a lot of good it did us. Jim Ramsey was the sheriff at the time. Did you know him?"

He nodded. "I know there was a big scandal about

his involvement in a murder and that Zack stepped into his shoes."

"William went to file a missing persons report, but Ramsey insisted there wasn't much he could do. Mom was of legal age. She'd taken her clothes and things with her, and if she didn't want to be a wife and mother anymore that was her right."

She'd had no right, Grace thought. She'd left behind three broken hearts that would never heal. "William hired a private investigator to search for her, but he never had anything to report, he never had a lead to follow."

Charlie was quiet for a long moment. "Why didn't you tell me this when we were seeing each other? It must have happened right before we met."

"Oh Charlie, there were a lot of important things we didn't talk about when we were together. We talked about whether we wanted to go out to dinner or stay in. You talked about your work and I talked about mine, but we didn't talk about what was going on with our lives when we were apart."

"You're right," he said flatly. "And it was one of the biggest mistakes we made. We should have talked about the important things."

Too late now. Grace looked out the window once again while a plethora of thoughts whirled through her head. It seemed as if the last two years of her life had been nothing more than a continuous journey of loss. First her mother, then Charlie, then William. And if something didn't break the case against her sister wide open, then Hope would be another loss.

A black, yawning despair rose up inside her. She'd been strong through it all, focused on getting from one day to the next without allowing herself any weakness.

At this moment, sitting next to the man who'd betrayed her trust, with thoughts of her mother and Hope heavy in her heart, she felt more alone than ever before.

"If I lose Hope, I won't have anything else to hang onto," she said. "My entire family has been ripped away from me, and I don't understand any of it."

"I'm going to see what I can do to find your mother," Charlie said.

She looked at him in surprise. "How are you going to do that?"

"I doubt if Jim Ramsey ever did anything to find her. It's tough for somebody to just disappear. She had a driver's license and tax records. With her Social Security number, we can start a search."

Grace frowned thoughtfully. "At this point, I'm not sure I care about finding her. Betrayal is a tough thing to get past."

He flashed her a quick glance. "Forgiveness is the first step on a path to healing."

"Forgiveness is for fools," she exclaimed with a touch of bitterness.

They didn't speak again for the remainder of the drive. The Beacon Juvenile Detention Center was on the south side of Oklahoma City. Set on twenty acres of hard, red clay, the building was a low, flat structure surrounded by high fences and security cameras.

The place had a cold, institutional look that Grace found horrifying.

As Charlie parked in the lot designated for visitors, a lump formed in Grace's throat as she thought of her sister inside.

Hope had never been anywhere but in the loving environment of William's home. How could she possibly cope with being locked up in this place with its barbed wire and truly bad kids?

"She doesn't belong here, Charlie," she said, as the two of them walked toward the entrance. "She isn't like the other kids in this place."

"I know, but right now there's nothing we can do about it." He reached for her hand, and again she was struck by how he seemed to know exactly what she needed and when.

She clung tightly to his hand, feeling as if it were an anchor to keep her from going adrift. The afternoon heat radiated up from the concrete walk, and Grace kept her gaze focused on the door.

Once inside, Charlie identified himself as Hope's lawyer and Grace as her sister. They were told to lock up their personal items, including Charlie's belt, and then were led to a small interview room with security cameras in all four corners and a guard in a khaki uniform outside the door.

Grace sat at the table with Charlie at her side and waited for her sister to be escorted inside. "We need to go back to the house, Charlie. We need to tear apart both William's and Hope's rooms to see if we can come up with something that will exonerate Hope."

"The sheriff and his men have already been through everything at the house," he said.

"Maybe they missed something." She heard the despair in her own voice. Being in this place made her feel desperate, for herself and for her sister. "You've got to do something, Charlie. I can't lose Hope."

"Grace, look at me." His eyes were dark, his gaze intense. "Right now we can't do anything to get Hope out of here. What I have to do is be prepared for when her trial comes up and make sure I do my job then. You told me when you came to me that it was because you needed a sneaky devil, and I was as close to the devil as you could find. You have to be patient now and trust that when the time is right, this sneaky devil will do his job."

Grace drew a tremulous sigh, the hysteria that had momentarily gripped her assuaged by the confidence she saw shining in Charlie's eyes.

At that moment the door opened and Hope walked in.

Charlie could tell the hour had passed too quickly for the two sisters, but at least Grace was leaving with the knowledge Hope was physically all right, although she was frightened and depressed.

It twisted his heart seeing the two of them together, how they'd clung to each other. Grace had remained calm and confident in front of Hope, assuring her that everything was going to be all right. It was only as they left the place that she seemed to wilt beneath the pressure and remained unusually silent.

They stopped on the way home for dinner at a little café that advertised itself as having the best barbecue in the state. The boast was vastly exaggerated. It was a quiet ride back, and Charlie could tell Grace's thoughts were on the sister she'd left behind. The sun was sinking low in the sky as they reached the edge of Cotter Creek.

He'd been stunned by what she'd told him about her mother. Charlie knew about grieving for a mother. He'd been devastated by the loss of his mother, and he'd had four years of preparing himself for her death. The death of a woman with cancer was understandable. The disappearance of a mother was not.

Hope was all she had left, and if he didn't manage to somehow come up with a defense for the young girl, then Grace would be truly alone and would probably hate him all over again.

He couldn't let that happen. As they drove down Main Street, he finally broke the silence that had grown to mammoth proportions. "We'll go back to the house tomorrow. I'm not sure we'll find anything helpful, but we'll search those rooms and see if anything turns up. I'll call Zack tomorrow and see if he's come up with anything new. We'll talk to Justin's roommate again and try to find a crack in the alibi."

He pulled up in her driveway and turned to look at her, wanting to take away the unusual slump of her shoulders and the dark look of defeat radiating from her eyes. He would prefer them filled with icy disdain.

"I swear to God, I'll make this right," he exclaimed. "I'll do everything in my power to make it right."

She broke eye contact with him and unfastened her seat belt. When she looked back at him, her eyes were filled with warmth, and she leaned across the seat and placed her lips on his.

Swift hunger came alive in him as he tasted those lips he'd dreamed about for so long. When she opened her mouth to him, he wanted to get her out of the car, take her into his arms and feel the press of her body against his, tangle his hands in her lush, silky hair.

The scent of her filled his head, dizzying him as the kiss continued. Charlie had always loved to kiss Grace. Her soft, full lips were made for kissing.

She broke the kiss long before he wanted her to and then opened her car door. "Don't bother walking me in," she said, as if to let him know the kiss had been the beginning and end of anything physical between them.

"Are you confusing me on purpose?" he asked, his voice thick and husky with the desire that still coursed hot and thick through his blood.

"I just figure if I'm confused you should be, too," she said, only adding to his bewilderment. "Call me in the morning to set up a time to go to the house." She slid out of the car and straightened up.

From the corner of his eye, Charlie saw a figure step around the side of her house. Everything seemed to happen in slow motion. He saw the figure raise an arm, heard the report of the gun and at the same time screamed Grace's name.

Chapter 8

Grace leapt back into the car just as she heard a metallic *ping* above her head.

"Stay down," Charlie cried, as he threw the car into reverse and burned rubber out of her driveway. She screamed and hunkered down in the seat as the passenger window exploded, sending glass showering over her back.

Her heart pounded so hard that she felt sick as Charlie steered the car like a guided missile. Her mind stuttered, trying to understand what just happened.

Somebody had shot at her. A bullet had narrowly missed her head. The words screamed through her head but didn't make sense.

As she started to sit up, Charlie pressed on the

back of her head to keep her contorted in the seat, and below the window level.

"Stay down. Are you all right? Did he hit you?" The urgency in his voice made every muscle in her body begin to tremble as the reality of what had just happened set in.

"No, I'm all right. I'm okay." Her voice was two octaves higher than normal, and she felt a hysterical burst of laughter welling up inside her. "If somebody is going to try to kill you, it's great when he's not a good shot."

Her laughter turned into a sob. "My God, somebody just tried to kill me, Charlie. What's going on with my life?"

"I don't know." His hand on the back of her head became a caress. "You can get up now. I don't think anyone is following us."

Tentatively she straightened to a sitting position, but she couldn't control the quivering of her body. "Did you see who he was?"

"No, he was in the shadows of the house and everything happened too damned fast. I'm taking you to my place tonight."

"If you think I'm going to argue with you, you're mistaken." She wrapped her arms around herself, attempting to warm the icy chill that possessed her insides.

"First we're going to take a couple of detours to make sure we're not being followed." As if to prove the point, he turned off Main, careened down a tree-lined street and then turned again onto another street.

"Charlie, why would somebody want to kill me?"

"I don't know, Grace. The first thing we're going to do when we get to my place is call Zack West. We need to report what happened."

He cursed beneath his breath. "I didn't see this coming. Jesus, if you hadn't jumped when you did, he would've nailed you."

Her trembling grew more intense. "Don't remind me." She brushed away the pieces of glass that clung to her. Her head pounded where she'd been hit before and she felt like she might throw up. "You're going to need a new window."

"That's the least of our problems right now," he replied, his voice still tense as his gaze continually darted to his rearview mirror.

They didn't speak again until they reached Charlie's ranch. He parked in front of the porch, got out of the car and came around to help her out.

It was only after she collapsed on his sofa that the shivering began to ease. As he got on the phone to call Zack, she stared out the window and replayed that moment when she'd seen the dark figure just out of the shadows, sensed imminent danger and dove back into the car.

What if she'd waited a second longer? What if he'd pulled the trigger a second sooner? The trembling she thought she had under control began again, and tears pressed hot in her eyes.

Somebody had tried to kill her. Why? *Why?* When Charlie hung up the phone, she looked at him, and he pulled her up into his arms.

"It's okay now. You're safe here," he said, as he held her tight. She burrowed her head into the crook of his neck, breathing in the familiar scent of him as her heartbeat crashed out of control with the residual fear.

He ran his hands up and down her back as he whispered in her ear words meant to soothe. Her trembling finally stopped, but still she remained in his embrace, unwilling to let go of him until the cold knot in her stomach had completely warmed.

There was a feeling of safety in Charlie's strong arms, and she needed that sense of security after what had just happened.

Finally she stepped back from him and sank to the sofa. "I can't believe this," she said, as Charlie began to pace back and forth in front of her. "How could this be happening to me?"

He went to the window and looked out, then began to pace once again, his lean body radiating with energy. "In light of what just happened, there's no way I think that the attack in the store was an attempted robbery," he said.

The cold chunk in her stomach re-formed as she stared at him in horror. "You think it was the same man as tonight? That he wanted to kill me that night in the store?"

"That would be a reasonable assumption. Give me a dollar."

"What?" She stared at him blankly as he held out his hand.

"Give me a dollar," he repeated.

She grabbed her purse from the sofa and pulled one out and handed it to him. "What's that for?"

He shoved the bill into his pocket. "You just hired me to be your professional bodyguard." His eyes were dark and simmered with a banked flame. "From now on you won't go anywhere, do anything, without me at your side. Until we know what's going on and who wants you dead, it isn't safe for you to be anywhere alone."

Grace leaned back against the sofa. Her life was spinning out of control and she didn't know why. Somebody wanted her dead, but she didn't know who. "Where's Rosa?" she asked, surprised that the housekeeper hadn't made an appearance yet.

"Today is her day off. She won't be back here until sometime tomorrow afternoon." Charlie once again moved to the window and peered outside, his back rigid with tension.

"Do you think whoever it was might come here?" she asked, fear leaping back into her voice. "If he recognized you, then what's to stop him from coming here and trying to get me again?"

Charlie turned away from the window and looked at her. "I won't let that happen." He walked over to the wooden desk in one corner of the room and opened the bottom drawer. "From now on anywhere we go there will be four of us. You and me and Smith and Wesson." He pulled out an automatic, checked the clip, then stuck the gun in his waistband at his back.

"I'm a hell of a shot and won't hesitate to pull the trigger if I think it's necessary," he added.

The sound of car tires crunching the gravel of the driveway drifted inside, and he turned back to the window. "It's Zack."

He opened the door to admit the lawman, and for the next twenty minutes Grace and Charlie explained to Zack what happened at her house and how it had been too dark for either of them to identify the man.

"You should be able to find a couple of slugs in my car," Charlie said. "One went into the passenger side and the other one shot out the window."

Zack nodded and looked at Grace. "And you don't have any idea who this person might be? No spurned boyfriends, no business problems of any kind?"

Grace shook her head. "I can't imagine who might want to hurt me. Do you think this has something to do with William's murder?"

Zack frowned. "I don't know what to think. I'll collect what evidence I can from Charlie's car and send some of my deputies over to your house to check for further evidence."

"There's something else I'd like for you to do," Charlie said. "Two years ago Grace's mother, Elizabeth, disappeared. I intend to do an Internet search to see if I can find out anything about where she might be right now, but you have better access to government records and can go places I can't. Would you check it out and see if you can find where she might be living now?"

"You think she might have something to do with all this?" Zack asked.

"No, that's impossible," Grace exclaimed. Her

mother might have deserted them, but she'd never have anything to do with the terrible things happening now.

Charlie and Zack exchanged a look that let Grace know they weren't as sure about her mother's innocence. "I'll check it all out and get back to you sometime tomorrow," Zack said. "I'm assuming that you'll be here?"

Grace nodded. "I don't want to go home right now."

Zack nodded with understanding. "That's a good idea. I recommend you don't go anywhere alone unless absolutely necessary and then take precautions for your own safety."

He got up from the chair where he'd been sitting, a weary frown on his face. "I don't know what in the hell is going on around here, but I'd sure like to get to the bottom of it."

"This has to put a new light on Hope's case," Grace said.

"We don't know that this incident is tied to William's murder," Zack replied. "And if it is, it doesn't necessarily do anything positive for Hope's case. The argument could be made that with you dead, Hope is the sole beneficiary of William's fortune."

Grace gasped. "That's a ridiculous argument," she exclaimed.

"I assume you'll be checking out Justin Walker's whereabouts for this evening," Charlie said.

"He's top on my list," Zack replied.

"You might also check out Hank Weatherford," Grace said. "Apparently there was some tension between him and William about some land William owns that butts up next to Hank's place."

Zack nodded. "Anything else you think of, no matter how small, call me."

"I'll walk you out," Charlie said, and the two men left the house.

Grace stared blankly at the front door, her mind reeling with everything that had happened—with all the possibilities of who might be responsible.

Did Hank want that five acres badly enough to kill for it? It seemed ridiculous to even consider such a thing, but thinking that Hope had somehow master-minded William's murder—and the attempted murder of Grace herself—in order to get all his money seemed equally ridiculous.

The other possibility—her mother—flirted at the edges of her mind, and although she wanted to dismiss it completely out of hand, she couldn't.

Pain blossomed in Grace's chest. Thoughts of Elizabeth always brought enormous grief, but this was different—more raw.

Maybe her mother had found another man and didn't know that William had changed his will so she was no longer the sole beneficiary. Perhaps she and her new man had decided to take out everyone who stood in the way of her getting that money.

It sounded crazy and sick, but Grace had seen enough to know that money could twist people into ugly semblances of themselves.

Or maybe what happened tonight had nothing to do with William's murder. *Somebody tried to kill me.* The words whirled around in her head, and again the cold knot retied itself in her chest.

She needed to think of something else, anything else. What she needed to do was make arrangements yet again for somebody else to open the store in the morning. She wasn't sure she'd be in at all.

Grace picked up Charlie's phone and dialed Dana's cell phone number. She answered on the second ring. "Dana, I hate to bother you, but could you open the store in the morning and work until Stacy comes in for her evening shift at four?"

"You know it's no problem," Dana replied. "I love working at the store. I'm just waiting for the time that you start sending me on buying trips, and I can take on more responsibility."

"What would that handsome husband of yours do without you if I sent you out of town?"

Dana laughed. "That handsome husband of mine would just have to cope, wouldn't he? Everything all right, Grace?"

"No, not really, but I appreciate your help with the store. I'll be in touch sometime tomorrow," she said, as Charlie came back through the door.

She hung up the phone. "That was Dana. I called her so she could open the store in the morning. She's a real jewel. Sometimes I don't know what I'd do without her." She was rambling, embracing thoughts of the store to keep away other, more troubling ideas.

"She wants to start going on buying trips for me. She has great taste. I probably should let her go."

Charlie's face blurred as tears filled her eyes. "She would do a good job."

"Grace," he said gently. "Why don't we get you settled in bed? Things won't look so grim in the morning." He held out his hand to her.

She took his hand and stood with a small laugh. "Somehow I don't think sunshine is going to fix any of this."

"Who knows? Maybe tomorrow Zack will find something that will identify your attacker."

She used her free hand to wipe at her tear-filled eyes. "I didn't know you were such an optimist, Charlie," she said, as they walked down the hallway toward the guest room she'd stayed in before.

"What are we going to do?" she asked when they reached the doorway. "How are you going to be my bodyguard, prepare a defense case for Hope and investigate all this? You aren't Superman."

He reached up and touched her cheek with a gentle smile. "Let me worry about it. You'd be surprised at what I'm capable of when I put my mind to it."

"Are you capable of getting me something to sleep in? I don't have anything."

He nodded. "How about one of my T-shirts?"

"Perfect," she agreed.

He dropped his hand from her face. "I'll be right back." He disappeared into the room at the far end of the hallway and returned a moment later with both a T-shirt and a toothbrush still in the package. "Try to get some sleep. We'll figure it all out in the morning," he said, handing her the items.

She nodded. "I'll see you in the morning." As he murmured a good-night, she closed the door between them and prayed that sleep would claim her quickly and banish all the horrible thoughts and images from her mind.

Rage, revenge or reward.

Charlie sat in his chair in the darkened living room and worked the motives for murder around in his head. No matter how he twisted everything, he couldn't make sense of it.

His heart accelerated in rhythm as he thought of that moment when he'd seen the figure in the shadows, watched as the figure raised his arm and knew that Grace was in danger. His heart had stopped then and hadn't resumed its regular, steady beat until they'd pulled up here at the ranch.

Moonlight filtered through the trees and into the window, making dancing patterns across the living room floor. He stared at the shifting patterns, as if in staring at them long enough something would make sense. Although he hadn't wanted to show his fear to Grace, the truth was he was afraid for her.

It was bad enough that somebody had tried twice to kill her, but almost as troubling was not having a clue as to the identity of her perpetrator.

Owning and operating a dress shop wasn't exactly a high-risk profession, and she'd insisted to Zack that there weren't any spurned lovers, no stalker boyfriends, nothing that could explain what was going on.

So what *was* going on? A dead man, a child facing

trial and two attempted murders. As crazy as it sounded, Charlie's thoughts kept returning to the missing mother. She was the one piece of the puzzle that remained a complete mystery.

Why had she left? Where was she now? After Grace went to bed, Charlie had done a cursory Internet search for her but found nothing.

The fact that Grace hadn't told him about her mother when they'd been dating indicated to him how little she'd thought of their relationship. He hadn't been important enough in her life to share that particular heartbreak.

He reached up and touched his bottom lip, where the feel of that brief kiss in the car lingered. Why had she kissed him? And if their relationship had meant nothing to her, then why did she hate him for how it had ended?

To say that she confused him was an understatement. What he didn't find confusing at all were his feelings for her. He loved her. It was as simple and as complicated as that. He'd never stopped loving her.

And she would never forgive him.

He released a weary sigh and glanced at the clock with the luminous dial on the desk. After two. Time to go to bed. He wasn't accomplishing anything here and needed to be fresh and alert tomorrow.

When he stood to go to his bedroom, he saw her standing in the doorway. By the light of the moon he could see her clearly—her tousled hair, the sleek length of her legs beneath the T-shirt, which fell to midthigh, and the fear that widened her eyes.

"Bad dream?" he asked, trying to ignore the white-hot fire of desire in the pit of his stomach.

"I don't need to be asleep to have bad dreams," she replied, her voice filled with stress. "I haven't been able to sleep. I've just been tossing and turning. I can't get it all out of my head—the noise of the bullet hitting the car, knowing that if I hadn't jumped into the car when I did another bullet might have hit me."

"You want something to eat? Maybe a glass of milk?" Although he tried to keep his gaze focused on her face, it slid down just low enough to see her breasts—her nipples hard against the cotton material. He quickly glanced up once again as every muscle in his body tensed. "Maybe putting something in your stomach will help."

"No, thanks. I'm not hungry." She took a step toward him, and he saw the tremble of her lower lip. "I was wondering if maybe I could sleep with you."

He knew she didn't mean sleep as a euphemism for anything else. She was afraid to be alone, and even though he knew how hard—no, how torturous it was going to be to lie next to her and not touch her, he nodded his head. "Sure, if that's what you want. My bed is big enough for the two of us."

"Thank you," she said gratefully.

He followed her down the hallway to the master bedroom and wondered how in the hell he was going to survive the night.

Chapter 9

Charlie tried to halt the rapid beating of his heart as she stood next to the bed. After he pulled down the covers, she slid in and curled up on her side facing him.

He placed his gun on the nightstand, then self-consciously unbuttoned his shirt and shrugged it off. It was silly to feel shy about undressing in front of her. She'd seen him naked more times than he could count, but that was before, in a different time under different circumstances.

Kicking off his shoes, he glanced at her to see that her eyes were closed. That made it easier for him to get out of his jeans. Normally he slept naked, but tonight he got beneath the sheet wearing his briefs, feeling as if he needed a barrier between them, even if it was just thin cotton.

"'Night, Charlie," she said softly, as he turned off the bedside lamp.

"Sleep tight, Grace," he replied. He squeezed his eyes closed, willing sleep to come fast, but how could he sleep with the scent of her eddying in the air and her body heat radiating outward to him?

He tried to count sheep, but each one of them had silky blond hair and a killer body beneath a white T-shirt. He knew she wasn't sleeping, either. He could tell by her uneven breathing that she was still awake.

They remained side by side, not touching in any way for several agonizingly long minutes. He gasped in surprise as she reached out and laid a warm hand on his chest.

"Grace," he said, her name nothing more than a strangled sigh that hissed out of him.

She scooted closer to him and trailed her fingers across the width of his upper body, tangling them in his tuft of chest hair. "What?" she whispered.

"You can't lie here next to me and touch me like that and not know that you're starting something."

"Maybe I want to start something." The words were a hot whisper against his neck. "I want you to hold me, Charlie. I want you to make love to me and take away the coldness inside me."

There was nothing he wanted more, but he didn't move. "You've had a scare, Grace. It's only natural that you'd reach out to somebody, but I don't want you to do something tonight that you'll regret in the morning."

Once again her hand swept across his chest and

he held his breath. "As long as you understand that it isn't the beginning of anything, that it's just sex, then I won't regret anything in the morning," she replied.

Jeez, how many men would have loved to hear from a woman that it was just about sex and nothing else? Still he hesitated. He didn't want to give her another reason to hate him. He told himself that one of them had to be strong.

She moved closer, molding herself against his side. "I know you still want me, Charlie. I've seen it in your eyes; I've felt it in your touch. I want you now. Not forever, but just for now."

Even though he would have preferred now and forever, he wasn't strong enough to stop himself from turning to her. Their lips met in an intense kiss that tasted of the sweet familiarity of past liaisons and of present fires.

Just that easily he was lost in her, in the taste of her, the scent of her and the heat of her body, so close to his. He cupped her face in his hands as the kiss continued, their tongues swirling together as their breaths quickened.

He pulled her into his arms, half across his body as his hands caressed her back and made their way to the bottom of the T-shirt.

He broke the kiss and plucked at the shirt. "Take it off. I want to feel your body next to mine."

She sat up and in one smooth movement pulled the shirt up and over her head. She tossed it to the floor at the end of the bed, then went into his arms once again.

Her soft, supple skin was hot against his, and he cupped her breasts, his thumbs moving over her hard nipples. The tiny gasp she emitted only served to ratchet up his desire.

He wanted her moaning like she once had beneath him, making those mewling noises that had always driven him wild.

She rolled over on her back, and he took one of her nipples into his mouth as she tangled her fingers in his hair. He teased first one, then the other nipple, sucking then flicking his tongue to give her the most pleasure.

"Charlie," she moaned, his name a sweet plea on her lips.

His hand moved down her flat stomach and lingered at the waist of her panties. Touching her was sheer pleasure, the smoothness of her skin making his blood thicken as he grew hard.

"Take them off," she said, and lifted her buttocks from the bed so he could pull the panties down and off. With her naked, he quickly took off his briefs. Then they came together—hot flesh and hotter kisses.

Although he was hungry for her, he wanted to take his time. He wanted it slow. He wanted to pretend that they had never stopped being lovers, that there was nothing bad between them.

He re-memorized the sweet curves of her hips, the silky length of her legs. His lips found all the places he knew would stoke her pleasure higher, and the taste of her drove him half mindless.

Grace had always been an active participant in lovemaking, and this time was no different. Her mouth and hands seemed to be everywhere—behind his ear, on his chest above his crashing heartbeat, along his inner thigh.

Knowing that if he allowed her to continue with her caresses, it was going to be over before it began, Charlie pushed her onto her back once again, and his fingers found her damp heat.

She arched her hips to meet his touch as she whimpered his name. Every muscle in her body tensed, and he knew she was almost there, almost over the edge. He quickened his touch and felt the moment when her climax crashed down on her. She froze and then seemed to melt as she cried his name over and over again.

Knowing he was about to lose control, he quickly disengaged from her and fumbled in his nightstand for a condom. His hands trembled uncontrollably as he pulled on the protection and then eased into her with a hiss of pleasure.

He froze, afraid that the slightest movement would end it all. The moonlight filtered through the curtains, dappling her face with enough light that he could see the bright shine of her eyes, a pulse beating madly in the side of her neck.

She closed her eyes, and he felt her tighten her muscles around him, creating exquisite pleasure for him. Her fingers dug into his lower back, and he slowly eased his hips back, then stroked deep into her.

The rush of feelings that filled him was overwhelming, not just the physical ones, but the emotional ones as well. She was hot, sexy and felt like home. She scared him more than any potential killer they might face.

He had confidence that he could keep her safe and sound from any threat, but he didn't know how to make her forgive him. He wanted her to be his woman forever, but she'd made it clear she was his just for now.

He'd had his chance with her and blown it. Now his job was to fix her life so that she could once again move on without him.

Grace woke up with the light of dawn drifting through the window and Charlie spooned around her back. She remained still, relishing the feeling of safety his arms provided, the warmth of his body against her.

Making love with him had been as magical last night as it had been eighteen months ago when they'd been an item. Charlie was a passionate man, a thoughtful lover who never took his own pleasure before giving pleasure to her. Her body still glowed warm with the residual aftermath of the night of love.

Had last night been a mistake? Definitely.

If she allowed herself, she could be as in love with Charlie as she had been before, but she wouldn't allow it. There was still a simmering rage inside her where he was concerned, a place where forgiveness could find no purchase.

She slid out of bed, wanting to get up before he awakened. She knew how much Charlie loved morning sex, and although there was a part of her that would have welcomed another bout of lovemaking with him, she didn't want to be available for compounding her mistake.

The last thing she needed to do was think about Charlie and her confusing feelings for him. What she needed to do was figure out why somebody would want her dead.

She used the shower in the guest room, hoping to let Charlie rest for as long as he could. She'd fallen asleep before him the night before and had no idea when he'd finally drifted off.

Charlie was mistaken. Nothing seemed clearer in the light of day, she thought, as she stood beneath a hot stream of water. William was still dead. Somebody was gunning for her and Hope was facing life in prison. No amount of morning sun could put a happy spin on things.

When she was dressed, she went into the kitchen, surprised to find Charlie making coffee. Apparently he'd been in the shower at the same time as her. His hair was damp, and he smelled of minty soap and that cologne that had always driven her half wild.

"Good morning," he said, and gave her a tentative glance.

"Don't worry, there aren't going to be any repercussions from last night," she assured him, as she sat at the table.

"That's good. I was worried that you'd accuse me

of taking advantage of you," he replied, pouring them each a cup of the fresh brew.

"I think I was definitely the one taking advantage last night," she replied dryly.

He set the mugs on the table then took the seat across from her. "Grace, we need to talk. We need to talk about us."

She held up a hand and shook her head. "Please, Charlie, don't." She steeled her heart against him, against the flash of vulnerability she saw in his eyes. "There's so much going on in my life right now. I can't think about anything else except getting Hope out of that horrible place and trying to figure out why somebody tried to shoot me last night."

He held her gaze for a long minute and then nodded reluctantly. "Okay, we won't do it now," he agreed, but there was a subtle warning in his words that let her know this wasn't finished—*they* weren't finished.

But they were, she thought, and the old, familiar anger rose up inside her. His betrayal hurt just like her mother's had, and she'd never forgive her mother nor was she ever likely to forgive him. She'd be a fool to trust him with her heart again, and Grace wasn't anybody's fool.

"You need to decide if you want to stay here with me or if you want me to stay at your place with you," he said. "There's no way I want you staying anywhere all alone right now."

She wanted to protest the plan, but she knew she couldn't return to her life as if nothing had happened. She frowned thoughtfully. "I'd really prefer to stay at my own place, but don't you need to be here at the ranch?"

"I've got a good foreman who can see to things," he replied.

Wrapping her fingers around her mug, she frowned again. "I hate the idea of taking you away from your life here."

He smiled, the gesture warming the gray of his eyes. "You bought my services as a bodyguard for a dollar. Until this thing is resolved, wherever you go, I go. If you want to stay at your place, then all I need to do is pack a bag."

"If you don't mind, I'd appreciate it," she said. Maybe her world would feel more normal if she were home among her familiar things. "I'd like to go back to the house today." She took a sip of her coffee and then continued. "We should talk to Lana and Leroy again. Maybe they will have remembered something helpful."

"I think they would have called if that was the case," he said. "But, if you want to touch base with them, we can do that. Have you thought about what you intend to do with the house and the property?"

"No. I suppose eventually I'll sell. I'll never live in the house, and I don't want it sitting empty forever." Grief for William pierced through her. He'd loved that house so much.

"The real estate market isn't great right now, but I imagine a home like that will move fairly quickly."

"I need to give Lana and Leroy a heads-up that at

some point they'll need to find another place to live. At least with the money William left to Lana I know they won't be out on the street." She sipped her coffee, thinking about everything that needed to be done to settle William's estate.

Somebody tried to kill you yesterday. The words jumped unbidden into her head. She took another sip of her coffee and tried to think of a single person she'd upset or offended.

"This can't be personal," she said aloud.

"What?" Charlie looked at her in confusion.

"Whoever is trying to kill me. It has to be about something other than dislike or anger at me personally. I know it sounds conceited, but I can't think of anyone who could hate me. I run a dress shop, for God's sake. I've never had a problem with anyone in town."

"We have a missing mother, a dead stepfather, a sister who we believe has been set up to spend the rest of her life in prison, and somebody trying to kill you. It's like somebody is trying to erase the entire Covington family."

"Surely you don't think my mother's disappearance has anything to do with what's happening now," she said.

He sipped his coffee, a new frown creasing his forehead. "I don't know. Last night I did a quick search on the computer for your mother but got no results." He swept a hand through his thick, dark hair. "I keep working everything around in my head trying to make sense of it, but I can't get a handle on it. Do you have a will?"

"No, I haven't gotten around to making one yet."

"So, if something happened to you, everything you own would go to Hope as your sole living relative?"

"I guess." She narrowed her eyes. "Charlie, I don't care how bad this looks, Hope wouldn't do this. Please, don't lose faith in her innocence."

"I'm just looking at all the angles," he said, and took another drink of his coffee. "Why don't we eat some breakfast and head to your place? I'll stow my stuff there, and then we can head over to the mansion to see what we can find."

It was after nine when they left the ranch to go to Grace's house. Charlie had a small suitcase in the backseat and his automatic pistol in a holster beneath his jacket.

The knowledge that he was carrying a gun to protect her sent a new rivulet of disquiet through her. The shooting the night before and the attack at the store had had a dreamlike quality to them, but his gun made them terrifyingly real.

"I really appreciate you staying at my place," she said, as they drove down Main Street toward her street. "I have a nice guest room where I hope you'll be comfortable." She wanted to make it clear there would be no repeat of last night, that she had no intention of him sleeping next to her in her bed.

"I'm sure I'll be fine," he replied. "You need to stop by the store for anything?"

"No. Dana will have things well under control. She should have a shop of her own. She has all the skills to run her own business."

"You've certainly made a success of it," he observed.

She frowned. "I suppose." Yes, she had made a success of her shop, but at what price? Certainly in the last two years she'd kept too busy to nurture her relationship with her sister. A hollow wind blew through her as she thought of the choices she'd made.

She had plenty of friendly customers, but few friends, and when she'd needed somebody to hold her close, to take away her fear, there had been nobody except the man she'd once dated, a man who had broken her heart. Yeah, right, some success she'd made of her life.

The wind coming in from the broken window felt good on her face. Charlie had cleaned up the glass before they'd gotten into the car. The plan was for him to hire someone to come out to Grace's house to replace the window. They'd use her car for the remainder of the day.

When they reached her place, Charlie pulled up in the driveway and cut the engine. "I'll come around for you," he said, pulling his gun from his holster. "We'll walk together to the front door with you just in front of me. I don't want a repeat of last night."

As he got out of the car, the reality of the situation slammed into her. Somebody had tried to kill her last night. Somebody had tried to put a bullet in her head.

She gazed around her yard and the house, looking for a shadow, a movement that would indicate somebody lying in wait for them. A new knot of tension twisted in the pit of her stomach.

He opened her door and pulled her out and against his chest. They walked awkwardly toward her front door, with him acting as a human shield against danger.

Grace didn't realize she'd been holding her breath until she unlocked the door and stepped into the entry hall. It was only then that she breathed again.

"Stay right here and don't move," Charlie said. "I want to check out the house." He kept the front door open. "If somebody is in here, I'll let you know and want you to run to the car and drive to the sheriff's office." He handed her the car keys, then disappeared into the living room.

Grace's heart beat frantically with fight-or-flight adrenaline as she held the keys firmly in hand and waited for him to return. What if somebody was here—lying in wait for them? What if that somebody bashed Charlie over the head or shot him?

Once again her breath caught in her chest as she stood rigid with taut muscles—waiting...hoping that there was nobody inside.

Finally he came back, his gun back where it belonged. "It's okay," he said. A devilish gleam lit his eyes. "The purple bedroom is hot."

She laughed as the edge of tension faded. "The purple bedroom is mine. You get the one across from it. Why don't you put your things in there? I'm going to change my clothes before we leave again."

"I'll just go get my suitcase from the car," he said. As he went out the front door, Grace walked down the hallway to her bedroom.

She'd always loved the color purple in all its

glorious shades. When she'd moved into the house, she'd decided to indulge herself by painting the walls of her bedroom lilac and finding a royal purple satin spread for the bed. The end result gave the aura of both relaxation and hedonistic pleasure.

Her dresser top held framed photos along with an array of perfume bottles and lotion. She walked over to the dresser and looked at the pictures. There was one of Hope in a pair of footed Christmas pajamas, her face lit with a beautiful smile.

There was also one of William, Hope and Grace. It had been taken six months after her mother's disappearance. The three of them had been at a carnival, and although they all sported smiles on their faces, the smiles didn't quite reach their eyes.

She turned away from the bureau and unbuttoned her blouse, then walked to her closet. Maybe today they'd find something at the house that would exonerate Hope. Even though logically she knew that Zack and his men would have gone over the crime scene with a fine-tooth comb, she still clung to the belief that somehow she and Charlie would find something that the authorities had missed.

She leaned against the doorjamb for a long moment, staring at the clothes inside the closet. Grace was exhausted even though she'd slept soundly after making love with Charlie. It wasn't physical fatigue but rather a mental one.

She grabbed a short-sleeved blue blouse from a hanger, then turned around. A scream welled up inside her and exploded out as she saw a face at her window.

Chapter 10

The scream ripped through Charlie, electrifying him with terror. He pulled his gun and raced across the hallway into her room.

She stood in front of the closet, her face a pasty shade of white. "He was looking in my window," she managed to gasp.

That's all Charlie needed to hear. He tore out of her bedroom, down the hallway and out the front door. He raced around the side of her house and spied a tall, lean figure running toward the fence that surrounded her yard. It was a privacy fence, and there was no way in hell he'd be able to jump it.

"Stop, or I swear I'll shoot," Charlie yelled, as the man leapt up to grab the top of the fence.

Unsuccessful, the man fell back to the ground then turned to face Charlie. It was Justin Walker. His eyes widened to saucer size as he saw the gun Charlie held in his hand.

Instantly he raised his hands. "Hey man, don't shoot me."

"What are you doing here?" Charlie asked, his gun not wavering from the young man's midsection. "Did you come back here today to finish what you tried to do last night?"

Justin frowned. "Last night? Dude, I don't know what you're talking about."

He looked genuinely perplexed, but Charlie wasn't taking anything for granted. "Get inside the house. I'm calling the sheriff." He gestured with his gun for Justin to move.

"Hey man, there's no need to call the fuzz. I wasn't doing anything. I just wanted to talk to Grace, that's all. I wanted to talk to her alone." As he protested his innocence, he moved toward the house where Grace stood at the back door, her eyes wide with fear.

"You have any weapons?" Charlie asked, as they reached the back porch.

"Hell no. I didn't come here looking for trouble," he exclaimed.

"Well, you found it," Charlie said. Despite Justin's protests, Charlie quickly patted him down, making sure the young man had no weapons on him.

Grace opened the backdoor. "Justin, what are you doing here?" she asked. She seemed to relax as she realized Charlie had things under control.

When they got into the kitchen, Charlie gestured for Justin to sit at the table. "I just wanted to talk to you," Justin said to Grace. "I was just going to stand at the window and try to get your attention, but then you saw me and screamed, and I freaked and ran."

"Maybe we should just call Zack and let Justin explain everything to him," Charlie said.

"No, please, don't do that." Justin slumped in the chair, an air of defeat in his posture. "He already thinks I killed Hope's stepdad. I don't need any more trouble from him."

"What do you want to talk to me about?" Grace asked. She remained standing next to the counter on the other side of the room from Justin. Charlie was standing as well, his gun still clutched in his hand.

Justin swept a hand through his dark, unruly hair. "I wanted to ask you about Hope. I just wanted to know if she was okay."

"Why do you care? According to you, the two of you were just casual friends, hang-out buddies and nothing more," Grace replied.

Justin's cheeks colored with a tinge of pink. "She was nice to me, okay? I liked her. When she turned sixteen, we were going to start officially dating. I just wanted to know if she was doing all right, that's all."

"She's fine, coping as well as can be expected," Grace said.

"Where were you last night?" Charlie asked.

"I was home, with my roommate."

Charlie narrowed his eyes. "Your roommate is a pretty handy alibi whenever you need one."

This time the flush of color in Justin's cheeks was due to anger, not embarrassment. "I can't help it if it's the truth."

"Should we call Zack?" Charlie asked.

Grace studied Justin's face for a long moment and then shook her head. "No, just let him go. I think he's telling the truth."

"I am," Justin exclaimed.

Charlie wasn't so sure, but he complied with Grace's wishes. "Go on. Get out of here. But if I see you around Grace again, I won't wait for the sheriff to ask you questions. I'll beat your ass myself."

Justin didn't speak again. As Charlie lowered his gun, he jumped out of the kitchen chair and ran for the front door. Charlie followed, making sure he left the house.

When he returned to the kitchen, Grace still leaned against the cabinets. "You okay?" he asked.

She nodded. "Now we know there was definitely something romantic going on between Hope and Justin." She looked dispirited, as if she knew this new information would only make things worse for Hope. "It will be easy for the prosecution to make a case that Hope killed William because William wouldn't let her see Justin."

"It doesn't change anything," Charlie replied with a forced lightness. "Go change your clothes so we can get out of here."

As she left the room, Charlie tried to get the sound

of her scream out of his head. His heart had stopped
when he'd heard her. He hoped he never heard that
particular sound from her again.

A few minutes later they were in her car and
headed to the Covington mansion. "I think tomorrow
I just might stay in bed all day," she said with a sigh.
"At least there won't be any surprises there."

"Unless I'm there with you," Charlie said, and
wiggled his eyebrows up and down in Groucho Marx
fashion. He wanted to make her laugh to ease the
tension that thinned her lips and darkened her eyes.

He was rewarded as a small giggle escaped her.
"You're wicked, Charlie Black," she exclaimed
before sobering back up. "I hope you're as good a
lawyer as you were two years ago. Hope is going to
need every one of your skills."

"I've already requested that Zack give me copies
of all the interviews he conducted with people immediately after the murder. I plan on getting all the
discovery available to start building our case. Believe
it or not, Grace, I'm working on it." He tapped the
side of his head. "I do my best work in my head long
before I commit anything to paper. I have a theory
about murder."

"And what's that?"

"I call it the three *R*s. Most murders are committed for one of three reasons: rage, revenge or reward."

"And which category do you think William's
murder falls into?" she asked.

He turned down off the main road and into the
long Covington driveway. "I'm still trying to figure

it out. The prosecuting attorney is probably going to argue rage—Hope's rage at a figure of authority who kept her from seeing the boy that she loved. Or he could possibly argue reward—that with William out of the picture she would be a very wealthy young lady."

She sighed. "Sounds grim."

He flashed her a reassuring grin. "Grim doesn't scare me. It just gets my juices flowing." He pulled up in front of the house and cut the engine, aware of Grace's gaze lingering on him. He unbuckled his seat belt and turned to look at her. "What?"

"Do you miss it? Being a lawyer? The adrenaline rush of the courtroom and the high stakes?"

He hesitated before answering, not wanting to give her a flippant response. "I'll tell you what I miss. I miss my father, who would have been proud of the man I've become over the last year. I regret the fact that I'm thirty-five years old and haven't gotten married and started a family of my own. To answer your question, no, there's absolutely nothing I miss about my old life." *Except you.*

The last two words jumped into his mind and for some reason irritated him. He wasn't sure if the target of his irritation was himself or Grace.

"Come on, let's get inside and see what we can find," he exclaimed.

Even though he had checked the rearview mirror constantly to make certain they hadn't been followed, he once again escorted her inside with his gun pulled and his body shielding hers.

Once they got inside, Charlie followed Grace to William's office, which was located in one of the bedrooms upstairs. As she sat at the desk and began to go through the drawers, he walked over to the window and stared out to the backyard. Grace still refused to go into the bedroom where William had been murdered, but Charlie had gone in and had found nothing to help find his killer.

He had little hope that she would find anything useful. She'd already been through the desk once before, but he knew she needed to do something to feel as if she were actively helping her sister.

Leroy had apparently been working hard. The flower beds in the backyard exploded in vivid blooms, with nary a weed in sight. The bushes were neatly trimmed and the grass was a lush green carpet.

Rage. Revenge. Reward. Somebody out there had a motive for killing William. If Justin and Hope had worked in concert to commit the murder, then why had she been passed out on the bed in an incriminating manner? Why didn't they just alibi each other?

Was it possible that the issue of those five acres had created such contention that Hank lost control and killed William? Hank was no young man, but it didn't take a lot of strength to stab a sleeping man in the back.

Charlie could smell Grace. Her dizzying scent not only fired his hormones, but also somehow touched his heart. Anger was building in him where she was concerned, an anger he didn't want to feel and certainly didn't want to acknowledge.

He knew he'd hurt her badly in the past, but he

was irritated by the fact that she refused to talk about it and clung to her sense of betrayal like it was a weapon to use against him at her whim.

He realized, though, that she was fragile now, and the last thing he wanted to do was add to the burdens she was already shouldering. He had to keep his emotions in check.

Once she had searched through the desk, she returned to Hope's bedroom. He stood at the door as she pulled open drawers and picked through the mess on the floor. She'd been through it all before and found nothing. He sensed her desperation but didn't know what to do to ease it.

It was almost three o'clock when he finally called a halt to her search. "Grace, there's nothing here," he said. "If there had been something, Zack would have found it, and if he missed anything, you would have found it by now."

She sat in the middle of Hope's bedroom floor, sorting through a box of keepsake items that belonged to her younger sister.

She put the lid back on the box and sighed. "I know you're right. I just feel compelled to do something to help. It doesn't feel right for me to work at the shop and go about my usual routine while everything else is falling apart."

"I know, but a daily routine is necessary, especially the part where we eat to stay strong. My stomach has been growling for the past hour."

She rose to her feet. "Why didn't you say something?"

He smiled and fought an impulse to reach out and tuck a stray strand of hair behind her ear. "I just did. But before we leave I'd like to check out the property that Hank and William had been arguing about."

She frowned at him. "Okay, but there really isn't anything there but a bunch of weeds and trees." Grace stood up, and they went downstairs.

"You once mentioned something about an old shed," he said, when they reached the front door. "You know what's in it?"

"Probably nothing. I think at one time it used to be a gardener's shed, but it hasn't been used in years." As she locked the door, Charlie once again gripped his gun.

He looked around the immediate area, seeking any threat that might come at them, at her. She turned from the door and stood just behind him.

The Covington place was isolated enough that it would be difficult for anyone to approach without being noticed. He felt no danger, saw nothing that would give him pause. While inside he'd spent much of the time at the windows, watching the road for any cars that didn't belong and checking the grounds for anything unusual.

"Where's that property?" he asked.

"Around back, behind Leroy and Lana's place."

"I want you to walk right in front of me. I don't think there's anyone around, but I don't want to take any chances."

"I'd like to stop by Lana's and let them know that I've decided to sell this place. The new owner might want to continue their services and let them remain in the cottage, but it's also possible they need to start making other plans."

The walk to the cottage was awkward, with her walking nearly on the top of his feet. As always, her nearness raised the simmering heat inside him, and he tried to ignore it as he kept focused on their surroundings.

Lana and Leroy weren't home. Nobody answered Grace's knock and no vehicles were parked in front of the place. "Maybe they both went to pick up Lincoln from school," Grace said.

"He seems like a nice kid." They headed for the side of the cottage.

"He's certainly the apple of their eyes," she replied. "Lana was pregnant when she married Leroy, and William and I were just grateful that he stepped up and did the right thing. It seems to have worked out well."

She pointed in the distance where the manicured lawn ended and an area of trees and overgrown brush began. "That's the land Hank was talking about. It never bothered William because it's so far away from the main house, but Hank's place is just on the other side, and I can understand why he'd want to see it cleaned up. The shed is on the other side of that big oak tree."

They headed toward the area where the shed was located. Charlie didn't want to leave any stone unturned.

He figured it was probably empty or full of gardening tools that had rusted and rotted over the years.

When they reached the wooden structure, Charlie returned his gun to his holster and eyed the old padlock on the door.

"I can't imagine why it would be locked," Grace said. "Nobody has used it in years. I wouldn't have any clue where to begin to look for the key."

"Who needs a key?" Charlie replied. He eyed the rotten wood around the lock on the door. Tensing his muscles, he slammed his shoulder into the door and was rewarded by splintering wood.

Another three hits and the door came away from the lock, allowing him to open it.

He pulled the door open just a bit and peered inside. The first thing he noticed was the unpleasant musty odor that wafted in the air. Then he saw the two flowered suitcases that sat on the floor just inside the door.

His heart began to bang against his ribs. Then he saw the sandal—a bright red woman's sandal. Inside it was the remains of a foot.

He reeled back and slammed the door. "We need to call Zack," he said, and turned to face Grace. Dread mingled with horror as he stared at her.

"Why? What's in there?" She tried to get past him to the door, but he stood his ground.

He grabbed her by the shoulders, his heart breaking for what he had to tell her. "Grace, stop. Listen to me."

She looked at him wildly, as if she knew what he was about to say. "Tell me, Charlie. What's inside the shed?"

"I'm sorry. I'm so damned sorry." He pulled her into his arms and held her tight, knowing she was going to need his strength. "Grace, I think it's your mother. Your mother's body is in the shed."

Chapter 11

Grace sat on the sofa in William's opulent living room, numb and yet as cold as the worst Oklahoma ice storm. She had yet to cry, although she knew eventually the numbness would pass and the pain would crash in.

It was late. Darkness had fallen, and still Zack and his men were processing the scene. Charlie was out there with them, but he'd insisted Zack leave a deputy with Grace.

Ben Taylor stood at the window, staring out in the distance where a faint glow of lights shone from the area behind the cottage.

For two years Grace had hated her mother for abandoning them. For two years she had cursed the name of the woman who had given birth to her. The anger was what had sustained her. Now it was gone and she had nothing left to hang on to.

She hadn't left them.

She'd been murdered.

The words flittered through Grace's head, but she couldn't grasp the concept, didn't yet feel the reality deep inside her.

The front door opened and a moment later Zack and Charlie walked into the room. Charlie immediately came to her side and sat next to her, his hand reaching for hers.

She allowed him to hold her hand. Somewhere in the back of her mind Grace realized his skin was warm against her icy flesh, but the warmth couldn't pierce through the icy shell that encased her.

"Zack wants to ask you a few questions," Charlie said gently.

"Of course." She looked at Zack, who sat in the chair across from them, his green eyes expressing a wealth of sympathy.

"Do you know of anyone your mother was having problems with at the time of her disappearance?" Zack asked.

"No." Her voice seemed to float from very far away.

Zack frowned. "Charlie mentioned that William had told you he and your mother had a fight the night before she disappeared."

She was having trouble concentrating. She felt as if she were in some sort of strange bubble, where things were happening around her and people were talking to her, but she really wasn't involved in any of it.

"Grace?" Charlie squeezed her hand.

She looked first at Charlie, then at Zack. "Yes, William told me they had an argument, but it wasn't a big deal. They were happily married, but like all couples they occasionally had disagreements."

She stared at Zack and then turned once again to gaze at Charlie. "What's happened to my family? Everyone has disappeared and now somebody is trying to make me disappear." Her voice had a strange, singsong quality.

"I need to get her home," Charlie said to Zack. "She's in shock."

"Yes, please take me home. I need to go to bed. I need to sleep. Things will be better in the morning, won't they, Charlie?"

He didn't answer her, but he wrapped an arm around her and pulled her against his side. "Zack, if you have any more questions for her, they can be asked tomorrow."

Zack nodded and stood at the same time Charlie helped her up from the sofa. At that moment Lana came flying into the room.

She looked around. "Is it true? Elizabeth is dead?" Zack nodded, and she began to sob.

Grace broke away from Charlie and went to her. She wrapped her arms around Lana and vaguely wondered why the housekeeper was crying for her mother and she wasn't.

"I need to ask you some questions," Zack said to Lana. "Both you and your husband."

Lana nodded and Grace stepped back from her.

"Do you know who would do this? Do you know who would kill my mother and pack her suitcases and stuff her in an old shed?"

"I don't know." Lana looked around wildly. "I don't understand any of this. First William and now your mother." Lana began to weep once again as Zack led her to a chair.

Charlie grabbed Grace by the arm. "Come on, let's get you home."

Once they were in the car, Grace leaned her head back and closed her eyes. "I'm so tired."

"We'll get you home and tucked into bed," he said.

"And I'm cold. I'm so cold. I don't feel like I'll ever be warm again." She wrapped her arms around herself and fought against the shivers that tried to take control.

"You will," he replied. "Eventually you'll get warm again and you'll laugh and enjoy life. Time, Grace. Give yourself time. It's true what they say about time healing all wounds."

Once again she closed her eyes. She knew eventually the agonizing grief over losing her mother would probably ease, but how could she get over her guilt? For two years she'd hated a woman who hadn't left them but instead had been brutally murdered.

Emotion swelled in her chest and made the very act of breathing difficult. She fought against it, afraid to let it take her—afraid that once she let it loose she would lose what little control she had left.

"Somebody must have hated us," she murmured, more to herself than to Charlie. "Somebody must hate us all, but I don't know who it could be."

She sighed in relief as Charlie pulled up in her driveway. All she wanted was to sleep—hopefully without dreams. It was the easiest way to escape the confusion and pain that had become her life.

Charlie helped her out of the car, and once they were inside he led her directly to her bedroom. She sat on the edge of the bed and tried to unbutton her blouse, but her fingers were all thumbs.

"Here, let me help," Charlie said. He crouched down in front of her and unfastened the buttons. There was nothing sexual in his touch, only a gentleness she welcomed as he pulled the blouse from her arms.

He retrieved her nightgown from the hook on the back of her bedroom door and carried it to her. "Here, while you put this on, I'll turn down the bed."

Dutifully she stood and took off her bra and pulled the nightgown over her head. Then she took off her pants, and by that time the bed was ready for her to crawl into.

She got beneath the covers and shivered uncontrollably. "Charlie, could you just hold me until I get warm?"

He quickly stripped down to his briefs and then slid beneath the sheets and pulled her into his arms. She welcomed the warmth of his skin as she shivered in his arms.

He stroked her hair and kissed her temple. "It's going to be all right," he said softly. "You're strong, Grace. You're one of the strongest women I've ever known. You're going to get through this."

"You don't understand. She wasn't just my

mother, she was my best friend." The words pierced through a layer of the protective bubble she'd been in since learning of her mother's death. "And I don't feel very strong right now." Tears burned her eyes as grief ripped through her.

Charlie seemed to sense the coming storm and tightened his arms around her. "Let it go, Grace," he said softly. "Just let it go."

"I never understood how she could have just walked away from me...from us. Oh God, Charlie, for two years I've hated a dead woman who didn't leave us by choice." She could no longer contain the sobs that ripped through her as the realization of the loss finally penetrated the veil of shock.

Charlie said nothing. He merely held tight as she cried for all she'd lost, for all she still might lose. She had always believed someplace deep in her heart that she would see her mother again, that somehow the wounds would be healed and they would love one another again.

That wasn't going to happen. Elizabeth couldn't rise up from the dead to spend even one precious instant with her children.

She cried until there was nothing left inside her and then, completely exhausted, she fell into blessed sleep.

"The initial finding is that she was probably strangled," Zack said to Charlie when he called the next morning. "Her larynx was crushed, and the coroner could find no other obvious signs of trauma. And there's no way she packed her own suitcases. The clothes inside were shoved in, not neatly folded. She was probably killed someplace else, then the suitcases were packed to make it appear that she'd left."

"And I suppose the suspect list is rather short," Charlie said dryly.

"Yeah, as in there isn't one." Zack's frustration was evident in his voice. "I've got the mayor chewing on my ass wanting answers as to what's happening in his town, and I don't have any answers to give him."

"I wish I could offer you some," Charlie replied.

"I interviewed both Lana and Leroy Racine last night. They remembered where they were on the day Elizabeth disappeared. Lana was in Oklahoma City getting her son a checkup with his physician and Leroy spent the day fishing. Other than that, I haven't had a chance to question anyone else. Hell, to be honest, I'm not even sure where to begin. I'm still trying to break Justin Walker's alibi for William's murder."

"You really think those kids killed him?" Charlie asked.

"I don't know what to think. I just collect the evidence and let the prosecuting attorney do the thinking. How's Grace doing this morning?"

"Still sleeping." And for that Charlie was grateful. He picked up his coffee from the table and took a sip. "Got any ideas about what's going on as far as the attacks on her?" he asked.

"I was hoping maybe you had some," Zack replied.

"I don't have a clue." Charlie frowned. It wasn't even nine o'clock and already his level of frustration was through the ceiling. "I don't suppose this new development changes anything with Hope's case?"

"A slick lawyer like you can probably make an argument that it should, but I don't think it will hold much weight. How do you tie a two-year-old murder into William's?"

Charlie blew out a deep breath. "I don't know, but in my gut I feel like they're all related—Elizabeth's and William's murders, Hope's incarceration and the attacks on Grace. Somehow they're connected, but I just can't get a handle on it."

"Well, if you do, I hope I'll be one of the first people you'll tell."

"And you'll let me know if anything new pops?"

"You got it," Zack replied.

Charlie hung up and stared out the window, his thoughts on the woman sleeping in the master bedroom. He was worried sick about her. She'd sat on the sofa in William's house like a stone statue, seemingly untouched by everything going on around her.

He'd always known she was a strong woman, but he'd known it wasn't strength that was keeping her so calm, so composed. Her brain had shut down, unable to handle any more trauma.

When the grief finally hit her, it had been horrible. Her sobs echoed in Charlie's heart, pulling forth his own grief for her. The worst part was knowing that he couldn't fix this for her. There was nothing he could say or do that would make her pain go away.

When she'd finally fallen asleep, exhausted by her river of tears, Charlie remained awake, his mind working overtime in an attempt to make sense of it all.

He could protect her from a gunman and make sure nobody could get at her without coming through him. But he couldn't protect her from grief, and that broke his heart.

Glancing at the clock, he was surprised to see that it was nearing ten. Grace never slept so late. He got up from the table and walked down the hallway to her purple bedroom, wanting to make sure she was okay.

She was awake but still in bed. "Hey," he said, and walked over to sit on the edge of the mattress. "How are you feeling?"

"As well as can be expected," she said. She sat up and pulled her legs up against her chest. Her eyes were slightly puffy from the tears, but Charlie thought she'd never looked as beautiful.

He reached out and smoothed a strand of her hair away from her face. She caught his hand and pressed it against her cheek. "I don't think I'm ready to face this day yet," she said softly.

"Then don't. There's nothing you need to do. If you want to stay in bed all day, nobody is going to complain. I'll even serve you your meals in here if you want me to," he said.

She smiled and reached up and pressed her mouth against his. He realized then that she must have gotten out of bed while he was on the phone with Zack, for her mouth tasted of minty toothpaste.

He tried to steel himself from the fire of desire that

instantly sprang to life inside him, but as she pulled him closer it was impossible to ignore.

A familiar ache of need began deep inside him, not just in his body but also in his heart. It was obvious what she wanted, and even though he knew he was a fool, it never entered his mind to deny her.

The kiss quickly became hot and hungry, and within seconds Charlie was naked and in bed with her. Last time, their lovemaking had been a slow renewal of old passion—a rediscovery between lovers—but now it was fast and hard and furious.

She encouraged him as he took her, her fingernails digging into his back, then into his buttocks. She cried out his name, whipping her head back and forth as she rocked beneath him.

He knew it was grief driving her to the wildness that possessed her. He held tight to her, as if to keep her from spinning off the face of the earth, and she cried out when she climaxed, a combination sob of pain and gasp of pleasure. He followed, losing it with a moan of her name.

Afterward he got up, grabbed his clothes and went into the bathroom to dress. Once again he felt a burgeoning anger swelling in his chest, and it was directed at Grace.

She had used him. He had the feeling that he could have been any man in her room just now. She'd just needed somebody and he was available.

She insisted she didn't want him and would never forgive him but pulled him into her bed and made him feel like he was the most important man in her world.

They needed to talk, but he was aware that now wasn't the time. She'd just lost her mother. She certainly wasn't in her right frame of mind, and he'd be a fool to attempt any meaningful conversation about the crazy relationship he now found himself in with her.

Just leave it alone, he told his reflection in the mirror. That's what a smart man would do. He drew a deep breath, sluiced water over his face and then did exactly what he'd told himself he wouldn't do.

"We need to talk," he said, when he returned to her bedroom.

Those beautiful blue eyes stared at him warily. "Talk about what?"

"About us, Grace. We need to talk about us." He refused to be put off by the vulnerable shine in her eyes.

She sighed, a tiny wrinkle appearing in the center of her forehead. "Do we really need to do this now?"

"We've put it off for eighteen months. I think we're past due for a conversation."

She raked a hand through her tousled hair. The sun drifting through the window caught and sparkled off her glorious golden strands.

His love for her blossomed so big in his chest he couldn't speak. How did you get into an unforgiving heart? How could he make her understand that he wasn't the same man he'd been in the past?

"Let me shower and have some coffee, then I guess we'll talk," she finally said with obvious dread in her voice.

He nodded and left her there with her hair shining

and her eyes filled with a sadness. He feared that he'd just made a huge mistake.

Grace stared at her reflection in the bathroom mirror. "What are you doing?" she asked the woman who stared back at her. "What are you doing making love with him when you hate him? Have you forgotten what he did to you?" No wonder he wanted to talk. She'd given him so many mixed signals it was ridiculous.

She whirled away from the mirror with a sigh of disgust. She'd let him get back into her heart. Somehow the drama of the past few days caused her to let down her guard.

She started the water in the shower and stepped in, hoping the stream would wash away the foolishness she'd entertained since he'd reentered her life and restore her to sanity.

When she'd come to him for help with Hope, she'd thought her anger and bitterness would shield her against any old feelings that might rear their head. But she hadn't expected his quiet support—his sensitivity to her every mood, his gentleness when she needed it most. She hadn't imagined his desire would be as fiery, as focused, as it had been before, and she certainly hadn't anticipated that he'd know when she needed a laugh.

She hadn't planned to fall in love with him all over again. She raised her face to the water, fighting against the new set of tears that burned her eyes. She couldn't go back. There was still a core of bitterness that remained inside her, an anger she refused to let go of for fear of being hurt again by him.

Stepping out of the shower, she grabbed a towel. She'd known this was coming. She'd known eventually they would talk about it. For weeks after she'd left him, he'd called, sent flowers and tried to communicate with her, but she hadn't given him a chance. The calls hadn't been answered and the flowers had gone directly into the trash.

Eventually he stopped reaching out to her, but there had never been any real closure between them. Now there would.

She dressed in a pair of bright yellow capris and a white and yellow blouse, hoping the sunny color would somehow bring warmth and comfort to her heart.

The one thing she couldn't think about was her mother. The grief would consume her. Her guilt would destroy her. It was better to stay focused on Charlie, to embrace the old rage that had once filled her where he was concerned.

She left her bedroom and found Charlie at the kitchen table. "The coffee is fresh," he said.

She nodded and poured herself a cup, then sat across from him, her fingers wrapped around the warmth of the drink. Grace was surprised to see a throbbing knot of tension in his jaw and the darkness of his charcoal eyes that looked remarkably like the first stir of anger.

"I can't imagine why you want to rake up the past," she finally said.

"Because it's there between us, because maybe if we talk about it, then you can finally let it go." He leaned back in his chair and studied her. "What I did was wrong, Grace. It was wrong on about a thousand different levels. Hell, I don't even remember that woman's name. I was drunk and she drove me home from the bar. It was a stupid thing for me to do, but I think we both need to accept some responsibility for what happened."

She sat up straighter in her chair and narrowed her eyes. "I certainly didn't encourage you to get stinking drunk and fall into bed with the first available woman." That old storm of anger whipped up inside her and the taste of betrayal filled her mouth.

"That's true and that's a mistake I'll always regret." A deep frown furrowed his forehead. "I'd won one of the biggest cases of my career that afternoon. Do you remember? I called you and wanted you to drive in, so we could celebrate, but you told me you had other plans for the weekend."

The heat of anger warmed her face. "So it's like the old song: if you can't be with the one you love, love the one you're with? If I wasn't available, it was okay for you to just find somebody else? That's not the way you have a loving, monogamous relationship."

"That was part of the problem," he exclaimed, a rising tension in his voice. "We never defined what, exactly, our relationship was. We never talked about it. We never discussed anything important."

He shoved back from the table with a force that surprised her and got up. "Hell, you didn't even tell me about your mother. You'd drive to my place twice a month for the weekend, but I didn't know what you did for the rest of the time. You never shared anything about your life here."

"And that makes it okay for you to cheat on me? Don't twist this around, Charlie. Don't make me the bad guy here." She embraced her anger, allowed it to fill her. It swept away the grief caused by her mother's death, the fear about Hope's future and the concern for her own personal safety.

He leaned a hip against the cabinets and shook his head. "I'm not trying to make you the bad guy. I'm trying to explain to you what my state of mind was that night. I was confused about you, about us."

"And while we were seeing each other how many other times were you confused?" Her voice was laced with sarcasm. "How many other women helped you clear your mind?"

"None," he said without hesitation. "You were always the one I wanted, but I never knew how you felt about me. I was afraid to tell you how I felt because I thought it would push you away." His voice was a low, husky rumble. "Tell the truth, Grace. I was just your good-time Charlie, available for a weekend of hot sex and laughs whenever you could work it into your schedule."

She stared at him in stunned surprise. "That wasn't the way it was, Charlie." Why was he twisting everything around and making it somehow feel like her fault? "Damn it, Charlie, that's not the way it was," she exclaimed.

He shoved his hands in his pockets and stared at her with dark, enigmatic eyes. "And the worst thing is we're back to where we started, only this time I'm your bad-time Charlie. Whenever you need somebody to hold you, to make love to you, you reach out to me because I'm the only man available."

She stood, her legs trembling with the force of her anger with him. She gripped the edge of the table with her hands. "You feel better, Charlie? You've managed to successfully turn your faults into mine. You've somehow absolved yourself of all guilt for cheating on me and made it all about my shortcomings. Congratulations," she added bitterly.

"I don't feel better. I feel sick inside." He reached up and swept a hand through his hair, and when he dropped his hand back to his side, his shoulders slumped in a way she'd never seen before. "I love you, Grace. I loved you then and I love you now and you've told me over and over again that you can't—or won't—forgive me. Well, I can't…. I won't make love to you again because it hurts too damn bad."

He turned on his heels and left the kitchen. A moment later she heard the sound of her guest-room door closing.

She sank back into the chair at the table, her legs no longer capable of holding her upright. This was what he did, she told herself. He twisted words and events to suit his own purposes. It was what made him a terrific defense attorney. It was why she'd contacted him to help with Hope's case.

He was an expert at making the guilty look innocent, at directing focus away from the matter at hand. He'd used those skills very well right now, but that didn't change the facts—didn't make his betrayal her fault.

Damn him. Damn him for telling her he loved her. And damn him for making her love him back. But just because she loved him didn't mean she intended to be a fool again.

He was right. She refused to forgive him, wouldn't take another chance on him. Her life was already in turmoil and that's what she had to focus on.

She had another funeral to plan. Her heart squeezed with a new pain as she thought of her mother. What she'd told Charlie about being friends with her mother was true.

They'd often met for lunch, and on most days Elizabeth would drop into the shop just to see what was new and spend some time with Grace. They'd shared the same sense of humor, the same kind of moral compass that made them easy companions.

So why had Grace been so quick to believe that her mother had done something so uncharacteristic as pack her bags and leave without a word? Instead of fostering her anger, she should have been out searching, beating every bush, overturning stones to find her mom. She should be thinking about Hope. God. She hated the fact that she was only allowed to see her at the detention center once a week. Hope was only able to call her every other day or so.

He loved her. The words jumped unbidden in her mind. Deep inside her, she'd known that he was in love with her. His feelings for her had been in his every touch, in the softness of his eyes, in the warmth of his arms whenever he'd comforted her.

And he was somewhat right about having been her good-time Charlie. When they'd met, she'd still been reeling from her mother's abandonment, and those weekends with him had been her escape from reality.

But why hadn't he seen that he'd been so much more than that to her? Why hadn't he recognized how much she'd loved him then? Maybe because she hadn't really shown him?

He was wrong about one thing. He was wrong to believe that when she made love with him he could have been anyone, that he just happened to be the man available. She'd wanted Charlie.

Grace felt as if she was born wanting Charlie, but that didn't mean she wanted to spend her life with him. That didn't mean she intended to forgive him and let him have a do-over with her.

They couldn't go on like they were, with him in her face every minute and in her bed whenever she wanted him.

It was time to let him go. She hoped he would still act as Hope's lawyer, but he couldn't be her bodyguard any longer. She'd have to make other arrangements.

It had been difficult to tell him goodbye the first time, but then she'd had her self-righteous anger to wrap around her like a cloak of armor. Now she had nothing but the realization that sometimes love just wasn't enough.

Chapter 12

Charlie walked out of the bedroom and back into the kitchen, but Grace wasn't there. She must have disappeared into her own room. He poured himself a cup of coffee and carried it to the window, where he stared outside.

How did you make a woman believe that you weren't the man you had once been? Losing Grace had shaken him to the very core, but it took his father's death to transform him.

His father hadn't liked the man he had become— a name-dropping, money-grabbing, slick lawyer who never managed to make time for the man who raised him.

Mark, Charlie's father, had called him often,

wanting him to come home and spend a little time at the ranch. Every holiday Mark had wanted Charlie home, but Charlie was always too busy. And then his dad was gone.

In the depths of his grief, Charlie came to realize his own unhappiness about the choices he'd made in his shallow life in the fast lane.

He'd recognized that what he truly wanted was to get back to the ranch, build a life of simple pleasures and hopefully share that life with a special woman.

When he fantasized about that woman, it was always Grace's face that filled his mind. He'd wanted her to be the one to share his life and give him children.

But it wasn't meant to be. There was no forgiveness in her heart, no room for him there. He turned away from the window as he heard the sound of heels on the floor.

He raised an eyebrow in surprise as he saw Grace, dressed in a cool blue power suit with white high heels and a white barrette clasped at the nape of her neck.

"I'm going into the shop for the day," she said. She walked over to where he stood and held out her hand. "Give me a dollar," she said.

He frowned. "What?"

"You heard me. Give me a dollar."

Charlie pulled his wallet from his back pocket, opened it and took one out. She took it from him and shoved it into the white purse she carried.

"I've just gotten my retainer back for your body-guard services. I'd still like you to continue with

Hope's case, but your services to me are no longer needed." Her cool blue eyes gave nothing away of her emotions.

"Are you crazy?" he exclaimed. "Have you forgotten that somebody is out to hurt you? Just because you can't trust or forgive me, isn't a good enough reason to put yourself at risk."

"I won't put myself at risk," she replied. "When I get to the shop, I'll give Dalton West a call and arrange for West Protective Services to keep an eye on me."

The idea of any other man being so intimately involved in her life definitely didn't sit well with him. Nobody would work harder than he at keeping Grace safe.

He set his cup down on the table. "Grace, for God's sake, don't let our personal issues force you to make a mistake. I can take care of you better than anyone."

She shook her head, her eyes dark with an emotion he couldn't discern. "I'm not making one. I feel like for the first time since William's murder I'm thinking clearly." She twisted the handle of her purse. "We can't go on like this, Charlie. It's too painful for both of us. I have enough things in my life to deal with right now without having to deal with you."

It surprised him that she still had the capacity to hurt him, but her words caused a dull ache to appear in the pit of his stomach.

"If you defend Hope, I'll pay you what I would pay any defense attorney," she continued. "And then we'll be square." She pulled her key ring from her purse. "I'd appreciate it if you're gone by the time I get home from the shop this evening."

"At least let me follow you to the shop," he said.

She hesitated and then nodded. "Okay."

He went back into the guest bedroom and packed what few things he'd brought with him. It wasn't until now that he realized how much he had hoped that they might be able to let go of the past and rebuild a new, better relationship.

Now, without that tenuous hope, he was empty. He carried his small bag down the hallway and found Grace waiting for him at the front door.

"Ready?" she asked. He noticed the slight tremble of her lower lip and realized this was just as difficult for her.

He nodded, and together they left the house. Charlie's car was in front of hers, the passenger window now intact. He walked her to her car door as his gaze automatically swept the area for any potential trouble.

When she was safely behind the steering wheel, he hurriedly got into his car. She pulled out of the driveway, and he followed her.

He could see her blond hair shining in the sunlight as they drove, that glorious hair that smelled vaguely of vanilla.

Again a painful ache swelled in his chest. He told himself it was good he got the opportunity to explain that terrible Friday night to her. He'd wanted her to know that he'd loved her despite what he had done.

Not that it mattered now.

He followed her down Main Street and parked in the space next to her. He was out of his car before she could get out of hers.

"I'll see you inside," he said, as he opened her car door.

He hovered at her back as she unlocked the shop and then they went in together. "I'll be fine now, Charlie," she said once she had the lights on and the Open sign in the window. "Nobody would be foolish enough to try to hurt me here during the middle of the day. People are in and out all day long."

He felt relatively confident that she was right. In the light of day in a fairly busy store, surely she'd be safe, but that didn't mean he intended to leave her safety to chance.

"You'll see to Hope?" she asked, and again her lower lip quivered as if she were holding back tears.

He nodded, the thick lump in his throat making him unable to speak for a moment.

"Charlie, thank you for everything you've done for me. I don't know how I would have gotten through the last week without you."

"I wish things could be different," he said, a last attempt at somehow reaching into her heart. "I wish you trusted that I'm different and realized how loving you is the biggest part of me."

Her eyes misted over and she stepped back to stand behind the cash register, as if needing a barrier between the two of them.

"Just go, Charlie." Her voice was a desperate plea. "Please just get out of here."

"Goodbye, Grace," he said softly, as he walked out the door and out of her life.

She watched him leave and had a ridiculous desire to run after him and tell him she didn't want him to go. Instead, she remained rooted in place as tears slowly ran from her eyes.

Angrily she wiped them away. It was better this way. They'd had their chance to make it work almost two years before and they'd blown it. Grace just wasn't willing to risk her heart again.

Stowing her purse beneath the counter, she tried not to think about the last time she'd been here.

Instead she went to the back room and dragged out a box of sandals that had come in so she could work on a new table display.

As she unpacked the cute, multicolored shoes, she tried to keep her mind off everything else. She needed a break. She desperately needed to not think about the murders or Hope and Charlie.

Here, in the confines of the shop, she'd always managed to clear her head by focusing on the simple pleasures of fabrics and textures. During those tough weeks after her mother disappeared, she'd found solace here. And when she and Charlie broke up, this place had been her refuge.

Today it didn't work. Nothing she did kept her mind off the very things she didn't want to think about. She had three customers in the morning and sold two pairs of the sandals she'd just put on display.

At noon she realized she hadn't made arrangements for lunch. Although the café was just up the street, she really didn't feel comfortable walking there alone. She should have packed a lunch, she thought, as she walked to the front window and peered outside.

She froze as she saw Charlie's car still parked next to hers. He was slumped down in the driver's seat but straightened up when he saw her in the window.

What did he think he was doing? They'd each said what needed to be said for closure. They'd said their goodbyes.

She opened the door, and before she could step out he scrambled from his car with the agility of a teenager. "What are you still doing here, Charlie?" she asked him, as he joined her at the door.

"It's a free country. I've got a right to sit in my car in a parking space on Main Street for as long as I want." He raised his chin with grim determination.

She narrowed her eyes. "What are you really doing?"

"Have you called West Protective Services yet?"

"Not yet. I was going to call after lunch."

"It's entirely up to you if you want to hire somebody else, but that doesn't mean I'm going to stop watching over you. I can guard you better than anyone you can hire, Grace, because I care about you more than anyone else. Don't worry, I don't intend to be an intrusion. There's really no way you can stop me short of getting a restraining order."

He'd often accused her of being stubborn, but she saw the thrust of his chin, the fierce determination in his eyes, and she knew it would be pointless to argue with him.

"Fine," she said, a weary resignation sweeping over her. "You can go now."

"What are you doing for lunch?" he asked.

"I'm not really hungry," she lied.

"Okay, then I'll just go back to being a shadow," he replied. He left her standing at the door and went back to his car.

She returned to her position behind the cash register and sat, trying to forget that she now had a shadow she didn't want and a heartache she knew would stay with her for a very long time.

Thirty minutes later her "shadow" reappeared in the store with a foam container from the café. He set it on the counter in front of her without saying a word, then walked out the front door.

Her stomach growled as she opened the lid. A cheeseburger was inside, its aroma filling the air and making her stomach rumble. She pulled off the top bun and saw just mustard and a pickle. Onions were on the side.

He'd remembered. After all this time, he still knew exactly how she liked her burgers. And it was this fact that broke her.

Tears blurred her vision as she stared at the burger and a deep sob ripped out of her. This time she knew what her tears were for. They were for lost love…they were for Charlie.

She only managed to pull herself together when the door opened and Rachel came in. "I just heard," she exclaimed, and immediately wrapped her arms around Grace's shoulders.

For one crazy moment, Grace thought she was talking about Charlie, but then she realized Rachel must have heard about her mother, and that made her tears come faster and harder.

All the losses she'd suffered over the last week came crashing back in on her. "Come on, let's go into the back," Rachel said. Grace locked the front door and allowed Rachel to lead her to the office. Grace sat at her desk and Rachel pulled a chair around a stack of boxes to sit next to her.

Grace grabbed a handful of tissues from a nearby box and dabbed at her eyes. "I've been so angry at her. I hated her for leaving and now I learn she's been dead this whole time."

"Does the sheriff have any leads?"

Grace shook her head. "None. Charlie thinks it might all be related, Mom's murder and William's." She began to cry. "Oh Rachel, I've made a mess of things. I've fallen in love with Charlie again."

"Grace, who are you fooling? You never stopped loving him," Rachel replied. "I saw him outside sitting in his car. What's really going on between the two of you?"

"Nothing now. Nothing anymore. He's just keeping an eye on me because of the attack the other night. And I want him to defend Hope when her case comes to trial." Grace decided not to go into the whole story about the shooting and how somebody was trying to kill her. "He says he loves me, that he always has."

"What are you going to do about it?" Rachel asked.

Grace sighed. "Nothing. I do think he's changed, Rachel. I believe that he's a different man than he was before, but I still have a knot of anger that I can't seem to get past where he's concerned."

"There are other good defense attorneys, Grace. If you really want to put him in your past, if you really have no desire to have anything to do with him, then find another attorney for Hope. Get Charlie Black completely out of your life."

Those words haunted Grace long after Rachel left the store. Grace ate the cold burger and considered her alternatives. She knew she should do what Rachel suggested, but she told herself that she wasn't convinced any other lawyer would work as hard as Charlie to defend Hope.

The afternoon was busier than usual. Prom was in less than a month, and more than a few high school girls came in to try on the sparkly gowns Grace carried just for the occasion.

When there weren't any customers in the store, Grace drifted by the window, oddly comforted by the fact that Charlie remained in his car.

"It's like having my own personal stalker," she muttered with dark humor at seven o'clock, as she turned the Open sign to Closed and locked the door.

She carried the cash register drawer to the back office to close out and sank down into the chair at the desk.

She was tired but didn't want to go home. Tonight she would be alone, without Charlie. She assumed he'd probably sleep in his car in her driveway, and while the idea that he would be uncomfortable bothered her, she would not allow her emotions to manipulate her into inviting him back in.

Let him go completely. A little voice whispered inside her head. *Or grab him with both hands and hold tight.* It has to be one or the other.

Because there had been more sales than usual during the day, it took her longer than normal to close out the books. It was almost eight by the time she locked up her desk. Still she was reluctant to leave.

She stood and stretched with her arms overhead and eyed the stack of boxes next to her desk. She should spend another hour or two unpacking the new products. There was a box of swimwear and another of beach towels and matching totes.

It wouldn't be long before summer was upon them. Where would Hope be this summer? Would she still be locked up in the detention center awaiting her trial, or would some evidence be found that would bring her home before the dog days of summer?

She would need to be mother and father to Hope now. She wouldn't be able to spend long hours here. She'd need to be available for her sister, to guide and love her.

As much as she loved the store, she loved her sister more. Dana could take on more responsibility and Grace could be what Hope needed, what she wanted.

She pulled the top box off the tall stack, moved it to her desk and opened it. It would take her about an hour to tag all the swimwear, and then she'd go home.

As she worked, she kept her mind as empty of thought as possible. It was just after nine when she finished. She was just about to leave her office when she heard a knock on the back door.

Who on earth…? She walked to the door and hesitated with her hand on the lever that would disarm the security alarm. "Who is it?" she yelled through the door.

"Grace, it's me, Leroy Racine. I need to talk to you. I remembered something…something about the night before William was murdered."

Was it possible this was the break they had been looking for? Grace disarmed the door and opened it partway to look at the big man. In the dark, she could barely discern his features. "What are you talking about?"

"The night before William's murder he had a visitor, a business associate of some kind. I was outside working, but I heard them yelling at each other."

Grace's heart leapt with excitement as she opened the door to allow him inside. "Come on into my office," she said, and gestured him into the chair where Rachel had sat earlier in the day.

Leroy sank into the chair and Grace sat at her desk. "I don't know why I didn't remember this before," he said.

"So, exactly what is it that you've remembered?"

Grace asked. She leaned forward, hoping, praying that whatever information Leroy had would point the finger of guilt away from Hope and to the real killer.

"It's really not what I've remembered as much as it is what I need to finish." He pulled a wicked, gleaming knife and leaned forward, so close to her that she could feel the heat of his breath on her face. "Tomorrow everyone will talk about how the robber who got away the other night came back here, only this time with tragic results. Don't scream, Grace, don't even move."

Leroy? Her mind struggled to make sense of what was happening. Grace stared into his dark eyes and knew she was in trouble, the kind of trouble people didn't survive.

Zack West's car pulled up beside Charlie's, and the lawman stepped out and walked up to his window. "Everything all right? You've been parked here for the whole day."

Charlie opened his car door and stepped out, his kinked muscles protesting the long hours in the car. "I'm just waiting for Grace to call it a day so I can follow her home." He shot a glance toward the darkened storefront. "I think she's working late on purpose just to aggravate me." He leaned against the side of his car and frowned. "Why are women so damned complicated?"

Zack laughed. "I don't know. I certainly don't always understand Kate, and we've been married for a while now." Zack headed back to his car. "I just wanted to make sure everything was all right here."

"Everything is fine," Charlie assured him. "I'm hoping she's going to call it a night pretty quickly, so I can get her home safe and sound."

Zack nodded, then got back into his car and pulled away. Charlie folded his arms and gazed at the shop.

How much longer was she going to be? He wouldn't put it past her to be cooling her heels intentionally, knowing he was sitting out here waiting for her.

Charlie had already made arrangements with Dalton West to help him keep an eye on her. Once Grace was back in her house, Dalton would take over surveillance on her place while Charlie went home and grabbed a shower and a couple of hours of sleep.

By the time Grace woke up the next morning, Charlie would once again be on duty for the day. He didn't care what she said. He wasn't going to leave her unprotected until they figured out exactly what in the hell was going on.

Eventually he'd need to figure out a way to cast her not only out of his thoughts, but out of his heart as well.

He checked his watch, then got back into his car and leaned his head back, waiting for her to call it a night.

Chapter 13

"Leroy, what are you doing?" Grace's voice was laced with the terror that coursed through her. She stared at him, trying to make sense of what was going on.

"What am I doing?" He smiled then, a proud, boastful smile. "I'm completing a plan that's been ten years in the making."

"What does that mean?" Grace slid her eyes toward the top of her desk, looking for something she could use as a weapon. Inside the drawer was a box cutter and a pair of scissors, but on top there was nothing more lethal than a ballpoint pen.

Leroy's eyes glittered darkly and he leaned forward, as if eager to share with her whatever was going on in his head. "It started when I met Lana and found out she was carrying William Covington's baby."

Grace gasped and stared at him incomprehensively. "What are you talking about? Lincoln is only ten years old. William and my mother were married at the time he was conceived. William wouldn't have cheated on my mother."

Leroy laughed, but there was nothing pleasant in the sound. "Ah, but he did. Your mother had flown to Las Vegas to help out one of her friends who was having a difficult pregnancy. Remember? She was gone for two weeks, and on one of those nights William and my lovely wife crossed the line. It only happened once, but that was enough for her to wind up pregnant."

She reeled with the information. Lana and William? What Leroy said might be true, but it still didn't illuminate everything that had happened over the last week and a half.

The fact that he hadn't lowered the knife and still held it tightly in his hand as if ready to thrust it into her at any moment kept a lump of fear firmly lodged in her throat.

If she screamed, he could gut her before anyone would hear her cry for help. She thought of Charlie in his car out front and wanted to weep because she had no way of letting him know she was in danger.

"What do you want, Leroy? Money? I have my cash drawer in the desk. Just let me unlock it and I'll give you everything I have."

"Oh Grace, I definitely want money, but I'm not interested in whatever you have in that drawer," he replied. "I've been a very patient man and soon my patience is all going to pay off." He must have seen the look of confusion on her face for he laughed once again. "William's money, Grace. That's what I'm after. Lincoln is a Covington heir—and why should he share an inheritance when he can have it all."

Grace had been afraid before, but as the realization of his words penetrated her frightened fog, a new sense of terror gripped her. "You killed William? It was you? And you set up Hope to take the fall."

Again a proud grin lifted the corner of Leroy's mouth. "It was genius. Your sister, she's a creature of habit. Every morning she makes herself breakfast and drinks about a half a gallon of orange juice. That girl loves her juice."

"You drugged it," Grace exclaimed.

"It was brilliant. She went back to bed and passed out. I killed William, trashed her room, smeared her with blood and put the knife in her hand. And before she goes to trial I'll make sure the prosecutor has all the evidence he needs to send her away for the rest of her life."

"I don't understand any of this," Grace cried, tears misting her vision as she tried to buy time. "Did you kill my mother, too?"

Leroy leaned back in the chair, but the knife never wavered. "Apparently William decided to come clean to your mother about that night with Lana. The next morning your mother came to the cottage wanting to talk to Lana, but she'd taken Lincoln into Oklahoma City for a doctor's appointment. You see, for me to make sure my stepson inherited all of William's money, I needed to make sure nobody else was going to inherit it. Your mother was the first obstacle in the way. I strangled her, and since nobody was home at the mansion, I packed a couple of her suitcases to make it look like she took off."

Grace closed her eyes as grief battled with terror inside her. Reward. Charlie had been trying to figure out the true motive of William's murder and now she knew. Money. William's money. Leroy wanted it all not for Lincoln, but for himself. With Lincoln being underage, Leroy and Lana would be in charge of the fortune.

What did Lana know? Was she a part of this? God, it would be the final betrayal to learn that the loving housekeeper had helped plot all these murders.

Grace opened her eyes and realized she was going to die here now if she didn't do something.

"I had to bide my time after your mother died. I knew I couldn't take out William too quickly or people would be suspicious," he said.

"People *are* suspicious," she said, barely able to hear her own voice over the pounding of her heartbeat. "You'll never get away with this, Leroy. When you try to collect William's money, the suspicions will only get bigger."

"Suspecting and proving are two different things.

William's murder is going to be pinned on Hope. Your mother's murder happened two years ago, and by the time I plant bugs in some people's ears it will all make perfect sense."

His dark eyes gleamed bright. "You see, the way the story will go is that your mother found out about William's night with Lana and was going to leave him. They fought and things got out of control and he killed her. Two years later, Hope began to suspect what had happened and believing that William was responsible for your mother's death, she killed him. And you, you're just the tragic victim of a store robbery. Nobody can tie up all the pieces so they point in my direction. You'll all be gone and a DNA test will prove Lincoln to be a rightful heir."

Grace knew she was running out of time. She had to do something to escape or at least to draw attention. Once again her gaze shot around, looking for anything that might help her.

The stacked boxes next to where he sat caught her eye. She tensed all her muscles, knowing it was very possible she'd die trying to escape him, but she would certainly be killed if she did nothing.

Now or never, she told herself as Leroy continued bragging about how smart he'd been to pull off everything. *Now or never,* the words screamed through her head.

She exploded from the chair and knocked down the stack of boxes. They toppled on top of Leroy as she ran for the door of the office, sobs of terror ripping out of her.

The sales floor was dark, lit only by the faint security lights and the dim illumination coming through the front window. She focused on the door. If she could just get out, Charlie would be there and everything would be all right.

She made it as far as the table display of sandals before she was tackled from behind. They both tumbled to the floor. Shoes fell on top of them as they bumped against the table.

Leroy cursed and momentarily let go of her. Frantically Grace crawled on her hands and knees into the middle of a circular rack of blouses, swallowing her sobs in an effort to hide from him.

If she screamed for Charlie, she would pinpoint her location to Leroy, who apparently hadn't seen exactly where she had gone. Even if Charlie heard her scream, she was afraid he wouldn't be able to get inside before Leroy killed her.

She could smell the man, the sour scent of sweat. She could hear him moving around the store, hunting her like a predator stalking prey.

Her body began a tremble she feared would move the blouses. Drawing deep, silent breaths, she tried to control the fear that threatened to erupt. She tensed as she heard Leroy's footsteps getting closer…closer still.

"Grace, you're just prolonging the inevitable," he said softly. The rack of blouses shook and despite her desire to stay silent, a slight whimper escaped her as she realized he knew where she was hiding.

She had to scream and she had to move. It was the only way Charlie might hear her and get out of his car to check it out.

At that moment, the knife slashed through the rack of blouses and a scream ripped out of her.

Charlie drummed his fingers on the steering wheel in time to the beat of the music from his radio. He was beginning to wonder if Grace was going to spend the entire night in the store.

Main Street had emptied of cars long ago, and most of the townspeople were now in their homes, watching television or getting ready for bed.

Charlie would love to be getting ready for bed, especially if Grace was waiting in it. He couldn't help but think of the last two times they made love and how he would happily spend the rest of his life loving her and only her.

What was keeping her from him? There had been moments over the past week when he hadn't felt the burden of their past between them and thought she'd gotten past her bitterness. He'd felt her love for him and entertained a tiny flicker of hope that there might be a future for them together.

He rubbed a hand across his forehead, weary with the inactivity of the day and thoughts of Grace. It was done. There was no point in trying to figure out what went wrong this time. Apparently she'd never really gotten over their past and refused to even consider any future with him.

He frowned as he saw a shadow move across the

plate glass window in front of the shop. Sitting up straighter, he breathed a grateful sigh. Good, maybe she was getting ready to go home.

He got back out of the car and stretched with his arms overhead, then shoved his hands in his pockets and waited for her to walk out the front door.

Again he saw shadowy movement inside the store and heard a noise—a scream. Alarm rang in his head as he yanked his hands from his pockets and ran to the front door. Locked.

"Grace?" he yelled and banged on the door with his fists. Wild with fear as he saw not one figure, but two, he looked around frantically, needing something he could use to break the door down.

He spied a heavy flowerpot in front of the storefront next door. As soon as he grabbed it, he threw it at the window.

The pot went through with a crash and the entire window cracked and shattered. Before the glass had cleared enough for him to get inside, Grace opened the front door.

She was sobbing and held an arm that was bleeding. "It's Leroy," she cried. "Leroy Racine. He ran out the back door. Charlie, he killed them. He killed them all and he tried to kill me."

"Get in my car and lock the doors," he said, refusing to look at her bloody arm. He was filled with an all-consuming rage. "Call Zack. My cell phone is on the passenger seat."

He pulled his gun and took off around the side of the building, knowing Leroy had to be using the alley for his escape. Leroy? As Charlie ran, a million questions raced through his head.

Leroy was a big man, not as fast on his feet as Charlie, and on the next block from Grace's shop he spied the man rounding a corner.

Charlie had never wanted to catch a man more in his life. As he raced, his head filled with visions of Grace being hit over the head with an object, of her being kicked in the ribs. The rage that ripped through him knew no bounds. He wanted to kill Leroy Racine, but first he wanted to beat the hell out of him.

"Stop or I'll shot," Charlie yelled, as he saw Leroy just ahead of him. "I swear to God, Racine, I'll shoot you in the back and not blink an eye."

Leroy must have recognized the promise in Charlie's voice, for he stopped running and turned toward him, a frantic defeat spread across his face.

At that moment the whine of a siren sounded in the distance, and Charlie knew Zack or one of his deputies was responding to Grace's call.

"Get down on the ground," Charlie commanded. "Facedown on the ground with your hands up over your head."

Leroy hesitated but must have seen something in Charlie's eyes that frightened him, for he complied. Charlie kicked the knife Leroy held in one hand and sent it spinning several feet away. He leaned over him and pressed the barrel of his gun into the back of Leroy's head.

"Don't try anything," he warned the big man. "Don't even blink too hard. One way or the other you're going away for a very long time. It's either going to be jail or hell."

At that moment Zack ran toward them, his gun drawn and his eyes wide as he saw Charlie. "He killed Elizabeth and William, set up Hope to go to prison and tried to kill Grace." Charlie's voice grew hoarse with anger. "His knife is over there."

"Charlie, you can step away from him," Zack said, his voice deceptively calm. "I've got him now."

Reluctantly, Charlie pulled his gun from the back of Leroy's head and straightened. Before anyone could stop him, he drew back his boot and delivered a swift kick to Leroy's ribs.

Leroy yelped and raised his head to look at Zack. "Did you see that? I want him arrested for assault."

Charlie looked at Zack, who shrugged. "I didn't see anything," Zack replied.

"I've got to check on Grace. She was hurt," Charlie said, as Zack pulled Leroy to his feet and cuffed him.

Charlie took off running in the direction he'd come from. He still didn't have any real answers, couldn't figure out why Leroy had done what he'd done, but at the moment answers didn't matter—only Grace did.

She saw him coming and got out of his car. In the light from the nearby street lamp, he could see that her cheeks were shiny with tears, and she held her arm against her side, one hand pressed against the opposite upper arm.

"Charlie," she cried, as he neared. "Thank God you're okay."

He reached her and pulled her gently into his arms, careful not to hurt her.

As he smelled the familiar scent of vanilla in her hair and felt the warmth of her body against his, Charlie did something he couldn't remember doing since he was a young boy and his mother had died—he wept.

It was nearing dawn when Charlie followed Grace home. The night had been endless for Grace. At the hospital, she'd received eight stitches in her arm and then spent most of the rest of the night with Zack, telling him everything Leroy had told her.

She was beyond exhaustion yet elated. Zack promised her that first thing in the morning he'd get the wheels of justice turning to release Hope.

Hope was coming home, and it was time to tell Charlie a final goodbye. When they reached her house, she pulled into the driveway and parked. Charlie pulled in just behind her.

She didn't have to be afraid anymore. She could get out of her car without waiting for Charlie and his gun to protect her. She no longer needed him as a private investigator, a criminal defense attorney or a bodyguard. It was time for them to move on with their lives.

She got out of the car with weariness weighing on her shoulders and the whisper of something deeper, something that felt remarkably like new heartbreak.

Charlie joined her on the sidewalk and silently walked with her to her front door. "You're going to be all right now, Grace," he said.

She unlocked the door and then turned back to face him. His features looked haggard in the dawn light, and she fought her impulse to reach up and lay her palm against his cheek. "Yes, I'm going to be all right," she replied softly.

"Hope should be released sometime tomorrow, and the two of you can begin rebuilding your lives." He reached a hand up, as if to tuck a strand of her hair behind her ear, but instead he quickly dropped his hand back to his side. "You don't have any reason to be afraid anymore. It's finally over."

She nodded, surprised by the rise of a lump in her throat. He stared at her, and in the depths of his beautiful gray eyes, she saw his want, his need of her and she steeled herself against it, against him.

"Then I guess this is goodbye," he said, although it was more a question, a plea than a statement.

Her chest felt tight, constricted by her aching heart. "Goodbye, Charlie." She said the words quickly, then escaped into the house and closed the door behind her. She leaned against the door and felt the hot press of tears at her eyes.

She should have been happy. The bad times were behind her, so why was she crying? Why did she feel as if she'd just made the biggest mistake of her life?

Chapter 14

"It's just a movie, Grace," Hope said plaintively. "We'll go straight to the theater, and when the movie is over, we'll come right back here."

Grace took a sip of her coffee and frowned at her sister. It had been a week since Hope had gotten out of the detention center and moved into Grace's house.

The spare bedroom was now filled with all things teenage. Grace welcomed the chaos, the laughter and the drama that had filled the last seven days of her life.

Hope's release wasn't the only positive thing that happened over the last week. Although Lana had been devastated to learn that the man she'd married had done so only for the sake of Lincoln's inheritance, the knowledge that he'd murdered William and Elizabeth had nearly destroyed her.

She'd come to Grace begging for forgiveness, both for the horrific things her husband had done and for her own mistake in sleeping with William on that single night.

She'd explained that William had been missing Elizabeth desperately and invited her to have a drink with him. One drink led to half a dozen and suddenly they were both making the biggest mistake of their lives.

She hadn't told William that she'd gotten pregnant. She met Leroy a month later, and when she gave birth William assumed, like everyone else, that Lincoln was Leroy's child.

Grace assured her there was nothing to forgive and made Lana promise that she would allow Grace and Hope to get to know Lincoln, who would share in the inheritance that William had left behind.

"Earth to Grace." Hope's voice penetrated Grace's thoughts. "So can I go to a movie with Justin or not?"

Grace sighed, wishing this parenting stuff was easier. "I don't know, Hope."

Hope reached across the table and took Grace's hand in hers. "Grace, I know Justin has made some stupid mistakes in his past, like dropping out of high school, but he's really a nice guy. He deserves another chance."

"You'll go right to the theater and come right back here?" Grace asked.

"Pinky swear," Hope replied, lacing her pinky finger with Grace's.

"Okay. We'll consider this a test run."

"Cool." Hope was out of the chair almost before the words had left Grace's mouth. "I've got to call him and tell him I can go."

As she ran for her bedroom, Grace leaned back in her chair and sighed. This would be the first time Hope would be out of her sight since coming home.

Maybe part of her reluctance in letting Hope go was because Grace didn't want to spend the evening alone. Being alone always brought thoughts of Charlie and a sadness that felt never ending.

She hadn't seen him in the past week, but every time she got beneath the sheets on her bed she saw him in her mind, felt him in her heart.

Forgetting Charlie was proving more difficult than she'd thought. She got up from the table and carried her coffee cup to the sink, then stood by the window and stared out into the backyard.

He'd accused her of holding back, of confusing him when they'd been dating. She remembered the night he'd called her, so excited by his big win in court that day, asking her—no, begging her—to drive in to celebrate with him.

The sheer force of her desire to be with him had frightened her, and she'd told him she couldn't make it. Hours later she'd changed her mind and decided to surprise him. Unfortunately she was the one who had gotten the biggest surprise.

Hope walked back into the kitchen. "It's all set. Justin will pick me up at seven."

Grace turned from the window and forced a smile. "And you told him you needed to be home right after?"

"Yeah, but I was thinking maybe after the movie Justin could come in and we could bake a frozen pizza or something. I think if you talk to him for a while, you know, get to really know him, then you'll like him."

"That sounds like a nice idea," Grace replied.

Hope walked over to stand next to Grace and looked out the window. "When Mom left, I thought nobody else would ever care about me," Hope said softly. "I figured if my own mother didn't like me enough to stick around, why would anyone else like me?"

Grace put her arm around Hope's slender shoulders. "I know. I felt the same way."

"But, then I met Justin and even though he had a reputation as a tough guy, he made me feel better. He told me I was pretty and nice and that it was Mom's problem, not me, that drove her away."

"And now we know that she didn't leave us at all," Grace replied.

They were silent for a few minutes, and Grace knew they were both thinking of the mother they had buried two days before.

Hope finally looked at her. "It's important to me that you give Justin a chance, Grace. You don't have to worry about him taking advantage of me, or anything like that. Justin knows I want to stay a virgin for a long time and he's cool with that."

"I promise I'll give him a chance," Grace replied.

Hope reached up and kissed Grace on the cheek. "I'm going to go take a shower and get ready. Seven o'clock will be here before I know it."

Once again she left the kitchen and Grace turned her gaze back out the window. She could definitely relate to those feelings Hope described, of believing that if her mother didn't love her enough to stick around that nobody else would really love her.

She'd carried that emotion into her relationship with Charlie, and despite her deep feelings for him, she'd kept a big part of herself walled off from him, certain that eventually he'd leave her, too. She had to be unworthy of love because her mother had found her so.

Charlie told her she needed to accept partial responsibility for the demise of their relationship, and he was right.

She had treated him like a good-time Charlie, flying into his life for fun and laughs but never sharing with him any piece of herself, of her life here in Cotter Creek.

No wonder he hadn't seen their relationship in the same way she had. She'd given him so many mixed signals.

And now it was too late for her, for them.

Charlie sat on the back of his favorite stallion and gazed at the fencing he'd spent the last week repairing. It had been grueling physical work, but he'd welcomed it because it kept his mind off Grace.

He hadn't even gone into town during the past week. When he needed supplies, he sent one of his ranch hands in to get them. Charlie hadn't wanted to run into Grace or even see her storefront.

He wondered if everyone had that one love who stayed with you until the day you died and haunted you with a bittersweet wistfulness.

Leaning down, he patted his horse's neck, then grabbed the reins and turned around to head back to the house. It was too bad there wasn't a pill he could take that would banish all thoughts of Grace Covington from his mind. He was just going to have to live with his regrets and the overwhelming ache of what might have been.

Just then, as he approached the corral, Charlie saw the car pull into his driveway. Her car. His heart leapt, then calmed as he cautioned himself with wariness.

Maybe something else had happened—a legal issue she wanted help with or a question that needed to be answered. As he dismounted from the horse, she stepped out of her car, the fading sunlight sparking on her glorious hair and tightening the lump that rose up in his chest.

She looked lovely in a turquoise and white sundress, with turquoise sandals on her feet and a matching purse slung over her shoulder.

She couldn't keep doing this, he thought, as he walked slowly toward where she stood. She had to stop using him as her go-to man.

"Grace, what's up?" he asked, his tone curt.

She leaned against her car door. "Hope just left to go to a movie with Justin."

He frowned. "And you drove all the way out here to tell me that? Gee, thanks for the info, but I'm not sure why I need to know that." He stuffed his hands in his pockets, afraid that if he allowed them to wander free he'd reach out and run a finger across her full lower lip.

"Earlier this evening Hope and I had a chat about our mother and how she felt when we thought she'd abandoned us. She told me she thought nobody would ever love her again, and I realized that's exactly how I'd felt."

She pushed off from the door, her eyes dark and so sad that Charlie felt her sadness resonating in his own heart. "I hope both of you feel better about things now that you know the truth," he said.

"I don't feel better," she exclaimed and her eyes grew shiny with tears. "Oh Charlie, you were right about me. I did use you, but somewhere along the line I fell in love with you."

"And then I got drunk and stupid and screwed it all up," he replied, as a hollow wind blew through him. "We've been through all this, Grace."

He sighed with a weariness that etched deep into his soul. "I can keep Hope out of jail for a crime she didn't commit and I can probably keep you safe from some crazy stalker, but I don't know how to get you to trust me again."

She took several steps closer to him and that amazing scent of hers stirred the desire he would always feel for her. Still he kept his hands firmly tucked into his pockets, not wanting a moment of weakness to allow him to touch her in any way.

"I swore I didn't believe in second chances, that only a fool would give a man her heart again after he'd broken it once." Again her eyes took on the sheen of barely suppressed tears. "And then I realized I'd never really given you my heart for safe-keeping the first time. How could you know you were breaking it when you didn't realize it was yours?"

Charlie stared at her, afraid to believe what he thought her words might mean. "Why are you here, Grace?"

"I'm here because I realize I'm a different person now than I was when we were dating. And if I can believe that I'm a different person, then why can't I believe that you are? I'm here because for the first time in a year and a half I don't have my anger at you to fill me up, to protect me. And without that anger all I'm left with is my love for you."

Tears fell from her eyes and splashed onto her cheeks. "I'm here to find out if it's too late for me…for us."

Charlie's heart swelled so big in his chest he couldn't speak. He yanked his hands out of his pockets and opened his arms to her.

She fell into his embrace and he held her tight, feeling as if he were complete for the very first time. The scent of vanilla and jasmine smelled like home. Grace smelled like home.

"Charlie?" She raised her face to look at him. "It's not just me anymore. I'm a package deal. Hope is and will always be a part of my life."

"I always wanted a sister-in-law," he replied.

"Sister-in-law?" Grace stared at him, and that sweet lower lip of hers trembled. "Is that some kind of a crazy proposal, Charlie?"

He dropped his hands to his sides and smiled at her. "Give me a dollar."

"What?"

"You heard me, give me one." He held out his hand.

She opened her purse and pulled out a dollar bill. He took it from her and shoved it into his back pocket. "You've now retained the lifelong services of a criminal defense attorney and bodyguard." He pulled her into his arms, his gaze warm and soft, relaxed. "Better yet, you've got my love through eternity."

She returned to his embrace. "All that for a dollar? You're cheap, Charlie."

He grinned at her. "Only for the woman I love." His smile faded and he gazed at her intently. "Marry me, Grace. Marry me and be my wife. Share my life with me."

Charlie's words filled Grace with a kind of happiness that she'd never before experienced. This was right, she thought. This was the first right thing that had happened in a very long time, and she had no doubt that it would last forever.

"Yes, Charlie, I want to marry you. I want you to be my good-time Charlie, my bad-time Charlie, my forever Charlie."

He kissed her then, a hungry yet tender kiss that

held both the regrets of the past and the promise of the future. He wasn't the only one with regrets. Grace knew that their future together might have begun sooner if she'd been less afraid of putting her heart on the line when they'd been dating.

"Better late than never," she murmured, as their kiss finally ended.

"Second chances, Grace. Sometimes that's all we need." His eyes glowed with a light that always weakened her knees and curled her toes. "How long does that movie last?"

She grinned. "Long enough," she exclaimed, and grabbed his hand. Together they ran for the ranch house where his bed and their future awaited.

* * * * *

KINCAID'S DANGEROUS GAME

BY
KATHLEEN CREIGHTON

Kathleen Creighton has roots deep in the California soil but has relocated to South Carolina. As a child, she enjoyed listening to old timers' tales and her fascination with the past only deepened as she grew older. Today, she says she is interested in everything – art, music, gardening, zoology, anthropology and history, but people are at the top of her list. She also has a lifelong passion for writing and now combines her two loves in romance novels.

For my family,
near and far;
I love you,
eccentricities, skeletons and all.

Prologue

Part 1
In a house on the shores of a small lake, somewhere in South Carolina

"Pounding…that's always the first thing. Someone—my father—is banging on the door. Banging…pounding…with his fists, feet, I don't know. Trying to break it down."

"And where are *you*?"

"I'm in a bedroom, I think. I don't remember which one. I have the little ones with me. It's my job to look after them when my father is having one of his…spells. I have to keep them out of his way. Keep them safe. I've

taken them into the bedroom and I've locked the door.
Except…I don't trust the lock, so I've wedged a chair
under the handle, like my mom showed me. Only now
I'm afraid…terrified even that won't be enough. I can
hear the wood splintering…breaking. I know it will
only take a few more blows and he'll be through. My
mother is screaming…crying. I hold on to the little
ones. I have my arms around them, and they're all trembling. The twins, the little girls, are sobbing and crying,
'Mama, Mama…' but the boys just cry quietly.

"I hear sirens…more sirens, getting louder and
louder until it seems they're coming right into the room,
and there's lots of people shouting. Then all of a sudden
the pounding stops. There's a moment—several
minutes—when all I hear is the little ones whimpering…and then, there's a loud bang, so loud we all jump.
We hold each other tighter, and there's another bang,
and then there's just confusion—voices shouting…foot-
steps running…glass breaking…the little ones crying…
and I think I might be crying, too."

Cory discovered he *was* crying, but he also knew it
was all right. *He* was all right. Sam, his wife, was
holding him tightly, cradling his head against her
breasts, and her hands were gentle as they wiped the
tears from his face.

"I'm going to find them, Sam. My brothers and
sisters. I have to find them."

Samantha felt warm moisture seep between her
lashes. "Of course you do." She lifted her head and took

her husband's face between her hands and smiled fiercely at him through her tears. "We'll find them together, Pearse," she whispered. "We'll find them. I promise you we will."

Part 2
In a diner in a small town in the Texas Hill Country

"I never thought it would happen," Cory said to Holt Kincaid over steak and eggs at the diner. "Not to Tony. He's always been…well, let's just say, he's somewhat of a lady's man. I didn't think he'd ever find…"

"The *one?*" Holt lifted one eyebrow. "Who's to say there's a *one* for everybody? Maybe some people just don't have *one* to find."

"Like you, for instance?" Cory's eyes narrowed thoughtfully as he picked up his coffee cup. "What's your story, Holt? I sense there is one—probably a helluva one, too."

Holt smiled sardonically but didn't reply.

After a moment Cory said, "So. What about my other sister? You said her name's Brenna, right? Where is she and when can I meet her?"

Holt let out a breath and pushed his plate away. It was the moment he'd been dreading "That's gonna be a problem."

"Why? What problem? You said the twins were adopted together, grew up in the same family. Surely they've stayed in touch. Brooke must know—"

"I wish that were true." Holt picked up his coffee and blew on it, stalling for time. But there was no way around it. It looked like he was going to have to be the one to break the news that would devastate the man sitting across from him. Never mind that he'd found three of his lost siblings—two brothers and now one of his sisters. The task wouldn't be complete until he'd found the last one as well.

"Mr. Pearson, I'm sorry to have to tell you, but Brenna ran away from home when she was just fourteen. Brooke hasn't seen or heard from her since." He spread his hands in utter defeat. "I have absolutely no clue where she is. Or even where to start looking."

Chapter 1

Holt Kincaid was no stranger to insomnia. He'd been afflicted with bouts of it since childhood, and had learned long ago not to fight it. Consequently, he'd grown accustomed to whiling away the long late-night or early-morning hours catching up on paperwork, going over notes from whatever case he was working on, knowing that what he didn't pursue would come to him on its own, eventually.

Not this time.

The only case he was working at the moment—the only one that mattered, anyway—was at a dead stand-still. The paperwork had been done. He'd been over his notes a hundred times. There was nothing more to be gleaned from them.

Over the course of his career as a private investigator specializing in missing persons cases—the cold ones in particular—he'd had to admit defeat only once. That one failure was the case responsible for a lot of the insomnia he'd suffered for most of his life, and the idea that he might have to add this one to the roster of his regrets weighed heavily on his mind. Sleep wouldn't come to him this night, no matter how coyly he played her flirting game.

Laurel Canyon was quiet now. There'd been sirens earlier, prompting him, as a longtime resident, to pause and sniff the air for the smell of smoke. But the cause this time—a traffic-stopping fender bender on the boulevard—had been cleared up hours ago. An onshore breeze rustled the leaves of the giant eucalyptus trees that soared above his deck, but in a friendly way, last week's Santa Anas being only a bad memory now. Late-October rains had laid the threat of brush fires low for the time being.

Holt had come to be a resident of the notorious Santa Monica Mountain community by happenstance rather than choice, but over the years it had grown on him. He'd found it suited him, with its shady past, the steep and narrow winding dead-end streets and pervasive aura of mystery. The huge old eucalyptus trees and rickety stairways and ivy-covered walls guarded its secrets well. As he guarded his own.

He'd also come to embrace the canyon's laid-back,
live-and-let-live attitude, a holdover from the sixties when
it had been the center of L.A.'s rock music scene. Now as
then, in Laurel Canyon the expression "goin' with the
flow" wasn't just a hippie slogan, but a way of life.

It had become his way of life: Go with the flow…
don't get emotionally involved…go about your business
and don't waste energy railing against things beyond
your control.

*Yeah. That was my mistake with this case. I got too
close. Made it personal.*

As with the first and still his greatest failure, he'd let
himself get too fogged in by emotions to see where the
answers lay hidden.

*Face it, Kincaid. Maybe there just aren't any
answers. Not in this life, anyway.*

Unbidden, as if a stubborn imp in his subconscious-
ness had again touched Replay, the case and the events
of the past year unfolded slowly in his mind, playing out
against the murmur of breezes through eucalyptus trees
and the intermittent *shush* of a passing car.

He'd taken on Cory Pearson's case for two good
reasons: First, because it presented a new kind of challenge. Typically, he'd be searching for a birth parent, a
child given up for adoption, an abducted child long ago
given up for dead by everyone except loved ones still
praying for answers. But this was a man searching for
four younger brothers and sisters. The children had been
taken from him when they were very young by a well-

meaning social services agency after their Vietnam vet father had shot his wife and then himself during a violent episode of PTSD. The four younger ones had been adopted by two different families while the oldest brother fought his way through a dismal series of foster homes and juvenile detention facilities, only to be denied access to his siblings' whereabouts when he finally reached adulthood.

A sad story, for sure, but one to which Holt had felt confident he could give a happy ending. These kids had vanished into the *system.* Systems kept records. And Holt was very good at getting old systems and old records to give up their secrets. That was his second reason for taking on the case of Cory Pearson's lost siblings: He'd expected success.

Holt didn't take on hopeless cases. He already had one of those, and it was more than enough.

Things had gone about as expected, at first. After months of tedious detective work, he'd finally gotten a line on the oldest boy, now working as a homicide detective in Portland, Oregon. The timing hadn't been great. Cory had dropped into his brother's life in the middle of a case involving a serial killer and had very nearly been mistaken for the killer himself. Thanks to a drop-dead gorgeous blond psychic who'd been helping out with the investigation, everything had turned out fine in the end, and the psychic—or empath, as she preferred to call herself—had recently become Cory Pearson's sister-in-law.

Cory's reunion with one brother was followed immediately, and without any further help from Holt, by the second. Finding his younger brother paralyzed as a result of a climbing accident, Cory'd been determined to bring him back to the life and the woman he'd loved and left. After epic battles with a wild river and a deranged killer, he and his wife, Sam, had been successful.

Two down, Holt had thought then. Two to go.

It hadn't been a piece of cake, but eventually he'd tracked down one of the twin girls. And again, his timing had been lousy—or, he supposed, depending on how you looked at it, fortuitous. He'd arrived in the woman's Texas Hill Country town to check her out only to find his client's baby sister had just been arraigned on charges of murdering her ex-husband —with the aid of a pet cougar, no less. Since both Cory and Sam had been on assignment and unreachable, Holt had called on Cory's best friend, a well-known part-Native American photojournalist named Tony Whitehall.

That had all worked out okay, too—again, depending on how you looked at it, since former confirmed bachelor Tony now appeared about to become his best buddy's brother-in-law, stepdad to a nine-year-old kid and co-caretaker of one helluva big kitty cat.

Holt had been riding pretty high that day, thinking he had the case as good as sewed up, since finding one sister meant finding both, right? Then the news had come down on him like a ton of bricks: Brenna Fallon had run away from home at the age of fourteen, and hadn't been heard from since. Her sister Brooke didn't know whether she was alive or dead. Holt didn't like remembering how he'd felt hearing that…the cold knot in his stomach, the sense of utter helplessness. This kid—though she'd be a woman in her thirties now—wasn't in any system. She'd gone completely off the radar. She could be anywhere. Or nowhere. She could very well be dead, or as good as.

He hadn't given up, though, even then. Giving up wasn't Holt's style. In the past two months he'd called in every marker, every favor he had coming and then some, and as a result had had people combing through cold case files and unclaimed Jane Doe remains in virtually every state in the union, plus Canada and Mexico. He'd personally checked out more bodies of young women dead way before their time than he'd ever expected to see in his lifetime, and armed with DNA samples from Brooke, had eliminated every one of them. Which was good news, he supposed.

But it still didn't give him answers. And three out of four wasn't going to cut it. He didn't think for one minute Cory Pearson would be content to have found three out of four of his siblings. The one he hadn't found was going to haunt him forever.

Nobody knew better than Holt Kincaid what that felt like.

He rubbed a hand over his burning eyes and turned away from the window, and from the mesmerizing sway of eucalyptus branches. Sinking onto the couch, he reached for the remote, thumbed it off Mute and began to click his way through ESPN's late-night offerings, rejecting an old George Foreman fight, some pro billiards and a NASCAR documentary before settling on a Texas Hold 'em poker tournament. Maybe, he thought, if he could get into the strategy of the game it would take his mind off the damn case.

He'd watched enough poker to know this wasn't a current tournament, more likely one from a few years back. He was familiar with some of the players, particularly the more colorful ones. Others, not so much. The commentators seemed to be excited by this event because of the fact that a woman had made it to the final table, something that evidently had been almost unprecedented back then. It didn't hurt any that the woman in question was young, blond and cute, either. Billie Farrell, her name was, and Holt thought he'd probably seen her play before. Anyway, she looked familiar to him.

Damn, but she looks familiar…

He felt an odd prickling on the back of his neck. Leaning closer, he stared intently at the TV screen, impatient with the camera when it cut to one of the other players at the table, tapping his fingers on the remote until it came back to the one face he wanted to see.

She was wearing dark glasses, as so many of the players did, to hide their eyes and not give anything away to steely-eyed opponents. She had short, tousled blond hair, cut in layers, not quite straight, not really

curly, either. An intriguingly shaped mouth and deli-
cately pointed chin, like a child's.

He really needed to see her eyes.

Take off your glasses, dammit.

He got up abruptly and crossed to the dining room
table that served as his desk, half a foot deep now in
manila file folders and stacks of papers he hadn't gotten
around to putting in files yet. Nevertheless, he didn't
have any trouble finding the one he wanted. He carried
it back to the couch, sat, opened the file and took out a
photograph. It was a picture of a fourteen-year-old girl,
computer-aged twenty years. He didn't look at the photograph—he didn't have to, because it was etched in his
memory—but simply held it while he stared at the face
of the poker player known as Billie Farrell.

He wasn't conscious of feeling anything, not shock
or excitement or anything in particular. Didn't realize
until he fumbled around for his cell phone and had to
try to punch the buttons that his hands were shaking.

It took him a couple of attempts, but he got the one
he wanted. Listened to it ring somewhere in the Texas
Hill Country while he stared at the TV screen with hot,
narrowed eyes. When an answering machine picked up,
he disconnected, then dialed the number again. This
time a man's voice answered. Swearing.

"Okay, this better be an announcement of the Second
Coming, or else I just won the Publishers Clearing
House sweepstakes. Which is it?"

"Tony. It's me, Holt."

"Dude. D'you know what time it is?"

"Yeah. Listen, is Brooke there?"

"Of course she's here. She's asleep, what did you expect? At least, she was—" There was a sharp intake of breath. "Wait. It's Brenna, right? God, don't tell me. You found her? Is she—she's not—hey, Brooke. Baby, wake up. It's Holt. He's found—"

"Maybe," Holt interrupted. "I don't know. I need Brooke—"

"I'm here." Brooke's voice was breathy with sleep, and shaky.

"Okay." Holt took a breath. Told himself to be calm. "I need you to turn on your television. ESPN. Okay?"

"Okay." Her voice was hushed but alert. She'd been married to a deputy sheriff once upon a time, so Holt figured maybe getting phone calls in the middle of the night wasn't all that unusual for her.

"I don't know which channel," he told her. "Just keep clicking until you find the poker tournament."

After a long pause, she muttered, "Okay, got it."

"Watch for her—the woman player. Okay, there she is. Tell me if—"

He didn't get the rest of it out. There was a gasp, and then a whispered, "Oh, God."

He felt himself go still, and yet inside he was vibrating like a plucked guitar string. "Is it her? Is it Brenna?"

He heard a sniff, and when she spoke in a muffled voice he knew Brooke was crying. "Oh, God, I don't know. It could be, but she was just a little girl when she... It's been so long. I'm not *sure*. I can't see her eyes! If I could just see her eyes..." And then, angrily, "Why doesn't she take off the damn *glasses!*"

Holt held the phone and listened to soft scufflings and some masculine murmurs of comfort while he waited, eyes closed, heart hammering. After a moment Tony's voice came again, gruff with emotion.

"Hey, man, I'm sorry. She can't tell for sure. It's been what—eighteen years? She says it might be her. But you're gonna go check her out, right?"

"Yeah," Holt said, "I'm gonna go check her out." He picked up the remote and clicked off the set.

An hour later he was in his car on I-15, heading east toward the rising sun and the bright lights of Las Vegas.

He hit the jackpot right off the bat. The casino manager at the Rio was new, but Holt found a couple of dealers who'd been around awhile, and had actually worked the poker tournament he'd been watching on ESPN reruns.

Although, even if they hadn't, they would have remembered Billie Farrell.

"Sure, I remember her. Cute kid. Pretty good poker player, too," Jimmy Nguyn said as he lit up a cigarette and politely blew the smoke over his shoulder, away from Holt and the other dealer. Jimmy was a guy in his late thirties with a Vietnamese name and an American-size body—five-eleven or so and hefty. He had a card-sharp's hands, though—big and long boned, with nimble, tapered fingers. He wore a pencil-thin moustache and his hair slicked down and looked like something out of a 1930s gangster flick.

The other dealer snorted and moved upwind of the smoker. She was a tall, angular woman with sun-damaged skin and long blond hair she wore pulled up in an off-center ponytail. She'd told Holt her name was Cricket. Now she popped a piece of chewing gum in her mouth, tossed the ponytail over her shoulder and said, "Come on, Jimmy, she was more than 'pretty good.'" She looked over at Holt. "She had talent, that one, plus charisma up the wazoo. That year, the one you're talking about? Came *this close* to winning a bracelet. Woulda been a big star in the circuit, if she'd stuck around."

"Stuck around?" Holt felt his stomach go hollow.

Cricket shook her head. "Quit right after that tournament you saw, didn't she, Jimmy? That's the way I remember it, anyway. I guess it was…I don't know… pretty hard for her to tough it out, after what happened."

"What did happen?" Holt kept his voice low, hiding the despair that was rolling over him like a bank of cold Pacific fog.

She shrugged and shifted around, looking uncomfortable. "Okay, well, she had this partner…"

It was Jimmy's turn to snort. "Guy was a real scumbag." He dropped his cigarette onto the parking lot asphalt and ground it to dust under his shoe as he said musingly, "Miley Todd was his name. Never did get what a young pretty girl like that saw in him. The guy cheated and got caught," he explained to Holt. "Got himself banned from the casinos for life."

"Billie was clean, though," Cricket put in.

Jimmy lifted a shoulder. "Yeah, okay, the kid probably was clean. But there'd have been talk. There's always talk. Rumor and innuendo—you know how it is. Carries a lot of weight in this town."

"I don't think that's why she quit," the blond dealer said, quick to jump to another woman's defense. "Billie was tougher than that. Tough as nails. What made her such a good player. If she'd wanted to stay, she would have."

Jimmy held up a hand. "I'm just sayin'…"

Cricket gave him a dismissive look and focused on Holt. "All I know is, she won pretty big that night—finished in third place—and she took her money and split. That's the last the poker world saw of her."

Holt hauled in a breath. "Okay, then, thanks for your time." He couldn't turn away fast enough. It was all he could do to keep his disappointment in check, and what he wanted more than anything was to slam his fist into something and cuss until he ran out of words bad enough. To come so close. And now it looked like he was right back at square one. Well, maybe not square one, since at least he had a name and a town.

"Hey," Cricket called out to him as he was about to open the door of his car, "you asking about Billie, I'm assuming you're looking to find her, right?"

Holt turned to look back at her. "Yes, I sure am."

"Well, then, don't you want to know where she is?"

* * *

"Excuse me, miss. Could you help me out here?"

Billie gave the hose nozzle a twist to shut off the water and lifted what she hoped was a helpful smile to the customer who was standing a few feet away with a bedraggled gallon-size Michaelmas daisy in one hand and a fading sedum in the other.

She'd noticed the guy wandering up and down the aisles, first because she'd never seen him before, second because he looked a lot like Clint Eastwood. In his prime. And third, because he didn't look like the sort of person to be browsing in a nursery on a weekday morning. He was wearing slacks and a sport-type jacket, for one thing, instead of jeans and a T-shirt. He wore a dress shirt with no tie, open at the neck, which gave him a casual, rumpled look in spite of the dressy clothes. Still, he looked out of place, Billie thought. Dirty Harry in a flower shop. And she had a pretty good sense for people who seemed "off" in any way. Her survival, for a good part of her life, had depended on it.

"Sure," she said, wiping her hands on her blue cotton apron. "What can I do for you?"

He shifted the two pots up and down, like he was trying to gauge their weight.

"I'm looking for something pretty with flowers. These look a little…I don't know…tired." He'd put on a smile, but it didn't look comfortable on him. As if, Billie thought, turning on the charm wasn't something that came naturally to him.

She studied him covertly from behind her sunglasses. "You'd have better luck with annuals this time of year. We're starting to get in some cool-weather stuff now. Be more in a week or two."

"Yeah, but they die, don't they? I'm looking for something you don't have to plant new every year."

Billie shrugged and nodded toward the pots in his hands. "Well, those two you got there are perennials. They'll come back every year."

"Yeah…" He said it with a sigh and a disappointed look at the sedum. "I was hoping to find something that looks a little nicer in the pot. Actually, it's for a gift." He gave her the smile again, along with an explanation. "My sister's getting married Saturday. They've bought this house here, and it looks pretty bare to me—one of those new subdivisions south of town. I thought maybe I'd get her some plants—pretty it up a bit."

"Ah, well…fall's not a good time for perennials. Sorry." She gave the hose nozzle a twist and turned the spray onto the thirsty crepe myrtles spread out in front of her.

"Look—" The guy set the two pots down next to the crepe myrtles and dusted off his hands. "I hate to be a pain in the ass, but I'm getting kind of desperate here."

I believe that's the first truthful thing you've said to me. She didn't say that, of course. She turned off the water and laid the hose carefully aside, out of the pathway, then angled another measuring look upward as she straightened. She could almost feel the guy vibrating, he was so tense. *Mister, I hope you're not*

planning on playing any poker while you're in town.
You'd lose your shirt.

All her defenses were on red alert. Clearly, the guy
wanted something, and she seriously doubted it was
potted plants. But if her danger instincts were aroused,
so was her natural curiosity—which admittedly had
gotten her into trouble more than once in her life.

Who is this guy? What does he want with me?

And most important of all, and the question she really,
really needed an answer to: *Who is he working for?*

Giving the man the smile he seemed to be trying so
hard to win, she said, "Well, there's no need for *that*.
Look, why don't you go with some kind of shrub? You
can get something with some size, so it'll look impressive up there with all the other wedding presents."

"Impressive. Okay, I can live with that. So, what've
you got?"

"Well, let's narrow it down a bit. First, since you
said this house is in a new subdivision, I'm guessing no
trees, right? So you'll need something for full sun. And
heat tolerant, obviously—this *is* Las Vegas." She turned
to walk along the pathway and the man fell in beside her,
strolling in a relaxed sort of way, reaching out to touch
a leaf as they passed. She gave him a sideways glance.
"How do you feel about cactus?"

He winced and laughed, as if she'd made a joke.

"I'm serious. More and more people are going with
native plants now to save water. Save the planet—you
know, go green."

"So to speak," he said dryly, and she found herself smiling and meaning it.

"So to speak." She nodded, conceding the point. "So, okay, no cactus. Evergreen, or deciduous?"

"Deciduous—uh…that means they lose their leaves, right?"

She looked at him and he grinned to show her he was kidding. This time she tried not to smile back. "You seriously are not a gardener, are you? Where are you from?"

"Nope," he said amicably, "definitely not a gardener. And I live in L.A., actually."

"Really. Most people in L.A. have some kind of garden."

"Not me. Not even a houseplant." He paused, then added with a shrug, "I'm not home enough to take care of anything living. I've got eucalyptus trees and ivy, some bougainvillea—that's about it. Nature pretty much takes care of those."

He halted suddenly and pointed with a nod. "What are those? Over there—with all the flowers?"

Billie gave him a look. "Uh…roses?"

"Okay, sure, I see that now," he said, throwing her a sheepish grin before returning to stare thoughtfully at the display of rosebushes. "Can you grow roses in Las Vegas?"

"We wouldn't sell them if they wouldn't grow here," she said shortly, and got a look of apology that made her feel vaguely ashamed. Her mind was skittering around like a squirrel trying to decide whether or not to run into traffic.

The guy is attractive and charismatic as hell, and he still smells wrong. Well, actually, he smells pretty good. Whatever he's using for aftershave, it was a good choice.

She hauled in a determined breath. "Actually, roses do very well in a desert climate. Less trouble with disease. You just have to give them enough water."

"Hmm. Roses kind of go with weddings, don't they?"

"Sure. I suppose so. Yeah."

"They'd definitely be impressive," he mused.

"Yes, they would."

"And they have pretty flowers."

About then Billie realized they'd both stopped walking and were standing in the middle of the aisle smiling at each other. Really smiling. And her heart was beating faster, for no earthly reason she could imagine.

Okay, I'm not a squirrel. I know what happens to squirrels who run into traffic.

She cleared her throat and walked on with purpose, making her way quickly to the rosebushes. "Your timing is good, actually. They put out a nice fall bloom, once the weather cools. Couple more weeks, though, and we'd be pruning them back for the winter."

The customer picked up a red rosebush in a three-gallon pot, read the tag and threw her a look as he set it back down. "Well, you've saved my life, you know that?" He moved aside a pink variety—he was a guy, of course, so no pink need apply—and picked up a butter-yellow with some red blush on the petals. "You're very good at your job. You must like it." He said it casually, maybe *too* casually.

"Yes, I do," she replied carefully, and felt her skin prickle with undefined warnings.

He straightened, dusting his hands. "If you don't mind my asking, how'd you come to work in a nursery? In this town, someone with your looks…" He smiled again, but his eyes seemed a little too sharp. A little too keen. "Seems an unusual career choice."

And again she thought, This guy better never try his hand at the poker tables—with a tell like that, he'd never win a hand. "Maybe," she said evenly, "that's why I made it."

Watching his eyes, she knew he was about to fold.

"Well…okay, tell you what," he said abruptly, all business now. "How 'bout if you pick out half a dozen or so of these—the nicest ones you can find." He reached for his wallet. "Can I pay for them and leave them here until Saturday? Because I'm in a hotel, and I can't exactly…"

"Sure." Suddenly she just wanted to be rid of him. "That's fine. Just tell them at the register. Six, right? I'll put a note on them, put them back for you."

He thanked her and walked away, rapidly, like somebody who'd just remembered he had somewhere to be.

Billie watched him as far as the cash register, then turned abruptly. Angry. At herself. And shaken. The guy had folded, no question about it. So why didn't she feel like she'd won the hand?

* * *

Holt was sitting in his car with the motor running and the air-conditioning going, although it was November and not that hot for Las Vegas. But considering it was midday and he was in the middle of a treeless parking lot, he was pretty sure he'd be sweltering shortly if he turned the AC off.

He wasn't pleased with the way things had gone with Billie Farrell. Definitely not his finest hour. He'd turned on the charm—as much as he was capable of—and had gotten nowhere.

So she was wary, on her guard. He hadn't wanted to push too hard, thinking he'd be better off to leave himself someplace to go with his next try. Which was why he was sitting in the parking lot staking out the nursery, waiting for her to come out so he could follow her, see where she lived, find out where she liked to go for lunch. Figure out how he might "happen" to run into her again. Maybe this time he'd offer to buy her a drink, or even dinner.

If he could just get her someplace indoors where she'd have to take off those damn shades...

Meanwhile, what in the world was he going to do with six rosebushes? Donate them to an old folks' home? He'd have to think of something. Hell, he didn't even *know* anybody who grew roses.

When someone knocked on the window of his car about six inches from his ear, he did three things simultaneously: Ducked, swore and reached for his weapon.

Then he remembered he wasn't carrying one at the moment, that it was currently in the glove compartment of his vintage Mustang. By which time he figured if anybody had been looking to do him damage it would already be lights-out.

However, he was still swearing a blue streak when the door on the passenger side opened and Billie Farrell slipped into the seat beside him.

Chapter 2

She looked flushed and exhilarated, almost gleeful—and why shouldn't she? She aimed a look at the open front of Holt's jacket, inside which his hand was still clutching his shirt in the area over his rapidly thumping heart.

"Well, I guess that tells me one thing about you. Whoever the hell you are. You're used to packin'."

"Actually," he muttered darkly, "I'm just checking to see if I'm having a heart attack. Jeez, Billie." He slid his hand out of his jacket and ran it over his face, which had broken out in a cold sweat. "What were you thinking? If I had been *packing*, I'd have probably shot you—you know that, don't you?"

She shrugged, but behind the dark glasses her gaze

was steady, and he could almost feel the intensity of it. "Nuh-uh. If you'd been packin' I'd have seen it when you took out your wallet. See, I notice things like that. That's because I used to be in the kind of business where you need to notice things like that. But then, since you know my name, you knew that already."

Holt returned the measuring stare, his mind busy trying to gauge how much further he could reasonably hope to carry on with his charade as a horticulturally challenged out-of-town wedding guest. Or whether he should just pack it in and go with the truth.

Not being happy with either option, he decided to go with something in between. He held up a hand. "Okay, look. I recognized you. I've watched you play. I admit it—as soon as I saw you, I knew that was you, and… well—" and it was only the truth, wasn't it? "—I wanted to meet you."

"It's been years since I played poker." Although she looked away and her voice was quiet, she didn't relax one iota.

And although he nodded and gave her a rueful smile, he didn't, either. "I watch old poker tour reruns on television when I can't sleep. The game fascinates me. I know it's got to be more about skill than just dumb luck, because the same people always seem to make it to the final table."

Her eyes came back to him, her lips curved in a half smile. "Oh, believe me, luck still has a whole lot to do with it." Her head tilted, and the dark lenses taunted him.

"Please tell me you're not planning on trying your hand at the game while you're in town."

"Well, actually…"

"Oh, lord." She faced front again and hissed out a sigh.

"What? Why not?" He straightened, genuinely affronted.

She laughed without sound. "Why not? Well, okay, go ahead, if you don't mind losing. Just do yourself a favor, stay away from the high-stakes tables."

"What makes you so sure I'd lose? I'll have you know I do pretty well at online poker."

"Sure you do, because nobody can see your face."

"What's that supposed to mean?" he demanded.

"You really want to know?"

"Yeah," he said, and meant it.

They were bantering, he realized, though there was nothing light or easy about it. The tension in the car was almost tangible, like a low-pitched humming, but something felt along the skin rather than heard through the ears. He had the impression she was playing him, flirting with him, deliberately trying to distract him from whatever his agenda was.

But, without being able to see her eyes, of course, he couldn't be sure.

"Mister—"

"It's Holt."

"Well, Holt, you've got tells a child could read. Okay?"

"Come on."

She smiled, and this time a pair of dimples appeared unexpectedly. "Look, don't get insulted. Most people have 'em and aren't even aware they do. That's why you see so many poker players wearing hats and dark glasses."

"Is that why you do?" he asked softly.

The dimples vanished. "Like I said, I don't play the game anymore. I guess I've still got the habit." She waited a couple of beats before continuing. "Do you even have a sister?"

Holt snorted and didn't bother to answer. He listened to the shush of the air-conditioning and the throb of the idling motor and the hum of that unrelenting tension, and Billie sat there and listened along with him. Patient, he thought. Probably one of the things that had made her a success at the poker tables. Because in spite of what she'd said, he knew it was more than just luck.

He exhaled, conceding her the hand. "Okay, so you made me." He paused, then said, "I'm curious, though. How come you're here? Sitting in my car? Making conversation?"

"Why not? It's a nice car."

Then it was her turn to huff out air, too softly to be called a snort. "You're familiar with that old saying, 'Keep your friends close, and your enemies closer'?"

He jerked—another tell, he was sure, but what the hell. "I'm not your enemy."

"Well, sure, you'd say that." The almost-smile played with her lips again. "Tell you what, Holt—is that a first name or a last, by the way?"

FREE BOOKS OFFER

To get you started, we'll send you
2 FREE books and a FREE gift

DETACH AND POST CARD TODAY!

IODIA

Mrs/Miss/Ms/Mr _____ Initials _____

BLOCK CAPITALS PLEASE

Surname _____

Address _____

_____

Postcode _____

Email _____

MILLS & BOON®

NO STAMP NEEDED!

® MILLS & BOON®
Book Club

FREE BOOK OFFER
FREEPOST NAT 10298
RICHMOND
TW9 1BR

NO STAMP
NECESSARY
IF POSTED IN
THE U.K. OR N.I.

"First. It's Holt Kincaid."

"Okay, so…Holt. Why don't I let you buy me lunch and you can tell me who you are and what you really want. And I'm willing to bet the farm it ain't rosebushes."

He laughed, then sat still and did a slow five-count inside his head. Then, still slowly, before he shifted from Park into Drive he reached up and unhooked his sunglasses from the sun visor and put them on. And heard her knowing chuckle in response.

He didn't *think* he'd let himself show the triumph he was feeling, but he was beginning to realize that with this lady, there was no such thing as a sure bet.

She directed him to an all-you-can-eat Chinese buffet place in a strip mall not far from the nursery, and since it was fast, convenient and kind to the pocketbook, Holt figured she was probably a regular there. That theory was confirmed when Billie gave a wave and a friendly greeting to the two women at the cash register—mother and daughter, by the look of them—and got smiles in return.

She breezed through the dining room, heading for a booth way in the back, one he happened to notice was turned sideways to the entrance so that neither of them would have to sit with their backs to the door. Somehow he doubted that was a coincidence.

"Is this okay?" she asked with apparent innocence. And although the lighting was low, she didn't take off those shades.

"Sure," he said, and she swept off to the buffet.

Because he didn't entirely trust her not to slip out while he was dithering between the kung pao chicken or the sweet-and-sour shrimp, Holt got himself a bowl of wonton soup and settled back in the booth where he could keep an eye on her. He watched her slip in and out among the browsing diners, adroitly avoiding reaching arms and unpredictable children, wasting little time in indecision, since she obviously knew exactly what she wanted.

And he felt an odd little flutter beneath his breastbone when it occurred to him he wasn't just watching her because she was someone he needed to keep track of. He was watching her for the sheer pleasure of it.

Okay, so she's attractive, he thought, squirming in the booth while a spoonful of wonton sat cooling halfway between the bowl and his mouth. *So what?* Given what he was pretty certain was her genetic makeup, that was no big surprise. So far, all of Cory Pearson's siblings had been exceptionally attractive people. Why should this one be any different?

And yet, she *was* different. He couldn't put his finger on what made her so, but she was. Not beautiful, and certainly not pretty—both of those adjectives seemed both too much and too little to describe her heart-shaped face and neat, compact little body. She wasn't tall and willowy, like her twin sister Brooke, and while her hair was blond and neither curly nor straight—also like Brooke's—hers was a couple of shades darker and cut in haphazard layers, and it looked like she might be in the habit of combing it with her fingers. He couldn't tell about her eyes, of course. But, maybe due to being unable to see past the shades, he'd spent quite a bit of time looking at her mouth. It fascinated him, that mouth. Her lips weren't particularly full, but exquisitely shaped, with an upward tilt at the corners. And then there were those surprising dimples. Her teeth weren't perfectly straight, which led him to surmise she'd run away from home before the mandatory teenage orthodontia had taken place. In an odd sort of way, he was glad.

What she was, he decided, was dynamic. There was just something about her that drew his gaze and held it, like a magnet.

"That all you're having?" She asked it in that breathless way she had as she slipped into the booth opposite him, carrying a plate loaded with an impossible amount of food.

"Just the first course." He stared pointedly at her heaped plate. "Is that all *you're* having?"

"Just the first course." She contemplated the assortment on her plate, then picked up her fork, stabbed a deep-fried shrimp and dunked it into a plastic cup containing sweet-and-sour sauce. "So, what are you, some kind of cop?" She popped the morsel into her mouth and regarded him steadily while she chewed.

Holt raised his eyebrows. "What makes you think that?"

"Oh, please." She forked up something with a lot of broccoli and bean sprouts. "You have cop written all over you."

He didn't know how to answer that, so he didn't, except for a little huff of unamused laughter. She was beginning to annoy the hell out of him, with this cat and mouse game she was playing.

He pushed his soup bowl aside, and instantly a very young Chinese girl was there to whisk it away and give him a shy smile in exchange. He watched her quick-step across the room while he pondered whether or not to ask Billie why she was so well acquainted with cops, since in his experience your everyday law-abiding citizen wouldn't be able to spot a cop unless he was wearing a uniform and a badge. He decided there wasn't much point in it, since he was pretty sure she'd only tell him what she wanted him to know—either that, or an outright lie.

He excused himself and went to the buffet, where he spent less time deciding on his food selections than on how he was going to handle the next round with Billie Farrell. He was beginning to suspect she might not be an easy person to handle. Maybe even impossible. He'd already concluded that asking her direct questions wasn't likely to get him anywhere. So maybe he ought to try letting her do the asking. See where that led him.

"So," he said affably as he slid back into the booth and picked up his fork, "where were we?"

"You were about to tell me you're a cop," Billie said, studying what food was left on her plate—which wasn't much.

"Was." He gave her an easy smile. "Not anymore. Haven't been for quite a while."

"Ah. Which means you're private. Am I right?" She glanced up at him and hitched one shoulder as she picked up a stick with some kind of meat skewered on it. She nibbled, then added without waiting for his reply, "Otherwise you wouldn't still have the look."

"The look…" He muttered that under his breath, then exhaled in exasperation and took one of his business cards out of his jacket pocket and handed it to her.

She glanced at it but didn't pick it up. "So. Who are you working for?" It seemed casual, the way she said it—but then, he couldn't see her eyes.

"Nobody you know." And he could have sworn he saw her relax, subtly. But then, with her, how could he be sure?

He watched her finish off the skewered meat then carefully lick the stick clean of barbecue sauce. Watched the way her lips curved with sensual pleasure, and her little pink tongue slipped tantalizingly between them to lap every possible morsel from the skewer. When he realized hungry juices were pooling at the back of his own throat, he tore his eyes away from her and tackled his own plate.

"So…let me get this straight. You're a private dick—"

"Investigator."

"Sorry—investigator, hired by somebody I don't know, and… What is it, exactly, you want with me?"

Chewing, he pointed with his fork at the card she'd left lying on the table. "If you read that, it says I specialize in finding people." He paused, took another bite. "I've been hired to find someone." He glanced up at her. "And I believe you might be able to help me."

"Hmm." She stared down at her plate while above the dark glasses her forehead puckered in what seemed to be a frown. "Why?"

"Why what? Why do I think you can help me?"

She shook her head. "Why do you—or the people you work for—want to find this person?" The dark lenses lifted and regarded him blankly. He could see twin images of himself reflected in them, which, of course, told him nothing. "There's all kinds of reasons to want to find somebody, you know."

"It's kind of complicated," Holt said, picking up his napkin and wiping his lips with it. Stalling because he hadn't decided whether it was time to put his cards on the table—and why was it everything that came into his mind seemed somehow related to poker? "But I can tell you, the people who hired me don't mean this person any harm."

"Yeah, well, there's all kinds of ways to do someone harm." She cast a quick look over her shoulder at the buffet tables, then abruptly slid out of the booth, leaving her almost-empty plate behind.

Leaving Holt to contemplate her words and complexities while he stared at her plate and a low-intensity hum of excitement vibrated through his chest. He was becoming more and more certain he'd found his client's last missing sibling, and equally certain she was never going to willingly admit to her true identity, for reasons he couldn't quite figure out. He was going to have to find another way to positively prove Billie Farrell was, in fact, Brenna Fallon.

The plate she'd left sitting on the table seemed to shimmer and grow in size as he gazed at it. For some reason the girl with the quick hands hadn't whisked it away yet, evidently being occupied elsewhere in the dining room. Billie was busy, too, heaping a salad-size plate with goodies from the dessert table. Holt threw them both a glance, then plucked the wooden barbecue skewer off of Billie's plate and wrapped it carefully in a clean paper napkin.

Billie had no idea what she was putting on her plate; the buffet table in front of her was a blur. Her heart was pounding, although she was confident nobody watching her would ever guess it.

Watching me…

Yeah. She could feel the detective's eyes on her, those keen blue eyes that wouldn't miss much. She knew she had the advantage on him, since she could read him pretty well and, unless he was a whole lot better than most of the other opponents she'd faced, he wouldn't be able to read her at all. But somehow she had to figure out how to get him to tell her more about who he was working for and exactly who they wanted him to find.

Okay, dummy, you know it has to be you they are looking for. The more important question is, why?

A week ago she'd have had to guess it was that jerk, Miley, trying to track her down. But he'd already managed to do that on his own, and besides, he'd be too cheap to hire a private dick. And even if he did somehow happen to have the money, he'd use it to get in a poker game somewhere.

Beyond that possibility, her mind refused to go.

But thinking about Miley Todd had given her an idea how to play this guy Kincaid. It was a strategy Miley had taught her way back when he was first teaching her to play poker: Start talking about herself, not a lot, just a little bit. Get her opponents relaxed and hoping for more. Then maybe they'd let their guard down and tell her what *she* wanted to know.

"So," she said in a breezy way as she slipped back into the booth, "where were we?"

"You were about to tell me whether you're going to help me find the person I'm looking for," Holt said absently, staring at her plate. "My God, are you going to eat all that?"

She focused on the mess before her and felt a wave of queasiness. Lord, was that *pudding?*

"What can I say? I have a sweet tooth." She picked up an almond cookie and nibbled on its edges while she studied him through her dark glasses. She tilted her head and let him see her dimples. "See, the thing is, how do I know if I can help you if I don't know who you're looking for?"

"A young woman," Holt said easily. "About your age, actually."

"Uh-huh…and you think she's here in Vegas?"

"I think she might be, yes."

"All right, here's the thing." She dropped the cookie

onto her plate, barely noticing that it landed in the pudding. "If I seem like I'm being a little bit cautious, it's because I've had to be. You understand? I've been in this town a long time. Nowadays, poker is pretty respectable, mainstream, but back when I first started playing, some of the people you brushed elbows with might not be the most upstanding citizens, if you know what I mean."

The detective nodded. "Like Miley Todd?"

She let go a little bubble of laughter and was grateful again for her shades. She picked up a grape and popped it into her mouth. "O—kay…so you've been checking up on me. Why am I not surprised?"

"I'm an investigator," he said with a shrug. "It's what I do." He pushed aside his plate and leaned toward her, forearms on the table. "Look, I know you and this guy, Todd, used to be partners, and that a few years back he got caught cheating and banned from the casinos."

Billie gave a huff of disdain. "He was an idiot. Card-smart, maybe, but people-stupid. A little bit of success and he started thinking he was smarter than everybody else."

"So, how did you get involved with this guy?"

She didn't move or gesture, but he could almost hear the doors slamming shut. It occurred to him that even without being able to see her eyes, he was learning to read her. "It was a long time ago. I was young—what can I say?"

He almost smiled at that, given how young she still was—a lot younger than he was, anyway. Instead, he said casually, the way he might have asked her if she liked wine, "What kind of partners were you? Professional, lovers…"

Unexpectedly, she smiled. "I'd be lying if I said I didn't see that coming."

He smiled back.

The air between them seemed to change subtly… become heavier, charged with electricity. She thought of the wild Texas thunderstorms she'd loved as a child, and realized with a shiver of fear that it was the first time in years she'd allowed herself to remember those times. She wondered why. *Why now, with this man?*

Still smiling, she hitched one shoulder. "I know how guys think. It was the first thing you thought of. But the answer is, no, we weren't lovers. Not that Miley didn't have ideas along those lines when he first met me." She picked up another grape and crunched it audibly between her teeth. "Until I told him what I'd do to him if he ever laid a hand on me."

"Ouch." He gave a pained laugh and shifted in his seat. Moments passed, and Billie could almost hear thunder rolling away in the distance. Then his gaze sharpened, focused on her again. "So…your partnership was strictly professional, then. I'm not clear on how that works in poker."

She shook her head, mentally reining herself in, sharpening her own focus. Reminding herself of her game plan. "Partnership probably isn't the right word. Miley was more like my mentor, I guess you could say.

Protector, too, sometimes. At first." She paused. "Vegas could be a rough town, back then." *Don't kid yourself, it still is.* "I'll tell you one thing, though." She sat back in the booth, as far as she could get from that plateful of sweets, having lost her appetite completely. "He was a good teacher."

He sat very still, regarding her without changing his expression, and it occurred to her that in a very short time he'd become very good at controlling those unconscious tells of his. Either that, or he'd been playing her all along. A small frisson of warning sifted coldly across the back of her neck.

"Do you ever take off those sunglasses?" he asked in the same soft, uninflected voice he'd been using to ask about her relationship with Miley.

"During a game, never," she shot back just as quietly.

"That's what this is to you…a game?"

"Sure it is. It's a lot like poker. We're both holding cards the other can't see and would really, really like to." She paused and gave him her game smile—confident, apologetic, serene. "And you know…sooner or later, one of us is going to have to call."

He expelled air in an exasperated puff, then looked over at the buffet tables, frowned and muttered, "I need some dessert," the way someone might say, "I need a drink."

"Have some of mine." Having obviously rattled him, she was enjoying herself again.

He aimed the frown at her, then at her plate. His eyebrows rose. "Is that pudding?"

"Yeah, and you're welcome to it." She slid the plate toward him, then rested her chin in the palm of her hand and watched him pick up his spoon, scoop up a bite of the stuff, frown at it, then put it in his mouth. She felt an absurd and totally unfamiliar urge to giggle.

"So…" Still frowning, he took another bite. "Who's going to call—you or me?"

"You really aren't much of a card player, are you?" She was feeling amused, relaxed, confident, sure she had the upper hand again. "If I call, you've got two choices—fold or show me your cards."

He stared at the spoon, his frown deepening. "Yeah, but you have to pay for the privilege, as I recall." His eyes lifted and shot that keen blue gaze right into hers. As if he could see through her dark glasses. As if he could see into her soul.

Cold fingers took another walk across the back of her neck. A reminder that with this guy she couldn't afford to let her guard down, not even for a moment.

"This isn't poker," she snapped, no longer amused, relaxed or confident. "And let's quit the poker analogies, which I could think of a whole lot more of, but what's the point? Here's the deal—I don't give a damn who you're looking for or who you're working for, and if you don't want to tell me, that's okay with me. Now—" she slid out of the booth and stood up "—are we done here?"

"The person I work for," Holt said, pushing aside the dessert plate and reaching for his wallet, "hired me to find his two younger brothers and twin sisters. So far, I've found the brothers and one of the twins." He took out some bills and laid them on the table, then looked up at Billie. "That twin's name is Brooke Fallon. Her sister's name is Brenna. She ran away from home when she was fourteen." He tucked his wallet away again and waited.

The silence at the table was profound, but inside Billie's head was the tumultuous crashing sound of her world falling apart.

"So?" she said, and could not feel her lips move. She was vaguely surprised to find she was sitting down again.

"So, I thought you might be my client's missing baby sister," he said softly, as he slid out of the booth. "And if you were, I thought you might be interested to know you've got a family that's looking for you."

She shook her head…pursed her lips, stiff though they were. "Sorry. Not me. Don't know her."

"Hmm," Holt said, gazing down at her, "if that's true, I'll be really disappointed. I guess I'll have to wait for the DNA to tell me whether I have to keep looking for Brenna Fallon, or whether I've already found her."

"Wait." A breath gusted from her lungs. She reached out and snagged his jacket sleeve as he turned away. "What are you talking about? I'm not giving you my DNA. You're not a cop, you can't—"

His smile was gentle. "Oh, but you've already given me what I need." He reached inside his jacket and pulled out what appeared to be a folded paper napkin. Unfolded it and showed her what was inside.

Only years of practice at keeping her face and body

under strictest control prevented her from blowing it completely. She stared at the thin wooden stick nestled in white paper in complete silence, and her mind was empty of thought. But somewhere in the primal recesses of her consciousness, a terrified child was screaming—*Run.*

Chapter 3

Still smiling, Holt tucked the folded napkin and its contents away in his inside jacket pocket. The smile was only for show. He didn't have any idea whether DNA could be recovered from the wooden skewer, and he didn't know whether Billie would see through his bluff. Or, as she would no doubt put it, *call* him on it.

Waiting at the cash register for the mother-daughter duo to process his credit card, with his peripheral vision he could see her still sitting just as he'd left her, staring straight ahead, apparently at nothing. He wondered what in the hell she was going to do now. Was she really going to let him just walk away? He was her ride back to the garden shop, of course, but it wasn't that far if she decided she'd rather walk.

What was going through her mind right now?

He wished now that he'd taken a little more time to study her playing style before rushing off to Vegas to meet her. He had no clue how this woman's mind worked.

He signed the receipt, tucked it and his credit card in his wallet and returned the wallet to his pocket, then turned to check once more on his erstwhile lunch companion. His heart did a skip and a stumble when he saw that the booth where she'd been sitting was now empty.

Swearing, he slammed through the double doors and half ran to the parking lot. She wasn't there. Since there was no way she could have gone farther in the time available, he reversed course and got to the restaurant's foyer just in time to meet her as she came out of the restroom, drying her hands on her jeans and looking completely unperturbed.

"Ah, there you are," Holt said, hoping she wouldn't pick up on the fact that his heart was pounding and he was breathing like a marathon runner. "I was about to go off without you."

"Yeah, right," she said as she walked past him and pushed through the double doors. She was smiling that damn little half-smile of hers, the one that made her seem ancient and all-knowing.

About halfway to the car she threw him a sideways glance and said in an amused tone, "Do you really think you can get DNA from a wooden stick?"

"I don't know," Holt replied. "I guess I'm about to find out."

She laughed. It was a low, husky sound, but like a shrilling alarm clock, it awoke the sensual awareness of her that had been dozing just below the levels of his consciousness. His skin shivered with it, a pleasurable sensation he tried without success to deny.

Determined to ignore it, he unlocked her side of the car and went around to do the same to his, since his restored 1965 Mustang didn't come equipped with power door-locks. He slid into his seat as she did hers, and from the corner of his eye he saw her run her hands appreciatively over the black leather upholstery. He was suddenly acutely aware of the warmth of the leather seat on his backside. Although it was comfortably cool outside, the air in the car seemed too thick to breathe.

He got the engine turned on and the air-conditioning going full blast, and as he was waiting for it to take effect, she said in that same throaty voice, "I really do like your car, by the way."

"Thanks." Good God, what now? Was she actually flirting with him?

"Did you restore it yourself?"

"No. I got it from a grateful client." He backed out of the parking place, then abruptly shifted gears and pulled back into it. "Tell me something," he said as he slapped the gearshift into Neutral. "Why should you be afraid of the DNA result anyway?"

"Who says I'm afraid?"

"It's not like you're wanted by the police," he went on, "or a suspect in a crime. All this is, is a family that's trying to find their missing sister."

Sister. Sistersistersister... Thank God he couldn't see inside her mind, see that word pulsing there like the gaudiest neon on the Vegas Strip. Thank God for the years of training that would keep him from knowing the pain she felt with every starburst.

"Yeah, well," she said, hating the gravel in her voice, "see, that's the thing. I'm nobody's sister. Okay?" *Don't deserve to be. Don't you understand? I lost that right a long time ago.*

"Pity," Holt said softly, putting the Mustang once more into reverse. "These are some nice people. You couldn't ask for a better family to be a part of."

Yeah, right, Billie thought, and it was all she could do to keep from erupting in derisive laughter. *Nice* didn't come anywhere close to describing the brother she remembered.

Then...something he'd said. Something that had been blasted out of her head at the time by the sound of that name: *Brooke Fallon*. But...she remembered now. He'd said *brothers*. Plural. But how could that be? She only had *one* brother.

"So, tell me about 'em," she said, concentrating everything she had on keeping her tone light, making her interest seem only casual. Inside her head was a cacophony of thoughts, a jabbering madhouse of incomprehension and confusion, a babel of questions she couldn't ask without giving herself away.

"Why should you want to know?" He tossed her a look as he headed out of the parking lot. "If you're not, as you say, the person I'm looking for, it's got nothing to do with you."

Panic seized her. It was only a few short blocks to the garden center; he'd be dropping her off in a minute or two. But she had to know. *She had to know.*

She could feel herself beginning to tremble inside. How much longer could she keep him from noticing?

She shrugged with elaborate unconcern. "Hey, it sounds like an interesting story, okay?" Paused at a traffic light, he looked over at her again, smiling sardonically. She gave him back her most winning smile. "I'd really like to hear it."

Holt felt a quickening, a swift surge of exultation. He'd never been fishing in his life, but he imagined this must be what a fisherman experienced when he felt that unmistakable tugging on his line. "It's kind of a long story," he said with doubt in his voice. "Don't you have to get back to work?"

There was a moment of absolute silence, yet he could hear her sigh of frustration like a faint breath, hear the crackle of tension in her muscles and joints like the rustling of fabric on skin. He wondered if it was because he couldn't read her the usual way, with his eyes, that he seemed to be developing the ability to pick up on her with his other senses.

The garden center loomed ahead. Holt slowed, turned into the parking lot. He pulled into the first empty space he came to and stopped, leaving the motor running, then looked over at Billie. She was sitting motionless, facing forward, and from her profile he could see behind her glasses, for once. Her eyes were closed. For some reason that jolted him, and he saw her in a way he hadn't been able to up till now.

Vulnerable.

"Yeah. Okay, sure." She let out a careful breath and gave him a thin, empty smile—no dimples, this time. "Listen, thanks for lunch." She opened the door, slid her legs out, then looked back at him. "And good luck finding her—the person you're looking for." She got out of the car.

He was in a quandary, letting her go. He wondered if this was what a fisherman would call letting the fish "run." If it was, he decided he didn't have the nerve for it. He had her hooked, he was sure of it. Had her almost literally in his hands. Yet, short of bodily kidnapping her, he couldn't reel her in. Not yet, anyway. He couldn't bear to let her walk away from him, but at this point, what choice did he have?

The funny thing was, he was pretty sure she didn't want to walk away from him, either. If she *was* Brenna Fallon, as he was dead certain she was, her insides had to be a mess right about now. He'd just dropped a hand grenade into her life. She had to have a million questions she was dying to ask but couldn't, not without admitting who she was. Or, to use another one of those damn poker analogies that seemed to be everywhere lately, folding.

Again, he couldn't be sure, since he hadn't watched her play very much, but he had an idea Billie Farrell didn't fold very often.

She'd paused, standing in the V of the open car door, and in that moment he heard himself say, "I'm going to be around awhile…"

She ducked down to give him her knowing half smile. "Right—for your sister's wedding."

He gave her back a huff of unamused laughter. "If you really want to hear the story, come by my hotel after work. I'll buy you a drink—or you can buy me one."

"A drink?"

"A beer…martini…something with an umbrella in it—hell, I don't care."

Her smile broadened. "How 'bout a Diet Coke?"

"Whatever turns you on," he heard himself say, and it wasn't something he was in the habit of saying.

"Where are you staying?" Her voice was both husky and breathless, and the frisson of awareness took another meander across his skin.

He gave her the name of his hotel, a good-size one located well off the Strip. She nodded. "I know where it is." She straightened and firmly closed the door.

Holt watched her walk away, watched a stiff November wind lift the blond feathers of her hair to catch the desert sunlight. And, after a while, let go of the breath he didn't know he'd been holding.

* * *

He was driving back to his hotel when his cell phone rang. Since he wasn't a big fan of people who tried to talk on their cell phones and drive at the same time, he picked it up and glanced at it to see if it was somebody he could ignore. When he saw who it was, he thumbed it on, said, "Hang on a minute…" and pulled into a strip mall parking lot. He turned into the first vacant spot he came to and turned off the motor, then picked up the phone again.

"Brooke—"

"Have you seen her? Is it her?" Her voice was high and anxious, on the edge of tears.

"I've just come from having lunch with her—"

"Oh God…"

"—and, to be perfectly honest, I can't be sure. She says she's not your sister, but…"

Now her voice dropped to a husky mutter. "I don't understand."

Holt sighed deeply. "Look, I'm pretty sure Billie Farrell and Brenna Fallon are one and the same. She's probably got her reasons for not wanting to admit it. I imagine it wasn't easy being on her own at fourteen. She's learned to be careful about who she trusts."

"Did you tell her—" Brooke expelled a breath in an impatient hiss and reined herself in. "Yes, okay. But the pictures I gave you—has she changed so much?" Her voice was wistful, close to tears again.

He ran a weary hand over his eyes; he was beginning

to feel the effects of a night without sleep. "Hard to tell. If I could just see her eyes…" He gave a huff of frustrated laughter. "But she wouldn't take off the damn dark glasses."

Brooke laughed, too, a small gulp. "I know, I keep watching the poker game over and over, screaming at the TV screen, *Dammit, Bren, take off the damn sunglasses!*"

There was a long pause, and then she said softly, "She has very distinctive eyes, Holt. Not like mine, or Cory's. Hers are…I guess they're what you call hazel. But they're sort of golden, actually. Almost the same color as her hair."

"According to Cory," Holt said, "those are your mother's eyes. Your brother Matt has them, too."

Billie was in her bathroom, huddled under the warm shower spray, trying to think.

She'd asked for the afternoon off, pleading illness, and since she'd never done such a thing before, ever, her boss had not only given it to her, but had expressed his concern for her health.

"Probably just a bug   one of those twenty four hour flu things," Billie had told him. And the truth was, she did feel kind of sick to her stomach.

She didn't know what to do. She really had not seen this coming. The thing with Miley, yeah; she always had suspected her past would come back to haunt her one day. She just hadn't thought the ghosts would come from so *far* in her past.

Every instinct she had was telling her to get the heck out of Dodge—she'd even gotten her old suitcase down out of the overhead storage in her parking garage, but had left it sitting empty beside the back door. Because what was the point? Holt Kincaid had managed to find her once, and he'd surely find her again, no matter where she ran. She couldn't go back on the streets where she could vanish into the legions of anonymous dispossessed; she wasn't fourteen anymore—she was a grown-up member of society, fully documented and therefore traceable.

What was she going to do? What *could* she do?

It was at that point in her panic that she'd headed for the shower. She did some of her best thinking in the shower.

So. What were her options?

Running would always be her first choice, but in this case, probably a bad one. Not only would it be futile, at best only postponing the inevitable, but there was the thing about *brothers*. Holt Kincaid had said brother*s*.

Admit it, Billie, you're dying to know what that's about. And, the man with the answers is dying to tell you.

So why don't you do it? Go see the man, buy him that drink—or let him buy you one—and see what he has to say. What are you afraid of?

Afraid?

That did it. She turned off the water and yanked back the shower curtain. Grabbed a towel and scrubbed her skin rosy and her hair into layers of spikes, every movement jerky with anger. If there was anything in the world Billie hated, it was being afraid. She was done with being afraid. Done long ago with feeling scared and helpless. Knowledge was power, right? These days, Billie Farrell was all about having the power. Which meant she had to have the knowledge.

And the man with the knowledge was Holt Kincaid.

The ringing telephone dragged Holt into consciousness from the depths of a sound and dreamless sleep. He groped first for his cell phone, then realized it was the room phone that was making the racket.

What the hell? he thought. A glance at the alarm clock on the nightstand told him it was three o'clock in the afternoon, since it was obviously daylight. Too early for Billie to be off work. He picked up the receiver and growled, "Kincaid."

"Hey, you up for that drink?"

"Billie?" He sat up and swung his legs over the side of the bed, scrubbing the sleep out of his eyes. "Where are you?"

"In the lobby. What's the matter, did I wake you up?"

"Yeah, well...I didn't get much sleep last night." He was wide awake now, and his heart was going a mile a minute.

"So you coming down, or what?"

"Yeah, sure. Give me five minutes."

"Okay, I guess I'll be in the bar. Want me to order for you?"

"Make it the coffee shop," Holt said, swallowing a yawn. "You can order me a cup of coffee—black."

As he lurched into the bathroom to splash water on his face and run a comb through his hair, he was wondering one thing: Would Billie be wearing her sunglasses?

In the parlance of Vegas, he was willing to lay odds on it.

Billie would have given a lot to be able to keep her heart from pounding when she saw Holt Kincaid standing in the entrance to the coffee shop. But although she'd learned to control a good many of her body's natural reflexes, pulse rate wasn't one of them.

Schooling her visible movements to be slow, careful, deliberate, she picked up her Coke and took a sip, then watched over the rim of the moisture-beaded glass as he spoke to the hostess, who pointed him toward the table where she was sitting. She smiled as she saw the hostess's body language change in the subtle and indefinable ways of a woman in the presence of a very attractive man.

He was attractive, no denying that. Wearing the same slacks, jacket and open-at-the-neck dress shirt he'd had on this morning, he didn't look quite so out of place in the hotel restaurant as he had wandering among the potted plants at the garden center. But no matter what kind of setting he found himself in, she thought, Holt Kincaid wasn't a man to fade into the woodwork.

The hostess's eyes followed him as he zigzagged his way across the almost-empty dining room, and so did

Billie's. When he pulled out the chair opposite her, she saw that he had a bedspread wrinkle across one cheek, and something in her chest did a peculiar little flip.

Another thing she hadn't learned to control—yet. She definitely needed to work on that.

Holt settled into the chair and reached for the cup of coffee steaming on the table in front of him, gave her a little nod of greeting and drawled, "Miss Billie."

"Wow," she said, lifting her eyebrows, "that didn't sound like California."

He drank coffee, grimaced and set it down. "I said I *live* in L.A. I was born and raised in Georgia."

"Really. You don't have an accent. Usually."

"I left the South behind fairly early on. It still crops up now and again, I guess."

Most people would have missed the slight flinching of the soft skin around his eyes when he said that, but Billie didn't. And she thought, *Aha. He's got ghosts in his past, too.*

She filed the knowledge away for future reference.

"Sorry about your nap," she said, and her eyes kept coming back to the wrinkle mark on his cheek. She had the strongest desire to reach out and touch it. Why did it seem so poignant to her? Something about that mark on the supercool, iron-hard Clint Eastwood clone brought to mind images of unexpected innocence...or vulnerability.

He regarded her while he drank coffee, then said, "I wasn't expecting you this early."

"Well, here I am." She lifted a shoulder, not about to

concede how badly she wanted what he had to give her. Billie didn't give her opponents that kind of advantage over her, not if she could help it.

Holt didn't say anything, just watched her over the rim of his coffee cup. She fought down impatient anger and said lightly, "You were going to tell me a story."

His eyebrows rose. He set down the cup. "Just like that? No social niceties?"

She gave a little tiff of sarcastic laughter. "Social *niceties?* What do you want to do, put money in the jukebox and dance?"

Unbidden, the thought popped into Holt's head that dancing with Billie Farrell might be a very nice thing. Unsettled by the notion, he gave her a thoughtful smile. For a moment the air between them did the sizzle and crackle thing, and then he thought, *What the hell am I doing?* He cleared his throat, shifted around in his chair and frowned. "I'm just trying to think where to start."

"How about, who hired you to find…this woman?"

He nodded. "Fair enough. His name is Cory Pearson."

"Never heard of him."

"No," said Holt, "of course you haven't. But the story begins with him. When Cory was a little kid his dad went off to fight in Vietnam. He came back changed— nothing like the loving daddy who used to tell his little boy bedtime stories he made up himself. He was moody and withdrawn…started drinking heavily, couldn't hold a job. It was a familiar story at that time.

"Anyway, as time went on, the family grew to include

four more children—two boys, and then twin girls. When their father was having one of his spells of PTSD, it was Cory's job to keep the little ones out of his way while his mother tried to talk her husband back from whatever hell he'd gotten lost in. Finally, one night when the little girls—the twins—were about two, their father had a violent episode during which he shot his wife and then himself."

"Good God," Billie exclaimed.

Holt nodded, picked up his cup and found it empty. A waitress appeared to refill it. He thanked her, waited until she had left, then went on. All the while Billie sat without moving, without seeming to breathe, even, her face gone still and pale as death.

"Since there was no other family, the kids were taken by social services. Evidently, no foster family could be found to take all five, so they were farmed out all over the system. Eventually, the four younger children were adopted—the two boys by one family, the twins by another."

Billie spoke almost without moving her lips, and devoid of all inflection. "What about Cory?"

"He was older, about twelve by that time. Too old for most adoptive parents to consider. He stayed in foster care for a while, but ran away so many times trying to find his brothers and baby sisters, that he eventually wound up in juvenile detention. By the time he graduated out of the system when he was eighteen, his brothers and sisters had vanished—adopted and gone."

Billie muttered under her breath.

Holt nodded. "He was just a kid, and a known troublemaker at that. What could he do?" He paused, cleared his throat and wondered whether, behind those dark lenses, there might, just possibly, be tears in her eyes. Was it his wishful thinking, or did her mouth have a softness about it he hadn't seen before?

As if determined to deny that, she cleared her throat and said harshly, "Okay, so he's hired you to find the four siblings—I get it. So why did he wait so long? Vietnam—that had to be…what, thirty years ago?"

Holt nodded. "That's a question Cory has asked himself. Mostly, I think he'd just given up. He managed to turn his own life around—went to college, became a journalist, a war correspondent. Fairly famous one, too—won a Pulitzer for his reporting on the Middle East wars. Was captured and held prisoner for a while himself." He paused. "It was while he was in an Iraqi prison that he met a man, an aviator who had been shot down during the first Gulf War and had been in that same prison for eight years. They were rescued together. Eventually, Cory married the man's daughter, Samantha. It was Sam who convinced Cory he needed to find his brothers and sisters. That's when he contacted me."

"Because you specialize in finding people." Billie's lips twitched slightly, too quickly to be called a smile.

"That's right." He spoke very softly now, too, watching her face. It occurred to him that she seemed to have gone a shade whiter, if that was possible. "As I said, I've found the two boys. Wade is a homicide detective in Portland, Oregon, and Matt is in Southern California—splits his year between teaching inner-city kids and being a whitewater rafting guide, which is quite a feat, considering a rock-climbing accident put him in a wheelchair a few years back. I also found one of the twins—Brooke. That was a couple of months ago. She told me—"

Billie stood up so abruptly Holt flinched back as if from an expected blow. "Like I said—can't help you," she mumbled, and there was no question about it now… her face was the color of cold ashes. She paused, then made a valiant attempt at a smile, obviously trying to backtrack, mend what for her had to be a catastrophic breakdown of her defenses. "Look…thanks for the Coke… Gotta go. Wasn't watching the time…I'm supposed to be—sorry."

She walked away, moving as rapidly through the dining room as the closely set tables would allow.

He didn't try to stop her, or follow her, either. He knew desperation when he saw it.

Billie managed to wait until she'd turned the corner and was out of Holt Kincaid's line of sight before she bolted. Fortunately, she'd played a tournament in the hotel and knew where the restrooms were. Even so, she barely made it into a stall before becoming wretchedly, violently ill.

Thankfully, the restroom was empty. She threw up until she had nothing left in her stomach, then collapsed onto the cold tile floor, pulled her knees to her chest and wrapped her arms around them in a vain effort to stop the shaking. The pressure of sobs was like an iron fist squeezing her chest, and she hauled in air in great gulps and clenched her teeth so hard in her determination to hold them back, her jaws screamed in agony. She tore off her sunglasses and dug the heels of her hands into dry, burning eye sockets. But no matter how hard she pressed, no matter how viciously she tried to scrub them away, the images came. Images she thought she'd blocked out of her mind forever. Memories of pain and fear and humiliation and shame.

Brooke...oh, Brookie, I'm so sorry. I'm so sorry. I'm so sorry...

Chapter 4

Holt was trying to decide whether he'd just had a major break in his case, or blown it completely. One thing he did know: He was never going to be able to figure out Billie Farrell or anticipate her reactions, so he might as well quit trying.

Cory Pearson's story had shaken her, no doubt about that. And if it had finally sunk in that she had three brothers she didn't know about, he could have expected some degree of shock. Given the color of her complexion, he wasn't all that surprised she'd felt the need to make a hasty exit.

But he hadn't expected her not to come back.

He'd waited for her for nearly an hour, nursing his

cup of coffee and smiling at the waitress whenever she appeared anxiously at his elbow. He'd figured once Billie regained her composure she'd have a jillion questions—or at the very least, be ready to stand fast on her denial of any relationship to his client. Finally, accepting the fact that his quarry had slipped away, he'd signed his tab and gone back to his room to plan his next move.

He was sitting on the edge of the bed gazing at the wooden skewer in its napkin nest and trying to calculate the odds a lab might be able to get a reading on Billie's DNA from it, when a knock came on the hotel room door. His heart jolted and skittered around a bit, but he was pretty sure his voice was calm as he called out, "Yeah, who is it?"

When he heard a gruff, "It's me—Billie," his heartbeat settled down to a hard, heavy rhythm he could feel in the bottom of his belly.

He opened the door and she pushed past him without a word, her momentum carrying her into the middle of the room, where she paused and looked around her as if she wasn't quite sure where she was or how she'd come to be there. Naturally, she was still wearing the shades.

He closed the door and walked around her, touching her elbow as he turned to face her. She flinched away from him like a contrary child.

"Brenna Fallon?" he asked softly.

The dark lenses regarded him steadily, revealing nothing but twin images of himself. Below them her face showed no signs of emotional turmoil, only a kind of poignant defiance. "Used to be," she said in a voice full of gravel. "A long time ago. I'm *Billie* now. Billie Farrell."

"Okay," he murmured, nodding cautiously.

She spoke rapidly, vehemently, arms folded across her chest. "You got that? I'm not that person you're looking for. I wasn't lying." She sucked in air, and he wondered if her heart was beating as fast as his was. "I'm not that person anymore."

Again he nodded. Seconds ticked by, counted in those thunderous heartbeats, while he gazed at her and she stared back at him. Then he lifted his hands and gently took the sunglasses off of her face.

Her eyes blazed at him, molten gold like the just-risen sun.

His breath caught, and he felt as if he'd been punched in the stomach. He'd known it—known she was Brenna—from almost the first moment he'd laid eyes on her. Of course he had. But maybe he hadn't known it in his *gut*. Until now.

"You have your mother's eyes," he heard himself say in a thickened mumble he didn't recognize.

More seconds passed—he didn't know how many. Then without warning she reached up, caught his shirt collar in her fisted hands and pulled his head down and kissed him. Kissed him hard, with hunger and desperation and who-knows what other emotions. And, at least for a while, gained his shocked and instinctive cooperation.

Might as well face it. He was never going to be able

to predict Billie Farrell's next move—or Brenna Fallon's, either.

She hadn't known she was going to kiss him—hadn't even known she wanted to. Kissing *anyone* was the farthest thing from her mind. For the first couple of seconds it seemed like the wildest, stupidest, most dangerous thing she'd ever done—and given her history, that was saying a lot. Adrenaline surged through her, prickling her skin and sending her heart rate rocketing off the charts.

Then…she *felt* him. Felt his mouth, silky soft on the surface, firm underneath…the warm, shocked puff of his breath, the solid bulk of his shoulders beneath her balled-up fists. And his response—she hadn't expected *that*.

She felt a moment of panic…thought, *I should stop this!* And discovered she didn't want to—for a number of different reasons. To keep from having to think about the bombshell that had just been dropped on her. But mostly…because it just felt so damn good.

Such a hard-looking man, and yet… *Who would've thought he would feel so good?*

She would have liked to go on kissing him a considerable while longer, but obviously he didn't share her desire. She became aware of his hands on her waist, felt them linger there a moment…then move with purpose to her shoulders. The pressure on her shoulders was gentle persuasion, at first, and his mouth still clung to hers in a way more wistful than hungry. Knowing what was coming, she made a soft, whimpering sound of protest, but his hands had already moved on to her arms, slipped along them until he could grasp her wrists. Before he could humiliate her completely by pulling her hands free of his collar, she gave up her grip and jerked away from him, furious and shaken. She would have fled, then, but he'd probably anticipated that, because he didn't let go of her wrists. And for a few seconds they looked at each other across their locked hands, both breathing hard.

Holt's eyes narrowed, and he said thickly, "You want to tell me what that was about?"

She lifted her chin and lowered her lashes, and injected her voice with a seductive bravado she was far from feeling. "Don't tell me you hadn't thought about it."

He gave her a sideways, wary look. "Uh…actually, no, I hadn't."

"Liar." But he went on looking at her, saying nothing. She felt cold and queasy. She knew her smile was congealing fast, and it was only pride that enabled her to produce a nice little pout and accompanying puff of laughter to go with it. "Okay, I think my feelings are hurt."

"They shouldn't be," he said dryly, "believe me. It's just against my principles to hit on my clients' relatives—or a woman who's emotionally vulnerable, for that matter." He gave a sharp little laugh and gallantly added, "But you sure don't make it easy."

She bit her lower lip as she smiled up at him and turned her wrists experimentally in his grasp. "You didn't hit on me, I hit on you. And who says I'm 'emotionally vulnerable'?"

He made a sound that was more snort than laugh and let go of her wrists abruptly, as if he'd just realized he was still holding them.

And it was only when he was no longer touching her, when she couldn't feel the warmth of his body and the strength of his hands, that Billie realized how much she'd been depending on those things—on *him*—for support. Now, without it, she felt herself trembling inside and didn't know how to stop. To her horror, she realized that what she wanted more than anything at that moment was for Holt to put his arms around her and hold her tight. She wanted to press her face against his chest and gather his shirt in her fists and breathe in the comforting scent of him.

Instead, she folded her arms across her chilled body, supplying herself with the hug she needed, and turned her back to him, preempting the rejection she knew was coming.

Oh no…where are my glasses? I feel so naked…

She would die before she'd ask Holt Kincaid to give them back to her, but…

You better do something about those eyes, Miley always told me, back when he first started teaching me to play poker. You're never gonna be a successful card player unless you cover those eyes. Every thought in your head is right there in your eyes.

"So it was just some kind of weird emotional reaction," she said stiffly, without turning. "I'm over it, okay?"

"Billie—Bren—"

She made a sharp gesture, cutting him off. "Look, I just came to tell you so you can go tell your client— Cory…whatever—that you found me. Okay? So it's over—case closed. Now you just go away. Leave me alone."

"Just like that?" His voice was soft now, and came from close behind her. A shiver ran down her back for no good reason. "Don't you want to meet them? They're your family, Brenna."

"I told you—it's *Billie*. That's who I am now. You got that?" She flung that at him over one shoulder as she moved away from him. "Family? Look, if you met my sister Brooke, you have to know about me and *family*. There's no way in hell I'm ever going back there. You can—"

"He's dead, Billie."

"What?" A small gasp followed the word, as if the spoken response had been automatic, and the shock a delayed reaction that came after.

Holt said it again, gently. "Your brother. He's dead."

When she slowly turned toward him, he watched her face, vulnerable and naked as a child's. Saw bewilderment, first, then something feral and raw he couldn't put a name to.

"How?" She whispered it, suspicious and wary. "When?"

"He was killed in a car crash a couple of years ago. Your parents, too. I'm sorry…"

But she had her defenses back in place now, and she hitched one shoulder only slightly as she turned away. "Hey—I'm sorry about my parents," she said gruffly. Then she went utterly still, and her voice seemed to come from somewhere else entirely—disembodied and devoid of emotion. "As for my brother…if there's a God, and any justice at all, he's in hell, right where he belongs."

"Don't you want to know about your sister?" Standing behind her, he watched her raise one hand to her face and wondered if she was wiping away tears, or perhaps feeling for the sunglasses that weren't there. "Brooke's had—"

She made a quick, jerky motion with the hand that had touched her face. Cleared her throat and said huskily, "I know about Brooke. It was on the news— about her getting arrested for killing her husband, and the mountain lion and all that."

"Then you know—"

"I know she's okay, that she's got a kid. She looks good—looks like she's doing okay." She whirled on him, suddenly, her face flushed and angry. "Look, what do you want me to say?"

Her sunglasses were in his shirt pocket. She looked so defenseless he was tempted to give them back to her, but instead he folded his arms over the pocket and the glasses and said softly, "She's got a new man in her life—a good man. I imagine she'd love to tell you about him…seems like the kind of thing sisters do." He paused. "She's dying to see you, Billie. *Brenna.* She misses you."

She turned her head and stared hard at nothing. He could see her throat work as she swallowed.

"And you have three brothers—real brothers, good, decent men, all of them. You have a *family.*"

Her eyes came back to him, bright with anger, and her lips curved in a smile of derision. "Family? You say that like that's supposed to be something great, right? Look, as far as I'm concerned, families are the reason for most of what's gone wrong in this world."

"Come on, Billie."

"*Don't.* Okay? Don't give me pretty speeches, because you just don't know." Her eyes were shimmering, fire and rain, although no tears fell. She paced a step closer to him, one hand upraised. "When I was on the street, all those other kids who were out there with me— why do you think they were there? Guess what? They had families. Families that *sucked.* Moms on drugs, dads on booze…I knew kids that had to leave home to get something to eat, or to keep from getting raped, beat up—or worse."

"Nobody said all families are perfect," Holt said evenly. "All the more reason to be grateful when you've got a good one. And you've definitely got that. *Now.*"

"Yeah? So *you* say." She paused, studying him thoughtfully, lips still curved in that mocking little smile. "What about you, Kincaid? You got a family? A 'good' one?"

She was good at reading faces, and his was kindergarten-easy. Once again she didn't miss the slight flinching around his eyes when he replied.

"No. No family."

"None?" She jerked back in feigned surprise, and inside she was gleeful…triumphant. *Aha—gotcha. So you have a skeleton or two in your family cupboard, Holt Kincaid.* "Come on. No parents? No brothers and sisters? Nobody?" She felt no guilt for taunting him. As far as she was concerned he deserved it for making her expose *her* emotions so cruelly.

Tight-lipped, showing none of his, he shook his head. "I was raised by my great-aunt, but she's gone now."

"Really." She watched him narrowly, her head tilted to one side. "So…what happened to your parents?"

He didn't reply, and his eyes had gone flat and gray as stones.

She stepped closer, and touched one of the arms that criss-crossed his chest. That, too, seemed hard as stone, but seemed to vibrate from some force deep within, and when she touched it, she felt the same vibration inside her own chest.

She looked up at him. "Hmm… So what was it? They die? Abandon you? Come on, Kincaid, I'll bet there's one helluva story there."

"I don't know you well enough to tell you that story," he said coldly, looking down at her without lowering his head so that his eyes were hidden by his lashes. His lips looked stiff and uninviting.

How could I ever have kissed them?
How could they have felt so good?

A shudder ran through her, and she shrugged to

hide it. She went on smiling, too, although she was seething inside.

I think…I hate you, Kincaid. Nobody makes me cry— nobody. But you came close. I'll make you pay for that.

She didn't know how, but she would find out what his story was, where he was most vulnerable. And she *would* make him pay.

And in the meantime, she still had an ace or two to play.

"That's easily remedied," she murmured, swaying seductively as she moved even closer to him, letting her hand slide upward along his arm, feeling the shape of warm, firm muscle beneath soft cotton.

Holt grasped her wrist hard. He couldn't seem to stop his body's response to her touch; all he could hope for was to keep her from feeling it. His smile felt hard and mean, but what else could he do? It was the only defense he had.

He hadn't expected this. Hadn't expected to be so attracted to her. Not just physically—he was confident he could have handled that easily enough—but in ways he couldn't explain. Ways that made him feel weak and vulnerable, even while some masculine instinct deep inside him kept wanting to protect and defend her.

As if, he thought wryly, this woman needed protection from him, or anyone.

"Is that something you learned on the street?" he drawled, hanging on to his smile with grim determination, even when hers wavered and he knew he'd hit a tender spot.

She wrenched away from him, the words she muttered under her breath a well known retort that invited him to perform a physically impossible act upon his own person.

"Billie—wait." Cursing himself silently, he managed to snag her arm before she reached the door. The look she shot him made a strange thrill ripple through his insides—something primitive, an irresistible challenge…a hurled gauntlet. His heart began to beat faster. He found himself recalling with uncomfortable clarity the way her mouth had tasted.

"Give me back my glasses," she said very softly, while her eyes seared him like molten gold, "and I'm outta here."

He released the breath he'd been holding. "Okay, look—that was out of line. I apologize." He waited for some sign she was willing to accept that, while the seconds thundered by in heartbeats he felt in his throat. "Don't go, okay? I really am sorry. And I do want to get to know you better…."

She glanced down at his hand, the one holding on to her arm, then angled a quizzical look up at him. And he realized his thumb was moving back and forth on the soft skin of her upper arm, stroking it. Caressing it.

Something lurched in his insides and he knew he was in big trouble. What he really wanted was to lift up his other hand and touch her cheek…then curve his hand around to the nape of her neck, cradle her head in his palm and kiss her—really kiss her, the way such a beautiful and fascinating woman should be kissed. He didn't do that, but he didn't stop stroking her arm, either. He watched his thumb caress the smooth, tanned skin for a moment longer, then lifted his eyes to hers and let his lips curve in a smile of genuine regret as he released her.

"…But not that way."

Liar.

She didn't say it out loud; she didn't have to. She could see the lie in his eyes and on his lips, written there plain as day. Plain as the numbers on a deck of cards.

She shrugged, folded her arms and sauntered past him, relieved to once again be far enough away from him so he couldn't feel her heart thumping. She flung herself into the only easy chair and said, "Okay…so I'm here. What do you want to know?"

He pulled out the hard-backed chair in front of the small table that served as both desk and TV stand, turned it around to face her and sat. For a moment he just looked at her, then leaned forward with his hands clasped between his knees. She found herself bracing— for what she didn't know.

"Tell me what it was like," he said in that quiet, almost whispery way he had that made her think unwillingly of lovers trading secrets in a tumble of sweaty sheets. "Out there—on the streets." He paused. She laughed nervously and looked away. His voice reached out to her…compelled her to respond even though she didn't want to. "How did you survive? How did you get off the street? Was it this guy, Miley Todd—your partner?"

"Yeah, I guess." She cleared her throat and shifted in the chair.

I don't want to do this. Don't make me go back there. Damn you, Kincaid.

But she knew she'd have to, if she wanted to win this game. Tell him everything. Go back there and live it all again. The pain, the loss…

Tell him, Brenna. It's the way you'll get him to go "all in."

She took a breath. "He found me at a bad time, I guess you could say. Or maybe a good time, I don't know." She forced a smile. "I'd just had a baby. Gave the kid up for adoption. So I was—"

He uttered a sharp obscenity and sat back in his chair. He didn't know what he'd expected to hear, but it sure wasn't that. Of all the things she could have said…

She was watching him, a smile playing around her lips but not even coming close to her eyes.

He rubbed a hand over his mouth and muttered, "How did it happen? I mean, were you—"

"Oh, it was consensual—more or less." She shrugged. "It was a cold winter…what can I say? You take warmth where you can find it, if you know what I mean. Things happen, okay?"

"I'm not judging—God, no." He exhaled, then shook his head. "I just can't imagine what it must have been like, to be out there alone, on the streets and pregnant besides."

"It was one of the better times, actually. I went to a clinic, and they got me into a shelter—a women's shelter, so it was pretty safe. Better than the others, anyway…I learned to stay clear of those."

"But you didn't stay. After…"

She seemed to have shrunk, somehow, sitting hunched in that big chair with her hands fisted on her thighs. Her face had a pinched look. She shook her head and he had to lean closer to hear her as she mumbled, "I got to hold her—just for a minute. It was a girl. Then they took her and I signed the papers and got the hell outta there. I just wanted to get as far away from that place as I could. Maybe you can't understand that, but that's just the way it was."

Maybe he didn't understand—how could he?—but he ached for her anyway. His throat ached. He cleared it, but still didn't think talking was a good idea, so he got up and paced restlessly to the window. It wasn't a spectacular Vegas view; his room did not face the Strip. Just an anonymous cityscape, darkening already to dusk, this late in November. He wondered if that cold wind was still blowing. In Vegas it was easy to lose touch with the world outside the hotels and casinos, but he knew there was a different world out there. Beyond the glitter and glamour of the Strip, Las Vegas was a city like any other, with its share of ordinary people leading ordinary lives, and criminals preying on both the innocent and each other.

"Miley Todd brought me here, to Vegas," Billie said, as if she'd read his thoughts. "I met him in Biloxi. He was playing poker in a tournament in one of the Gulf casinos, and I was working the main drag, picking up food money from the tourists doing card tricks…scams, actually. I guess Miley thought I had a good head for cards."

He turned back to her, discovering he'd lost his taste for asking questions. The images she'd already painted in his head were going to be tough enough to forget; he didn't need any more.

Funny—he'd never really thought about the term *empathy,* not until he'd run into the first of Cory Pearson's siblings, the Portland homicide cop, Wade Callahan, and the woman who'd recently become his wife. Tierney Doyle Callahan was an empath, a psychic who could read other people's emotions, and she'd met Wade while working with the Portland P.D. to catch a serial killer.

Meeting Tierney had gotten Holt to wondering whether he might have a wee touch of the empath himself, since he'd always had kind of a knack for getting inside the heads of the people he was searching for. An ability to think: *If I were that person, what would I do? Where would I go?* Not that he'd lay any claim to being psychic, but the fact was, a lot of the time he'd be right.

Brenna Fallon's story had grabbed him by the throat from the first time he'd heard it. He remembered vividly the clenching in the pit of his stomach when Brooke told him her twin sister had run away at fourteen to escape their adoptive older brother's sexual abuse. The photos Brooke had given him then had become burned into his brain, filling his nights with dreams of that fragile child-woman out there somewhere on some cold, mean street, vulnerable to every kind of predator and peril. Until a couple of days ago he'd all but given up hope of ever finding her, and then he'd had the incredible good luck to catch that poker game on late-night television.

Now…he slept no better, although it was a thirty-year-old woman's face that haunted him. Haunted him in ways he hadn't counted on.

"You want anything to drink? Or eat?" he asked, frowning, remembering the way she'd lurched out of the coffee shop downstairs, looking decidedly green around the gills. Chances were, he thought, she'd lost most of that Chinese food he'd bought her.

He knew he'd been right yet again when she smiled wryly.

"Yeah, actually, I am."

He picked up the phone, pressed the button for room service, then looked over at her and raised his eyebrows.

"A BLT on wheat and a chocolate shake would be fine."

He nodded, and she watched him while he gave the order, adding a cup of black coffee for himself. Noted the way his hair hugged the back of his head and receded—only a little bit and very attractively—at the temples. There were touches of silver there, too, and she wondered for the first time how old he was. Not that it mattered, she told herself. What did matter was that he was attracted to her, and she could use that to her advantage. She told herself the shiver of excitement she could feel running like a current under her skin was only the thrill of the game, the same excitement she always felt when she knew she was holding the winning hand.

He hung up the phone and looked over at her, eyes narrowed in a Clint Eastwood squint. She looked back at him, and the shiver beneath her skin coalesced in the center of her chest, a tight ball of warmth.

Take it easy, Bren, don't be too obvious or you'll scare him off. He's got scruples—who would've guessed a P.I. would have those?

She eased herself carefully back in the chair, elbows on the chair's arms, her hands clasped across her middle. "So, what now? You want to hear more about my misspent life?"

"No," he said, still frowning at her in that thoughtful way, "I really don't."

"O—kay." What now? She returned his gaze unflinchingly, but inside she felt off balance, as if she'd missed a step in a dance. She had to pause an awkward moment in order to pick up the beat, and her voice sounded artificial even to her own ears when she finally said, "So, tell me about yours, then."

"Nothing to tell." It was brusque, a door slammed in her face with such finality she caught her breath in a small, involuntary gasp. He sat on the edge of the bed and leaned toward her, hands clasped between his knees. "What I would like to know," he said in a hard voice, "is why you don't want to even meet your brothers. Cory especially. He's been looking for you for a long time, you know. He was the one who protected you when you and Brooke were small. You were just babies, and he kept you safe when your father went on his rampages. He sheltered you both in his arms the night your father shot your mother and then killed himself. Without a doubt your father intended to kill you all. You'd be dead, too, if it hadn't been for Cory."

She lifted her shoulders and felt herself shrink into them, as if under the weight of Holt's steady regard. "Don't remember it," she muttered, angry with herself for letting him get to her. "Don't remember him."

He didn't say anything, and after a moment she got up and began to pace in the cramped room. Didn't want to, but couldn't seem to help herself. "Look, I don't know those people. I don't want to know them." Couldn't keep her voice from shaking, either. She turned on him, furious. "Damn you. I don't need this kind of hassle."

"Just…meet them." His voice was gentle now, and somehow that was worse. "Is that too much to ask? Just let me take you to them."

She bent closer to him, dangerously close. He was sitting on the edge of the bed, his face almost on a level with hers. She could see the pores in his skin, the beard stubble on his cheeks, the lines radiating from the corners of his eyes, the silvery shadings of blue in his eyes. It made him suddenly too real, too human.

A lump formed inside her chest and rose into her throat, and for one horrible moment she was terrified she might break down.

Tense with the task of holding off that threat, she

spoke rapidly, forcing words through clenched teeth. "Okay—you want me to go with you to meet these people? I'll make you a deal. You find people, right? Okay, then, you find my daughter. I want to see my daughter first. You find her for me, *then* I'll go with you to meet my so-called brothers."

"And your sister," he softly reminded her, looking deep into her eyes. "She wants to see you, too."

She couldn't stay so close to him, not for another second. She let out breath in a gust and straightened. "Yeah sure—whatever." About to turn away from him, she jerked back for one more shot, her finger upraised in a gesture of command. "But first, *you find my baby girl.*"

Chapter 5

Holt was dead certain Billie had no expectation in the world he'd actually be able to find her daughter, that it had only been her desperate attempt to put him off that made her ask such a thing. He was pretty sure he knew, now, what was making her fear a reunion with the sister she'd left all alone to deal with their nightmarish family. He didn't have to be psychic or even an empath to recognize the flash of panic and guilt in her eyes whenever he'd mentioned her sister. It wasn't the unknown brothers she dreaded meeting; he doubted that part had even completely sunk in yet. No, he was certain the person Brenna Fallon couldn't face was Brooke.

Unfortunately for Billie, she didn't know Holt

Kincaid very well. Didn't know about the resources and the network of contacts he'd established over the course of more than twenty years spent doing the very thing she'd asked him to do: Finding people. Particularly those given up for adoption, or the birth parents of adopted children. It was what he *did*, and he was good at it. He'd told her that, but evidently she hadn't believed him.

In any case, since she hadn't exactly volunteered her home address he was pretty sure she wouldn't be expecting him to show up at her front door less than a week after their showdown in his hotel room. Much less with her daughter's name and address in his shirt pocket. But here he was.

She lived in a modest stucco bungalow in a quiet neighborhood not far from the Strip. Built sometime in the nineteen fifties or sixties, he estimated. It was a neighborhood of mature trees and few signs of children, possibly in transition from its elderly original residents to young married couples buying their first home. Most homeowners, including Billie, had opted to forgo the upkeep of traditional lawns in favor of water-saving and maintenance-free gravel, although lining Billie's front pathway was an assortment of pots and containers filled with a profusion of autumn-blooming flowers and plumes of decorative grasses. A white-painted rail fence separated the front yard from the sidewalk and driveway, and a large tree with narrow gray-green leaves Holt thought might be an olive shaded the front entrance. The

November wind rustled the leaves above his head as he made his way among the flowerpots to the front door.

Nice, he thought, and wondered why he was surprised. She did work in a plant nursery, after all.

He was searching in vain for a doorbell and had just lifted his hand to knock when he heard a thump from inside the house. Not loud, not the sound of breakage, but as if someone had dropped something heavy, or possibly slammed a door. Immediately after that came the sound of voices raised in anger.

He threw a quick glance over his shoulder, his hand already going to the weapon strapped in a holster at the small of his back. There was a car—a nondescript gray Dodge sedan—parked in the driveway. He'd noted it, but had assumed it was Billie's. It hadn't occurred to him she might have visitors—or more likely *a* visitor, since one of the voices he was hearing was Billie's. The other was definitely a man's.

Given what he knew of Billie's past, Holt had some bad ideas about what might be happening inside the house. Not wanting to make a possible bad situation worse, he decided against knocking or calling out to her. Instead he flattened himself against the wall beside the front door and leaned cautiously to look through the window. He couldn't see anyone in the living room, but he could still hear the voices, which seemed to be coming from the back of the house. Keeping his head down and with his gun in his hands, carried low and to one side, he ran swiftly and silently along the side of the house, following a concrete walkway. At the corner of the house he halted and peered around into the back-yard. He could see more flower-filled pots and, adjoining a covered concrete patio, a small free-form swimming pool, empty of water.

He could hear the voices clearly now. The man's voice, high and strained: "You *know* what they'll do to me. Are you gonna just let—"

And Billie's. "*Don't.* Don't you dare put this on me. I *can't help you.* Don't you get it? I can't."

"Hey—that's bull. You *won't.* And that's the kind of thanks I get? You little—"

"Don't threaten me, Miley." Her voice was vibrant with anger, and Holt heard a note of fear, too.

Billie Farrell—afraid? That got to him more than anything else. He tightened his grip on his weapon. Drew in a breath and held it, every muscle adrenaline-primed and poised for action.

"You and I are *done.*" Billie spat the words like bullets, in a voice that did not tremble. "I told you. After that last tournament. I paid you back. I don't owe you anything."

"You paid me *diddly!*" Miley was whining now. "What'd you make, a quarter mil? You give me a lousy twenty-five G's! What'd you do with the rest of it?"

"It's none of your business what I did with it. I don't have it. You got it? I can't help you. Now, get out of my house. And don't you *ever* come here again, you hear me? Stay away from me!"

"Jeez, Billie, all I'm askin' for—"

"Out...*now!*"

"This ain't over! I'm not—" There was a sharp exclamation and some vehement swearing, followed by, "For Chrissake, put that away—are you *crazy?* I'm going, okay? I'm *going.* Jeez…"

Footsteps thudded through the house. The front door slammed, and a moment later Holt heard the car start up in the driveway. Slipping his gun back in its holster, he swiftly crossed the patio, gave a warning knock, then thrust open the backdoor.

"Hey, are you okay—" The question died with a sharp intake of breath.

A few feet away, Billie had whirled to confront him, eyes blazing fire. Now she uttered a small, horrified squeak and collapsed back against the kitchen counter, one hand covering her mouth. In the other, Holt noted, she was gripping a rather large knife.

It took him about a second to get to her, and he was swearing vehemently under his breath as he gently took the knife—a serrated bread knife, it appeared—from her unresisting fingers. Then, in a little flurry of motion that could only have been spontaneous, she came into his arms.

What could he do? He dropped the knife onto the countertop and wrapped his arms around her. Which lasted about a second, barely long enough for him to register the fact that she was shaking, and that her hair smelled nice, and that her body felt incredibly good right there, snugged up against his.

She gave a furious gasp and thumped his chest with

her fists as she pushed away from him. "*Jeez,* Kincaid. What are you doing here? Are you friggin' *nuts?*" Her voice was shrill and breathless. She glared at him for a moment, then spun away from him, and as she did she caught sight of the knife lying where he'd dropped it on the countertop. She recoiled and jerked back to him, one hand clamped to the top of her head. "I could have— what if I'd—*dammit,* Kincaid!"

"I'm assuming that was your former partner Miley Todd." He kept his tone mild, figuring at least one of them ought to try to keep calm.

Her laugh was a sharp bark of anger. "Yeah…the man's a weasel." She turned back to the counter, picked up the knife, opened a drawer and dropped the knife into it, then closed it carefully.

Stay calm, Billie. You've already given too much away. What's wrong with you, throwing yourself at him like that? Since when do you need a man protecting you?

Oh, but admit it…it did feel good.

Yeah…too damn good.

She could feel him there, just behind her. *Too close.* If she turned now she could hardly avoid touching him.

"What did he want?"

"Money—what else?" She closed her eyes and willed him away.

Which seemed to work, because his next question came from a slightly greater distance. A foot or two. Breathing room at least. So why did she now feel off balance and precarious, as if she'd been left teetering on the brink of some great abyss with nothing to hold on to?

"So, what's his story?"

She had room to turn and face him now, so she did—carefully. He was leaning against the refrigerator, arms folded on his chest, regarding her with that narrow blue gaze of his. She leaned back against the counter and deliberately copied his stance. "You are the nosiest guy I ever met, you know that?"

He smiled. "Goes with the job."

She hadn't expected the smile. For some reason and without warning, a tightness gripped her throat. Unable to speak for a moment, she looked at the floor and gave a little sigh of laughter, then caught a breath and lifted her eyes back to his "What are you doing here, Kincaid? I'm not even gonna ask how you found me."

Without a word, he reached into his shirt pocket, pulled out a folded piece of paper and handed it to her.

"What's this?" she demanded as she took it. She unfolded the piece of hotel stationery. On it, neatly printed in block letters, was a couple's name: Corrine and Michael Bachman. Below that was an address in Reno, Nevada. Below *that* was a name, circled: *Hannah Grace.*

Billie couldn't feel her fingers. She stared down at the paper. The words danced...shimmered...blurred.

She didn't know what to do.

I won't cry. I can't cry. I sure as hell am not going to

*throw myself into his arms, not again! But I don't know
what to do.*

"This is her—my daughter?" Her voice felt scratchy,
and sounded unfamiliar.

"That's her." His voice was gentle—damn him. It
would have been better if he'd been brusque. She could
have handled that. Gentleness...not so well.

"Huh." She shook her head, struggled to find breath.
Pulled air in, then let it out. "That easy, huh?"

"If you know where to look." His hands had a
strange, tingly feeling, an urgent need to reach for her...
touch her. Hold her. He kept them firmly tucked between his folded arms and body.

"Wow," she said, and he watched her struggle to
find something else to say and finally give it up and
just laugh, the kind of laugh that meant anything but
amusement. Her throat moved convulsively and his
ached in sympathy.

"Can I—" she said, at the same moment he said,
"Would you like to see her?"

And even though he knew it was what she wanted
more than anything in the world, he saw panic flash in
her eyes. "From a distance," he added gently, and she
nodded in a dazed sort of way.

A moment later, though, she did a startled double
take and said, *"Now?"*

"Sure, why not? You have the day off so might as well."

"How did you—"

"I stopped by the garden center looking for you

first. They told me you were off today. And tomorrow, too, right?"

"Yeah…" She looked down at the piece of paper in her hand, fingered it restlessly, as if she didn't know what to do with it. Then she tossed it onto the countertop. "It's so far. It would take forever to drive to Reno."

Holt smiled. "Who said anything about driving?"

Billie stood on the sun-bleached airstrip and watched the red-and-white plane taxi toward them, sending up puffs of dust that went spiraling away in the midday breeze. The plane looked way too small to hold three people. It looked like a child's toy.

She sucked in a breath, which did nothing to relieve the knots in her stomach.

It's happening too fast. It's too much, first Miley shows up, and now this.

Her past was catching up with her. More than that. It seemed suddenly to be looming over her like a gigantic tsunami wave, one breath away from drowning her. She felt dizzy, a little sick. She wanted to lie down somewhere and go unconscious for a while until the world slowed down, or she caught up with it.

She'd had the same feeling before. Too many times before. In the past, her remedy for this feeling would be to run, to just go, get away as far and as fast as she could.

I should have gone. Should have left the day I saw him there in the garden center, picking out plants. I knew he didn't belong there. I knew he was bad news.

So, why don't you go now? What's stopping you? Nobody's forcing you to get on that ridiculous toy airplane.

The plane coasted to a stop. Beside her, Holt touched her elbow, then went jogging out onto the packed-earth runway. The plane's single prop slowed and finally stopped, and the door opened and the pilot crawled out onto the wing, then jumped to the ground. He ambled over to meet Holt, and the two men clasped hands, then went in for the brief back-thumping that passes for hugging among guy-friends. Then Holt turned and beckoned to Billie.

She hauled in another breath she didn't seem to have room for.

Why don't I go? There's the answer, right there. I hate it, but it's there and there's nothing I can do about it. It's him—Holt Kincaid. What good would it do me to run? He'd only find me again. I can't escape the man.

And somewhere way in the back of her mind a voice she didn't want to listen to was saying, *Why would you want to?*

"I want you to meet my friend Tony," Holt said, reaching out to touch her arm, drawing her closer. "He's the man who's going to take us to Reno."

The man's hand swallowed hers and his smile seemed to light up the already sun-shot day. He reminded her of a Humvee—big and square and formidable, and he made her feel safe.

She nodded and managed a breathless, "Hi," and his whiskey-colored eyes crinkled with laughter.

"Hey—it's all good. I promise I'll get you there and back in one piece." He clapped his hands together like an enthusiastic child and beamed at her. "Okay. Are you ready? Well, hop in, then.

"You get to ride shotgun," he told her as he guided her up onto the wing. To Holt he added, "Sorry, buddy — you get to sit on the floor. I took out the passenger seats to make room for my equipment and extra fuel."

"I guess it's a good thing it's not a long flight," Holt said dryly.

"I'm a photojournalist," Tony explained to Billie. "So I've got lots of stuff. Plus, the places I go don't always have convenient airfields with fuel pumps."

"Uh-huh," Billie said. She had her head inside the plane now, and was trying not to stare at the array of instruments across the front of the cockpit. She glanced back at the two faces smiling encouragement at her from below. "Um...I can sit on the floor. Really. I wouldn't mind." *Because back there where nobody can see me, maybe I can curl up in a fetal ball and stay there until we land....*

The two men chuckled, as if she'd said something funny.

"Never flown in a small plane before, huh?" Tony's eyes were warm with sympathy. "You'll be fine—I promise not to do anything crazy. Just buckle up...settle back and enjoy the ride, okay?"

"Okay." She gave him the smile he seemed to want, but the truth was, she did feel a little better. It was just something about him, the laid-back, effortless charm that made her forget about thirty seconds after meeting him that he had a face resembling a cross between a bouncer in a biker bar and a benevolent pit bull terrier. Whatever it was, she just had the feeling she could trust him.

As she settled into the passenger seat she looked over her shoulder and found Holt's eyes on her. Something in their watchfulness made a shiver go through her.

What about him? Do I trust him?

Why do I have to ask myself that? I must trust him, or I wouldn't be making this insane trip with him, would I?

If that's so, why does he make me feel…off balance? Unsure of myself? Scared?

Yes—scared. The truth was, Holt Kincaid frightened her. She hadn't thought of it quite like that, until she'd met Tony and realized the difference. Tony was a stranger to her, and yet, he made her feel safe. Rather like having a big brother…

Brother? Wait. No. Could this be…

The thought popped into her head, and just as quickly she rejected it. No, this man had the deep-mahogany skin tones and broad cheekbones that hinted at Native American origins, and besides, Holt had told her her brothers' names, and none of them had been Tony.

Still…the thought lingered. *Brother…I have brothers? Holt says I do. Real ones.*

And from the thought, as if from a planted seed, feelings began to grow inside her. Feelings she couldn't define, because she'd never felt them before. Feelings…

like warmth, and…comfort, and whatever the opposite of loneliness was called. Perhaps belonging?

All this went through her mind in the few seconds while she stared into Holt Kincaid's eyes. Then she drew a shaken breath and turned in the high-backed red velveteen seat and pulled her seat belt across her chest. And as the little airplane's engines caught and the seat beneath her began to vibrate, as Tony donned headphones and muttered into a radio microphone, inside her chest she quivered with excitement and apprehension and anticipation, and something that felt—impossibly—like joy.

At the same moment, on the floor behind her seat, strapped uncomfortably to the wall of the passenger compartment, Holt was wishing he'd never gotten Billie to take off her sunglasses. Those eyes of hers…he'd never seen anything quite like them. And as the Piper Cherokee shot down the runway and lifted into the cloudless Nevada sky, he knew the hollow feeling in his stomach had nothing to do with the abrupt change in altitude.

No use kidding himself—it wouldn't change the fact that the unthinkable had happened. He was in grave danger of falling in love with his client's baby sister. Falling in love with a woman with two names and more complications than anybody he'd ever met. A woman he wasn't sure he'd ever be able to completely understand. How was that even possible?

Not that he knew much about it—falling in love—from personal experience, anyway. It hadn't ever happened to him before, and he'd come to believe, with pretty much equal parts regret and relief, that it never would.

Right now, with his backside growing numb from its contact with the floor of a vintage Piper Cherokee, he couldn't even recall exactly when it had happened. Looking back, it almost seemed as if it had been that very first moment, when he'd first caught a glimpse of her face on his TV screen, half hidden behind a pair of mirrored sunglasses, and there'd been that electric shiver across his skin. He'd been carrying her picture around in his pocket for weeks, but the sense of recognition was more than that.

But he doubted that was true. It only *seemed* like he'd known her, or at least had been looking for her, all his life.

Fanciful stuff, and he was not a fanciful man. Nor did he believe in things like fate and destiny. No, he told himself, this was just biology, a simple matter of chemistry, which was maybe even harder to explain.

With her face pressed against the side-window glass, Billie watched the strangely colorful desert terrain give way to the curving avenues of Reno's suburbs. She's down there…somewhere, she thought. *Hannah Grace. My daughter.*

Why did I ever ask him to find her? What was I thinking?

Why don't I feel anything?

It was as if her subconscious mind had thrown up a firewall around her emotions. Self-preservation?

But I want *to feel something. I* should *feel something…shouldn't I? What's wrong with me? I'm going to see my child. My baby. She was a part of me, and I gave her away. And I can't feel anything!*

She could remember feeling. She remembered that day…remembered the awfulness of it. But it was only a *memory* of pain, not the feeling of it.

"She had dark hair," she said, and was vaguely surprised to discover she'd spoken aloud. Tony looked over at her, and his warm-whiskey eyes were hidden behind aviator's sunglasses. "I remember being surprised by that," she told him, not really knowing why she did. "That she could have dark hair, you know? Because I don't."

"Lots of babies have dark hair when they're born," Tony said. "Then it falls out and grows in a whole different color. So you can't tell anything by that. She could have blond hair now. You never know."

She gave a laugh that hurt, then drew a shaky breath. After a moment she looked over at him and said, "You sound like you know a lot about babies. Do you have kids?"

He shook his head, but smiled. "Not yet. I've just got a whole bunch of sisters with kids—lotsa nieces and nephews. I'm planning to, though." And his smile seemed to glow with warmth and promises and secret intimacies.

"So you're married?" Billie asked, wondering why the smile of a man so obviously in love should make her feel wistful.

Tony chuckled, a sound that matched his smile. "Not yet. Planning to be, though."

She drew another uneven breath and forced a smile. "She must be somebody special," she murmured, wishing it didn't sound so trite when she meant it with all her heart.

She wondered why he laughed, then, as if he knew a delicious secret.

The airfield north of Reno was much larger than the dirt airstrip in the desert near Las Vegas. Since it had once been an air force base and now served as home to the air tankers used in fighting forest fires in the nearby Sierra Nevada Mountains, its runways were long, wide and smooth—a factor for which Holt's backside gave thanks. Tony guided the Cherokee to a flawless landing, then taxied onto the expanse of tarmac where they were to park. Before leaving Las Vegas, Holt had called and arranged for a taxi to meet them, and he could see it waiting for them in the parking lot next to the airport office building.

Tony cut the engine and turned to give Billie a thumbs-up and a smile. "See? Told you I'd get you here."

Holt managed to get himself straightened out and limbered up enough to open the door and exit the plane first, Tony being occupied with the unknown details involved in concluding a flight and buttoning down his aircraft. While Billie was slowly unbuckling herself from her seat harness, he gingerly stretched his legs and aching back, then turned to give her a hand climbing down, if she needed it.

But she was still crouched in the doorway of the plane, poised as if for a leap off a high diving board, and her face was bleached to the color of desert sand.

"Airsick?" he said gently, even though the gnawing sensation in the pit of his own stomach told him that wasn't her problem, not by a long shot. He held out his hand to her and added, "You'll feel better once your feet are on the ground."

She gave him a withering look as she crept onto the wing, then hopped, with a nimbleness he envied, to the ground. "I've changed my mind," she announced, glaring at a point somewhere off to his right. "This is stupid. I don't know what I was thinking. Take me home."

Her teeth were chattering. Holt took the jacket she was carrying folded over one arm and, while she transferred her glare to his face, slipped it around her shoulders. Her eyes seemed too big, too fiery for such a small, pixieish face, as if the heat and turmoil that fed them was trying to consume her from the inside out. He wanted so badly to take her face in his hands, hold it, protect it like some fragile, delicate blossom, soothe the burning with his kisses. He could barely contain himself, she touched him so.

"You'll be fine," he said in what he'd meant to be a murmur but sounded instead like a growl. To emphasize his words, he tugged the two sides of her jacket he was holding, giving her a little shake. Her sunglasses slipped out of one of the jacket pockets and fell onto the tarmac. He bent down and picked them up, unfolded and slid them onto her face. It was like closing a door on a roaring furnace.

He couldn't resist stroking the spikey feathers of her hair behind her ears as he settled the earpieces in place, and his voice held more gravel as he said, "Better now?"

The lenses held steady for a long moment, and then she gave him the ghost of a smile. He let out a silent breath and hooked his arm around her shoulders, and as he did he cast one quick look back at Tony Whitehall, crouched in the doorway of the Piper Cherokee, giving him the thumbs-up sign.

She didn't speak a word on the twenty-minute ride into Reno, just kept looking out of the window of the cab, keeping her face turned away from him.

When they turned into the residential neighborhood of curving streets and stucco houses of the northwest part of the city, Holt said in tentative encouragement, "Looks nice—nice trees…nice houses."

She nodded but didn't reply or look at him.

"Nice place to raise a kid," he offered, and she didn't reply to that, either.

He checked his watch, then leaned forward to tap on the cab driver's shoulder. "This is okay—pull over right here."

"You sure? The address you gave me is a couple houses farther on down."

"Yeah, I know. This is fine. Might be a few minutes… keep the meter running." He'd explained their mission to the cabbie before they'd left the airport, not wanting to alarm him when they might appear to be stalking a child.

"No problem," the cabbie drawled as he pulled in to the curb and shifted into park. "Long as you're payin' me, I got all day."

Around them the neighborhood was stirring to life. Cars pulled into and out of driveways and came and went along the street. Two boys on bicycles whizzed by the waiting cab; children's voices mingled with the slap of running footsteps on sidewalks and pavement. Doors slammed.

"School just let out," Holt murmured. "Shouldn't be long now." He was looking over his shoulder, through the back window of the cab, intently watching the children coming along the sidewalk in clusters of twos and threes, sometimes more. The boys were untidy knots of motion, hopping, whirling, punching, pushing, laughing, the girls more sedate, heads together, arms linked, giggling and sharing secrets. Here and there a child walked alone, head bowed over a handheld electronic gadget or cell phone, thumbs busily punching buttons, oblivious to all else.

"There she is," he said suddenly. He put his hand on Billie's shoulder and pointed past her, directing her attention out the side window to the three girls now coming into view a block away. "Purple pants, pink jacket—see her?"

Billie's head moved, a quick up and down. Other than that she seemed to have gone still as stone—except that beneath his hand he could feel her body quivering.

"She's blond," he said softly, his lips near her ear. "Like you."

She nodded again, and this time made a sound, a very small hiccup of laughter.

After that there was stillness, except for the cabbie's raspy breathing and the ticking of the meter, while they watched the three girls pass by their taxi with only a brief, incurious glance. Two houses farther on, the girl in the pink jacket detached herself from her friends with a wave and a little pirouette and ran up the driveway, her blunt-cut blond hair bouncing on her shoulders, to disappear inside the open garage.

Billie sat motionless. Holt caught the cabdriver's eye in the rearview mirror and nodded. The car moved away from the curb, moved along the street past the house where the girl in the pink jacket lived and turned the corner.

There was a soft sigh of exhaled breath as Billie turned from the window at last and sat back in the seat. Her head swiveled toward him. "It's a pretty name— Hannah Grace," she said. "Isn't it?"

Her glasses gazed at him, blank, bleak…empty.

"Ah, Billie…" he said, and then was silent. What could he say?

You touch my heart. You make me want to wrap you in my arms and keep you from ever again knowing heartache, loss, despair.

The words would feel awkward and sound silly coming out of his mouth. He wasn't a poet, a man comfortable with words and feelings.

He put out his arm and was only mildly surprised when she let him pull her close. Her glasses bumped awkwardly against his shoulder, and he reached across with his free hand and removed them. She nestled her face in the hollow of his chest and arm, but he knew by her stillness she wasn't crying. He wondered what it would take to make this woman cry.

Chapter 6

It was late by the time they got back to Las Vegas.

They had taken time out for a fast-food hamburger before leaving Reno, which was pretty much Holt's customary choice of cuisine, anyway. He had noticed Billie barely touched the salad she'd ordered, although she did help herself to a few of his French fries. Then, at the Vegas airstrip Tony couldn't let them go without getting one of his cameras out of the back of the plane and snapping a bunch of pictures, mostly of Billie.

She had been good-natured about it, probably figuring it was pretty much to be expected, given that Tony was a photographer. Naturally, she didn't know the real reason he wanted those pictures, which was that

Brooke, twin sister to Brenna and the woman Tony Whitehall planned to marry and start having kids with in the very near future, would surely have skinned him alive if he'd come home without them. That was a revelation both Holt and Tony had agreed would be better kept for another time…another place.

Billie hardly spoke a word on the drive back into the city. She hadn't said much during dinner or the flight from Reno, either, except to answer direct questions, usually accompanied by a distracted smile. And the closer they got to her neighborhood, the less Holt liked the idea of dropping her off at her front door and leaving her alone. He told himself it was because he didn't want to risk giving her a chance to cut out on him. They'd had a deal and he'd kept his end of the bargain, and now *her* moment of reckoning was at hand. He had no idea in the world what was going on inside her head right now, but he did know she had a history of running when things got rough.

But he knew in his heart that was only part of it, and that the whole truth was both simpler and more complicated than that. The truth was, he didn't want to leave her. Period.

He pulled into her driveway and turned off the Mustang's motor and got out of the car, expecting her to tell him he didn't need to come in, that she'd be fine, thanks for everything and good night.

She didn't say that. She didn't say anything at all, just walked beside him along the avenue of potted plants, up the steps and onto her front porch. Holt kept his hands in the pockets of his windbreaker to keep from touching her, putting his hand on her back…the nape of her neck. He told himself it would only have been a touch meant to give comfort and sympathy. Which was a lie. But even if it had been the truth, he didn't know that he had the right to offer her anything so personal, or that she wouldn't misunderstand if he did.

There was, he realized, a lot he didn't know about Billie Farrell. Or Brenna Fallon, either.

She'd forgotten to leave a porch light on, so there was only the dim glow of the streetlights to see by as she unlocked the front door, pushed it open, then turned to look at him.

"You want some coffee? Or a Coke, or something?" She'd thrust her hands into her jacket pockets, and her shoulders looked hunched and defensive.

"Sure," Holt said. "Sounds good."

He followed her into the dark house, across the living room and into the kitchen beyond. There was more light here, shining in from a porch light outside, above the back door. Without turning on the kitchen lights, Billie shrugged out of her jacket and dropped it onto a chair beside the dining table, then went into the kitchen's work space to make coffee. Holt took off his jacket and draped it on the back of a chair, then went around the table to look out the window into the backyard.

He was about to ask her why there wasn't any water in her swimming pool—just to make conversation—

when something crunched under his feet. He froze—outwardly. Inside, adrenaline was exploding through his veins. He knew what broken glass felt and sounded like when he stepped on it.

"Billie," he called quietly. But she had the water running and didn't hear him.

He was beside her in three strides, maybe less. She turned startled eyes to him as she reached to turn off the faucet, and he pressed a finger against her lips before she could utter the exclamation poised there.

"Shh," he whispered, his lips close to her ear, "I think you've had a break-in. Window's broken. Stay here while I check the house."

She nodded, eyes wide above his cautioning fingers, and he gave her neck a reassuring squeeze before he left her.

He took his weapon from its holster in the small of his back and began a room-to-room sweep of the house, gratified at how quickly it came back to him from his cop days, long years past. How natural it seemed. He cleared every room, closet and cubbyhole as he'd been trained to do, and when he was satisfied the intruder was no longer in the house, he retraced his steps to the kitchen, where Billie was calmly filling the coffeemaker as if nothing out of the ordinary had happened.

He switched on the lights, tucked away his weapon and reached for the phone that was sitting on the counter. She looked over at him and said, "What are you doing?"

"Calling nine-one-one." He paused, phone in hand,

to frown at her. "Somebody broke into your house. I'm calling the cops. And before they get here you need to check and see what's missing."

She shook her head and went on filling the coffee-maker, silently counting out spoonfuls of coffee. Her lips were pressed tightly together, and her movements were jerky with anger. When she'd finished counting, she set the coffee can down with a clank and snatched the phone out of his hands.

"Come on, Billie, you need to report it."

She stared down at her hands, gripping the edge of the countertop, the knuckles white knobs against the pale blue tile. She wondered how, just a short time ago, she could have wished to feel something. Now, she felt ready to burst with feelings. Feelings she didn't know what to do with, or how to even name. She felt angry, but didn't know who to be angry with. She felt sadness and grief and regret and longing and fear, so much of everything she wanted to find a hole somewhere and crawl into it, cover her eyes and ears and wait for it all to go away. She wished she could cry, at least, but she'd lost that ability a long time ago.

Then there was Holt. This man who'd made such a shambles of her nice, ordered life. This man taking up so much space in her kitchen she felt as if there wasn't enough air left for her to breathe. She wished he'd never happened, wanted to hate him, wanted to be angry with him, at least. And she was. *Oh, she was.* And yet, she couldn't bear to think of him going away now and leaving her alone.

"It was just that stupid Miley," she said between clenched teeth.

"You don't know that."

Having no other place to send it, she threw him a look of bitter fury. "I know, okay? I don't need the hassle. Let it go."

He leaned against the counter and folded his arms, and his calm only infuriated her more. "Why are you so sure it's him?"

She picked up the coffeemaker's glass carafe and rounded on him, words tumbling from her lips in a rapid mutter. "Because I know him. This is just the kind of thing he'd do. Hang around, wait for me to leave, then just…waltz in. He figures he'll find what he's looking for, and if not, well, he thinks he's going to scare me, at least. I told you—the guy's a weasel."

"What's the story with this guy Miley?" He asked it as he took the carafe from her hands and turned to the sink to fill it with water.

She stared at his shoulder, unable to bring herself to lift her gaze higher. She couldn't look at his face. Not now. She was too full of feelings already. In silence she watched him pour the water into the coffeemaker, set the carafe in place and switch it on. Then he turned to her, the question he'd asked repeated in his sharp blue eyes and upraised eyebrows. She caught a breath and said, "Do we have to go into this now?"

"Yeah, Billie, I think we do." He leaned against the counter and folded his arms, and she could see no quarter in his face, or hear any gentleness in his voice. "I heard him threaten you. He scared you enough that you pulled a knife on him. So, yeah. We need to go into it *now.*"

For a long moment she just looked at him, her heart-shaped face set and angry, and Holt was conscious of a little thrill of combative excitement. But he was more determined than she was, or maybe she was simply beaten down by the emotional bombardment she'd taken today. Anyway, after a moment she closed her eyes, let out a hiss of breath and muttered something under her breath. Something that meant capitulation.

She postponed it as long as she could, though, opening cupboards and banging drawers and taking milk out of the refrigerator in angry silence. With everything assembled, she stood and glared at the gurgling coffeemaker as if doing so could make it finish its job faster and give her a few more moments reprieve while she poured and served. When it became clear that wasn't going to happen, she lifted her hands and let them drop, then turned on him.

"I was going to tell you the whole story—the other day, in your hotel room. You're the one that told me you didn't want to hear it."

"Yeah, well…" What could he say? He couldn't very well tell her what had been in his thoughts that evening…couldn't tell her how she'd haunted him, and how the pictures she'd painted of her life on the streets still did. "I didn't know the guy was still around. I thought he was past history."

"Yeah, well…so did I." She closed her eyes and he could see her fighting for control. After a moment she hitched in a breath as if girding for a difficult task. Clearly, he thought, this wasn't a woman accustomed to laying her troubles on someone else.

"Okay." She exhaled slowly. "He showed up about a week ago—a few days before you did, actually. He said he'd managed to come up with the buy-in for the big no-limit hold 'em tournament that starts in a couple days at the Mirage."

"I thought he's been barred from playing," Holt said, frowning.

"He is. Which is why he wanted me to sign up instead."

"Ah."

"I told him no," Billie said, her voice tight and vehement. "I'm done with that life. Don't have any desire to get back into it."

"I take it he didn't take no for an answer."

"He did not. Turns out he had a pretty good reason not to."

The coffeemaker chose that moment to announce the conclusion of its task with a belching, gurgling crescendo, and she turned to pick up the carafe. She poured two cups and handed him one, then set about doctoring her own cup with cream and sugar. She stirred, tasted, then leaned her backside once more against the counter, arms again folded, cup in one hand. She didn't move to sit down at the table, and neither did he.

Her eyes had a dark glint that wasn't amusement. "Miley always imagines he's smarter than everybody else. Or that everybody else is dumber, maybe. Anyway, he'd borrowed money from some pretty scary people to finance some scheme or other, and things evidently didn't turn out the way he hoped they would, so now he owes these guys some serious money."

"How serious?"

She drank coffee, frowned as she swallowed. "Seven figures."

"What? *Millions?*"

"Well, not *millions*. Little over a million, actually."

"Why would he think you could help him with that kind of money?"

Her smile was sardonic. "You don't follow tournament poker much, do you? A major tournament like the one at the Mirage, the winner will take home way over a million dollars. Even the runners-up get pretty big bucks. You know that tournament I was in, the last one before I quit? That was a fairly small one. I went out in third place, and my share after taxes was over a quarter mil."

Holt nodded. "I heard him say that. Sounded like he thinks you've still got it." He watched her closely while he sipped his coffee.

Her gaze hardened and slid past him. "Yeah, well, I don't."

"Why do you suppose he thinks you do?"

She gave a little huff of laughter and gestured with

her cup. "Maybe because of the way I live? Do I look like I just spent a quarter of a million bucks? Even if I paid cash for this house—which I did, by the way— and even considering I already gave him a chunk of the money—"

"Why did you? By the way…"

She drank the last of her coffee and put the cup on the counter. She felt calmer, now, at least. Talking about past history seemed to be helping take her mind off the present. She shrugged. "I guess…I felt like I owed him. It was the first time I'd played without him, and he'd put up part of the buy-in. So, I gave him his share and I figured that was it. We were done."

"So," Holt said, "let me get this straight. Your ex-partner gets in trouble with some loan sharks, he's desperate, he comes to you to ask you to get into a poker tournament in order to win the money to bail him out. You say no dice and he comes back, this time demanding money which he thinks you have stashed away from your last big tournament win. You tell him you don't have it, he threatens you, you pull a knife, he leaves,…is that why you think he's the one who broke in here today? You think he came back looking for the money?"

She shrugged and held out her hands. "What else?"

He frowned. "Who keeps that kind of money stashed in their house?" She just looked at him. The lightbulb evidently went on, and he sucked in air. "Ah—I get it. You lived on the street…"

"…and, I was used to hiding my stash of whatever

I'd managed to acquire. Even after I met Miley, I didn't have much use for banks. He probably figures I'm still like that."

"Are you?"

She snorted, making it clear it was all the answer she was going to give him. After a moment he said, "So, it was true, what you told him? You really don't have the money to give him?"

She straightened with an indignant jerk. "Yes, it's true. Do you think I'm that heartless? The guy's a weasel, but he saved my life, probably. Of course, I'd give him the damn money. If I could."

Holt waited. The silence grew electric, and he knew she wouldn't tell him unless...

"Okay...sorry," he said, reaching past her to set his coffee cup in the sink, "but I have to ask. What *did* you do with it? The money?"

There was another long pause.

"Billie?" he prompted softly. She was so close to him...arms folded on her chest as she gazed intently at the toe of her shoe, scrubbing away at the vinyl tile floor. He couldn't see her face, just the top of her head, and her hair looked unbelievably soft. He lifted his hand and his fingers hovered...

Then, abruptly, she lifted her chin and shook back her hair and her eyes met his in defiance, as if she were about to confess a major sin. "I put it in a trust."

"A...trust." He felt a moment's confusion, jarred by how near he'd just come to touching her in a way he'd never have been able to explain, at the same time wondering why this was so hard for her to admit. It seemed a reasonable enough thing to do. Responsible, even.

"Yeah," she shot back curtly, "like, you know, a trust fund?" She looked away, then, and mumbled something he couldn't hear.

"I beg your pardon?"

Her eyes snapped back to him. "For her—my daughter. For Hannah Grace."

He didn't know what to say. Words seemed to pile up on each other in his throat, forming a hard knot. He shook his head, and she stared at him almost accusingly.

"It's why I asked you to find her, okay? So I could put it in her name. Her real name. It's for…you know—college and…stuff."

"Jeez, Billie…" His face felt stiff. He lifted his hand and rubbed it, but it didn't help much. His arms, his face, his whole body ached with the need to reach for her… hold her…help her.

He didn't know what to do. Only one other time in his life had he felt so powerless—and that was a time he resented being forced to remember now, if only by way of comparison. How had he gotten himself to this point? When had he become so tangled up in this woman's life? When had she become so important to him?

It occurred to him then that they'd been standing there looking at each other for quite a long time, in silence. And when Billie spoke, it was a moment before he could be certain he'd understood her.

"Would you mind staying with me tonight?" she said softly.

There was a part of him, then, that wanted to take a page out of her playbook—bolt, get the hell out of there, run for his life. He was not a man equipped to deal with emotional demands. He lacked, or so he had always believed, the ability to give of himself emotionally. The ability, in short, to *love*. And he'd always considered himself lucky because of it—love, after all, being notorious as the cause of pain, anxiety, insecurity, disappointment and so many other negative emotions he could never hope to name them all. The positive aspects of love, highly touted in song and verse, he'd always considered not worth the cost.

But now, standing here facing this woman, with her golden eyes holding a burden of anguish that seemed too great for any one person to bear, he was coming to the realization that he'd been wrong. Wrong about his own ability to love, anyway. And, at the moment, the hazards and burdens of loving someone still seemed terrifying, and to far outweigh the supposed joys.

What should he do? It was late; he knew he should refuse the offer, make his excuses and go. To leave her now seemed…unthinkable. But to stay with her, wouldn't that be taking advantage of a vulnerable woman?

Of course she was vulnerable—what other reason could she have for asking him to stay? He doubted she even liked him very much. She'd kissed him once, that's true. But only, if he remembered correctly, because she'd just gotten one helluva shock.

He'd been strong enough to walk away from what she'd offered him that night, hadn't he? What had changed? Why did it seem so much harder now?

The answer was obvious: *You've changed, Holt.*

Yes, but she hasn't. And she's had more than one shock today.

"If you need me to, sure," he said calmly, as he tried to pluck words of reason out of the chaos of his thoughts. *She's had a break-in, you idiot. She's uneasy about staying alone. That's all it is.* "Be glad to. I'll, uh…just bed down on the couch. If you've got a pillow and a blanket…"

She tilted her head and made a derisive sound. "Jeez, Kincaid, what are you, *twelve?*" Her eyes met his, bright and brave. "I'm not asking you to a damn sleepover. I don't need you to protect me. I don't want you to sleep on the couch. Don't you get it? I want you to stay with *me.*"

He didn't say a word, not one word. Just stood there and looked at her, and for once she couldn't read him at all.

Her first impulse was to hit him—anything to jar that stony expression off his face. Her second was to cover her face, hide her eyes. But she wouldn't give him the satisfaction of knowing how devastating his rejection was.

She felt cold, and any moment now she was going to start to shake.

It took all her courage not to look away and all her strength just to make her facial muscles form a smile. "Well, I sure as hell am not gonna beg," she said, and pushed past him, wanting only now to get away.

His fingers closed around her upper arm, and her response was automatic. She jerked back against his grip, and for a few seconds there was a kind of silent tug-of-war, her desperation against his greater strength.

Finally, he said in a low growl, "For God's sake, Billie—" and she gave a sharp little cry as he pulled her into a hard embrace.

It was what she'd wanted, what she'd asked for. She had no idea why she went on fighting him; her reasoning mind had deserted her. She'd managed to get her arms folded up between her chest and his and refused to let herself give in to the temptation his body offered... the warmth, the strength, the comfort she yearned for.

"Don't do me any favors," she managed to get out between clenched teeth as she struggled.

Above her head she heard a small gust of a laugh, and when she looked up in fury, his head swooped down with the quickness of a hunting hawk. She had time only for a muffled and wordless protest, and then her mouth was no longer hers to control. He simply took it... claimed it...made it his.

And she had no objection. Her reason had already fled, and the same primitive imperatives that had made her fight him so mindlessly now compelled her to surrender. She felt herself growing weak and soft, and all her muscles becoming pliant. Her head fell back because her neck would no longer support it, but that was all right, because his hand was there to provide a cradle for it instead. Of their own accord her arms abandoned their barricade and crept around him like soldiers quitting the battlefield. And it was then, when her guard had been vanquished and she was left defenseless, that she felt it begin...the insidious invasion of emotions she'd been holding at bay for so long. First the ache...in another moment there would be tears.

I can't...I can't.

From somewhere, some reserve she didn't know she had, she found the will to pull herself back from the edge. Back...from the brink, yes, but not from *him*. No...because he felt too good, and she needed him too much.

And so, finding her mouth once again hers to control, she now gave it up to him. And remembered as she did how good he'd felt before when she'd kissed him. And wondered why she'd waited so long to kiss him again.

Her senses returned and they brought her pleasure, something she'd almost forgotten these past few days, and was surprised she could still experience. He smelled good...that elusive aftershave she'd noticed before, and the warm, earthy scent that was essentially, unmistakably *male*. He tasted pleasantly of the coffee they'd both been drinking. Her ears were filled with muted sounds, like the throbbing of distant drums...heartbeats and soft sighs and murmurs, and the *shush* of skin on skin. But mostly, the sense that dominated, that ruled, that overwhelmed, was *feeling*.

Every nerve ending in her body seemed to be alive and humming, quivering with eagerness for his touch.

And everywhere he touched her the pleasure was almost too intense to bear. So intense it brought tears to her eyes, and because she could not, *would not* cry, she laughed instead. A soft little gulp of laughter, caught in the sweet warmth of his mouth.

She felt his lips curve against hers in an answering smile, and she lifted one hand to touch his face. Her fingertips tingled exquisitely from their contact with the roughness of beard and the vibrant warmth of skin beneath, and her smile blossomed against his. She was shaking now, with silent laughter that was her only available release for the emotions that theatened to overwhelm her, and she felt his hand touching her face in much the same way she touched his.

It seemed a long time that they remained like that, lips touching, alternately forming smiles and kisses, fingertips exploring the vibrant, constantly changing landscape of each other's faces, bodies melding so naturally together she almost didn't notice the intimate ways they'd begun to shift and cling.

Then he let a breath out, long and slow, and his hand moved to cup her cheek, fingertips combing into her hair as he lifted his head and pressed a kiss to her forehead. She tensed then, waiting for him to release her, wondering how she'd bear it when he did. But instead he whispered words against her sweat-damp skin.

"Does this feel like I'm doing you a favor?"

Chapter 7

She needs me, Holt thought. *That's all this is.*

She needs me, he told his conscience, *and I'm not walking out on her.*

Gotcha, his conscience replied. *Reading you loud and clear.*

For a while then, blessedly, he didn't have to think at all. Kissing Billie, he was discovering, was a full-time occupation, an all-encompassing pleasure, one that involved every part of him, including his brain. *And your heart, too? Yeah, what about that, Holt?*

But that, too, was something he didn't have to think about. At least, not then.

That fascinating mouth of hers, with its impish little

up-turn at the corners…who would've thought it could feel so lush and ripe and full of sweetness? And her hands—card-player's hands with their nimble fingers—no surprise that they should be so clever, but who would've thought they could also be gentle, almost tender in the way they touched his face. In stature she was petite, her body small and compact, well-muscled and tidy…but who would've thought she could feel so soft, and fill his arms so completely.

Then, once again they were breathing in ragged little gusts of air, clinging to each other, and Holt wondered if she was trying as hard as he was not to show how shaken she felt. If she was wondering, as he was, what to do next.

About then was when she said, "Okay," and cleared her throat, pressed her palm against his chest and stared at it. He could see her forehead wrinkle with a frown.

"Yeah," he said, and cleared his throat, too, not really helping much.

"This is the really awkward part," she said, and valiantly lifted her face to meet his eyes. "I don't suppose you, uh…came prepared for this. I mean, I understand if you don't have anything, but the thing is, I'm pretty sure I don't. I'm covered for the pregnancy thing—yeah, learned my lesson there—and I'm clean, too. Had myself tested before Hannah Grace was born, and I've been careful since, but I don't expect you to just trust me. I mean, you'd have to be pretty stupid to—"

"Billie," he said, "shut up." He kissed her again, but

a shorter time than before. When he lifted his head she started to say something else, so he kissed her again, for a lot longer, and this time when he released her mouth she just licked her lips and stared at him, slightly cross-eyed.

"You'd be stupid to trust me, too," he said softly, "but I think we're both in luck. I drove down from Reno and came straight here this morning. I've got my overnighter in the car. I'm pretty sure there's something in there."

She was gazing at him in wonder. Her dimples flashed, and his heart gave a little leap, the way it did when he caught a glimpse of a deer dashing across Laurel Canyon Boulevard in the early, early morning.

"Hold that thought," he murmured, then touched a kiss to the tip of her nose and left her.

All the time he was getting his suitcase out of the Mustang, locking up, heading back to the house, he refused to let himself think about anything except what he was doing at that moment in time. *Don't think, don't analyze...stay in the here and now.* That's what he told himself whenever a glimmer of thought tried to sneak past his mental firewalls: *Here and now. That's all that matters.*

Back in Billie's house, he found she'd turned off the lights in the kitchen. Following the glow from the hallway, he made his way to its source, which was the larger of the two bedrooms he'd cleared earlier while checking for intruders. He'd noticed then that although it lacked frills, it was a distinctly feminine room, done in neutral tones of cream and tan, with accents of black and green. There were plants near the windows, which were curtained now against the darkness, and Audubon prints and Ansel Adams photographs in simple frames on the walls. Now, with Billie added to the setting, he realized how perfectly the room suited her. And what an intimate thing it was, to share that room with her. He wondered if she knew.

She was standing beside the bed, which was neatly made, with an assortment of throw pillows casually arranged on top of the spread. The only light came from the lamp on the table beside the bed, which she'd evidently just switched on. She lifted her head and smiled at him, but without dimples.

"Okay, Kincaid, this is your chance," she said in a tone that wanted to be airy, the tension she was trying to hide betrayed by only the slightest of tremors.

He set down his overnighter and returned the smile in a tentative way. "Chance? For what?"

"To change your mind." She turned to him, moving her body side to side in a way that suggested a wavering of will. "You know—the moment's passed and we've both cooled down...pulses steady. Isn't this where reason and common sense usually step in?"

"And have they?" When she only clasped her arms across herself and looked away without answering, he persisted gently, "Are *you* having second thoughts?"

She gave a sharp little laugh and brought her eyes back to him. They seemed to shimmer in the lamplight.

"I asked you to stay with me, remember? Because I, um—" She closed her eyes and struggled with it, and he took pity on her and mentally filled in the words she couldn't bring herself to say.

You need me.

"Billie, no, I haven't changed my mind. If you need me, I'll stay."

She looked at him for a long moment, smiling that little half smile, then slowly shook her head and whispered, "Kincaid, you are such a Boy Scout."

"Boy Scout?" He gave a surprised huff of laughter. "Don't think I've ever been called that before. And why is it," he added wryly, "I get the feeling you don't mean that as a compliment?"

"I do, actually. I haven't met that many Boy Scouts in my life...." She studied him thoughtfully, and her eyes seemed to kindle. He felt their heat from where he stood, two full arm's lengths away. "Who would've guessed. That's sure not what I thought of when I first met you."

"Yeah? What did you think of, then?" He realized they were speaking in low murmurs, the tone lovers use to exchange erotic suggestions under cover of darkness, though there was still that distance between them. A distance that seemed vast and unbridgeable.

"Harry Callahan," she said.

"Who?"

"You know—Clint Eastwood movies...Dirty Harry..."

He burst out laughing—he couldn't help it.

"You know," she said, watching him with her head

slightly cocked, "I think that's the first time I've ever seen you do that."

"Do what?"

She gave a little shrug. "Never mind—it's gone now. It was nice while it lasted, though."

She turned to take the pillows off the bed, saying over her shoulder as she did, "Bathroom's across the hall—it's all yours." She didn't see him go.

She told herself not to think, but, as thoughts will, they came anyway. *Why am I doing this? I guess I know why, I know what I think is why, but why do I need him when I've done all right without him up to now?*

She began to undress, her fingers stiff and cold on the zipper of her jeans, tossing her clothes in the general direction of the dresser on the other side of the bed. It seemed too…intimate, too personal, to leave them lying where he would see them when he returned.

When he returns…

She tried not to think about how it would be. How he would look.

His body…

I wish he'd make this easier for me. He's leaving it up to me to call the shots. I understand why, but I almost wish he'd take the lead. Funny…who would've thought he'd turn out to be so damned nice?

I don't need him to be nice. I need him to kiss me again. I need him to hold me. I need him to not let me think….

She lifted the corner of the bedclothes and crawled between the sheets, shifting herself all the way to the other side of the bed to leave room for him. The sheet rasped across her goose-bumpy skin like sandpaper. She was shivering, and no matter how hard she tried she couldn't make herself stop.

Holt left the bathroom and crossed the hall, his shaving kit in his hands and images of Billie in his mind. Not voluptuous, fantasy images—he didn't have enough intimate knowledge of her body nor enough prurient imagination to provide material for those—but flashback images of her face in all its different moods, constantly changing, like a kaleidoscope. He didn't try to stop them. It was better than thinking.

He hadn't any expectations of what he'd see when he walked back into her bedroom, but even so, the scene that met his eyes jolted him in ways he couldn't explain. He wished there had been a camera in his mind, some way of freezing that moment in his memory. Not a scene that could be considered sexy or erotic, not in the usual sense: Her face—just her face, her body a surprisingly small disturbance beneath the covers—nestled in a pile of pillows, its features indistinct, its outline blurred in the soft lamplight though the colors were pure and vivid, like a watercolor painting on silk. But for a moment he felt a weakening in his knees and that odd dropping sensation in his chest, and the need to remind himself all over again what he was doing here.

She needs you, Kincaid—that's all this is. Be good to her…handle with care…and when the time comes, let her go.

She raised herself on one elbow and watched him walk toward her, wearing all his clothes and carrying what appeared to be a small toiletries kit in his hands. She searched his face for a hint of a smile. Instead, his eyes seemed to burn her, and she wondered how blue eyes could do that.

"I left the light on for you," she said in a rasping voice. "You can turn it off, if you want to."

He placed the kit on the table beside the lamp and looked down at her. "Would you like it off?" he asked as he began to unbutton his sleeve cuffs.

She shrugged, and he reached for the lamp. "No— wait," she said breathlessly, "leave it on."

Why was this so hard? Why did it feel so awkward?

Because you never asked a man to share your bed before. Always before, sex was something that just sort of happened, or it was his idea and you went along with it. It was fun and games. Or two warm bodies obeying a biological urge. Whatever.

So…why does this feel like something more?

Because you're using him, maybe? Because you have a conscience after all?

But if she did, it was playing hide-and-seek with her, ducking out of sight again as she watched his fingers work their way down the front of his shirt, then pull the two halves apart and at the same time free of the waistband of his pants. It shouldn't have been a big thing to her, this first glimpse of his body, so the little hitch in her breathing caught her by surprise. She searched his face for some sign that he'd noticed, but his intent expression, the slight, compassionate frown, didn't waver. She caught her lower lip between her teeth and watched him fold his shirt in half and lay it on the floor beside the night table, then take his gun out of its holster, check it briefly, then lay it carefully on top of the shirt.

His body pleased her; with not much fat to hide the pull and tug of tendons and ligaments, she could see the way muscle moved beneath pale skin in sculpted patterns. She liked that he wasn't tan—which she thought showed a lack of vanity—and that the hair on his chest was beginning to gray a little, to match the silver at his temples.

"Are you always so neat and tidy?" she asked in a voice that felt unreliable, and was surprised when he smiled.

"No," he said, as he unzipped his pants, "but I do try to be a well-behaved houseguest."

She let go a small gust of nervous laughter. "Houseguest. Is that what you are?"

He didn't answer, but reached instead to turn out the lamp.

The bed jolted as he sat on the edge of it, and wobbled with his movements as he divested himself of the rest of his clothes, shoes and socks. She felt the cold caress of wind when he lifted the covers and slipped easily between them. She waited for him to reach for her, to come to her, and she thought resentfully, *Do I have to ask him to hold me?* She couldn't seem to stop shivering.

"Billie," his voice came out of the new darkness, "are you cold?"

"No," she said, furious. *Just hold me, dammit.*

He gave a little growling sigh and put out his arm and she scooted over into its curve. He drew her close to him and she nestled against his body, but didn't relax. He could feel her shivering, and her body's shape felt warm and silky but unyielding, like a sun-warmed sculpture in polished marble.

He'd never thought of himself as a sensitive person, but uppermost in his consciousness was the thought: *I want to do this right. For her.*

He didn't want to think about what that meant.

Though it was dark already, he closed his eyes. And though he'd never seen her body, he began to see it now with his hands...his fingers.

She was small—he'd known that. But beneath skin as soft and fragile as something newly born her muscles were firm, her bones strong. Woman-strong. His mind's eye followed his hand along the graceful, sweeping curve of her spine, down into the valley, then up the gentle rise...and the roundness of her bottom seemed custom-made to fit his hand. Moving slowly on, even the jut of her pelvic bone seemed soft to him beneath the velvet drape of her skin, and her belly, covered in that same velvet, quivered when he stroked it like the hide of a restless tiger. He rested his hand in the hollow below her rib cage and let his fingers play for a moment along the undulations of muscle and bone while she sucked in her stomach and her breathing hung suspended. Then, slowly, he raised his hand along her ribs to cover one small, round breast.

Small, yes…but it filled his hand to perfection. He heard her breath sigh between her lips, and realized only then that she'd turned her face into the hollow of his neck. The warmth of her sigh poured over his skin like liquid sunlight. Her legs were shifting, too, one knee drawing up to rest on his thigh.

"You're not shivering anymore," he whispered, stirring the feathers of her hair. She didn't reply. He counted the thumps of her heartbeat against his arm, then added, "It's okay if you just want to go to sleep. You've had a long day. You don't need to feel—"

"Hush up, Harry," she said. "Just kiss me."

After that it was easy. What was it about kissing this man, she wondered, that blew every conscious thought out of her head? When he kissed her a warm darkness seemed to settle over her, the darkness of a sultry summer night, and the air felt like melted butter on her skin. She heard only the hum of her own life forces, and maybe his, too, and the song they made filled her head and her whole being, as compelling, as hypnotic as the throbbing rhythm of drums. His mouth…his kiss…became her world, and she never wanted it to end.

But it did—it had to. And she gasped a breath, tangled her fingers in his hair and growled from the depths of her need, *"Don't…stop."*

"I won't," he whispered. His hands cradled her head; his thumbs stroked her cheekbones…her temples. His body became a blessed weight, an all-encompassing embrace. He whispered it again, into her mouth. "I won't...stop...."

Holt came awake with two realizations clear in his mind. One, he'd slept well and without dreams, at least none he recalled. And two, Billie was very close by. For a few moments then, he kept his eyes closed and let his other senses flood him with evidence of her presence: Her breathing, an uneven cadence to it that told him she was awake; a fresh, sweet scent reminiscent of flower gardens with a hint of toothpaste that suggested she'd been up and perhaps showered; a humid warmth that was simply woman, and uniquely *her*.

He opened his eyes and discovered she was sitting cross-legged on the bed next to him, hands clasped, elbows resting on her knees, watching him. Her eyes were dark and unreadable in the thin early morning light. His first impulse was to hook his hand around her neck and pull her down for a good-morning kiss, but because he was aware of the fact that she'd brushed her teeth and he hadn't, and that there was something vaguely wary about the set of her shoulders, he settled for a murmured, "Mornin', sunshine," instead.

She leaned down to kiss him, but in a brief, distracted way.

He muttered, "Hmm... Sorry—you smell good and I don't. Be right back..." and rolled out of bed and headed for the bathroom.

When he came back, she was still sitting where he'd

left her, wearing a T-shirt a few sizes too big for her that made it impossible for him to tell if she was wearing anything else underneath. But since it was obviously early, barely daylight, and she didn't seem to be eager to be up and about, instead of reaching for his clothes, he got back into bed, too.

She cleared her throat, a sound full of portent. "Hey, Kincaid…"

He turned on his side and pulled the sheet up over his hip, propped his elbow on the pillows and leaned his head on his hand. "Billie?" he said somberly.

"I want you to know something, okay?" Her voice sounded blunt and self-conscious. A suspenseful little pulse began to tap-tap in his stomach. She closed her eyes briefly and held up one hand. "Look, don't get me wrong—last night was great. I mean—" she gave a breathy laugh and her voice dropped an octave "—more than great—really, it was—" She looked away, obviously stalled, and he saw her throat move with a painful swallow.

The tap-tapping in his belly became his heart going thump-thump… "Billie," he said gently, "it's okay, spit it out." He offered an encouraging smile. "I sense a *but* in there somewhere."

She hauled in a breath that lifted her shoulders, and the words came out in a rush. "I just want you to know, you don't have to be afraid I'm going to be making, um, you know…demands. I don't expect you to say nice words…stick around…ask me out—stuff like that."

She paused, frowned, and he murmured a tentative, "Okay…" But she wasn't finished.

"I mean, look, let's face it, you're not a forever kind of guy, right? I just want you to know I'm cool with that. Because for one thing, I'm not a forever kind of woman, either." She gave herself a little concluding shake and her gaze came back to him, fierce and intent. "So—we straight on that?"

He gazed back at her. There was a weird, fluttery feeling in his chest, and he didn't know whether it was laughter or tenderness. He settled for a smile. "Yeah, Billie, we're straight. No forevers, no expectations, no nice words." He paused a beat. "Does this mean I don't get to tell you you're beautiful?"

She jerked back as if he'd insulted her. "You're making fun of me."

He lifted his hand and brushed her cheek with the backs of his fingers, ran his thumb lightly across her lower lip. "I'd never do that."

She licked her lip where he'd touched it. "I told you, you don't have to say things like that to me, just because…"

"I know I don't have to…just because. I can say it if it's true, though…right?"

She clasped her hands tightly together and hugged her arms against her sides like a self-conscious child, and didn't answer. What he wanted to do at that moment was take her down into the tumbled sheets and show her without the pretty words just how beautiful she was to him. Instead, he let his hand fall away from her and said softly, "I have one question, though. You don't know me all that well…so how do you know what kind of guy I am—forever-wise?"

She unclasped her hands and held one up, thumb extended. "One, you're not married." A forefinger joined the thumb. "Two, you've never been married." Another finger. "You're in your forties, you live alone—" her hand returned to join its mate in her lap, and she shrugged. "Obviously not somebody who's into commitment." She tilted her head. "Just out of curiosity, what happened?"

"What…happened?"

"To make you that way. I mean, you know why I'm the way I am. So, what's your story, Kincaid? Come on—give. It's only fair."

He just stared at her, his face stony, and her heart did a weird little skip-hop she'd never felt before. She wanted to reach out and touch his face the way he'd touched hers—a way no man had ever touched her before, that she could recall. She wanted to touch him like that and say the words that were in her mind.

Who hurt you, Holt? Who made you afraid to trust anyone with your heart?

"You're right," he said, just when she'd been sure he wouldn't answer. "It is only fair. So, here it is, my reason—my *excuse,* I should say—for choosing to remain unencumbered by…emotional attachments." His hand reached out for her again, this time to lie briefly on her shoulder, then brush lightly down her arm. And his eyes held hers like a hypnotist's, with that ice-blue gaze she was beginning to realize was anything but cold.

"I was five years old. I remember it because I'd just had my birthday party, and there was a pony." A smile flickered briefly. "I think that was the first and last time I was ever on a horse. Anyway, a couple of days later, my parents left me with a babysitter and went out to dinner and a movie, and never came back."

He said it so matter-of-factly, it was a moment before it registered. She did a little double take, then whispered, "What happened? Was it a car crash?"

His hand continued its idle journey up and down her arm. "Their car was found in the movie theater parking lot. My parents never were. They just disappeared."

She stared at him, appalled, half-disbelieving. "That's…crazy. People don't just disappear."

"Actually, they do—more often than you'd suppose." His eyes dropped to his hand, which had left her arm to brush across the front of her T-shirt where her nipples had beaded against the clinging cloth.

She shivered. "What happened? To you, I mean?"

"Well, my babysitter told me lies, at first. Everybody did. About how my parents had had to go away suddenly, but they'd be back soon. Eventually, I was sent to live with my mother's aunt. She was a school-teacher—unmarried. She did the best she could, I'll give her that." His smile was wry, his eyes forgiving. "Let's just say she wasn't a warm and fuzzy sort of person." He shrugged in a dismissive way that didn't alter the smile. "She died when I was seventeen, and I joined the army soon after. When I got out of the service, I decided I wanted to become a cop—a detective—so I could find out what happened to my folks."

"And did you?" It was hard to keep her voice steady, with his roving hand straying downward, stroking lightly across her thigh...

"No," he said. "But I found out I was more interested in finding missing people than catching bad ones, so I quit the force and that's what I've been doing." He didn't say any more, and a certain wariness in his eyes told her he probably wasn't accustomed to saying even that much.

That awareness made her feel chastened and humble, at first. Even, in an odd sort of way, vulnerable, too. But then a new feeling began to grow in her, one she remembered experiencing only once before in her life—the day her daughter was born. Something so primal she couldn't even put a name to it. Or didn't want to. But whatever it was, it filled her with a new kind of power and purpose.

All the while this momentous thing was happening inside her, she was looking into Holt's eyes and he was gazing back at her. His hand was sliding under her T-shirt and finding her nakedness all open to him, his for the taking. First, she gasped...shuddered...melted. Then, with her new inner strength, whispered, "No..." and leaned over to find his mouth, and at the same time was unfolding herself, finding her way inside the covers to sink against him and lay her body full length on his.

He made a sound low in his throat and his hands were big and warm on her back, stroking downward to hold her buttocks, then on to her thighs. But when he urged them apart, she murmured once more, "No..." mingling the word with the dark, sweet essence of his mouth. And then she slid down his body, slowly, kissing every part of him she met on the way, her heart growing quivery at the incredible sleekness of his skin. His hands were light on her sides, letting her slip between them, and his breath escaped him in the gentlest of sighs when she nestled her face in his warm, damp hair and kissed him there.

When he could take no more, he pulled her up to him and lifted his own body to meet her, and they found each other like old lovers after too long a time apart. He wrapped his arms around her, one low on her spine, the other cradling her head, and she brought her legs around his waist and arched to press her torso against his, nesting her breasts in the tickling softness of his chest hair.

Her mouth found his and she opened to him with no reservation at all, and would have gladly lost herself there, but for the sharp gasp that rushed from her throat when he seated himself deep inside her. He caught the gust of breath in his own mouth and held them both still, feeling the off-rhythm thumping of their combined heartbeats, until one or the other—maybe both—of them began to tremble.

Then he tore his mouth from her and in a rasping whisper said, "Billie...I—"

And for the third time she said it, a low, guttural

sound from deep in her throat. "*No*—no words. Just…
make love to me."

"I will…I am…do you feel me loving you?"

And she answered, "Yes…yes…yes…" until she
began to shake with dizzy laughter, the kind that sometimes comes with tears.

The next time they woke it was noon, or almost. This
time hunger drove them out of bed and back to the
kitchen, where a chilly November breeze was blowing
through the broken window. While Billie made coffee,
Holt taped a flattened cardboard cereal box over the
hole, then turned on the noontime news.

"I usually eat peanut butter toast for breakfast,"
Billie called from the other side of the counter. "Is that
okay with you?"

"Yeah…fine," he said absently, watching the crawl
across the bottom of the television screen. He heard the
thump-click of the bread being pushed down in the
toaster and turned to say over his shoulder, "Hey, there's
an Amber Alert."

She was coming toward him, rounding the end of the
counter carrying a steaming cup of coffee, smiling. Her
eyes went past him to the screen, and the smile seemed
to dissolve into a look of utter bewilderment. "Holt?"
she said, with almost no sound. The cup in her hands
began to wobble, and he snaked out a hand and rescued
it just in time to keep it from crashing to the floor.

He was licking his hand where the scalding coffee

had slopped over and burned it when he turned back to the news broadcast. Then he no longer felt the scald. He felt as if all the air in his body had been sucked out of him.

Billie moved beside him in stunned silence, and together they stared at the face on the screen…the face of a little girl about ten years old, a little girl with blond hair and magical golden eyes.

Chapter 8

"*Hannah Grace Bachman disappeared this morning while walking to school in this quiet suburban neighborhood just northwest of Reno. She was last seen wearing...*"

"This can't be a coincidence," Holt said unevenly. "Who do you know who'd—"

"It's got to be Miley." Her voice was tight and breathless, like his was, both of them sounding like someone who's just taken a blow to the stomach. "Who else could it be? He's the only one who knew...but how could he have known where she was? I didn't even know until you gave me that piece of paper—" Her face crumpled—for one brief moment—then settled into a mask of rigid control. She turned in a swift, unbalanced jerk and gripped the edge of the countertop to steady herself. "The paper—the one with her name and address—where is it? I put it down, right here. Did you see it? When we got home last night? It's not here. It's not *here,* Holt—"

"Miley must have found it when he broke in here yesterday," he said, more calmly than he felt. "Probably right after we left. He was looking for the money, you said. I guess he figured he'd found a way to get it out of you."

"This is my fault." She was pacing, hugging herself, her face still empty of all emotion. Only her eyes were alive, crackling with rage, and he understood now why she wore the sunglasses when she played cards. "I should never have asked you to find her. It was stupid. Why did I think I had anything to give her? It was selfish, that's what it was. Stupid and selfish. God, I can't even—"

"Cut it out. You may be the reason this happened, but it's hardly your *fault.* Look, there's one good thing, at least. He's not likely to hurt her, right?"

She stopped pacing to give him a hard look. Then she seemed to deflate as she sagged back against the counter. "I don't know. Miley's a weasel and a coward, but he's desperate. Plus, the people he owes money to probably wouldn't hesitate to hurt him and anybody else if it'll get them what they want. And like I told you—I can't get to the money. At least, I don't know how to get to it. It's in an 'irrevocable trust'—whatever that means."

"It means you can't get to it," Holt said grimly.

"Okay, so what should we do?" She seemed to vibrate with energy. He thought of a warrior, adrenaline-charged and primed for battle.

He picked up the remote and thumbed the television off. "The first thing we have to do is go to the police."

"Go to…the police." She said it the way someone would who hasn't had many reasons to be reassured by that prospect.

He took her gently by the arms. "Think, Billie. That cabdriver is going to do so for sure, the minute he sees that Amber Alert. If he hasn't already. I'm expecting to hear sirens any second."

She stared at him as if the words weren't making sense, and what he wanted to do more than anything in the world was pull her into his arms and just hold her for a while, until the shock of this had diminished, or at least let her know he was there to prop her up if she wanted to break down.

Fat chance of that, he thought. And anyway, there wasn't time. He planted a quick kiss on her forehead and was about to release her when the phone rang, making them both jump and clutch at each other.

She stared at it as she might a coiled rattler, then looked back at him with a question in her eyes. He nodded. She walked over to the counter, wiped her hands on her bare thighs and picked up the phone.

Her heart banged inside her chest like something trapped and trying desperately to get out. She tried to take a breath, but there was no place to put it, so she held it and managed a raspy, "Hello?"

When Billie heard the voice on the other end she almost dropped the phone. She wanted to hurl it through the window…pound it against something until it broke into a thousand pieces.

"Hey, Billie, you watchin' television? You seen that Amber Alert thing they got goin' right now?" The voice sounded high, excited. Scared.

He better be scared because I'm going to kill him, she thought.

Her rage-fogged vision cleared enough so that she could see Holt trying to get her attention, his eyebrows raised in a frowning question. She threw him a look and gave a jerky nod, and he mouthed the word *speaker.*

She jerked the phone away from her ear, but the buttons on it were shimmering and out of focus, and her hands were shaking too hard to do anything with them anyway. Holt took the instrument out of her hands, punched a button, and Miley's voice came slinking into the room.

"—you better turn it on. I'm not kiddin'—"

"I've seen it." She felt like flint, the stuff of ancient spears—brittle, hard, capable of killing. "If you hurt her—"

"Jeez, Billie! What kinda guy do you think I am? I'm not—"

"I know what kind of guy you are, Miley—the kind who'd do anything to save his own ass. And if you touch one hair on my daughter's head—"

"Hey. You got no room to threaten me. I'm holding the cards, here, not you. You give me what I want, I give her back to her parents, good as new. It's as simple as that."

Billie looked at Holt, then closed her eyes so he wouldn't see her fear. Her fingers tightened around the phone, which had grown slippery in her hand. "Look I told you the truth, Miley. I don't have the money. I can't give you what I don't have."

"Hey…that's cool. You don't have the quarter mil anymore—I get it. So, you just have to win some more. I got the buy-in money and you're all signed up."

Her stomach went cold. "What are you talking about?"

"The tournament—at the Mirage. You're in. All you have to do is show up—and win, of course. You win the tournament, you give me what I need, the kid here goes home, and you get to take home what's left of the pot. Everybody wins."

"You are insane," she said, unable to keep her voice steady. "I haven't played a hand in more than three years. I'm out of practice. And what if the cards don't go my way? You can't seriously think—"

"You think I'm not serious?" His voice went shrill. "You think this isn't serious, what I'm doing here? This oughta show you how serious I am. This is my *life* I'm talkin' about. You better win, Billie. You hear me? You *better* win, and win big. Or else this kid isn't ever gonna see her mommy and daddy again."

"Miley, wait! At least tell me—"

But there was nothing but a dial tone. She let the

phone slip from her fingers and never even saw where it fell. Her knees buckled. She felt Holt's arms come around her and allowed herself to be held, and to hold on to him, for a moment. Just a moment. Then she pushed away from him, straightened and said hoarsely, "I'm okay. I'm okay."

He let her go. She turned in a lost sort of way and combed the fingers of both hands through her hair. Coughed, and threw him a fierce look. "So…I guess we really have to go to the cops, huh?"

"Yeah, we do. We're going to be their number-one suspects the minute that cabbie puts two and two together."

"What makes you think they're going to believe us?" she said in a bleak voice. "And if I'm in jail, how am I going to—"

"I thought about that, too. I think I know somebody who can help us."

"So, you still have friends in law enforcement?"

"You could say that." He gave her a dark smile. "Go get dressed so we can get out of here before the cops show up on your doorstep. I'll tell you about it on the way."

He waited until he heard her closet door slide back, then picked up the phone from the counter where she'd dropped it, hoping there was caller ID. There was. He hit the button for incoming calls, and at the same time he was opening and closing drawers, looking for pencil and paper. He found what he needed on the third try, scribbled down the number of the last call and tucked the paper in his shirt pocket. Then he took out his cell phone and scrolled down through his speed-dial list to the one he wanted.

A brusque voice answered on the second ring. "Portland P.D., Homicide, this is Detective Ochoa—can I help you?"

"Uh…yeah," Holt said, "I'm looking for Wade. IIc anywhere around, by any chance? This is a friend of his—Holt Kincaid—I think we met last spring, during that serial killer thing…"

"Holt Kincaid…oh, yeah—the P.I., right? Sure, I remember you. Wade's out of the office, but I'll tell him you called."

"He on a case?" Holt's hopes of help were sinking fast.

The Portland detective chuckled. "Nah…I think he went home to have lunch with his wife. You know how these newlyweds are. If you have his cell or home number, you might try him there."

"Thanks," Holt said, and disconnected. Letting out an impatient breath, he checked his speed dial again. This time he got voice mail.

"Hey, Wade, this is Holt Kincaid. Give me a call back on my cell when you get this message. Thanks." He hesitated, then added, "It's important."

He disconnected and was searching his phone book for more options when Billie came in looking flushed, tucking the tail of a black long-sleeved pullover shirt into the waistband of khaki cargo pants. She looked ready to take on the world, he thought. All she needed was a flak vest with big letters on the back that said SWAT.

"Ready?" She sounded out of breath.

"Yeah." He tucked his cell phone in his pocket, snatched up his jacket from the chair back he'd hung it on last night—a lifetime ago. "You happen to know where the police station is?"

Naturally, his cell phone rang on the way, and just as he was maneuvering through erratic lunch-hour traffic. He fumbled the phone out of his pocket and handed it to Billie.

"Here…I don't talk and drive. Tell him I'll be with him as soon as I find a place to park."

He heard her say, "Holt Kincaid's cell phone…" and then, "Yeah, he's right here. He just has to find a place to park. Hold on." She held the phone face down on her thigh. "He says it's Wade, returning your call."

"Yeah, I know." Muttering under his breath, Holt made a right turn down a side street and into the parking lot of an auto parts store. He pulled into an empty space and left the motor running. Billie handed him the phone.

"Hey, buddy," he said.

Wade's voice came back to him, sharp with suspicion. "Who was I just talking to?"

Holt said, "Uh…" and glanced over at Billie.

"You call me outta the blue, tell me to call you back, it's important. So I do, and a woman answers the phone. You found her, didn't you? Brooke told us you thought you might have. Tell me that wasn't my baby sister I was just talking to."

"Uh…" said Holt again, but this time at least he had the presence of mind not to look at Billie. "Yeah…and I'll tell you all about that later. Right now, though, we've got a bit of a situation. May have. I don't suppose you have any friends in the Las Vegas Police Department?"

"We?" Wade's tone was instantly serious. "Is my sister in trouble with the law? *Again?* My God, Kincaid, is this another situation like Brooke's?"

"No, no—nothing like that. At least…I hope not. May need you to put in a good word for us, though. If you wouldn't mind."

"Mind? Hell, I'll do better than that. I've got some personal time coming. How 'bout I see you there in… say, what?" There was some muffled mumbling, and then, in the kind of quiet voice he'd probably use to calm distraught witnesses: "Tee's already looking up flights. She says it's important, and you know I don't argue with her about things like that."

"Wade? If you wouldn't mind, it might be a good idea to bring her along, too."

Wade gave a snort of laughter. "You think she'd let me leave her behind? She's just reminded me we haven't really had a honeymoon yet, plus she's never been to Vegas. We're on our way, my friend. You just hang in there—and in the meantime, you take good care of my baby sister, you hear me?"

"I mean to," Holt said softly, and disconnected. He looked over at Billie and found her watching him, and for once he couldn't read her eyes. "What?" he said as he handed her the phone, more sharply than he meant.

Her gaze didn't waver. She took a quick little breath, hesitated another second, then said slowly, "I've just been remembering something. You told me one of my brothers is named Wade, and that he's a cop in Portland, Oregon. Tell me the truth, Kincaid. Was I just talking to my brother?"

"Yeah, you were." And because he suddenly realized his own emotions were piling up behind the dam of his self-control, and he for sure didn't want to deal with her family issues, he put the Mustang in Reverse and backed out of the parking space.

"And he knows it was me?"

"Yep."

"And he's coming to help us? Just…like that?"

"You're his sister," Holt said flatly, as the Mustang lurched out of the parking lot and back onto the street. "It's what families do. Help each other when they need it. Get used to it."

She didn't reply, and he drove for a good way in silence.

It wasn't until he was pulling into the parking lot at the police headquarters that it hit him. He gave a sharp bark of laughter, and Billie's head jerked toward him.

"I just thought of something," he said, grinning and slowly shaking his head. "You're not gonna believe this. This brother of yours. He's a police detective, right?" She nodded in puzzled agreement. "And guess what, his last name is *Callahan.*"

She still looked uncomprehending, so he added in exasperation, "You said it—*Dirty Harry*, remember?"

She covered her eyes with one hand, laughing silently.

Billie had been in police stations before. Those past experiences had not been pleasant, and so far this one wasn't any better. She felt nervous and scared, for a lot of good reasons, but more than that, she felt *angry*. Betrayed. Those memories, those feelings…she thought she'd steered her life into a place where she'd never have to feel like that again. Yet, here she was. And she didn't know who to be mad at. Who to blame.

"I hate this," she whispered to Holt, and it seemed so natural now to tell him how she felt, although she'd never done that with anyone else before. "The way they look at you. They make me feel like I've done something bad even when I know I haven't."

"That just means you have a conscience."

He, at least, seemed unfazed by the fact that they'd been questioned, together and separately, for several hours. Meanwhile, Holt's Mustang and cell phone had been gone over with all the diligence the LVPD forensics teams could muster, and their identity documents checked and rechecked. Billie had even volunteered a sample of her DNA to corroborate her claim that she was the missing girl's biological mother. Which, as Holt had pointed out when she'd told him she was going to do it, could also work against her, since it would seem to give her a motive for kidnapping. Now they were together again, in a small, square room without windows, without much of anything in it except for a metal table and several hard chairs, and the single, unwavering eye of a video camera high in one corner.

"Do you think they believe us?"

"I think they'd like to." He was sitting relaxed in his chair, arms folded on his chest, and his eyes, resting on her, were calm. "Problem is, we're all they've got. And we're so perfect for it. Biological mom hires private investigator to find child she gave up for adoption, they go to see the kid, and the next day she's abducted? Doesn't get any more perfect than that." He smiled wryly. "Hell, I'm not even sure *I* believe us."

Her lips felt numb; she couldn't make herself smile back. "But...they'll check at the airport, won't they? They'll ask Tony. He'll tell them he brought us back here last night."

"Yes," Holt said gently, "and I'm sure they've already done that. Doesn't mean we—you—couldn't have hired somebody like Miley to kidnap your daughter."

She put a hand over her eyes and whispered, "Oh, God." After a moment she took her hand away and glared up at the video camera. "They're probably listening to us right now, aren't they?"

"Probably."

"They know I have a rap sheet, I guess...." Her stomach felt raw and sore, and there was a sick, sour taste in her mouth. "From when...I was on the street."

Yes...all the miserable, stupid things I did then, to stay alive. Panhandling, shoplifting, trespassing...but at least— She blurted it out. "I want you to know, I never did drugs. And I never turned tricks."

He sat up suddenly. Felt as if she'd slapped him. "My God—Billie..."

"You believe me, don't you?" She stared at him with hot, dry eyes.

The air between them was like a solid thing. He wanted to reach through it to touch her, but it seemed impenetrable. He said huskily, "I believe you. But it wouldn't matter to me if you had. I'd never judge you."

"Yeah, you would. And it would matter. You might not think so, but it would. You know why I didn't?" Her gaze didn't waver, just seemed to grow hotter and brighter—and at the same time more distant. Like stars. "I didn't because I figured if I was going to do that I might as well go back home. At least there I'd have food and a warm place to sleep."

What could he say? The effect of the words and that hot, hard gaze was enough to make him feel cold and shaky clear through to his insides. Staring back at her, he kept seeing all those battered young bodies he'd had to look at, in so many morgues, in so many cities, laid out cold and still with clean white sheets covering the evidence of how cruelly life had treated them. So many without names... All he could do was look at her and hope she'd understand his silence.

After the longest ten seconds he'd ever lived through, she sat back and exhaled sharply.

"Why are they still keeping us in here? They've asked us everything they possibly could. What are they waiting for?"

He cleared his throat. "Well, I think—" And just then the door opened to admit the Las Vegas detective they'd spent so much time with earlier in the day. Right behind him were the two people Holt wanted most in the whole wide world to see. "I think—" he finished, grinning as he rose to his feet "—for this."

As he went to greet his visitors, he caught a glimpse of a face gone white as chalk, and he knew then that what scared Billie Farrell—or Brenna Fallon—more than the entire Las Vegas Police Department combined was this moment, and what was about to take place. Meeting this man—Wade Callahan.

My brother.

She had no recollection of having risen to her feet, but she must have. Now she stood with her hands on the tabletop to steady herself and watched them come into the stark little room.

She saw him first—a tall man with broad shoulders and a slightly rumpled look, a face with a rock-solid jaw wearing a hint of beard shadow, close-cropped brown hair and heavily lashed eyes a deep, dark shade of blue. Right now those eyes were frowning and aimed straight at her, even while he was busy shaking Holt's hand and clapping him on the arm. Then he pushed past everyone else in the room, and tables and chairs, too, and she was swallowed up in the biggest, strongest hug she'd ever known.

Except, unbelievably, that big, strong body was shaking. She could feel the hard edge of his jaw pressed against her head, and her feet didn't touch the floor as he whispered, "Hey, baby sister. Nice to finally meet you. I'm your brother Wade."

She didn't dare speak. Didn't dare laugh, or even draw breath. She was so fragile, her self-control so tenuous, one word...just one sound...would smash it to pieces.

Then there was a sound, and she didn't break after all. A soft, almost comical, "Ahem..."

Wade released her with a shaken laugh. "Yeah...all right, I know. Sorry, Tee..." He turned to bring the other person, the woman, forward, although he kept Billie tucked in the curve of his arm. "Hey I want you to meet my wife. This is Tierney. Tierney...this is my sister Bren—"

"It's Billie," Holt said, from somewhere nearby.

The woman was lovely, with tousled blond hair and clear, beautiful blue eyes, so different from her husband's indigo, and worlds apart from Holt's hot-cold steel. She had sun-kissed skin, a scattering of freckles and a warm and generous smile. Something about her made Billie think of flowers.

"Hi, Billie," the blond woman said softly, and held out her hands to take Billie's. "Friends and family usually call me Tee." Her hands felt warm...so warm, and Billie realized hers were like ice.

"You read people's emotions," she said gruffly. "Holt told me." She tried to smile. "Guess this must be pretty intense, huh?"

Tierney's smile blossomed. "Oh, don't worry—I can block most people's most of the time." She gave Billie's hands a reassuring squeeze. "Think how awful it would be if I didn't."

But her eyes held Billie's for a few moments longer, and…it was the oddest thing. She wasn't psychic, she was sure of it—at least, she'd never even thought of such a thing before—but suddenly there was a voice inside her head, a voice that wasn't really a *voice* at all, more of a feeling, impossible to describe. And in words that weren't exactly words, but so clear it seemed as if they were words, it was saying, *You're not alone…we love you. No matter what happens, we're here with you now.*

"So," Holt said, "here's what we want you to do."

They were in a small squad room now—Holt and Billie, Wade and Tierney, several members of the Las Vegas Police Department assigned to the kidnapping case, and a couple guys from the FBI. They were scattered among the several desks in the room, some peering at computer screens or talking quietly on telephones.

Holt was sitting on the edge of a desk and Billie was standing in front of him, straight and stiff as a mannequin. He had his hands on her arms, but it wasn't enough. He wanted her *in* his arms. Wanted to do whatever he needed to do to get that dazed, scared, brave, stoic, *frozen* look off her face.

"You just need to buy us some time, okay?"

He waited for her nod and a barely audible, "Yeah, sure."

"All you need to do is to show up for the tournament, hang in for as long as you can. Give us time to find where he's holding her."

Her eyes looked flat and hopeless. "How can you? How can they? He could be… She could be anywhere."

He lowered his voice to a murmur and tipped his head toward the detectives poring over their computers in the room behind him. "These guys know their stuff, and they haven't been sitting around on their asses. They have some leads—they're working on those now." She just looked at him, clearly unconvinced. He forced a smile. "Plus, you've got me. I find people, remember?"

"Kincaid." One of the LVPD detectives—Holt was pretty sure his name was Vogel—held up an arm and beckoned him over to the desk where he was hunched over an array of electronic equipment along with a tech guy and one of the FBI agents. "I think we're ready here."

"Yeah…coming." Holt slid his backside off the desk but kept one hand on Billie's shoulder as he guided her over to where the three men were waiting. Her shoulder felt small-boned and defenseless, and he had to remind himself she was anything but.

The techie was a slightly overweight guy with

thinning red hair cut short and flat on top. He looked about nineteen. He handed Billie a phone, and Vogel said, "Okay, what I want you to do is call this guy Miley Todd back at the number he called you from. That's this number right here." He smoothed a piece of paper on the desk with one hand, and Holt recognized the note he'd scrawled before leaving Billie's. "We know it's a cell phone," Vogel went on, "so we can't trace it. But what we can do is try and ID the tower the signal's coming from. Understand? That'll narrow our search area. So we need you to keep him talking as long as you can. Can you do that?"

She nodded, and Holt saw her throat move. He thought she looked scared to death.

"Tell him you need proof he's got Hannah," he said, drawing her eyes to him, putting all the strength and confidence he could muster into the look he gave her. "Tell him you need to know she's all right. Keep him on the line as long as possible."

She nodded again. The techie donned a pair of head-phones and pointed to her. She took a breath, let it out and punched in the number. A moment later, everyone in the room could hear the *brrr* of the distant ring.

Once. Twice. Three times. Holt was willing to bet nobody in the room took a breath. Then there was a click, and a voice, high and scared and one he'd heard before, said, "Yeah—who's this?"

"It's me—Billie." Holt couldn't believe how calm she sounded. Angry, yeah, but definitely not scared.

Miley, on the other hand, was freaking out. Holt wouldn't have thought his voice could get any higher, but it must be hitting close to high C.

"Billie? What the hell! How'd you get this number?"

"Caller ID, you moron," Billie replied, and several people in the room had to stifle laughter.

"Hey, you better watch who you're callin' names, okay? I'm not kiddin' around here. You better not be talking to the cops, either, you hear me? Billie? You hear me? No cops!"

"Yeah—" she cleared her throat; her eyes were closed "—yes, all right. Just…calm down, okay? Look, I'm doing what you want, I'll be in the damn tournament when it starts tomorrow. I just want—" her eyes flicked to Holt's for one panic-stricken moment, then she caught a quick breath and rushed on "—I need to know she's okay."

"I told you, I'm not gonna hurt her. That's all you need to know."

"Yeah, but she's probably scared to death. Let me talk to her, okay? Just let me tell her—"

"Hey, I know what you're doing." His voice went up the scale again. "You're trying to keep me talking so you can trace this call. You better not be tryin' to trace this call, you hear me? Won't do you any good anyway, 'cause the kid's not here."

Billie's fingers were gripping the phone so hard her knuckles were white. "Where—"

"Yeah, right, like I'm gonna tell you? Somewhere

safe, is all you need to know. Somewhere you won't find her, neither, not without me. So you just better not be talkin' to the cops. Because if the cops do find me? If anything bad happens to me, you're never gonna find her. You hear me, Billie? Nobody's ever gonna see that little girl again."

Chapter 9

The weather turned warmer that evening. The wind had died down; the front, or whatever it was, had moved on east. This being the desert, the temperature had dropped with the coming of darkness, and Holt knew it would be chilly by morning, but for now it was pleasant enough that the tourists were out strolling the Strip in droves.

Billie and Holt had had dinner with Wade and Tierney, who had flipped a coin to decide which of the touristy mega hotel/casinos they should stay in for their first trip to Vegas, and belated honeymoon to boot. The Venetian had won the toss. Holt and Billie had left the newlyweds waiting for their turn at a gondola ride and had driven back to Billie's in time to meet the police technician who'd be setting up a monitor on Billie's landline.

While Holt and the techie had their heads together over the electronics, Billie had wandered out onto the patio in the backyard. After seeing the techie—whose name was Riley—to his van and locking up the house, Holt found her there, sitting cross-legged on the deck beside the empty pool. She wasn't wearing a jacket, just the long-sleeved pullover she'd put on that noon after getting the phone call from Miley. Her SWAT outfit, he thought, smiling to himself. And at the same time his heart felt curiously heavy.

"Hey," he said, and she looked up at him, smiling just a little, but not saying anything.

"What are you doing out here in the dark?" he asked, although it wasn't really dark, with the light from the kitchen pouring through the windows and a three-quarter moon bright overhead. He sat down beside her, not cross-legged—his joints were no longer comfortable with such extremes—but with his feet dangling over the side of the pool.

She looked down at her linked hands. "Just…you know. Thinking about stuff."

"Yeah, well…I guess you've got a lot to think about."

She took in a breath and shook back her hair. Looked up at the night sky. "Actually, I was thinking about the Grand Canyon."

What could he say to that? Considering everything that had happened to her in the past day or so, it seemed…unexpected. To say the least. Finally, he just said, "Yeah?" hoping she'd explain.

Instead, she asked, "You ever been there?"

"Nope," he said. "How about you?"

She shook her head. "Always wanted to. I meant to. I mean, I think everybody should see it, don't you? It's one of the most amazing things on the planet, and it's right *there*. So close. And I've never been. Don't you think that's…I mean, it just seems *wrong*." Her voice had an odd little vibration in it.

It awakened a corresponding hum in his own chest, and he started to tell her something, then realized just in time that what he'd been about to say was, "We'll go. When this is over. I'll take you." As if it was a given they'd be together then.

"How come you have a pool with no water in it?" he asked after a moment.

She gave a little half laugh, then shrugged. "I don't know, it just seems like too much trouble. I mean, my parents had one, and they were always needing to do something to it—clean it, disinfect it, strain stuff out of it, fix the filter, heater…I think it's kind of like owning a dog. You know? Ties you down."

It occurred to him that he did know. That he knew exactly what she meant, because he was the same, Hell, he didn't even have a potted plant. "You've got plants," he said. "Aren't they a lot of trouble, too?"

"Yeah, but if they die it's not a big deal, you just throw them away and get new ones." There was something defensive about the look she gave him. "Nobody cries for a plant."

"No strings," Holt said.

"Right." After a moment, she took in another of those breaths that seemed like a portent—as if she'd turned some sort of mental page. "I was just thinking…it would be kind of nice to have water in the pool right now. I sort of wish I did. It would be nice to just…drift in the water…in the dark. You know?"

"So you wouldn't have to think," Holt said softly, and she gave a light laugh and said, "Yeah…"

Then she looked at him, and the naked longing in her face made him inhale sharply. He wondered if it was really the pool she was talking about at all, or if it was the strings she missed. Or if he was only projecting his own loneliness onto her. Loneliness he hadn't even been aware of until now.

He cleared his throat and said carefully, "I don't have a pool, but a warm bath or shower sometimes works for me."

She shook her head, and he could see a wistful smile. "Not the shower. Showers always make me think—it's sort of like a brain lubricant for me."

"Bath, then." He got to his feet and held out a hand to her. "Come on—I'll run it for you. Got any bubbles?"

She was laughing when he pulled her up, but the laughter died quickly, and a second later she was in his arms. Not the way it had been with them before, with the chemistry and fireworks and pounding heartbeats, but quietly, gently, with her arms wrapped around his waist and her cheek resting against his chest. He held her that way for a while, until he felt a tremor run through her. And in that moment, and that small shudder, he knew he wanted it, too—the water in the pool, the potted plants, a dog, maybe…most of all, *this*. A woman to hold, to share the Grand Canyon with, to run a warm bath for. *No…not a woman. Just this one.*

"You're cold," he said with gravel in his throat. "Let's go inside."

What is this I'm feeling? Billie thought. *Not scared, not lost…but like I've been that, and then somebody came to find me and he's got his arm around me, and now it's almost as if I've never been anything but safe and warm. And most of all, not alone. I can barely remember what it felt like, all those years of being alone. As if they were a dream that's gone from your head when you open your eyes.*

But how can that be, when the truth is, this *is the dream, and one day soon I'll wake up and he will be gone…*

"I don't think I have any bubble bath," she said. "Would dish soap do?"

"I guess. It softens hands…" he intoned, and she stifled a laugh against his soft cotton shirt.

In the kitchen, she got the bottle of dish soap from under the sink while Holt locked the door and turned off the lights, and they walked down the hall without touching. In the bathroom, she turned on the light, then stood holding the bottle of soap while he turned on the water in the bathtub, tested the water temperature and put in the old-fashioned stopper. When he finally straightened and his eyes reached for her across the brightly lit room, her heart stumbled.

What do I do with a man like this? she wondered. *This man with his steely eyes and a face almost as hard, but with a mouth that hasn't forgotten how to smile and makes me forget everything, even who I am. This man who's as much a loner as I am, maybe more, and yet he's here, with me, in my bathroom, running me a bath as if I'm someone who needs caring for and he's someone who's used to caring. Where does a man like this learn about caring? Softness? Gentleness? Love? I had parents, at least for a while. And a sister. Who did you have, Holt Kincaid?*

Almost without knowing she did, she handed him the bottle of soap. He poured some into the thundering stream of water, and a few tiny, perfect bubbles flew upward and drifted toward the light.

"Okay," he said, setting the soap bottle on the edge of the tub, "that should do it. Unless you'd like some music?" She shook her head. His eyes blazed into hers, and they, far more than the steam rising from the filling tub, made the room suddenly feel like a summer night in the tropics. "Okay, then, I'll get out of your way...." He paused beside her, laid one hand gently on her shoulder and leaned down to touch a kiss to her forehead. And would have gone on by and left her there, except...

She caught him by the hand. "Stay," she said, and

though it was barely a whisper, it bore the weight of command.

He stood looking down at her, not smiling, and she was glad he didn't smile. It would have ruined it if he'd smiled, even a hint of one. But his eyes were somber, and blanketed with unspoken questions.

She tilted her head toward the tub, rapidly filling with bubbles, and murmured, "Here. With me. The tub's big enough." And now it was she who smiled. "That's one of the good things about buying an old house."

He still didn't say anything, but reached past her to turn off the light.

"Why—" she began, and felt his fingertips touch her lips.

"Shh," he whispered. "Wait a minute."

And even before he'd finished speaking, moonlight was already pouring into the room, replacing the harsh man-made illumination and cloaking everything in softness and mystery. She made a wordless sound of approval and her fingers found the buttons on his shirt.

"Better turn off the water," he murmured in her ear, "or we'll have a flood."

She nodded and turned to comply, and he took advantage of the moment to nudge off his shoes and put his gun in a safe place on top of the toilet tank. Then she was back, her movements fluid in the charcoal filter of moonlight. Her shirt was gone without her seeming to have touched it; less than a second later he felt her fingers on his skin, the buttons of his shirt already undone. Her bra was the stretchy sports bra type, and she divested herself of it with what seemed like sleight of hand—a flourish of raised arms, a little shake of her head, and her small, perfect breasts were unveiled like a marble statue in a moonlit garden.

He felt his pulse leap in his throat and reminded himself once again to shield. To slow the tempo of his desire. To find *her* beat. This was her music they were dancing to.

The cargo pants—and whatever was underneath—made a shushing sound as they fell. Naked and unselfconscious as a child in the half darkness, she reached for his arm and held it for support as she used the toe of one foot to push the pants off the other, taking the shoe with it. The same procedure with the other foot, an impatient kick that sent everything to some distant corner, and her hands were back on the waistband of his pants. Her nearness made his head swim.

And while there was no conscious seduction in the way she undressed both herself and him, at the same time it seemed to him an intensely *intimate* thing. This house, this room, this moment… This, he realized, was her place of mystery and privacy, and for some reason she'd invited him in. He understood that there was a kind of innocence in the way she offered, and that it wasn't about sex, at least not at this instant, but more about the sharing of her innermost self. He felt both humbled and incredibly blessed. *What,* he wondered, *could I have done to deserve such a gift?*

She took his hand and he held on to her while she stepped into the pile of foam, then she steadied him while he did the same. There was no sound except for the faint hissing of disturbed bubbles. Then he heard the sound of unspoken delight, an indrawn breath, as she lowered herself into the water. He slid down behind her, holding his own breath as the water level came near but didn't quite reach the edge of the tub. There was a loud gurgle as water rushed into the overflow outlet. He eased back against the end of the tub and pulled her onto his chest, and she put her foot over the hole to keep the water level from dropping. He wrapped his arms around her and settled his chin on her hair, and she sighed, then laughed low in her throat.

He concentrated on clouds drifting across blue autumn skies…sunlight sparkling on water…the swaying of eucalyptus branches outside his bedroom window far away in Laurel Canyon. Anything to keep his mind off the lithe, slippery body draped across his.

"How's that?" he asked carefully, trying not to jostle anything, and she replied softly, "Nice."

Then she was silent for a long time, so long he might have thought she'd gone to sleep, but for the rapid tap-tapping of her heart against his arm.

"Holt, I'm scared." She said it the way she might have said, "My back itches." *Please scratch it for me.*

She didn't add that unspoken request, but he knew the response she wanted from him at this moment was the same as if she had.

"About the tournament tomorrow?" Her head moved on his chest, nodding. "You'll be fine," he said. And because he knew she wouldn't be satisfied with the automatic pat on the head, he added, "You're very good— I've seen you play."

"I haven't played in a long time. I don't know the new faces."

He lazily scooped a handful of warm water and smoothed it over her thigh like oil. "All you have to do is—"

"—buy you some time. I know." She stirred restively, to his increasing discomfort. "But what if I can't? What if I go out tomorrow?"

"You won't."

"How can you say that? You saw me play one time. And I'm sorry, but you don't know diddly about poker."

"True. But," he added after a pause to think about it, "I'm a big fan of Kenny Rogers."

She squirmed again, trying to look up at him. "Kenny—"

"You know, the song…"

"Oh— 'The Gambler.' Right."

"What is it he says? To play your cards right all you need to know is when to hold and when to fold. Is he right?"

She gave one of her little whiskey laughs. "Uh…you do know he wasn't really talking about poker, right?"

Now it was his turn to shift position, trying to find a place for her that would still allow his brain to function.

When he had her more or less settled, he pressed his face into her hair, inhaled the sweetness of her scent, then murmured, "It's an analogy, sure. They keep cropping up, these poker analogies—did you ever notice that? Maybe because they're so perfect?"

She lay quiet, now, in his arms. "Life's just one big poker game?"

"Isn't it? Think about it. You don't get any say in what cards you're dealt, it's all about how you play your hand." He paused and wrapped his arms more tightly around her. "You have to know when to walk away, when to run. And you do. Don't you?"

"Seems to me," she said in a sad, quiet voice that wrung his heart, "I'm pretty good at running. Always have been."

"Maybe..." His hands wanted to stroke her again... caress her. This time he let them, and he said huskily, "But not this time."

Like a playful otter she turned in his arms, twisted around so she could look at him, and he took her face between his hands and held it while he looked into the shadows that hid her eyes. "Right now, when it counts, you're still at the table. You could have walked away, but you didn't. You stayed in the game."

The sound she made could have been a laugh or a sob; it was too dark to tell. He brought her face to his and kissed her. "That's all you have to do tomorrow, Billie—stay in the game. Make it to the next round. Okay? Win us another day."

He waited for her nod, but instead she slithered upward and kissed him, and went on kissing him while her legs adjusted themselves around him in the confines of the tub. He groaned, groping blindly for willpower in the exotic jungle his senses had made of his reason. Blessedly, he found it, but allowed himself to savor, just for a moment, the hot, tight feel of her body around him. When he eased her away from him, every nerve and muscle in his body echoed her squeal of protest.

"The water's getting cold and my backside's numb," he said in a whisper.

"Wuss," she murmured.

"And the condoms are in the other room."

"Oh—right."

Weakened by laughter and desire, he let her pull him to his feet. Then he took the towel she gave him and wrapped her in it and carried her to her bed.

It was different this time. Billie couldn't have put into words why, exactly, but it just was. Sure, there wasn't the newness, the first-time nervousness, the collision of conscience with need, but it was more than that. Of course, a lot had happened—was still happening—but it wasn't that, either. Something was different inside *her*.

The shape and taste of his mouth, the prickle of his beard-rough face on the palms of her hands, his hard, long body and big, gentle hands—these things she hadn't even known before yesterday. Yet, now she felt as if she'd always known them.

This morning I told him I wasn't a forever kind of

woman, yet now I keep hearing the word forever *whispered over and over inside my head like a bit of song that won't leave me alone.*

But he hasn't changed. He still is not a forever kind of man. So where does that leave me?

Vulnerable. I could get hurt.

"What?" he whispered, staring down at her face in the darkness, his chest gone tight with tenderness. His fingers were cradling her head, and his thumbs, caressing her cheeks, had felt wetness there. "Billie…what's wrong?"

"Wrong? Nothing's wrong…must've missed a spot with that towel," she said, and her laughter was languid and sweet, so he thought he must have been mistaken.

Except that, when he bent his head to kiss away the moisture, he found it tasted faintly salty, like tears.

The ballroom at the Mirage was a zoo, a seething hive of humanity with a noise-level approaching damage limits. *Where did all these people come from?* Billie wondered as she stood in the entrance to the ballroom, searching the crowd for familiar faces. In the years since she'd last played in a major tournament, the popularity of no-limit hold 'em appeared to have exploded.

Yes, but it's still the same game, she reminded herself. The most important thing to have in a tournament of this size was still self-discipline. That, and a lot of luck. Miley had taught her that much, at least. Right now, she knew, the field included a whole bunch of really terrible poker players, most of whom would be gone by the end of the night's play. Later, when the players had been winnowed down to the top few, skill would make a difference. But on the first day of a tournament this size, it was mostly about luck. And discipline.

Billie knew she'd need both to make it through to tomorrow's play.

Just buy us some time, Billie. Give us one more day.

"Hey—Billie Farrell, is that you?"

She turned to find the source of the voice, and it was a moment before she recognized one of the familiar faces on the tour. During play he'd be wearing a hooded sweatshirt and huge sunglasses. Without his disguise he looked deceptively young and harmless. "Hey," she said. "Yeah…it's me. Couldn't stay away."

"Well, welcome back—as long as you're not at my table. What number are you at?"

She checked the card in her hand. "Uh…twenty-six."

He flashed a grin. "Thank you, Lord. Well—see you later. If we're both still around." He touched her elbow and moved off into the crowd.

Well, here goes, Billie thought, and followed.

She found her table and took her place, nodding at the players already seated as she placed her backpack under her chair. In the backpack were a bottle of water, a can of high-energy drink, and several granola bars. She wouldn't be drinking much; bathroom breaks could be few and far between. If she lasted that long. Also in the backpack were her sunglasses. She took them out and put them on, then arranged her allotment of chips on the table in front of her.

The last few players took their seats. So did the dealer, blank-faced and anonymous. A loud buzzer sounded, and the noise in the ballroom died to a suspenseful murmur. The tournament had begun.

She watched two cards come slithering across the blue-green table toward her. She put her hand over them and tipped up the corners. Ace-queen, suited. She laid the cards flat and sat back in her chair, her face an impassive mask.

Not a bad way to begin, she thought.

"O—kay," Detective Vogel said, "this is the area we're lookin' at, right here." He thumped the map on which he'd just drawn a large circle with a red marking pen, then turned to his audience. This consisted of Holt, Wade, Tierney and a couple of the LVPD detectives. The rest of the team were busy on the computers, and the FBI guys had been keeping a low profile, letting LVPD take the lead in the case. "Here's I-15. The tower's just off the interstate. He had to be somewhere in this range."

"What the hell's out there?" one of the detectives asked.

"Uh…Arizona?" somebody said, and got a few snorts of laughter in response.

Somebody else said, "A whole lotta desert."

"Well, there's Valley of Fire State Park." This came from out in the middle of the squad room, where Sergeant Sanchez, the only woman on the team, had been staring intently at a computer monitor. She glanced up and added, "Google Maps," by way of an explanation.

"Valley of Fire? Never heard of it," Vogel said.

"Says here," Sanchez went on, reading from the monitor screen, "it's Nevada's oldest state park."

"Where are you gonna hide a kid in a state park? There's nothing out there." Vogel ran a hand over the gray stubble of his brush-cut hair, then aimed a question at the group at large. "How're we coming on the credit card records? Anybody? Jeez Louise…"

One of the other squad members picked up a stack of papers and waved them as he wove his way around the desks. "We're going over them now. So far the only thing we've got just verifies the general location. The guy got gas at a station off I-15, right around the time he made that call to Ms. Farrell."

"Would you mind if I take a look?" Holt asked quietly.

"Have at it," Vogel said, and the other detective handed over the printout with a shrug.

Holt scanned down the list, then went over it again, while the briefing went on, suggestions and questions and reports fading to background noise.

"Find something?" Wade asked in an undertone.

Holt looked up at him, frowning. "Maybe." He tilted the sheet so Wade could see it and pointed. "Look how many times he stopped for gas. Here, here and here."

He and Wade looked at each other, then at the rest of the group.

"Got something?" Vogel asked.

"I don't know," Holt replied. "Seems like he's using an awful lot of gas. What kind of vehicle burns that much gas? And might be found in a state park?"

"An RV," Vogel said, swearing under his breath.

There was a brief little silence, then everybody shifted into Drive at once. The room seemed to crackle and hum with activity, and Holt felt the excitement like a current of electricity under his skin.

Vogel was spouting orders in a rat-a-tat-tat voice, like an arcade popgun.

"Sanchez—find out if there's camping in that park. Everybody—find out whether the suspect has an RV registered to him. If not, find out if he's got any friends or relatives, neighbors who own an RV. Find out if there've been any reports of stolen RVs in the past forty-eight hours. Come on, people, let's go! Clock's ticking!"

It was late when Holt got back to Billie's place, but even so, he beat her there. He parked on the street and looked at the dark house and empty driveway and told himself that was a good sign, that it meant she hadn't gone out of the tournament yet. At least, he hoped that was what it meant.

He didn't have a key to her house, so he turned off the engine and headlights and settled down to wait.

It wasn't the first time he'd had to sit in his car and wait for someone to show up...for something to happen. He'd been doing stakeouts since his early years on the force. To pass the time back then, he'd think about the case in progress, go over every detail, much the same way he did now when he was battling insomnia, only in his mind. This time, though, instead of cold facts and hard details, his mind kept filling up with images. Faces. Some of them were hazy and indistinct, some soft-edged, like old photographs. Some were painful, stark and vivid.

Brenna Fallon, fourteen years old, in a photograph with worn edges...

Gaunt faces, with empty eyes...the faces of homeless teenagers gathered under an overpass to keep out of the rain...

Billie sitting in the moonlight on the edge of an empty swimming pool, her face wistful as she talks about the Grand Canyon...

And not a face, but me, standing with my arms around her and my chin on her hair, looking in awe at the Grand Canyon...

My mother's face, not from memory, but from a photograph Aunt Louise had sitting on the piano...

Wade and Tierney, the way they look at each other...

Tony and Brooke. And what is it about the faces of people in love? Do I imagine it, or is there something that seems to shine from inside them, like a house with all the windows lit up?

He wasn't sure what woke him...hadn't been aware of falling asleep. He sat up straight and stared at the dark windows of Billie's house, and the cold seemed to seep into his bones. A cold that wasn't only from the temperature outside, which was definitely dropping, but also the chill of what he understood was loneliness.

He was staring at those dark windows when headlights came sweeping across the white rail fence and the still, gray branches of the olive tree, and Billie's car pulled into the driveway.

She got out of her car and waited while he climbed out of the Mustang and walked up the driveway to meet her. The chilly desert night reached into the collar of his jacket and coiled around his ears, but he didn't feel it. She didn't say anything, just reached for his hand, and he walked with her along the pathway between the flowerpots. His heart was beating hard and fast, and he tried to think of what he could say to her to make her feel better. To let her know whatever happened, it wasn't her fault, and she hadn't failed.

They reached the bottom of the porch steps. She caught a quick breath and turned to him.

"I made it. Tomorrow…round two," she whispered, and came into his arms in a rush that left him without breath.

Chapter 10

"It'll be a lot different the second night of the tournament," Billie said. "Quieter."

"Hmm…" Holt's hand was stroking up and down her back, keeping a lazy rhythm with the slow up and down movement of his chest beneath her cheek.

Her eyelids drifted down, and she had to fight to make her lips form words. "There'll still be a crowd, just…most of 'em will be in the spectators' gallery. There'll be…I forget how many tables—around twenty, I think—each with nine players. The winner at each table advances to the next round."

"So," said Holt, "I guess there's twenty players left for that round. How many tables?"

She managed a feeble head-shake. "Four tables, usually. But that's when some of the big-name poker stars sit in, so it comes out to six players per table. And from that point on it'll probably be televised."

"And that's tomorrow night?"

"Yup. So…even if by some miracle I make it to the semi-final round, that's still only…"

"One more day." His chest lifted, then slowly settled with a long sigh. His arms tightened around her and she felt a stirring in her hair and then the warm press of his lips. "Give us that, love, and we'll find her."

"Promise?" she whispered, smiling because she knew how silly a thing it was to ask. And aching in her throat because he'd said the word *love* and she knew it didn't mean anything at all.

He responded, "Yeah, I promise." But of course it wasn't a sure bet and not even in his hands, so how could he make such a promise?

And yet…it was good to hear, and she felt her eyelids suddenly floating on a film of moisture she didn't understand at all. It couldn't possibly be tears, because for one thing, she never shed tears, wasn't even capable of it. And for another, what she was feeling right then was his nice, solid chest under her cheek and the steady thump of his heartbeat in her ear, and his arms strong and warm around her. So why would something so sweet and good and wonderful make her cry?

* * *

Holt left Billie sleeping and stole out of the house at zero-dark-thirty the next morning. He'd asked Billie for one more day, and he didn't want to waste a minute of it if he could help it. He picked up some fast-food drive-through breakfast biscuits and coffee and went straight on to police headquarters, figuring he'd be the only one of the team working the kidnapping in the squad room at that hour. Instead, he found Vogel and Sanchez and a couple of the others already there, sitting on desk corners scarfing down doughnuts and slurping coffee out of disposable cups. He handed around the sack of bacon-and-egg biscuits and helped himself to one before he picked a roosting spot on a desk opposite Vogel. He waited while the detective took a huge bite of his sandwich, chewed, then swallowed it down with coffee.

"Caught a break," Vogel said, waving what was left of the biscuit in its paper wrappings in the general direction of the rest of the squad. "Sanchez managed to track down a cousin of Todd's who says she loaned her RV to him the day before the kidnapping. Also gave us his current address." He took another bite. "Evidently, he's been bunking with his girlfriend. This cousin said he and the lady showed up asking if they could borrow the RV because they wanted to 'go camping.'"

"You've been busy," Holt said, sounding a lot calmer than he felt.

Vogel nodded as he chewed. "We got a unit sitting on the girlfriend's place. Car in the driveway, no sign of the RV."

Holt drank coffee and cleared his throat. "You figure one's holed up there and the other's staying with the kid in the RV?"

Again Vogel nodded. "According to what Todd told your friend Billie, finding him isn't going to get us the kid, so my guess would be the girlfriend drew the short straw. Anyway, we don't want to move on the girl-friend's place until we know more about who's where. What we really need is to find that RV." He nodded toward the big screen in the front of the squad room. "Question is, how? It's gonna be like looking for the proverbial needle in all that."

Holt stared at the screen with narrowed eyes. He assumed what he was looking at were satellite photos of the search area. The Valley of Fire. A turbulent sea of red and gold, carved by wind and water over millions of years. Incredibly beautiful, but desolate. And vast.

"We'll have eyes in the air at first light—" Vogel looked at his watch "—right about now, actually. But even with choppers and planes, it could take days. There must be a million places out there to hide an RV. And God knows how many RVs are out there right now. How the hell are we gonna know if it's the right one?"

"I think I might know somebody who can help with that," Holt said, reaching in his pocket for his cell phone.

Opened it, found his batteries were on life support, shoved it back in his pocket and frowned at the room. "Anybody know the number for the Venetian?"

Vogel gave him a skeptical look. "You're thinking the *psychic?* Even if I believed that stuff—and I'm not sayin' I do or I don't—how's she gonna help?"

"She's an empath—picks up on emotions. Figured maybe if she got close enough, she might be able to home in on the vibes of a scared little girl." Holt gave an offhand shrug and downed the last of his coffee. He wasn't about to waste breath trying to convince somebody of something he'd seen proof of with his own eyes. Something like that you either believed or you didn't. "Figured it couldn't hurt, right?"

Vogel stared at him for a moment, then tossed his empty coffee cup in the general direction of a trash can and pointed at his squad as he slid off his desk perch. "Sanchez—get me the Ven—"

"Already on it," Sanchez drawled, cradling a phone next to her ear.

"Got another phone I can use?" Holt sent his trash after Vogel's. "My cell phone's…"

"Sure—use that one right there." The detective was already halfway across the room, yelling at somebody else. "Hey, Turley, those choppers in the air yet? Get me the tower out at—"

Holt picked up the phone on the desk behind him and tucked it under his jaw while he took out his cell phone again and found the number he wanted in his phonebook. He put away the cell phone and punched in the number. After a couple of rings a sleepy voice answered.

"This better be Publishers Clearing House…"

"Tony, it's me," Holt said, then listened to some swearing. "Look, you know I wouldn't call this early if it wasn't important. Where are you? How soon can you get back to Vegas?"

"Never left," Tony said, in the middle of a huge yawn. "Brooke's on her way here. You didn't think she was gonna stay away once I e-mailed her those pictures I took—you kiddin' me?"

Somebody was definitely on his side, Holt figured. He let out a breath. "Man, you don't know how glad I am to hear that. Need another favor, my friend. Listen, will that toy of yours carry three passengers?"

"Three? Sure, if I leave my cameras, and if two of you don't mind sitting on the floor."

"Okay," Holt said, "get your gear and meet us at the airstrip. Can you be there in an hour?"

Billie woke up and knew before she opened her eyes that it was later than she'd ever slept before. A sickening lurch in her stomach reminded her she'd not only overslept, she'd also failed to show up for work.

Too late to worry about that now.

For a few more minutes she lay in her bed, listening to the silence of an empty house. Wondering why she'd never noticed before that the silence had a weighted, suspenseful quality, as if the house itself was holding its breath, waiting for something to come and fill the void. A voice, a laugh, a country song playing on a radio, the morning news on television, the tinkle of silverware on plates…

She got up, pulled a T-shirt on and wandered out to the kitchen, where she found the light blinking on her message machine. Three messages, the digital readout on the police recorder said. She punched the button, heard two hang-ups, then Holt's voice.

"Mornin', sunshine. Don't worry about going in to work. I called your boss. In case he asks, you're having stomach problems. I figured that covers a lot of territory, so you can fill in the blanks however you want to. So…rest up, whatever you need to do, for…you know, tonight. I don't know if I'm supposed to wish you luck, or not. So…break a leg, or whatever you say in the world of professional poker. Just hang in there, darlin'. And…I'll call you later. Okay…'bye."

She stood for a moment, her finger poised to play the message again, just to hear his voice. Told herself that was stupid, and went to make coffee instead. She was measuring coffee into the basket when the phone rang, making her jump so that the grounds went all over the countertop instead. She wiped most of them into the sink, brushed her hand off on the front of her T-shirt and picked up the phone, her heart already lifting into a quicker, more hopeful cadence, knowing it must be Holt, calling her back as he'd said he would.

"Hey," she said with a softness in her voice she hadn't even known would be there.

"Where you been? I been callin' you all morning."

Cold rage washed over her. She wrapped her arms across herself and shivered. "Miley."

"Yeah, it's me—who did you think? So, you did it, didn't you? Went to the cops. I told you—"

"Don't be stupid. The cops, the FBI—they're all over it without any help from me. What did you think was going to happen? You grab a little girl off the street and her parents aren't going to notice? Jeez, Miley, what were you thinking?"

"I told you what I'm thinking. You just need to win that tournament and everything's gonna be okay. I know you made it to the second round, so that's good. You just keep winning and everything's gonna work out."

"Miley, you know what the odds are of winning that tournament? Even if I was the best player in the world—"

"You just better be the best. You hear me?" His voice turned menacing. "You better win, Billie."

There was a click, and then nothing. Billie looked over at the recorder the police technician had set up, but it had nothing to tell her, either. She carefully returned the phone to its cradle and pressed her knotted fist against the cold flutter in her belly. *Stomach trouble—yeah, right.*

Find her, Kincaid. Please…find her.

* * *

Holt shifted, trying to find relief for his backside without taking his eyes off the tapestry of red, purple and gold unfurling beneath him. On the other side of the plane, Wade was sitting facing backward with one knee drawn up, the other stretched out in front of him, face pressed against the window. In the front seats, Tierney and Tony were also staring down at the incredible desert-scape known as the Valley of Fire. Aptly named, Holt thought, especially considering whoever had come up with the name probably hadn't had the opportunity to see it from the air, with the sun low in the sky, painting parts of the incredible rock and sandstone formations with scarlet and gold and casting others into purple-and-indigo shadow. He'd heard Tony cussing a few times, bewailing the absence of his cameras, but it had been a long time now since any of them had said anything.

They were running out of time. Out of daylight, and out of time. The odds against Billie making it to tomorrow night's final table were…what? A thousand to one? He was no math wizard, but it had to be huge.

Hang in there, love…

But under that thought, his emotions were so much more. More raw, more complex. He didn't realize how much more, until Tierney threw him a quick glance and he saw how haggard and strained her face was.

"Sorry," he said softly, and she smiled.

Wade looked up at his wife. "How're you holding up, babe?"

Her smile wavered, but she murmured, "I'm fine."

"Anything?" Wade asked.

She shook her head. She'd reported some interesting pickups over the course of the long afternoon, so they knew what they were trying to do was possible, at least. But so far, nothing that might have been the emotions of a frightened little girl.

"We're losing the light," Tony said, telling them all what they already knew. The canyons below were more purple now than gold.

Holt watched the Cherokee's tiny shadow undulate across the landscape, playing hide-and-seek with the shadows. Then watched it fade and disappear as the sun sank below the horizon. He strained to see a pinprick of light, but there was nothing but deepening darkness. It occurred to him it was like a vast ocean of sand and rock, and they were looking for a single tiny lifeboat.

"Let's try one more pass," he said. "A little bit more to the north this time."

The plane droned on toward the north, and the silence inside the plane grew heavier. When the left wingtip dipped into a sharp bank, Holt's heart sank with it.

"Gotta call it a day, folks—sorry," Tony said. "Running low on fuel."

"That's okay, buddy, you did—" Holt got that far and was interrupted by a sharp gasp.

"Wait! Wait—go back!" Tierney turned to them, her face rapt, her blue eyes bright. She put her hand up to cover her mouth, because she was laughing along with the tears.

The accountant from New Jersey went all-in on a straight draw that didn't come through for him, and Billie's table was down to three—Billie, an Internet player from New Zealand who looked about fifteen and a middle-aged guy wearing several gold chains, who chewed constantly on a toothpick and kept staring at Billie's cleavage. Which was actually okay with her, since she'd gone to some trouble to produce the cleavage by means of an extremely uncomfortable push-up bra she'd bought in a moment of insanity and she almost never wore.

Most of the other tables were done, or down to their last two players. Billie had been playing conservatively, biding her time, trying to hold on as long as possible. But inevitably, her pile of chips had shrunk, and it was clear her two remaining opponents were running equally low on patience. The looks Toothpick Guy sent her now were more annoyed than lascivious.

On the next hand, Billie drew pocket tens. The wonder kid from New Zealand, the chip leader, folded. Toothpick Guy checked, but looked a little too smug about it. Billie checked, too.

The Flop was ten, deuce, three. Billie stared at the cards, confident her glasses would keep her eyes from betraying her. She waited as long as she could get away with, then bet a thousand. Toothpick Guy promptly saw her bet. Exuding confidence, but not too much.

The Turn card shot onto the table. Another deuce. Again Billie stalled. A full house wasn't a sure thing, but she was almost out of chips. This hand was probably as good as it was going to get, and besides, what choice did she really have?

She went all-in.

Toothpick Guy's smug smile faded when he saw her full house. He had pocket queens, both red. Two pair, queen high.

Time really did seem to stand still. She knew she was holding her breath, and even her heartbeat seemed to have been suspended.

In slow motion, the dealer dealt the final card—The River. It was the queen of spades.

Toothpick Guy let out a gusty breath and leaped from his chair, hands clapped to the sides of his head in joy and relief. Billie sat motionless.

It's over.

There was a shimmery noise inside her head that blocked out all other sounds: Her own voice saying the right things as she rose from the table and extended her hand to the two surviving players. The New Zealander, saying something sympathetic to go along with his rather sweet smile. Toothpick Guy, all teeth and graciousness now that he'd won. She felt people patting her on the back as she turned, no doubt wishing her well, and she didn't hear that, either.

I failed, Holt. I couldn't do it. Hannah Grace, I'm sorry. I'm so sorry...

Blind and deaf, somehow she wove her way through the ballroom—through the casino, through the rows of slots with their garish lights and dinging bells and avid, oblivious worshipers...through the vast and crowded lobby, noisy with people enjoying the glitz, glamour and excitement of Vegas. Cold air slapped her in the face, and she came to with a start, realizing she was on the sidewalk apron just outside the main entrance, under the portico where limos and taxicabs deliver their passengers. She hesitated, shivering, then began walking rapidly, not knowing or caring where she was going.

"Billie!"

Somewhere, lost in the shimmering noise inside her head, she heard someone calling. Calling her? Or was it her imagination? Didn't matter, she didn't want to talk to anyone, or see anyone. She kept walking.

"Billie—wait!"

That voice. The voice she'd been both hoping and dreading to hear. She turned, quaking inside, holding on to her self-control by a gossamer thread. And saw Holt farther down the drive, making his way toward her, dodging around people, pushing past some. She started toward him, then halted, unable to make her legs take another step.

Then he was there, reaching for her, but she put out her hand to stop him from pulling her into his arms.

"I'm out," she said, words coming rapidly in a hoarse

voice, blunt and unforgiving. "I couldn't do it. I tried, but I lost. I didn't—"

"Billie—listen to me." He was shaking his head, gripping her arms. And smiling.

None of that registered. "I'm sorry, Kincaid. I couldn't—"

He gave her a little shake. "Billie, it doesn't matter. Don't you understand? It's okay. We've got her."

In that instant, time and space did strange and impossible things. Time stopped. The universe shrank down to the tiny space that included only herself and the man holding on to her…holding her up…holding her together. She stared at him and heard a distant voice asking, "She's okay?"

And Holt's lips moved and formed the words, "Yeah…she's okay. She's with her parents. Hannah's fine, Billie. She's fine."

The bubble popped. Sound rushed in. Sound and movement and thought. "What about Miley?" she asked. "Did they get him?"

"He's in custody."

"What's going to happen to him?"

She asked it in a hard voice, but there was something about the way she held herself… Holt stared down at her dark lenses, reflecting bits of light from the neon circus of the Strip, then reached up and gently took them off. Her eyes gazed back at him, dark and defensive, and he marveled that someone with a heart so battered and bruised could still find room in it for a rat like Miley Todd.

"You care about him," he said softly.

She hitched a shoulder. "I don't want—I mean, he did save my life."

Holt slipped an arm around her and tucked her against him as he started walking along the hotel drive. "I think the guy was actually glad to see the cops show up. Probably thinking, better them than the guys he owed money to. Anyway, he's probably going to be talking to the feds about witness protection in exchange for telling them about the guys he was in hock to. Turns out they're part of a pretty big organized crime syndicate the feds have been trying to bring down for a long time. Don't worry about Miley Todd—I have a feeling he's going to land on his feet."

She drew a long, shaky breath. "I can't believe it's all turned out okay." She hesitated, then craned to look at him. "She's really all right? She must have been so scared. You're sure—"

"See for yourself." And while she stared at him uncomprehendingly, he lifted his arm and signaled to the LVPD squad car parked in a fire lane a little farther along the drive. The car door opened. "Billie," he said gently, "there's someone here I think you should meet."

Billie froze, seemed to become rooted to the concrete sidewalk. "No." Her voice was a terrified whisper. "No, no—I can't…"

A little girl was getting out of the squad car, still clutching the teddy bear they'd given her at the police station while they were waiting for her parents to arrive.

Billie was silent, although he could feel her shaking. She lifted a hand and pressed her fingertips to her lips.

He watched the girl's parents get out of the car. These were two very decent, ordinary people—not young and a little dowdy, maybe—the kind of people you'd expect to find at PTA meetings and on the sidelines at soccer games. The mom first—and she was the kind of mom you'd feel good about coming home to if you were a kid, Holt thought, because you'd know there was going to be something good to eat waiting for you in the kitchen, and a hug to go with it. Then the dad—the kind of dad you knew would be there to catch your bicycle when it wobbled, and who would tell you no when you asked if you could do something you knew in your heart was stupid and dangerous. The kind of people his own parents could have been. Would have been.

"They must hate me so much," Billie whispered.

He looked down at her and smiled. "I don't think these people are capable of hating."

But she went on standing there, looking at the couple standing with their hands on their daughter's shoulders, both protecting and encouraging. She seemed incapable of taking a step. She looked up at Holt, and the longing in her eyes squeezed his heart.

He gave her a nudge and, in a gruff-sounding voice he didn't entirely trust, said, "Go on—go meet your daughter."

Still she hesitated. "She…she knows who I am?"

He nodded. "Her mom said she's been asking about her birth mother. She wants to meet you."

"And...it's okay with them? Her mom and dad?" She sounded both disbelieving and hopeful.

"Yes," he said softly, "it's okay."

He took her hand, then, as if she were a child afraid of the dark. Guided her a few steps closer to the three people waiting beside the police car, then experimentally let go of her hand. She looked up at him and he smiled and nodded, then watched her walk on alone to meet her daughter. His face felt stiff, his throat tight and achy, and he folded his arms and straightened, making himself taller, sturdier, as if that would make him feel less alone.

Then he wasn't alone, as Wade came from one side to clap a firm hand on his shoulder, Tierney from the other to slip her arm around his waist.

"Look at her—not a tear," Wade said. He nodded toward his wife, who was openly weeping. "Tee's a basket case."

"Billie doesn't cry," Holt said. His arm was around Tierney's shoulders, and he gave her a squeeze. "Hey, I thought you could block."

She sniffled happily. "Who wants to block emotions like these? They're the good stuff. They feed my soul."

Holt didn't answer her; he never got the chance. Because just then two things happened, almost simultaneously.

A taxicab came barreling up the drive and zipped into

the space just ahead of the police car and right next to Billie and the Bachman family.

And Tierney stiffened, clapped a hand over her mouth and whispered, "Oh, God."

Instantly concerned for his wife, Wade said, "You okay, babe? What's wrong?"

"Nothing. Nothing's wrong," she replied, laughing as new tears slid down her already wet cheeks. "Wait— just wait."

The taxi's back door flew open and a woman climbed out—a tall, blond, beautiful woman—followed closely by Tony Whitehall. Billie looked up and turned to face the newcomers, her face frozen in a puzzled frown. And Holt felt as if he was watching a tableau, all its players poised in the moment just before the scene's dramatic climax.

Then…there was sound, and motion.

Brooke Fallon Grant marched up to her twin sister and said furiously, "Well, dammit, Brenna, you wouldn't come home, so I've come to get you!"

And Holt watched in shock as Billie—or Brenna— burst into tears.

The tidal wave of emotion that swept over him then was more than he knew what to do with—and definitely more than he wanted anyone to witness. He spun around, hands lifted, chest heaving, searching blindly for a private place, a hole to crawl into, a shelter where he could be alone and find a way to deal with the upheaval within him. But instead of aloneness, once again he found himself surrounded, arms wrapped around him, a strong hand gripping his shoulder.

"It's okay," Tierney whispered, hugging him tightly. "It's beautiful, isn't it? That's *family.*"

And Wade said brusquely, "Well, Holt, my friend, looks like your job here is done." He paused while Holt coughed, cleared his throat, looked up at the lights and tried to laugh. "Have you told Cory and Sam yet?"

"Ah," Holt said, and cleared his throat some more. "Got a call in to them. Expect they'll be here soon." He hauled in a chestful of air and wondered why the achievement of something he'd been working toward for so many months didn't make him feel happier.

Tony came wandering up just then, his pit-bull face looking like it didn't know whether to laugh or cry. He shook Wade's hand with the two-handed grip that passed for hugging between guys, nodded toward Holt, sniffed and said, "Boy…this is something else, huh?" Then the three men stood silently and a little apart, arms folded on their chests, watching the two sisters. The two women had their arms around each other, heads close together, laughing, nodding, wiping eyes, laughing again…crying.

Tierney moved to stand close to Holt's side, and he thought it was strange that he didn't feel any need to widen the distance between them. There was something about her that he found comforting. Maybe, he thought, because he knew he couldn't hide his feelings from her anyway, so why worry about it.

"Does she know how you feel about her?" she asked quietly after a while.

He gave a soft huff of laughter. "No, I'm sure she doesn't. And I intend to keep it that way."

"Why?" She waited for him to answer, and when he didn't, she said, "If it makes a difference, she loves you, too." He still didn't reply, and he heard a sharp little intake of breath. "But it isn't that, is it? I think…for you that almost makes it…harder."

When she paused, his mind flashed back to the night before, in Billie's bathtub, with her all slippery and weightless on his chest, the weight all inside, where his heart should be.

Life's just one big poker game…

You don't get any say in what cards you're dealt, it's all about how you play your hand.

You have to know when to walk away, when to run.

"It's too big a gamble for you, isn't it? Loving some-one…"

He threw her a look he knew she didn't deserve— hard and mean and born out of the darkness he could feel starting to close in around him. "If you mean, am I willing to risk losing somebody I love, the way I lost my parents—yeah, it's too big a gamble." *I can't do it. It just hurts too much.*

"Oh, Holt, this is *Vegas*," Tierney said, and her voice was tender—not only the voice he heard with his ears, but the one he *felt*, deep inside his mind. "Don't you know…the greater the risk, the greater the reward? And sometimes the reward far outweighs the risk."

He could only shake his head, unable to speak.

Just then Billie looked up. Still flanked by and holding on tightly to her sister, she lifted her head and looked straight at him, and her tear-streaked face broke into a radiant smile. It was simply the most beautiful thing he'd ever seen in his life, more beautiful than any sunrise. Could even the Grand Canyon be more amazing?

If I could just wake up to that smile every day, he thought, *it might be worth the risk…*

What the hell. He held out his hand and she let go of her sister and came to him in a blind rush. He wrapped his arms around her and pressed his face into her hair…took a deep breath, closed his eyes…and went all-in.

Epilogue

"**P**earse, could there *be* a more perfect day for a wedding?"

This was, of course, a rhetorical question, which Sam's husband knew better than to answer. He smiled at her, and she settled back in her folding chair as she added with a sigh, "Or a more perfect spot for one. This was a brilliant idea, havin' it in the Portland Rose Garden. I've got to hand it to Wade and Tee for comin' up with it."

"It was a good choice," Cory agreed. "A good compromise."

Sam snorted. "What compromise? The brides' hometown down in Texas has bad memories for both Brooke and Billie—I'm never gonna be able to call her Brenna,

Pearse, I'm sorry—and Las Vegas just seems a little bit tacky, if you know what I mean. So where were they gonna go? I think this is perfect. Not only is it the most gorgeous place I've ever seen, but it's where it all started, sort of." She knew she was chattering, but couldn't seem to help it. Her emotions were all over the place these days. "Well, not where it *started,* I suppose that would've been back home at Mama's house in Georgia, but it's where you first laid eyes on Wade. He was the first brother you found, and you first met him right here in this rose garden. And now…here we all are. Together."

She reached over and took her husband's hand and squeezed it, then sniffed. "Tell me the truth, Pearse—did you really think this day would come?"

Cory lifted her hand to his lips. "Never doubted it."

"Oh, come on, Pearse, don't lie to me. Don't you sit there and tell me there weren't a few bad moments. Like right here in Portland, when Wade mistook you for a serial killer and almost shot you?"

Cory rubbed ruefully at the back of his neck. "Yeah, that was a bad moment, all right. Especially when the real killer took that opportunity to take Tee hostage, and then shot Wade. For a while there I thought I'd found him only to lose him for good."

"And," Sam pressed on, "how about that day in the Kern River Canyon, when that woman almost ran us off the road, trying to kill Matt—"

"But she didn't," Cory pointed out, "and as a result, he and Alex found each other again."

"Finding your little brother in a wheelchair," Sam said softly. "That wasn't your best moment, either, Pearse."

"No…" He took a breath and smiled. "But that little brother of mine has taught me an awful lot about courage and inner strength. Like you did, Sammie June."

She nodded, and for a moment was silent. A soft breeze stirred through the evergreens that encompassed the rose garden and carried the sweet scent of the blossoms with it. Recorded chamber music floated on the warm spring air and the sun was gentle on her skin. Everything was beautiful, and in spite of that, she shivered.

"I don't know, though…I don't think anything your brothers put us through could hold a candle to your sisters. My lands, Pearse—when I think Brooke might have gone to prison—or worse—for murdering her ex-husband, when she was totally innocent…."

"I know. Thank God for Tony. And Holt. None of it would have happened without him."

She couldn't help but notice her husband's voice was husky, too. Weddings have a way of doing that, Sam thought.

She sat up straight. "Look—here they come. It's starting."

The men were coming along the pathway between rose beds flush with their spring bloom. The minister, first, wearing cream-colored robes. Then both grooms—Holt tall, straight and solemn, sunlight glinting off the silver at his temples…Tony a bit shorter and broader, solid as a mountain, his beautifully rugged face split in an irrepressible grin. Right beside him was Brooke's son, Daniel—such a handsome boy, so tall and blond, like his mama—looking up at the man who was about to become his new daddy as if the sun rose and set at his say-so. Then Matt in his wheelchair and Wade right behind him, both brothers handsome as sin. *Like their brother,* Sam thought with a misty glance at her husband.

The music rose in volume and quickened in tempo, and there was a rustling among the assembled guests as most of them turned to watch for the arrival of the bridal party. It was a small group, most of Sam's family having decided to wait for the big reception they were planning to throw for the happy couples back in Georgia. The whole staff of Penny Tours, Matt and Alex's river-rafting company, had driven up from California together in one of the company vans, and of course quite a few of Wade's fellow cops from the Portland P.D. were there in their dress uniforms. Most of the rest of the crowd consisted of Tony's family— his mom and sisters and kids, the husbands and brothers standing in back of the rest since they'd run out of folding chairs.

Then…the first of the brides' attendants started down the aisle. *So beautiful,* Sam thought, and felt a fluttering in her chest as she watched the little girl float toward her, carrying her basket of roses and wearing a simple ankle-length white dress. Hannah Grace waved shyly at

her mom and dad, who smiled and waved back from
their seats in the front row across from Sam and Cory.

Then it was Alex's turn, and she was grinning at the
bunch from Penny Tours as if to say, *Hey, look at me,
I'm wearing a dress!* Then Tierney, radiantly, gloriously
pregnant, with eyes only for Wade, already teary-eyed
from what Sam guessed must be an overwhelming
banquet of emotions.

The music paused…a hush fell over the assembly,
and over the gardens beyond. Then there was a collec-
tive sigh of breath as Brooke and Billie came from
opposite sides of the garden to meet at the back of the
aisle. They looked at each other, and Brooke lifted a
hand to brush something from her twin sister's cheek.
Then they both laughed, and turned…and waited.

Cory squeezed Sam's hand as he rose from his seat
and went to meet them. He kissed each of his sisters on
the cheek, then each one took an elbow, and they started
up the aisle together.

Oh, Lord, that's done it, Sam thought. She clapped
a hand over her mouth, but tears were already welling
up and spilling over, and she didn't have a tissue, of
course, to save her life. She watched through a blur as
Cory handed over the brides to their respective grooms,
then came back to take his seat. He handed her a hand-
kerchief as he settled into the chair beside her, waited
for her to mop her cheeks and blow her nose, then
reached over and took her hand.

"Thanks," she whispered soggily. She leaned her

head on his shoulder. "Oh, Pearse, look at them up there. All of them together...did you ever imagine anything like this?"

Cory's laugh sounded wistful. "To tell you the truth," he whispered back, "I always imagined them the way I saw them last. You know—little. Just babies."

Sam drew a long breath, gathering courage. "Well, darlin', it sure does look like there's about to be a baby boom in your family. You don't look out, your family's apt to be as big as mine."

Her husband laughed without sound. "I don't think there's much danger of that—the Starrs have a pretty good headstart."

Another breath she didn't really need. "And...they're about to get bigger, too. By at least one."

He threw her an interested smile, eyebrows raised. "Really? Who's pregnant this time?"

"Oh, for Lord's sake, Pearse!" She glared at him in exasperation. And watched his face go blank, then pale with shock.

"Samantha?"

"Yes?"

"Sam—when did you? When were you...? And you're telling me this *now?*"

"It seemed like a good time."

"Does this mean—are you quitting the CIA? Are you going to quit flying? What—"

"Well, now, we'll cross that bridge when we come to it," she said serenely.

"Sam, when—"

She squeezed his arm and nodded toward the gazebo. "Hush up, Pearse. It's beginning."

* * * * *

*Mills & Boon® Intrigue brings you
a sneak preview of ...*

BJ Daniels' Montana Royalty

*Devlin Barrow wasn't like any cowboy
Rory Buchanan had ever ridden with. The European
stud brought status to her ranch – as well as a
trail of assassins and royal intrigue.*

Don't miss this thrilling new story in the
WHITEHORSE, MONTANA *mini-series available
next month from Mills & Boon® Intrigue.*

Montana Royalty
by
BJ Daniels

The narrow slit of light between the partially closed bedroom curtains drew him through the shadowed pines.

He moved stealthily, the moonless darkness heavy as a cloak. The moment he'd seen the light, realized it came from her bedroom window, the curtains not quite closed, he'd been helpless to stop himself.

He'd always liked watching people when they didn't know he was there. He saw things they didn't want seen. He knew their dirty secrets.

Their secrets became *his* dirty little secrets.

But this was different.

The woman behind the curtains was Rory Buchanan.

He began to sweat as he neared the window even though the fall night was cold here in the mountains. The narrow shaft of light from between the curtains spilled out onto the ground. Teasing glimpses of her lured him on.

As he grew closer, he stuck the wire cutters he carried into his jacket pocket. His heart beat so hard he could barely steal a breath as he slowly stepped toward the forbidden.

The window was the perfect height. He closed his left eye, his right eye focusing on the room, on the woman.

Inside the bedroom, Rory folded a pair of jeans into one of the dresser drawers and closed the drawer, turning back toward the bed and the T-shirt she'd left lying on it.

He didn't move, didn't breathe—didn't blink as she began to disrobe.

He couldn't have moved even at gunpoint as he watched her pull the band from her ponytail, letting her chestnut hair fall to her shoulders.

She sighed, rubbing her neck with both hands, eyes closed. Wide green eyes fringed in dark lashes. He watched breathlessly as she dropped her hands to unbutton her jeans and let them drop to the floor.

Next, the Western shirt. Like her other shirts and the jackets she wore, it was too large for her, hid her body.

Anticipation had him breathing too hard. He tried to rein it in, afraid she would hear him and look toward the window. It scared him what he might do if she suddenly closed the curtains then. Or worse, saw him.

One shirt button, then another and another and the shirt fell back, dropping over her shoulders to the floor at her feet. She reached down to retrieve both items of clothing and hang them on the hook by the door before turning back in his direction.

He sucked in a breath and held it to keep from crying out. Her breasts were full and practically spilling out of the pretty pink lacy bra. The way she dressed, no one could have known.

She slid one bra strap from her shoulder, then the other. He could hear her humming now, but didn't recognize the tune. She was totally distracted. He felt himself grow hard as stone as she unhooked the bra and her breasts were suddenly freed.

A moan escaped his throat. A low keening sound filled with lust and longing. He *wanted* her, had wanted her for years, would do anything to have her…

Instinctively, he took a step toward the back of the ranch house. Rory was alone. Her house miles from any others. Her door wouldn't be locked. No one locked their doors in this part of Montana.

The sound of a vehicle engine froze him to the spot. He dropped to the ground behind the shrubs at the corner of the house as headlights bobbed through the pines. The vehicle came into view, slowed and turned around in the yard. Someone lost?

He couldn't be caught here. He hesitated only a moment before he broke for the pines behind the house and ran through the woods to where he'd hidden his car.

As he slid behind the wheel, his adrenaline waned. He'd never done more than looked. Never even contemplated more than that.

But the others hadn't been Rory Buchanan.

If that pickup hadn't come down the road when it did...

The sick odor of fear and excitement filled the car. He rolled down his window, feeling weak and powerless and angry. Tonight, he could have had her—and on his terms. *But at what cost,* he thought as he reached for the key he'd left in the ignition of the patrol car, anxious to get back to Whitehorse.

He froze. The wire cutters. He didn't feel their weight in his jacket pocket. His hand flew to the opening only to find the pocket empty.

INTRIGUE

Coming next month

"As far as I know, no one's tried to kill me before."

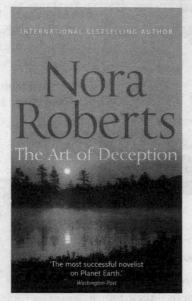

Famous artist Phillip Fairchild forges and sells famous works and is planning to sell the stolen Rembrandt which Adam Haines is investigating.

Phillip's crimes may be harmless, but someone else is not. An attempt is made on the life of Phillip's daughter. And what had been an exciting game becomes dangerously real.

Available 6th August 2010

www.millsandboon.co.uk

millsandboon.co.uk Community

Join Us!

The Community is the perfect place to meet and chat to kindred spirits who love books and reading as much as you do, but it's also the place to:

- **Get the inside scoop from authors about their latest books**
- **Learn how to write a romance book with advice from our editors**
- **Help us to continue publishing the best in women's fiction**
- **Share your thoughts on the books we publish**
- **Befriend other users**

Forums: Interact with each other as well as authors, editors and a whole host of other users worldwide.

Blogs: Every registered community member has their own blog to tell the world what they're up to and what's on their mind.

Book Challenge: We're aiming to read 5,000 books and have joined forces with The Reading Agency in our inaugural Book Challenge.

Profile Page: Showcase yourself and keep a record of your recent community activity.

Social Networking: We've added buttons at the end of every post to share via digg, Facebook, Google, Yahoo, technorati and de.licio.us.

www.millsandboon.co.uk

2 FREE BOOKS
AND A SURPRISE GIFT

We would like to take this opportunity to thank you for reading this Mills & Boon® book by offering you the chance to take TWO more specially selected books from the Intrigue series absolutely FREE! We're also making this offer to introduce you to the benefits of the Mills & Boon® Book Club™—

- **FREE home delivery**
- **FREE gifts and competitions**
- **FREE monthly Newsletter**
- **Exclusive Mills & Boon Book Club offers**
- **Books available before they're in the shops**

Accepting these FREE books and gift places you under no obligation to buy, you may cancel at any time, even after receiving your free books. Simply complete your details below and return the entire page to the address below. You don't even need a stamp!

YES Please send me 2 free Intrigue books and a surprise gift. I understand that unless you hear from me, I will receive 5 superb new stories every month, including two 2-in-1 books priced at £4.99 each and a single book priced at £3.19, postage and packing free. I am under no obligation to purchase any books and may cancel my subscription at any time. The free books and gift will be mine to keep in any case.

Ms/Mrs/Miss/Mr _____ Initials _____

_____

Surname _____

Address _____

_____

_____ Postcode _____

E-mail _____

Send this whole page to: Mills & Boon Book Club, Free Book Offer, FREEPOST NAT 10298, Richmond, TW9 1BR